The Collected Stories of
BERTRAND RUSSELL

Compiled and Edited by
BARRY FEINBERG

SIMON AND SCHUSTER   NEW YORK

Copyright © 1972 by George Allen & Unwin Ltd
Published by Simon and Schuster
Rockefeller Center, 630 Fifth Avenue
New York, New York 10020

First U.S. printing
SBN 671-21489-6
Library of Congress Catalog Card Number: 72-90594
Manufactured in the United States of America

Acknowledgements

Thanks are due to the following for their co-operation in making available certain material included in this book : the Bertrand Russell Estate; the Bertrand Russell Archives at McMaster University, Hamilton, Ontario; the Gaberbocchus Press; George Allen & Unwin Ltd; the Estate of Goldsworthy Lowes Dickinson. A special debt of gratitude is owed to Edith, Countess Russell, for her invaluable advice throughout the preparation of this volume. Thanks are also due to Kenneth Blackwell, Barbara Feinberg, Ronald Kasrils, Rosalind de Lanerolle and Franciszka Themerson, for their generous assistance.

Contents

Preface

The life of Bertrand Russell was of legendary proportions. A selfless and compassionate crusader for human liberty, Russell was relentless in pursuit of truth and justice. His energy and concern persisted until his death at the age of 97. Russell's writings, expressed with masterful clarity of thought and style, include more than sixty books, all but a few of which have been kept in constant demand. His major studies have had a critical impact on diverse fields of learning; his popular writings have influenced the ideas of millions. But for the less formal side of Russell and a fuller appreciation of his more intimate qualities, especially of his sense of fun and his delighted perception of absurdity, we must turn to his autobiographical and purely imaginative writings.

Not the least of his more personal and light-hearted occupations was inventing stories and relating anecdotes. It is the purpose of this volume to present a complete collection of Russell's stories both published and unpublished, fictional and factual, including transcriptions of his tape-recorded anecdotes told for the amusement of his family and a few privileged friends.

One of Russell's essential gifts was his ability to express complex ideas with great elegance and simplicity. His facility for lucid prose won him the Nobel Prize for Literature in 1950, although he had not, at that time, published any fictional writings. His first book of fiction appeared in 1953, in the form of five short stories under the title of *Satan in the Suburbs*. One of the stories, 'The Corsican Ordeal of Miss X' had already appeared during December 1951 in *GO*, a London magazine. It was published anonymously and readers were offered a prize for identifying its author. No one succeeded, but as Russell recalls in his *Autobiography*, 'one of the characters in the story is General Prz to whose name there is a footnote saying, "pronounced Pish"; and the prize was given to a man who wrote to the magazine: "This is Trz (pronounced Tosh)."* The 'Corsican Ordeal' was not Russell's first attempt at writing fiction. Almost half a century earlier, he had written several stories of which only one, a novella, still survives. Entitled 'The Perplexities of John Forstice', it is published here for the first time. It was completed in 1912, shortly after the end of Russell's first marriage and during the early months of his relationship with Lady Ottoline Morrell. In this same period, the publication of *Principia Mathematica* had brought to a close almost ten years of prodigious effort. Not surprisingly the novella reflects, in the perplexities posed for the main character, Russell's personal situation at the time.

Ever since the writing of 'A Free Man's Worship' in 1903, Russell's power as a prose stylist had been apparent, but he had never before turned his pen to purely imaginative composition. When he had finished 'Perplexities', therefore, he was anxious to seek the views of his literary friends. Joseph Conrad who had been generous in his praise of Russell's books was interested but critical. Goldie Lowes Dickenson was much more sympathetic as appears from a 1912 letter to Russell : *. . . It seems to me a very great piece of writing. That is banal. I mean a very beautiful expression of some of the things hardest to say and most worth saying. I do really think it has the quality of the best seventeenth-century prose, which is the highest praise one can give. . . . You are the only man I know well who seems like myself to be aware of being on a pilgrimage. I feel often that I wish it were not so, that one ought not to be so side-tracked from the normal more or less instinctive life as I feel myself to be and as I think you feel yourself to be. It goes deeper with me, and is more inevitable than with you, because my temperament has condemned me to love passionately where there is no possibility of response or fruition. The compensation is that out of all that pain and dissatisfaction there does emerge a kind of insight. But the lone-liness is sometimes intolerable. And it comforts me to find you, by another route, wandering in the same region. There are many, I suppose, if one knew them. For them you will I hope publish this. You will find audience few but fit.*[1]

In spite of this encouragement, Russell decided against publishing the story and it lay forgotten among his papers until 1968, when he was asked to reconsider his decision. He changed his mind provided that the following assessment 'appear prominently in any publication of it' : *Whilst I am satis-fied with the first part of the work, the second part represented my opinions during only a very short period.*[2] *My views in the second part were very sentimental, much too mild and much too favourable to religion. In all this I was unduly influenced by Lady Ottoline Morrell.*[3]

His marriage to the American writer, Edith Finch, in December 1952 brought him great happiness. Her love and companionship rescued him from a prolonged period of pessimism and despair begun in the early thirties and strongly manifested during the years of the war. The dedication to Edith in his *Autobiography* sums up Russell's feelings :

> *Through the long years*
> *I sought peace.*
> *I found ecstasy, I found anguish,*
> *I found madness,*
> *I found loneliness.*
> *I found the solitary pain*
> *that gnaws the heart,*
> *But peace I did not find.*

Now, old and near my end,
I have known you,
And, knowing you,
I have found both ecstasy and peace
I know rest.
After so many lonely years
I know what life and love may be.
Now, if I sleep,
I shall sleep fulfilled.

Russell's newly felt harmony with life was, undoubtedly, a major cause of his return to fiction writing. But where his writing of 'Perplexities' was intensely personal and totally serious, the later stories are notable for their relaxed objectivity, poignant wit and, above all, the author's enjoyment in his own creations. In his Preface to *Satan in the Suburbs*, Russell describes the pleasure he derived from inventing his stories : *To attempt a new departure at the age of eighty is perhaps unusual, though not unprecedented: Hobbes was older when he wrote his autobiography in Latin hexameters. Nevertheless, a few words may be in order, to mitigate any surprise that might be felt. I do not think that the reader's surprise to find me attempting stories can be greater than my own. For some reason entirely unknown to me I suddenly wished to write the stories in this volume, although I had never before thought of doing such a thing. I am incapable of critical judgement in this field, and I do not know whether the stories have any value. All that I know is that it gave me pleasure to write them and that therefore there may be people who will find pleasure in reading them. The stories are not intended to be realistic – I am afraid disappointment awaits any reader who is led to search for Ghibeline castles in Corsica or diabolical philosophers in Mortlake. Nor have they any other serious purpose. The one which I wrote first, 'The Corsican Ordeal of Miss X', attempted to combine the moods of 'Zuleika Dobson' and 'The Mysteries of Udolpho', but the others, so far as I am aware, have less relation to previous models. I should be very sorry if it were supposed that the stories are meant to point a moral or illustrate a doctrine. Each of them was written for its own sake, simply as a story, and if it is found either interesting or amusing it has served its purpose. . . .*
However free and spontaneous their writing may have been the stories are, inevitably, richly invested with his social and ethical views. Fourteen years later in his *Autobiography* he was able to be more explicit about his intentions :
. . . The writing of these stories was a great release of my hitherto unexpressed feelings and of thoughts which could not be stated without mention of fears that had no rational basis. Gradually their scope widened. I found it possible to express in this fictional form dangers that would have been

deemed silly while only a few men recognised them. I could state in fiction, ideas which I half believed in but had no good solid grounds for believing. In this way it was possible to warn of dangers which might or might not occur in the near future. . . .

Whatever uncertainty Russell felt about the merit of his stories was reinforced by his difficulty in finding an enthusiastic publisher. '*I found a reluctance on the part of both editors and readers to accept me in the role of a writer of fiction. . . . Everybody wanted me to continue as a writer of doom, prophesying dreadful things.*' But he was sustained in his efforts as a story teller by his own delight in their creation and also because he '*often found fables the best way of making a point*'. He later regretted that none of his tales were ever given a wider public airing through dramatisation in film or theatre and '*especially that none of the "Nightmares" have been made into ballets*'.

Many of Russell's stories had their origin in spoken rather than written form. At the time of their invention he was also relating and recording onto private tapes a series of anecdotes based mainly on autobiographical reminiscences. A very few of these were later incorporated in his three-volume *Autobiography*, but for the most part they are published here for the first time. The anecdotes complement the purely imaginative material in this collection because of their overwhelming sense of spontaneity and irreverent fun. In transcription the anecdotes read as smoothly and incisively as his more carefully prepared prose. This is not surprising as Russell was able to construct whole books in detail in his mind; once committed to paper his material seldom needed alteration. The sparsely corrected manuscripts of his more formal writings are evidence of this remarkable process.

Included together with his stories and anecdotes are three unpublished children's stories, told for the amusement of his own children in the late 1920s, a collection of aphorisms, and finally an auto-obituary which, though inaccurate in its prediction of 1962 for his own demise, exactly anticipates and parodies the biased judgement of many of the obituaries written at the time of his death.

Owing to the variety of forms employed by Russell in composing his stories, it was felt necessary to depart from the original presentation of the published items and arrange them together with appropriate unpublished material in a new sequence within five sections.

The bringing together of these writings pays tribute to another facet of Russell's rich and many-sided career. It is hoped that his wish that the stories might entertain and teach a wider audience will now be brought closer to fulfilment.

[1] Extract from Lowes Dickinson's letter, dated 21 July 1912, reproduced by kind permission of his niece, Mrs Mary Brownlow.
[2] 'Perplexities' is, in fact, in three parts. Russell, almost certainly, intended his reservations for the third part of the story.
[3] Extract from Russell's letter to Anton Felton, his literary executor, 6 April 1968.

The Influence of Fiction

Two views of fiction: as art and as a social force, Tolstoy, What is Art?
    Neither more important than the other
    No relation whatever between the two - effect of good art may be
        none or bad. e.g.: Shakespeare & Dostoevsky
Advantages of fiction:
    Can be more true to life
        Especially in fear-ridden societies
    Can develop a point of view dramatically in complete purity & to
        the logically utmost point. e.g.: Yahoos & Heathcliff
    Where exact truth is the aim, limitations cause aesthetic ruin;
        but when truth is not claimed, imagination has free play
As a social force:
    American novels, both good & bad, tell truths which cannot be told
        straightforwardly, without social obloquy. e.g.: Steinbeck's
           as against
    Grapes of Wrath & Beecham the Lecturer.
                          China
    Fiction more widely persuasive. e.g.: Oliver Twist & Malraux on
Fiction emancipates man from the tyranny of fact & liberates the
    Imagination.
    Imagination, not slavery to fact, is the source of whatever is good
    in human life.

Notes for a speech to the Authors' Club, 11 February 1953

PART ONE

LONGER STORIES

'The Perplexities of John Forstice', described by Russell as 'a novel, in the manner of Mallock's New Republic', is published here for the first time.

'Satan in the Suburbs' was the title story to Russell's first collection of fiction published in 1953 by The Bodley Head. 'Zahatopolk' and 'Faith and Mountains' first appeared as the 'other stories' in *Nightmares of Eminent Persons and Other Stories* published in 1954 by The Bodley Head. In his Preface to that book Russell commented:

'Zahatopolk' is designed to be completely serious . . . 'Faith and Mountains', may strike some readers as fantastic, but, if so, they must have led sheltered lives, as appears from the following:

"Taking its cue from the Coronation of Queen Elizabeth II of England this year, the National Pickle Association started a search for an American girl with the name of Elizabeth Pickle to be the ruler of Pickledom during 1953.—The *Peanut Journal and Nut World.*" (Quoted from the *Observer*, June 28, 1953.)

I wish Elizabeth Pickle all success!

The Perplexities of John Forstice

Everyone was astonished by the change in John Forstice, when he returned after his year of absence.

He had been a single-minded enthusiast, innocent as a child in worldly matters, wholly wrapped up in his test-tubes and calculations, known to physicists as a brilliant investigator of the constitution of matter, but appearing to others as an unsophisticated kindly dreamer. In an interval between two investigations, he had become dimly aware of a witty and charming young woman who was among his pupils, and – whether by his initiative or by hers – had married her. But after a fortnight's honeymoon at Cromer, to the indignation of her younger admirers, he became absorbed in a new series of calculations, and for years did not see her again except as a dim phantom half hidden by a mist of symbols. Even of the town in which he lived he knew nothing but the way from his house to the laboratory and the lecture-room.

Now he had just brought to an end a vast research, to which his last four years had been devoted. In spite of his child-like modesty, a feeling of satisfaction pervaded his thoughts as he reflected on the astonishing and yet solid results achieved by a combination of ingenious experiment and mathematical skill. A sense of emptiness and freedom, of unusual openness to impressions, of escape from the narrow concentration of a great task, left him the leisure of mind to enjoy the beauty of the sunny afternoon in May; for years past he had not noticed spring flowers or heard the song of birds, and as he walked he wondered at the blindness that had passed them by.

Forstice was doing a thing he had never done before : he was going to a garden-party. He had anxiously consulted his wife as to what he should wear on such an anomalous occasion; fortified by her opinion, he now had no misgivings on that subject, although he still suffered from a certain shyness and struggled against an impulse to turn back and go home.

It so happened that Mr Hatfield Lane, the famous Empire builder, had come down for the week-end, and was to be seen that afternoon at the garden-party, to which Forstice had been invited because the distinguished guest had expressed a wish to meet him. To his surprise he found Mr Lane, whom he had imagined as a sedate man of affairs after the model of the statues in Parliament Square, engaged in light *badinage* with a circle of admiring ladies. The great man, however, who prided himself on the universality of his interests, and moreover respected physics as the basis of engineering, which was to him the essential condition of Empire, had heard of some of Forstice's minor discoveries, and at once began to cross-question him as to the progress of his work. Forstice answered briefly and hesitatingly, disappointing his interlocutor by his deficiency in the power of self-advertisement. Very soon he dropped out of the conversation and remained a listener while the ladies resumed their attacks.

Gradually the party began to fade away. When almost all were gone, an intellectual lady who had arrived late came with a serious air and said: 'Mr Lane, whenever I meet a great man I like to carry away a great thought. I believe that you know more of the world than any other living man. Do tell me whether there is more good than evil in the world, and whether the amount of good is increasing.'

'My dear lady,' replied the Empire builder, 'I know nothing of good and evil, which are terms that I have never been able to understand. I only know that I like some things and dislike others. As to that, there are many more of the things I dislike in the world than of the things I like. What with the ascendancy of snivelling Little-Englanders, the treachery of the Admiralty, and the dishonest incompetence of the War Office, I find the world at present very little to my taste.'

'But,' she answered, 'apart from these troubles, which we may hope are temporary, do you see any tendencies in the world which give you pleasure?'

'Yes,' he said, 'there are some. The great problem of modern times is the harnessing of inferior races to the industrial machine. The Blacks, when they are left alone, are so contented that they won't work. But civilised government and civilised taxation are rapidly spreading discontent among them, and there is hope that soon all will have to work to live. I want to exploit to the utmost the natural resources of the earth. Why? I hardly know why, but I suppose in order to make men richer.'

Forstice, who had never taken any interest in political questions, was puzzled by this answer. 'But will the Blacks be richer when you have succeeded?' he asked.

'I don't know about the Blacks – it is bad for them to have more than the bare necessaries; they only spend their surplus in drink and become demoralised.'

'Then you propose to make them discontented without expecting that in the end they will be the better for your efforts?' Forstice persisted.

'Well, I suppose that is what it comes to – but the world was not made for the Blacks, nor yet for the average of White men. It is a world where the strong prosper and make things advance, while the weak must submit to be tools in carrying out the purposes of the strong.'

'And does such a world content you? Do you wish it to go on existing, or would you be glad to think that it was soon coming to an end?' asked Breitstein the pessimist financier.

'Personally, I wish it to go on existing, because I am one of the strong. But if I were one of the weak, I suppose I should feel differently. And of course the weak are the vast majority.'

'Then you like the world,' said Forstice, 'because the many are sacrificed to the few, and you are one of the few?'

'If you choose to put it that way, yes, although I should have preferred a less brutal way of putting it.'

By this time, no one remained except Breitstein, who, having long ago seen through Empire-building along with everything else, listened with kindly tolerance to Lane's naïve enthusiasm; and Shifsky the Socialist, who had stayed, although with growing indignation, in order to acquire material for a description of the modern capitalist with which he meant to adorn his next speech. At this point, he could endure silence no longer, and burst vehemently into the discussion.

'Don't believe him, Forstice,' he exclaimed, 'Lane may be strong for the moment, but the future is not for him and his strong man. The weak have been exploited too long by the strong; everywhere they are uniting, and by union they in turn will become the stronger. And the very energy of Lane and his allies only increases the forces against him. Every ounce of African gold which his helpless negroes are driven to extract from the mines which he calls his diminishes the purchasing power of wages in Europe, and intensifies the labour unrest which must in the end bring about the downfall of capitalism. Then at last we shall have justice, and the world will be a place where even those who love mankind can be happy.'

'Bravo,' said Lane, 'that will make an excellent peroration the next time you meet the united class-conscious proletariat in the back parlour of some East-End public house. I must leave you to persuade Forstice of your millennium if you can. But with Breitstein at hand to prick your bubbles, I should think you will have a difficult task.'

But Breitstein merely smiled a lazy smile, and left Shifsky to develop his hopes uninterrupted.

'Poor Lane,' said Shifsky as soon as his back was turned, 'he is pathetic with his self-confidence and his belief in his own strength. He really believes that human will – particularly his will – can alter the course of events. But Man is a mere embodiment of economic forces, a mere channel of the world-desire which sweeps through him as through everything else. Mankind is like a vast organ, with pipes of many sizes: Lane, I admit, is one of the largest, but he fancies he is the wind that blows through the other pipes. He sees himself controlling the destinies of Continents, one of a band of heroic pirate Vikings, the circumcised Northmen of our day. But he is only one of the penultimate phases of capitalism, as it works out its own destruction by the inherent logic of competition. A few more forced amalgamations, a few more internecine combats, and the people, happier than Caligula, will find that their enemies have only one head. Whether

19

that head is the head of Lane (poor fellow) or of another, its fall will inaugurate the reign of Communism and justice, of whose kingdom there shall be no end. Then no one will be very rich, and no one will be poor; wars will cease, useful inventions will no longer be suppressed by trade rivals, and all life will be conducted with the order and regularity of the Post Office.'

'Then do you think,' Forstice asked, 'that there would be no evils apart from poverty?'

'Yes,' he said, 'I am sure of it, and poverty is due to bad laws. Alter the laws, and the earth will become a Paradise.'

'I like your Post Office Paradise,' said Breitstein, yawning. 'I hope I may live to be the serpent in it, and drive men out of it by the knowledge of good and evil, especially the latter. I like, too, your view that there is no evil except poverty, because as I have much more than you would give to your Postmaster-General, I must be happier than any one in your Paradise, which is a consoling reflection. Besides, it is a comfort to have done with art and science, literature and philosophy, friendship and all such trifles. When I was very young, they persuaded me that all these things had some value, but now, like you, I think poverty the only evil and wealth the only good. So I spend my days in the City, and divide my evenings between flirtation and stamp-collecting. Stamp-collecting interests me more, because there is more difference between stamps than between women, but its joys grow rarer because my collection, I am sorry to say, is nearly perfect.

'But I think much of your Paradise already exists. Consider for instance the City Clerk, the finest flower of our civilisation: day after day he travels in the same corner of the same train, hangs his coat and hat on the same peg, and greets his wife in the evening with the same cheery platitude. How admirable! how perfect! with all the splendid regularity of the stars in their courses, and like "the most ancient heavens, fresh and strong". No foolish passions distract his breast, no "moving about in worlds not realised". The halfpenny paper, the fog, the price of coal – these are tangible sensible topics, with which even a civilised man may occupy his rare and unwelcome moments of leisure. Later on, the marriage of his virtuous daughters to younger editions of himself, the easy success of his sons without the struggles that made him the man he is, may worthily fill an occasional evening with a respectable friend. Whatever may be our professions, we all really agree with you in admiring this manner of life; for the whole effort of preachers, philanthropists, and social reformers is directed to increasing its amount and heightening its intensity.'

'What a ghastly travesty of the Socialist's ideal!' exclaimed Shifsky. 'Of course art and all such things will flourish under Socialism as never before. It is the hurry and pressure of competition that kills them in our present society. But I have no patience to argue with such effete flippancy.'

And with these words he went, not even saying good-bye.

'Would you mind,' said Forstice, 'telling me what is your real opinion? I gather you were not quite serious in what you said, and that you do not think the world would be good even if every one were prosperous and well-behaved. All these problems are new to me; I do not know what to think, and if you can help me I shall be really grateful.'

'I am tired of this garden,' Breitstein replied; 'come out into the fields and I will try to answer your question.

'My view of life,' he began when they reached the fields, 'is not a very cheerful one, and I don't myself see much use in expressing it. But I suppose your motive is scientific; if you are making a statistical classification of people's opinions, you may as well have mine along with others. Our friend Shifsky thinks that if life were freed from its obvious misfortunes, all would be well; I think that the real misfortune would only be intensified a thousandfold. The real misfortune to my mind is *ennui*, absence of interest in anything. Poverty, physical pain, unhappy affections – all such things I regard as blessings, because they prevent boredom. No great misfortune has ever come to me. I have always been well-to-do, healthy, able to secure affection wherever I desired it. But I am pursued day and night by an utter weariness of life, an intolerable lack of desire. In youth I had some slight intellectual interests, but unfortunately for me I had good abilities, and found learning so easy that it seemed not worth-while. Metaphysics held me longest, because I thought it the most difficult; but soon I saw that what is thought difficult is really impossible, and that what is possible is easy and uninteresting. Alpine climbing, at first, gave me a little excitement; but when all the risks had grown familiar, when I had become famous by the ascent of virgin peaks in various parts of the world, the mountains became as dull to me as Piccadilly. I have found the same experience in what is called love. The pursuit is sometimes interesting, but conquest is usually too easy; and even when conquest is hardest, unutterable *ennui* returns in the moment when the goal is attained. The pleasures of gambling lasted me rather longer, because the conflict is sharper and more intellect is brought into play. Sometimes on the Stock Exchange, in contests with the best practitioners of the art, when ruin or a great fortune hung in the balance, I have felt a pleasant titillation; but there, too, invariable success has abated my zest. You may wonder why I continue to live. I hardly know – perhaps I feel suicide too pronounced a step, a little vulgar in fact; and – well yes, if you want the truth – my poor old mother rejoices in my successes and knows nothing of my inward indifference to everything. But when she is dead I shall no longer have any tie to life.'

'Then you would be glad if you thought the whole world would come to an end tomorrow?'

'Glad? Yes, only that is too strong a word – I should feel a mild satisfaction.'

'You are the first man I have ever met who has felt as you do,' said

Forstice, 'and what is strange, you are the first who has had no complaint to make of outward circumstances. I don't understand how this can be; I must try to get to the bottom of it.'

Wearied with his long afternoon of unfamiliar thoughts, Forstice walked slowly homeward. The pessimism of Breitstein bewildered him. 'I had always imagined,' he said to himself, 'that a man who is invariably successful must be happy, yet Breitstein is utterly miserable. Am I happy? I never asked myself the question before. I suppose I was happy while my work absorbed me. But then I never reflected; perhaps if I had done so, I should not have been happy. And now Breitstein says that all is worthless: pleasure and pain, work and play – he sees no value in any of it. I wonder whether he is right. Most people I see are blinded by the instinctive wish to live; he alone among my acquaintances is not. Perhaps it is only instinct that makes people continue to live; perhaps, if we were reasonable, we should all agree with Breitstein. I must think of this question reasonably, without prejudice, as I should think of a question in physics. But if Breitstein is right, there can be no balancing of the goods against the evils in the world, because the goods are all dust and ashes: as soon as they are stripped of the glamour of desire, they are seen to be of no account. I do not see how his opinion can be tested. I wonder whether there is any other way of approaching the question? If there is another way, I must try to discover it.'

At this point in his reflections he reached home.

After dinner, instead of going to his study, as he usually did even on a Sunday, he resolved to ask his wife what she thought of Breitstein's views. 'My dear,' he said, 'do you find happiness in life, or do you think all human hopes are dust and ashes?'

But instead of answering, she burst into tears, to his infinite distress; and in spite of all his efforts, it was a long time before he could discover the reason. 'Do you know,' she said at last, 'that in all the years of our marriage this is the first time you have shown any real interest in me? We have lived side by side, yet utterly separate; you were so absorbed in your projects and your calculations that often you did not hear what I said; when you were at leisure, you were tired, and wished only for relaxation. Don't think I undervalue what you do; if I did, I would not have borne the long solitude to which your work has condemned me. But since you have asked, I will tell you what I had meant to keep from you as long as possible.'

She then told him that a year ago, when he believed her to be paying an ordinary visit to her mother, she had had an operation for cancer; now the cancer had recurred, and operation was no longer possible.

Forstice, utterly overwhelmed, forgot all his previous preoccupations, and became conscious, for the first time, of the affection which his absent-mindedness had concealed both from her and from himself. Filled with remorse, he saw with terrible distinctness all the loneliness of her life with him, and especially of the last twelve months; in instant response, with a wild yearning to bridge the gulf, and repair in some degree the wasted years, his whole being went forth to her, in longing to make his passionate sympathy felt and known; all his abstract interests were thrust out utterly, leaving only a great elemental human devotion. Through long months of growing misery he showed a boundless solicitude and care; the tenderness and understanding of his thought for her increased as her pain increased; every little service that was possible was an alleviation of his grief, and an occasion for showing the depth and strength of his love.

Not only towards his wife, but towards all with whom he came in contact, a new impulse of tenderness possessed him, giving a new insight into their needs and aspirations. The doctor, the nurse, the maids, even the faces he passed in the street, were no longer to him, as hitherto, mere shadows, hardly reaching to the centre of consciousness: they became to him now living and real, as real as his own grief. With a sympathy which he had never known before, he saw the thoughts and feelings of others; the force of one great devotion set free the pent-up waters of love towards all the world.

Everywhere around him he saw strife and greed, eager grasping after pleasures bought by others' pain, a thirst for mastery as the completion of one's own being. Hard, heartless faces passed him in the street, full of struggle and fight, full of the bitter determination that Self should succeed at whatever cost to others. Those others too he saw – broken wrecks, helpless and hopeless, wandering aimlessly, with vague eyes and halting step. But he gave love to all – the tyrant as much as the victim, the rich and prosperous as much as the destitute. True, the love brought its own pain – some were in misery, some had discord in the soul, some lived in a blind and headstrong devotion to evil; and for each of these, love brought a separate drop of sorrow to fill the ocean of compassion. But beneath all this load of pain, beneath the anguish and remorse of his private sorrow, some new hope, some glimmering of what was almost joy, began to dawn in his soul, bringing an unintelligible hint of solemn peace beneath all the bitterness of loss.

Day by day his love increased, down to the last solemn hours when in her final colloquy with Death the things of this world grew remote, the eternal silence called, and other voices were hushed. All anxieties and frets seemed to him then a very little thing beside the majestic mystery of Death; shame held him dumb, and rebuked even the passionate outcry of his nature against the destruction of a cherished life. Death, it seemed, was something greater and deeper than our judgements of good and evil, the undeviating march of Fate, revealing the littleness of our human world of hopes and fears, the greatness of the unruffled world of outer night. Bowed, crushed, with a wild rebellion held in check by a new awe, he went forth from her deathbed bewildered, not knowing what remained standing, yet knowing that some new wisdom was struggling into birth, making all his

23

previous thought seem small, trivial, unstable, mere thistle-down to be blown away by the first breath from the unknown.

II

The sense of a hitherto unsuspected wisdom, now dimly felt but not yet fully known, remained with Forstice in the empty days that followed his wife's death. He found that he could not attach the same importance as in former times to abstract work and the things of the intellect; they, he felt, were fair-weather friends who had proved faithless in the hour of need, after making him blind for many years to the love which, until the last sad months, had called to him in vain. Human affection alone, at this time, seemed to him to give value to life. He was lonely, full of doubts, without any moral compass to guide his course; yet in the value of human affection he felt a basis on which to build. To his surprise, he found himself no longer troubled by Breitstein's pessimism. It now seemed clear to him that there are things in life which are not dust and ashes, but the reason for this conviction remained obscure. With reviving interest, he felt an overwhelming necessity to discover the reason; and with this intention, he decided to leave his native town and enlarge his knowledge of mankind.

For one year, it was decided, Forstice's post was to be filled by a substitute, leaving him free to travel and reflect. He travelled in many countries, and spoke with men of many races. The sense of an undiscovered mystery never left him; yet, when he endeavoured to put into words the vague thoughts which beset him, he found himself baffled always by the terrible solidity of the world of common things. To his scientific habit of mind, it was hard to believe that any wisdom could come through the apparent revelation of a moment. Sometimes he would almost decide to put away the search, but again and again it was revived by some influence from the beauty or the horror of nature or of human life; again and again, although as yet unsupported by reason, the belief returned that, somehow, human life is of infinite value and is redeemed by some hidden splendour.

At length, returning, he found himself in Florence, and paid a visit to his friend Forano the mathematician. To him he spoke of his doubts and his vain attempts to solve them. 'Come with me,' replied Forano, 'to the next meeting of the "Amanti del Pensiero". Did you never hear of them? They have always been few, but they have existed now for a century. Many great men have been among them, united only in the belief that clear candid thought is the greatest of human activities. In their early days, Leopardi was the leading spirit among them; then Mazzini for a time in spite of his exile; now for many years no one man has been dominant. They meet this day week; lay your problem before them, and although I cannot promise that we shall solve it, I think I can promise an interesting discussion.'

When the evening came, Forano took him to a small dingy room behind a café, where about ten or twelve men were assembled, some silently smoking long thin cigars, others excitedly discussing with a wealth of gesture. He was introduced to all, and after a few mutual compliments (rather awkward on his side), he told his difficulties in much the same way as he had told them to Forano, who was now the first to open the discussion.

'I have no doubt,' he said, 'that many things in the world make it worth preserving; for my part, as is natural, it is mathematics that I value most. In the essence of mathematics there is something of which the value is not to be measured by its usefulness or by its educational importance, but is in some way not commensurable with common goods. Daily life, human relations, the pleasures of hearing and seeing, so far as I have experienced them, are not such as would make me desire this world to endure; others may find more in them, but to me they lack perfection, and what lacks perfection seems of no account. In mathematics I see perfection, and with perfection a kind of restfulness which I find nowhere else.

'I suppose the foundation of the mathematical impulse is pleasure in a proof – not in the proof of some conclusion already valued, but in proof for its own sake, quite regardless of the question what it is that is proved. This pleasure seems to be twofold: partly the delight in human capacity, partly the aesthetic delight in logical structure. Both these elements exist throughout mathematics, and the further we penetrate the greater they become.

'It is not only the possibility of discovering proofs that gives satisfaction to the mathematician, it is also the nature of the objects with which he deals. Everything in the everyday world seems haphazard, uncertain, approximate; in the mathematician's world, everything is necessary, certain, exact. In the everyday world, everything is changing and passing; in the mathematician's world, everything is eternally the same: his truths and his concepts are nowhere subject to the power of Time. In the everyday world, nothing is solid or reliable: the strongest affections fade, the closest friends grow cold, and by our own wantonness we estrange the few who might be faithful. But mathematics never changes, never refuses its help when we require it, is never offended by a temporary neglect.

'Mathematics gives most joy when life gives most disgust. Remote from the passion and sordidness, the weakness and failure of our human world, the mathematician enters upon a calm world of ordered classic beauty, where human will, with its violence and uncertainty, counts for nothing; with joyful resignation he contemplates the unchanging hierarchy of exact, certain, shining truths, subsisting in lofty independence of Man, of time and place, of the whole universe of shifting accidental particular things. With a kind of proud self-abasement, like that of the mystic in communion with his God, the mathematician feels at once the vastness and strength of

25

the non-human world of mathematics, and the enhancement of Man's glory by his power of knowing and loving such a world. In the sublimity of the world of abstract thought, he finds a joy which outweighs the short-comings of the world of will and emotion; in its chiselled perfection of form, his thirst for worship finds an outlet. And so long as any perfection, however rare and however difficult, can enter into human life, he feels that the world does not exist in vain.'

The next to speak was the philosopher Nasispo. 'I agree entirely,' he said, 'as regards the beauty of the mathematical world, and the proud submission of thought to truth. But I do not think it is necessary – at least, I do not think it always will be necessary – to ignore the world of actual existence in order to achieve what the mathematician values. His ideal world seems to me needlessly remote from our actual universe; so regarded, it cannot bear fruit in the ordinary relations of life, but only in the intellectual cloister to which the mathematical ascetic retires from the cares and temptations of the world. I believe that the same attitude which the mathematician adopts towards the abstract world is possible also towards the world of existence, and that thereby all our emotions towards common things can be ennobled.

'The great merit of the mathematician's world, apart from its beauty, is its timelessness: through this, the mathematician's thoughts are not of things subject to generation and decay, and are freed from the restlessness and anxiety which besets hopes that are at the mercy of Fate. But even what is most transitory – the summer lightning or an infant's smile – has some share of eternity: eternally it is true that such a thing once was, eternally it remains part of the history of the universe, eternally its essence subsists in the abstract world. For a brief moment, it takes on the colour and substance of actual existence; through all the ages it remains something which once had life and actuality. Perhaps, under the influence of practical desires, we attach too much importance to the passing existence, too little to the unchanging subsistence in the world of Being. Perhaps, if we could survey all time in one divine intuition, if we could rise above our hopes and fears into the region of untroubled contemplation, we should see the flight of Time as a thing of far less importance than it seems to actors entangled in the unknown drama. What is best in human life is brief; even the mathematician's joy in his eternal world is soon interrupted by fatigue or the business of the day. To eager desire, what is gone is of no account; only what is and what is to come gives value to life. But what is, is transitory; and what is to come, is uncertain. Thus desire begets despair, and Time brings into the world still-born even the joys to which some brief moments of life might have been accorded.

'But to contemplation not fettered by desire, whatever has been is eternal: all the beauty and wonder of a moment shines on for ever in the world of Being. The true philosopher will so discipline his heart and so foster the spirit of contemplation that he will see the eternity incarnate in the passing show; while the bodily life of beauty flies, its eternal soul lives on in his remembrance. His life must still be in time, and still itself be transitory; but his thought, while it persists, may be freed from slavery to Time: he may see the world with the vision of the eternal, and find again, even in what is most brief, the untroubled calm of the mathematician's abstract world.

'To the eternal vision, the actual world is no longer haphazard, uncertain, or inexact. To our piecemeal view, it seems such; but to an all-embracing view the whole is eternally necessary, determined, precisely what it is and not otherwise. The joy and peace of this contemplation is Spinoza's intellectual love of God, that "infinite love with which God loves himself", and the soul which is filled with the intellectual love of God is at one with all other souls inspired by the same love. In this contemplation consists our eternal life; for in this contemplation, Self and Time and all that makes division is transcended. Not fully, to us bound in the trammels of the flesh, is this contemplation possible; but dimly, in moments of mystic insight, we can rise above our usual grovelling bodily vision into a transfigured world, where the Whole emerges from its parts, and the majesty of the cosmic order is revealed.

'To those who have known this vision, all love, all affection, all desire, are transformed: they lose the terror and the madness and the insistence that beset the slave of Time, and become filled with the vast calm of contemplation; the greatness and eternity of the universe impregnates every minutest portion, and the fear of loss is softened by the mystic timelessness of what is loved. Good and evil, to this vision, are swallowed up in the infinity of the world; and a boundless joy, the joy of union, fills the soul with worship and love and the peace of eternal life.'

The next to speak was the poet Pardicreti. 'Although I agree,' he said, 'that the attitude both of the mathematician and of the philosopher is one of those that it is good to take towards the world, still there is something in me that rebels against any closed system, any finality, any abiding city for the soul. My mathematical friend, I felt, treated mathematics a little too much as if it were Abraham, and he could rest eternally on its reasonable bosom. And Nasispo, too, made his good purely contemplative, purely receptive. But Man is active as well as contemplative, creative as well as receptive. There is in life something of adventure and daring, which I should not wish to forget: imagination can impose beauty upon the world, and bring into existence much of the vision which its hopes reveal. It is not only the world as it is in itself that is interesting, but also and chiefly the world as illumined by men, the reflection on the outer darkness of the central fire in the soul. Consider what we poets have made out of the stars; and in themselves, if science knows everything, they are only bits of matter wandering aimlessly through space.

'Even if we do not travel a step outside science, there is still – perhaps more than ever before – a grand Lucretian epic to be written on the subject of Matter. Matter, like mathematics, exhibits at once the littleness and the greatness of Man, littleness in outward power, greatness in thought and passion. Humbling to the vanity which centres the universe about schemes of human salvation, Matter is at the same time an incentive to the pride which will not be turned aside from its purposes by an indifferent world.

'The unknown inhuman wildness of the universe is more delightful to me than the orderly schemes of theologians, because it leaves more play for imagination, for possibilities, for the unending search after something greater than our minds can conceive. I do not desire a God: I want a world where there is always something to be done, a virgin forest in which to hew a way, a night to illumine with beacon fires, an infinite chaos with a core of cosmos gradually growing; I desire to possess my soul in face of an alien universe, and to learn to love it and make beauty out of it without assimilating it to Man.

'A strange belittling of the universe is involved in all anthropomorphism. What is important to *me*, the primitive man thinks, *must* be important to the universe. The whole scheme of salvation is an endeavour to preserve this instinctive sense of self-importance: through successive refinements, all religion which is directed primarily to human destiny prolongs this simple-minded faith that the universe cannot be indifferent to what is of over-whelming importance to us. Day after day and night after night, men look out upon the vastness of the world: the sea beats upon the shore, the sun rises and sets, the starlight reaches us after years of lonely voyaging through space. Age after age, matter is hurled through the void, never resting, never attaining a goal, clashing, smashing, destroying and again creating, blindly, endlessly, yet with the cold regularity of perfect mechanism. In the midst of this huge unthinking world, a few little specks on one of the smallest of the planets passionately claim that they are the centre about which all revolves: defying Copernicus, they range the moral order still in concentric spheres about this little earth, and imprison the great wild universe within the tame walls of their tidy imaginations; God made the sun to light the day, the moon to light the night, and the stars to guide the belated traveller to his home. When this crude anthropomorphism has been refined by philosophy, men still believe that all reality is like human minds in being spiritual. Their loves and hates, their hopes and fears, are still indications of the purpose of the universe. Because man's activities have purposes, and because the universe is ceaselessly active, they suppose the universe, too, must have a purpose.

'Thus without reason man projects himself upon the world: by schemes of salvation, by metaphysical theories, he makes the universe subordinate to himself, smaller than himself. And in so doing, he shuts himself out from the greatness of which he is capable—the greatness of impartial contemplation, the greatness of rising above human hopes and fears, the greatness of seeing undismayed the majestic mystery of the passionless indeflectable cosmos. Not by such means is human salvation to be achieved, but by going forth freely, open-eyed, to toss on the uncharted sea. There, in the soul gifted with courage, human ideals grow to meet and grapple with the greatness of their apparent foes; hope and despair become world-embracing, and end at last in reconciling man to the universe by the discipline of desire and the victory of thought.

'The mind of Man, almost helpless in the midst of the vast wild world, is the meeting-place and focus of all the abysses of space and all the procession of the ages. Sense and passion, the mirror and the central fire, strangely blended, at once reveal and transform the world; and as imagination darts the light of passion now here, now there, its sudden rays pierce the astonished darkness of the outer night, and the mirror of sense reveals undreamed-of visions to the soul.

'But beyond the farthest depths that the fire of passion can illumine, felt rather than seen, there is something which is not darkness, some mystery, some glory. All great poetry, whatever its nominal theme may be, strives after the revelation of this glory. Graceful images, exquisite pictures of outward beauty, deep thought, profound passion even, will not make poetry truly great: the one quality needed is the indefinable quality of magic. A cadence, a single word rich with ages of poignant feeling, a hint of the life-in-death of ancient loves, will bring the sudden disquieting doubt, the sudden unimaginable hope, making our solid daily world rock and dissolve in mist, revealing behind the shows of sense – what? No man can say; yet this unknown something is the life of all the highest beauty, the goal of the poet's aspiration, the one supreme glory in comparison with which all else is dross.'

The next to speak was Chenskoff the Russian novelist, who had come as the guest of Pardicreti. 'Like my friend Pardicreti,' he said, 'I think the highest quality of all art, as of poetry, is magic, the suggestion of another world behind the world of common sense. And like Forano, I have not found in human relations anything that could satisfy the craving for beauty; glimpses there are of an unsurpassable splendour, but the littleness of envy and the daily round, or the crashing thunderbolts of the world of matter, seem always to prevail against them.

'But there is one thing in human life that I feel to be of deep importance, one thing for which mathematics, or any pursuit that is remote from emotion, cannot provide an outlet. That one thing is Pain – not the accidental pain of day to day, but the infinite pain that lies at the heart of life. I doubt if there can be really great achievement except through pain; it is pain that gives clear, sure beauty, the sense of having been wrought in the fire. It is pain that gives the quality of yearning; without that, a man

29

may be an appreciator, but not a creator. All supreme beauty makes us travel on in thought to things beyond human life, the things of vision, that are just suggested in the greatest things the world contains. That is what makes the madness of it all – the vision just beyond our reach, that we long to bring to earth and fix – but it flies, and only echoes of it fill the soul with longing. The artists and madmen and creators are those who have seen heaven for a moment; and they wander through the earth trying to see it again, feeling nothing else counts, all else is exile – and all that the earth contains cannot content them, because it is not heaven, not the glory that has blinded them to common things.

'Perhaps we of the chaotic North are not yet capable of the detachment, the impersonal intellectual vision, which two thousand years of civilisation have given to the descendants of Roman greatness. To me, human life has always appeared struggling and passionate, and by contrast, before I had found an outlet for the infinite pain, I sought relief in whatever was least struggling and least passionate – calm, unfeeling Power, Necessity marching to its conclusions over the recurring generations of crushed lives and bleeding souls. A cold joy came to me from Pardicreti's Epic of Matter, the unhasting solemn procession from the nebula to the Solar System, to Life, at last to Man, and thence, in all likelihood, back to universal Death, an unending inevitable development, proceeding with unchanging regularity, producing human hopes, ideals, and despair as a trivial incident in its march. I loved waste solitary places, rocky headlands where sea and land contended for mastery in a solemn recurring rhythm, where man and every living thing could be forgotten, where the outward tumult of the waves soothed my inward restlessness, and made me receptive of the unbending calm that lay beneath the noise and foam. Feeling, I thought, turns men from their purposes, makes them weak, irregular, and despicable; to have no feeling is to be strong. I longed to march through a predetermined development with the ruthless consistency of the material world, to be as regular, if necessary as cruel, as though I were a mere embodiment of lifeless force. Contempt for myself and all mankind, a proud passion to transcend the vanity of human existence, upheld me in this worship of the eternal sublimity of fate.

'But this detachment, passionately as I sought to achieve it, was rendered impossible for me by the infinite pain which I felt to be the ultimate truth of life. The laughter of children, or the bright-eyed energy of youth, attacking the old world with the ever-new freshness of untested faith, would rouse in me an almost unbearable anguish – the vision of the awful journey that lay ahead, crushing out gaiety, hope, desire, in the long agony of life. Late at night, I would go out into the starlight to feel the wind on my forehead and hear it in the trees – coming none knew whence, going none knew whither, wandering eternally round the world like an unquiet ghost that longs for rest but can find no rest while Time endures. Like the night-wind, humanity wanders homeless through life, coming out of the unknown, returning again into the unknown darkness, restless, seeking it knows not what, longing for an abiding city only to be found in extinction, passing through the earth like the wind, and like it leaving not a trace behind, weary with a whole eternity of pain, in which the dumb striving of the universe becomes conscious and moans and throbs in travail. Sunset skies, memories of childhood, tales of vanished love, would rouse in me that infinite pain on which I felt that all life is built – all the energy and idealism, all the frenzy, madness, and wickedness of the world. Intoxication, cruelty, lust, restless activity, are all inspired, I felt, by fear of that infinite pain; but all are unavailing, since all fail to find an escape from the pursuing spectre. This pain is unlike all other pain; it is a revelation, in a flash, of some part of the inmost secret of life, filling the whole soul with utter longing for some other world than this, some heaven, unimaginable, indescribable, where there could be rest not purchased by extinction. Blindly and helplessly, men reach out for this or that, they snatch the cup of water from each other's parched lips, and spill the precious drops in the burning desert sand, but the infinite pain remains. Some become insane and find a futile happiness in a world of lies; some seek forgetfulness in sensual orgies; some hope for relief through a life of doubtful battle, others through a treadmill round of trivial duties; many, after the terrible sorrows of childhood, escape the pain by escaping from real life into a mere automatic bodily survival.

'And looking back over my own life, I saw the same dread of the infinite pain, driving me hither and thither in restless passion, making my life a fever except in a few rare moments of courage which had partially redeemed it. Suddenly, as with a new insight, I saw that all the noise and fury was mere cowardice, mere shouting in the night to keep the ghosts away. There was, I saw, another way to deal with this pain, to turn and fight it, to face it and subdue it and make it minister to wisdom; to take it into the soul and endure while it stabbed and stabbed again; and so to rise above it, and learn through it the vision of heaven, the mysterious unity of all life in the search for liberation. The mystery is revealed in the conquest of pain by acceptance, in the vision which sees undismayed the deepest horror in the dark caverns of the soul, in the paean that celebrates the flaming mystic marriage of pain. And in the marriage of pain the soul dies to self, for self is the terror and the flight; it lives to Life, to the whole world, to love for all that struggles and suffers and lives.

'And I saw that, although all real life is passion, there are passions of different kinds: there are the passions of escape, restless, insistent, finite, parting man from man, growing in frenzy as escape grows more impossible; and there are the passions born of the marriage of pain, which are infinite, uniting man to man, sweeping over the whole soul like a wind from the sea, bearing with them the assurance that they fulfil the supreme purposes

31

of life, embodying all its greatness, its splendour, its poignant sorrow and its unquenchable yearning after another world.

'All life is built on the infinite pain, and from this pain there is no escape. The attempt to escape leads only through growing terror to madness; but acceptance of the pain leads, through a moment of unimaginable anguish, to a new life, free, boundless, and so filled with mystic glory that the pain, although it still lives and gives life, no longer dominates and no longer makes all existence a burden almost too heavy to be borne. Each free Soul is a fire sending forth its flaming light and heat into the vastness of nature's night, conquering some portion of the wild universe for human ideals and human worship. Its life may be brief, but it is not the life of a slave or a coward; it is a life of conquest, of creation, making some part exist of that imagined heaven which would still the infinite pain. Pain is the gateway to the good, and survives in the best we know; but beyond the best we know, dimly, haltingly, we conceive another best, not perhaps attainable by man, but shining through the glory of the heavens and the earth, almost incarnated in love, hauntingly leading us on like distant music over the darkening sea.'

The last to speak was Giuseppe Alegno, an unobtrusive, silent man, not famous like the others, living alone on the very modest salary of a small post under Government. His few intimate friends loved his delicate reverent sympathy, his poignant humour, and the gentle wise sorrow with which he regarded the combats and follies of mankind. Too kindly to permit himself the luxury of despair, too tentative and concrete to give his assent to any gospel, he never directly revealed his inmost view of life; and even now, he contented himself with doubts and illustrations.

'The chief thing that has impressed me,' he said, 'during the discussion, is, what a fine thing it must be to be a great man. For a poor devil who has to spend his days cooped up in a dingy office, it is pleasant to think that others have more agreeable professions, and I do not doubt that the joys of your pursuits are worthy of all the praises you have bestowed upon them. But if I might be the spokesman of ordinary mortals, I should suggest that we exist on our own account, and not merely as material for the lordly imaginations of men of genius. We common people, who are, after all, the great majority of mankind, are too limited, too full of daily cares, to appreciate the refined delights of your various heavens. We cannot understand mathematics and philosophy, we are indifferent to poetry, and music only pleases us when we can dance to it. We like novels well enough, but they must be about lost wills or amazing murders, not about the mystic marriage of pain.

'This morning I had a long conversation with my old washerwoman. Her face is wrinkled like a withering apple, her eyes tired but still shrewd, her legs stiffening with rheumatism, her arms red and rough from the wash-tub. Her husband, she tells me, gambled, then stole, then went to prison, where he died years ago. Her only son is at the war; she cannot read, and feels doubtful whether he is still alive. His wife died lately, leaving four young children whom the old woman has to care for as best she may. The children, of course, are subject to all the troubles of childhood: just now it is whooping-cough, at other times it is measles or teething, but always it is something. Her clients often fail to pay, and her rent is often hard to find. Now what would you advise me to say to her?

'Forano, I suppose, would ask her to rejoice in the proof that her clients owe her a large sum of money which she is not likely to get, and in the non-human truth of a subtraction-sum which makes it likely that her landlord will soon turn her out. Nasispo would tell her that, although the whooping-cough may pass out of the world of existence, it will whoop on for ever in the world of Being. Pardicreti would tell her to admire the inexorable order of the motions of matter when the steam blinds her and the smell of soap-suds on a summer's day overwhelms her. Chenskoff would tell her to thank her stars that she has enough finite troubles to keep off the infinite pain which besets those who have time for it. But I doubt if she would find much very real comfort in any of these sublime reflections.

'I suppose you want to know what I say to her. But I don't say anything. I keep an eye on the newspapers and try to reassure her on the subject of her son; when her situation is worse than usual, I sometimes help her with her rent; but in the main I merely listen to her without doing anything. Once I asked whether she hoped to go to heaven, but she said her father was a Garibaldino who hated the priests and taught her to disbelieve all that they preached. I did not see how to instruct her in any of your fancy religions that are not taught in churches; so I reminded her that the eldest boy would soon be old enough to earn money, and promised that I would help him to get employment.

'All that has been said in our discussion about the aristocratic goods enjoyed by great men is no doubt true, and I do not deny its importance. But as a universal gospel it is defective. "First become a King, and then enjoy your Kingdom" – that is really your advice. But we cannot all be kings, and we live in democratic times, when ordinary mortals refuse to be ignored. Either you must make your gospel as accessible to the poor and needy as Christianity has been, or you must find some other gospel which does not demand exceptional powers in the disciple.

'Why do men and women continue to live at present? Most, no doubt, from mere instinct; but this motive, as civilisation advances, will become less and less general. With those who reflect, the usual motive is the dependence of others. Human life is such a cunningly devised network that, although pain is nearly universal, most human beings, by a voluntary death, would increase the pain for others. And so the machine goes on, grinding out suffering; and so, I suppose, it will go on till the human race is extinct.

I do not believe what is needed is a gospel, but merely courage, and the habit of not reflecting on our own misfortunes. If you ask what purpose is served by human life in general, and whether it would be better if it should cease, I can only say I do not know. But if any purpose is served, it must be one that can enter into the daily lives of common man, not a rare and difficult good, realised only by the few, to whom all the other millions are to be ministering slaves. Show me a heaven that is open to my washerwoman, and I will join your religion; but if you are to go to heaven and leave my washerwoman to perdition, I will not bow down before your unjust God, however great may be the joys he offers to his chosen worshippers.'

III

While the 'Amanti del Pensiero' were discussing, very varying thoughts and feelings passed through the mind of Forstice. Except Forano and Chenskoff in their belittling of human affections, each speaker in turn convinced him, and he was feeling his question almost answered when Alegno again plunged him into perplexity. The pessimism of Breitstein, he had come to see, was the self-centred pessimism of spiritual death: any genuine interest in any other human being made it impossible. But the pessimism of Alegno was the outcome, obviously, of a very real interest in other human beings. Was it possible that even he was blind to something which could exist in the humblest lives, some good as infinite as that of the philosopher and the poet, but not dependent, like theirs, on a knowledge and a capacity only possible to the few? Some instinct told him that it must be so; but in articulate thought he could not answer Alegno. Doubt still held him and he saw that his search must still continue.

At this time, with his doubts still unsolved, he was summoned home to England by the illness of his uncle Tristram Forstice. Having been left an orphan while still a boy, John Forstice had come into the guardianship of his uncle, a kindly, slightly sentimental, country gentleman, with scientific interests and probably good scientific capacity, but remaining an amateur for lack of early training. To him John as a boy owed much in the way of opening larger horizons, and suggesting possibilities of discovery which stimulated his growing delight in the world of science. Tristram Forstice, who had never married, was now an old man, living alone in a big rambling house, inherited from his father, on a desolate part of the Anglesey coast. Half the house was shut up, and in the garden the paths were overgrown with weeds, unclipped box hedges choked the roses, and old trees lay rotting where the winter storms had uprooted them. Outside the garden, the sea moaned day and night, and rain and mist shrouded the wind-swept moors. The old man, now growing rapidly weaker and visibly nearing his end, lived daily more and more in memories of the past – of his parents, of John's father, of other brothers and sisters whom he had survived; gradually he almost ceased to distinguish John as an actual living being, confounding him with the earlier generation who were more present to his mind.

There was in the neighbourhood only one other big house, now let, built in the reign of Charles II by Robert Belasys the politician, and inhabited, until the last thirty years, by his descendants. John had heard it said that his uncle had wished to marry Catherine Belasys, the last of the family; but she had married an unknown penniless artist, who, after causing her much unhappiness, had become insane. When he at length died, gossip had again expected that she would marry Tristram Forstice; but to the astonishment of all and the indignation of many, on the death of her only child, a delicate boy, which happened very soon afterwards, she retired from the world into a sisterhood, where she still lived, devoting her time and her money to the relief of suffering among the poor.

Beyond these few outward facts and unsubstantiated conjectures, John had known nothing as to his uncle's part in the life of Catherine Belasys. Now, however, his uncle began to speak of her, at first seldom and briefly, but gradually more and more. He spoke of her as she appeared in girlhood, sometimes busy with the labourers and their families, whose needs she always knew, at other times dominated by the sea and the mist, brooding on the transitoriness of human things, and so haunted by the sense of man's impotence as almost to lose her hold on life. Of her marriage he spoke little; but John felt that it had been due to an impulse to free herself from the paralysing influence of her surroundings, a swift passionate effort to live in the present and the future, to escape from the dominion of the past and the unchanging world of nature.

'Her beauty,' Tristram said, 'was not like the beauty of other women; it spoke to the soul, not to the senses. All the sorrow and pity of the world lived in it; often, watching her face in repose, I felt an almost unbearable sacred anguish, a pain piercing down and down till its sharp point touched my heart, rousing the infinite home-sickness of the exile from a remembered heaven. The spirit of the sea was in her beauty, all its wildness and all its eternal strength. But deeper even than strength, compassion shone from her eyes and made all her motions gentle. I never felt her young: she seemed always to me the immortal mother of sorrows, old as human life, inflexible as fate, tender as the first warm breath of spring.'

Tristram Forstice was sinking fast, and often now became incoherent, wandering in his talk, or living again among scenes of childhood. On one of the latest days on which his mind was clear, he spoke at last without reserve of Catherine.

'When I am dead,' he said, 'I wish you to go to Sister Catherine with a message from me. Tell her that I loved her to the last; she knows that my love began as soon as I was of an age to love, but I wish her to know also

35

that it continued to the end. There was a time – a very brief time – when she returned my love. We were to have married; but her boy, whom she watched over with a tense and terrible anxiety because he was delicate and she feared his father's madness, fell ill and died. Rightly or wrongly, she felt that her love for me had led her to take less thought than usual for the child, and remorse rose like a dividing spectre between us. And even if that could have been overcome, she had suffered too much: her capacity for personal happiness was exhausted, and all the joys of love were dead irrevocably. No life was possible to her except a life wholly devoted to others, and we parted – not without some bitterness on my side. I wish you to tell her that I have long since understood, long since ceased to feel bitterness; that our little moment of happiness has lived in my memory; that my heart has built a precious shrine for the ashes of dead hopes, and has enriched it with whatever of wisdom the lonely years have brought. I have no belief in a future life, I do not delude myself with the thought of a meeting in heaven; and after spending half a lifetime with her image, I could not face her actual presence even in another world. But one last word of love and understanding I do wish to send.'

He then gave his nephew, out of a locked box by his bedside, a journal and a packet of letters – Catherine's and his own, for she had returned his when she went into the sisterhood, but had not wished him to return hers. The journal he wished his nephew to read as soon as he was dead; the letters were to be dealt with as Sister Catherine might decide. Soon his strength failed him and he ceased to speak; not many days afterwards he died.

Through the night, in the silence of the almost empty house, John Forstice read his uncle's journal, living over again the long sorrows and brief joys of the love which had just been ended – a love silent and solitary, except for one short interval. The journal began while Catherine was still a girl and Tristram was little more than a boy. After a period of growing hope, held in check by the diffidence of inexperienced love, her future husband appears: proud and shy, Tristram stands aside, inwardly raging, foreseeing disaster, doing nothing to avert it. With her engagement, the journal ceases for some years. It begins again when Tristram, after a long absence, returns to his father's deathbed, and learns of the madness of Catherine's husband. In various ways he is of use to her in her distress; his love flames up after the years during which it has been buried; gradually, bit by bit, it wins a timid response, and hopes of happiness appear. Then, after her husband's death, there are a few weeks of joy; but even during these weeks he feels her spirit constantly escaping from him into a vast passionless world of eternal things into which he cannot find an entrance. Very soon the catastrophe of the child's death shatters his hopes. The final parting, although he knows it to be inevitable, fills him with impotent rebellion; its very inevitability makes it the more cruel, and increases the anger which he directs by turns against fate and against Catherine. Slowly a calmer mood returns, and he finds in memory a possession of which nothing but death can deprive him. But never for a moment does he doubt that passionate love is what is of most worth in his life; that whether it brings joy or whether it brings sorrow, it is still the only thing that can concern him profoundly. Slowly he learns to turn his love to other uses, to universalise it and make it minister to sympathy and wisdom. The last entry in his journal, after many struggles, arrives at the philosophy which inspired the kindly affectionateness of his later years : 'No, passionate love is not to be judged by its duration, or by the happiness or unhappiness that it causes. Those who look at it from without, seeing only the restlessness and the havoc that it brings in its train, may be pardoned if they judge that the world would be better without it. But those who know it from within willingly bear the pain, the heartache and the weariness of lonely years: these things are as nothing beside the moment of spiritual meeting in the silent ecstasy of union. There is in all human intercourse, to those who have the power of love, some disquieting hint, some wistful suggestion, of a mystical world where solitude is overcome, where the walls that divide each separate soul from its comrades are broken down, where the division between Self and Other is of no account. But accidents of time and place, the business of life, superficial disagreements, the barriers of insistent egoism, and mere poverty of feeling, make the realisation of such a world impossible here on earth. Only in some unknown heaven, in the communion of just spirits made perfect, imagination hauntingly suggests an unattainable ideal. One small portion of this ideal, in rare moments, the passionate lover achieves; and in comparison of what those moments reveal, all else in the world seems of little worth; he feels himself at once rising to a dizzy pinnacle among the stars, and sinking deeper and deeper into an ocean of joyful death. *Verweile doch, Du bist so schön* is not the language of the greatest passion. The greatest passion knows that mortality cannot live at such a height or such a depth, and longs for death to prevent the return to common earth. An infinite poignant pain, of more worth than any mundane joy, inter-penetrates and heightens the happiness of love's fruition; for the world and the finiteness of the human soul cannot long permit the full infinity of mystic passion. But all the greatest things, however brief their outward life may be, seem, in some unintelligible way, to live for ever in a remote world of light. In that world of light, the lover feels, the soul might share the eternity of its love, if the moment of utter perfection could be immortalised by swift death. But the world returns with its cares, the heaven seen for a brief space is closed again, and worship is left in place of the living epiphany. But the epiphany has brought its own wisdom, for all true worship is wisdom. Through love, something of the infinity of every human soul is revealed; something of the reverence and tenderness of love goes out towards all mankind; and something of the shining glory of love irradiates all the stunted lives of imprisoned souls. To the man who has once known love, despair of the world is not possible; for through all failures and sorrows there remains the memory of that joy and the knowledge of what is possible in human life.'

Immediately after his uncle's funeral, John carried out his last wishes by visiting Sister Catherine, the Mother Superior (as she now was) of a sisterhood in a dark smoky manufacturing town. He was shown into a large bare room, with an oilcloth on the floor, empty except for some books, a table, and a few hard chairs. What sort of woman would he find, he wondered, as he waited full of nervous dread. Would she be a cold formal nun, who would receive him and his message with a heart dead to the world, or even with disapproval? In these unknown surroundings his fear grew greater; already he felt his voice and manner loud and coarse. How should be bring himself to deliver a message from a lover here? But his imaginings were cut short by a Sister calling him to the Mother Superior's room.

As he went in, he saw the beaming face of a little girl, bending up to kiss, with evident devotion, a dim face shrouded in a dark veil – he heard afterwards that she was one of the many adopted orphans. As the child disappeared, he saw a small frail form enveloped in a dark blue serge habit, a face soft in skin but deeply lined with lines of suffering, and giving at once the impression that hardly any body remained round that vivid glowing soul. At once he knew how foolish all his anticipations had been; as he stood looking down at those wonderful far-seeing eyes that looked at him, he felt at once that to her he could give his message simply and fully. A hand with long sensitive fingers was put on his arm; 'Come and sit here,' she said. He looked round the room: rigidly plain, but somehow with a feeling of simple beauty and sweetness in it; books and some religious pictures covered the walls; beside her chair were a few dim and faded photographs, one of a young boy. In one corner was a *prie-Dieu* and a crucifix. The only ornament was a bunch of flowers that the child had just left.

As he began to speak, the face opposite him, or rather the eyes, lost the smile he had felt so welcoming, and there came a look that seemed to give almost too much silent suffering understanding, the outcome of tragic sorrow and renunciation; but besides this and above it all there was something he had never seen before in all those he had met, a sort of gentle tender radiant light, that saw something, worshipped something, he could not see, some ever-present vision of light and love. As he talked, the long thin fingers were clasped together, the eyes rested on him; but from time to time he saw them look up and out, as if bringing all the tale of love and devotion that he laid at her feet up to some other Presence. Was there any tinge of warmth or satisfaction for the devotion that he brought her? No, he felt; in that soul where Self was renounced, none; only overwhelming reverence and deep emotion. When he mentioned some of his uncle's kind deeds, and his generous affectionate manner of life, her whole body seemed to quiver with gladness.

At length she spoke; her voice appeared to come from far away, as if from another world, yet it had notes of strangely poignant feeling, holding an agony of compassion for all the sorrows of mankind. Her vivid memory of tiny details about his uncle surprised him. Gradually she passed on to speak of the heavenly love, avoiding mention of beliefs which she knew he could not share.

'Yes, human life contains much that is bad, more of bad, perhaps, than of good, by the common standards of the market-place. But the bad is limited, circumscribed; it is possible to see the whole of a bad thing, to isolate it and pass beyond it. Much also of what is thought to be good, is limited in the same way, but not all. Have you ever, perhaps in a moment of the profoundest sorrow, seen a light break through from beyond, felt as though you were floating out on an invisible boat into the infinite ocean of Being, to a region beyond the storms of our rock-bound human shores, where strife never comes, where pain and sin seem to be absorbed in the oneness of infinite love, where beauty, which in our nether world has the terror of death-bringing lightning in the night, shines with a steady radiance that illumines the world foreshadowed in our restless yearning? In that world, Truth no longer frowns like an avenging God; for the goods which Truth forbids are not the goods of that world, the evils which Truth reveals are powerless against the peace of that uncharted sea. In that world, there are no boundaries; our human powers cannot reach the limits of its joy. Those who have known its freedom cannot again wholly confine their thoughts within the prison of finite hopes and fears in which their previous life has been immured. They know that in every human spirit there is something that is infinite and divine, perishable, perhaps, and obscured by the mists of restless desire, but yet of greater import than all the rest of what makes man's life; they know that only in the victory of the divine can peace be found. To every human spirit they give a love which is the expression of the infinite, a love seeking nothing for itself, scarcely seeking for others those lesser goods that a more finite love would demand, but aiming always at freeing the infinite in others from the trammels of earth.

'And to those to whom this liberation has come, utter despair is no longer possible; through pain, through the loss of those they love, even through the seeming degradation of those whom they would most wish to help, they see still shining the sun of that transfigured world, they know that somehow, inexpressibly, in spite of sin and grief, human life has a value which is infinite, reaching out to the stars, embracing the whole universe, uniting all that is past and all that is to come in a vast whole of love. For love is the good and love reveals the good; love is the sun that shines through the casements of our prison, and love is the power that unlocks the prison gates and makes us free citizens of the world of light. While love lives, the world deserves to last.'

When she became silent again, what had she said? A great deal to him, yes; more than he could account for. He felt almost bewildered, as though he had made a new discovery; but it was not her words that had said so much, for after all they were few – it was something else. Her words had come as from a soul filled with infinite love, tender sympathy, and reverence; they had come with some unknown and vibrating value. Love deep as his for her was in her heart for the man who was dead, of that John felt convinced; but even if he had known of it before he died, would it have satisfied his longing? Probably not; for was it not a love hitherto unknown to him, a love taken up and fused into the love of her God? Self and desire purged away in the fire of suffering, leaving a love passionate still, yes, but only – he could dimly imagine – passionate to give not to receive. He could picture her hour after hour on her knees, looking up, or bowed in worship and reverence, holding in the arms of the soul that being who after all these years was so precious to her. Long silence had not touched or dimmed those prayers – her look alone showed that.

Was there regret for all she had missed? Sorrow and anguish for the pain she had caused, perhaps; but above it all, he felt again, there was a faith, obstinate and unfailing, that she had but withdrawn herself from his life to leave him in more powerful, more enfolding, and more infinitely tender hands.

A chapel bell aroused him from his musings. 'Ah, is it already time for Vespers?' she said. He went; but as he held that emaciated hand, he felt, in spite of unbelief, an irresistible desire to bend in reverence before her, to say, 'You will bless me too, won't you?' As if dimly conscious of his thoughts, she looked up with glowing eyes and said: 'You he loved, and you gave him tender care and comfort in those last days. I shall never forget you.' Again her words were few, but her look spoke much more.

As he walked away, some instinct made him look up at the house, and rather to his surprise he saw her standing at a window with a sad look; he felt she was looking at him as the last link with that past now outwardly and visibly for ever at an end. As he looked up, the second Vesper Bell rang; she turned slowly away and disappeared.

In the street, rain was falling, children begrimed with sooty mud were quarrelling and crying, men returning from their work were laying bets in loud tones on the result of the next football match, from a neighbouring factory a torrent of sordid girls poured forth with harsh laughter and brutal jests, bumping into Forstice with oaths as he tried to make his way through them. For a moment the contrast was greater than tense nerves could bear; then the thought of universal love returned, and he began to see, no longer with his own eyes, but with those eyes of vision that had been filling his soul with new light. Outwardly degraded as they were, each of those spiritually stunted human beings seemed to him of infinite value, with some hidden beauty buried beneath the visible horror. The new insight which the last hour had brought could not, he felt, be all delusion; yet it was hard to find a place for it beside his other beliefs – the belief that the soul dies at death, that Matter rules the world, that spiritual forces are powerless against natural laws, mere shining bubbles on the surface of the hurrying stream.

Absorbed in a profound questioning, he soon ceased to see or hear the sights and sounds of the street; in a dream he reached the station, in a dream he travelled home. Through all his thinking, that voice and those eyes still spoke to him: he could not share the beliefs which inspired them, yet he could not doubt that they held some wisdom of immeasurable importance to mankind, some truth as true as any of the truths of science. He remembered the feeling of the mystery of life which had come to him when his wife died, the haunting sense of an undiscovered infinite value in human existence which had been only deepened by all the evils that he had seen. He remembered the unreasoning instinct which had kept him from acquiescing in the pessimism of Alegno. That secret in which Wisdom was shrouded he felt that Mother Catherine possessed; and yet, and yet, how could it be disentangled from the God, the life of prayer, the belief in the power of the Spirit, with which in her it was entwined?

Day after day, in a passion of thought, the same problem held him; hour after hour, sitting or slowly pacing backwards and forwards, he saw side by side the two truths, the truth of science and the truth of vision; struggling to make them combine, he saw them still apart, still mutually destructive, yet still both true. Very slowly, with much doubt, not without some loss in the glory of the vision, he found a kind of possibility of union, not clear-cut or definite, not adequate or fully satisfying, yet enough to persuade him that a union could exist, and that neither need be wholly sacrificed to the other.

Gradually he came to see that most of the good and evil we seem to find in the world is a reflection of our own feeling: love and hate, desire and aversion, cut the world in two, fill it with strife, make it fragmentary, the battleground of a doubtful warfare. But there is another way of viewing the world, more receptive, more impartial, a way filled with welcoming acceptance. When this way of feeling is strong, it makes us think of the world as wholly good, no longer fragmentary, but one, because one emotion goes out to the whole. The heart of this feeling is reverence, a wondering sense of infinity in everything. The beauty created by the artist rouses this feeling, and embodies his restless search for the ideal infinite beauty which he feels to be somewhere, everywhere, close at hand always, yet just hidden by a veil that at any moment may be torn asunder.

But the mystical acceptance of the world subsists side by side with the horror of cruelty and lust; and thus a conflict grows between the vision and the facts of our daily world. And so the mystic comes to feel that our daily world is unreal, or less real than the world of his worship: behind the world of sense he imagines another world, more perfect and more real. But here the verdict of science is absolute: if the vision is to have a real place, to be a source of wisdom, not of illusion, it must accept the everyday world, retaining the mystic's feeling without the mystic's belief as to the nature of the universe.

But the vision seemed to bring with it acquiescence; nevertheless we cannot acquiesce in pain and cruelty and lust. So long as the world of science and the world of vision are both regarded as having the same reality, this contradiction must remain. We can love those who inflict pain, who are cruel or lustful; we feel that they are blind, and be filled with compassion for their ignorance of all that gives value to life; but although we may love them, we cannot passively acquiesce in their blindness, or cease to wish them different.

Two truths, not wholly separable one from another, are revealed by the vision, and survive the critical scrutiny of science. The first of these gives a contemplation of the actual world more vast, more free, more impersonal, than the view of daily life: by rising above the mists of desire, away from the belittling, distorting influence of hopes and fears, we can attain at moments, however imperfectly, to the divine all-embracing intuition of the universe, free from the *here* and *now*, free from the prison-house of Self, revealing the Whole, eternal and infinite in spite of the brevity and limitation of every part when seen in a separate isolation. The great cold outer world, although it may not satisfy our mundane desires, is, to the eyes of vision, splendid, full of wonder, full of unhasting inevitable sublimity. Towards other human beings, the eyes of vision are the eyes of love: not of the love which asks, but of the love which gives. Man, like the rest of nature, is part of the eternal Whole; to the eternal vision, all his deeds have their predetermined place, all are from the beginning of time necessarily what they are not otherwise, no more exposed to indignation than the revolutions of the heavenly bodies. But Man, unlike what we know of mere matter, is endowed with the power of thought and feeling; in every man's heart the infinite pain, the infinite longing, make the inmost fibre of our life, call out to us for love and sympathy; and when the vision has effaced Self and quieted indignation, no obstacle hinders the free outpouring of love in response to this call.

The other truth which the vision reveals is the possibility of a life here on earth immeasurably greater than the life of the human society as it now exists. The world of vision exists only in fragments; it is a possible world, not quite the actual world; partly real, but partly hoped for. The goods of vision are infinite: they outweigh all other goods and evils. It is in man's power to realise them: in each individual's power partially, in the power of mankind as a whole fully. All that is greatly evil in the world is due to human beings, and would cease if they lived in the vision. Poverty, illness, the prospect of death, separation from those we love, none of these make the vision impossible, although some make it more difficult of attainment. It is not outward events that make the difference, except as they affect our way of feeling towards the world: the way of feeling is everything. Pain and pleasure are not of much account, except when they dim the vision. Success and failure are of almost no account.

There is a finite and an infinite way of feeling about everything; the infinite way is aware of heaven as a living possibility here on earth. The heaven of the mystic vision does not yet exist, except in dim struggling fragments entangled in earth; the artist, the lover, and the saint see it in aspiration, and help the fragments to grow and emerge from their earthly integuments. The heaven of the vision would exist fully if all men possessed the vision fully: only the finiteness and limitation of men's thought and feeling prevents our birth into the free life.

The fullest vision requires the fullest knowledge, the fullest worship, the fullest love; all these are the outcome of reverence, reverence not only to what is deemed specially worthy of reverence, but to everything, to the mystery of existence, to the infinity embodied in every particle of the Whole. Loyalty to science is not hostile to the vision, but a necessary outcome of it. Indifference to knowledge is a kind of irreverence, an assumption that our ignorant imaginings surpass what really is. All search for truth is a kind of reverence, a kind of worship, and all fear of truth a blasphemy.

It is through reverence that the infinite enters into human lives. A very little leaven of the infinite will redeem a whole life. The good life is not contemplation only, or action only, but action based on contemplation, action attempting to incarnate the infinite in the world. A life devoted to knowledge or beauty or love is a life inspired by the vision, a life in the infinite. Human existence, in spite of all its pain and degradation, is redeemed by any portion, short or long, great or small, of knowledge or beauty or love; and the greatest of these is love.

These thoughts shaped themselves slowly in Forstice's mind during the lonely days which he spent in his uncle's house, in the midst of accounts and legal business and the sorting of papers, while the autumn rain beat on the window panes, and the howling gales carried the leaves in swirling eddies through the air. But now his year of absence was ended; with a pang that seemed like a second death he bade farewell to the scene of the joys and sorrows that had become a part of his own life, and with resolute hope he returned to the study and teaching of physics in which the remainder of his days were spent.

Satan in the Suburbs
or Horrors Manufactured Here

I

I live in Mortlake, and take the train daily to my work. On returning one evening I found a new brass plate on the gate of a villa which I pass every day. To my surprise, the brass plate, instead of making the usual medical announcement, said:

HORRORS MANUFACTURED HERE
Apply Dr Murdoch Mallako

This announcement intrigued me, and when I got home I wrote a letter asking for further information, to enable me to decide whether or not to become a client of Dr Mallako. I received the following reply:

Dear Sir,

It is not wholly surprising that you should desire a few words of explanation concerning my brass plate. You may have observed a recent tendency to deplore the humdrum uniformity of life in the suburbs of our great metropolis. The feeling has been expressed by some, whose opinion should carry weight, that adventure, and even a spice of danger, would make life more bearable for the victim of uniformity.

It is in the hope of supplying this need that I have embarked upon a wholly novel profession. I believe that I can supply my clients with new thrills and excitements such as will completely transform their lives.

If you wish for further information it will be given if you make an appointment. My charges are ten guineas an hour.

This reply made me suppose that Dr Mallako was a philanthropist of a new species, and I debated with myself whether I should seek further information at the cost of ten guineas, or should keep this sum to be spent on some other pleasure.

Before I had resolved this question in my own mind, I happened, on passing his gate one Monday evening, to observe my neighbour Mr Abercrombie, emerging from the doctor's front door, pale and distraught, with wandering, unfocused eyes and tottering steps, fumbling at the latch of the gate and emerging on to the street, as though he were lost in some entirely strange locality.

'For God's sake, man,' I exclaimed, 'what has been happening to you?'

44

'Oh, nothing particular,' Mr Abercrombie replied, with a pathetic attempt at an appearance of calm, 'we were talking about the weather.'

'Do not attempt to deceive me,' I replied, 'something even worse than the weather has stamped horror upon your features.'

'Horror? Nonsense!' he replied testily, 'his whisky is very potent.'

Since he evidently wished to be rid of my inquiries, I left him to find his own way home, and for some days I heard no more of him. Next evening I was returning at the same hour when I saw another neighbour, Mr Beauchamp, emerging in the same condition of dazed terror, but when I accosted him, he waved me off. The next day I witnessed the same spectacle in the person of Mr Cartwright. On the Thursday evening Mrs Ellerker, a married lady of forty, with whom I had been on friendly terms, rushed from his door and fainted on the pavement. I supported her while she revived, but when she recovered she uttered only one word, whispered shudderingly; the one word was 'never'. Nothing further was to be got from her, although I accompanied her to the door of her house.

On the Friday I saw nothing, and on Saturday and Sunday I did not go to work, and therefore did not pass Dr Mallako's gate. But on Sunday evening my neighbour, Mr Gosling, a substantial City man, dropped in for a chat. After I had supplied him with a drink and settled him in my most comfortable chair, he began, as was his wont, to gossip about our local acquaintance.

'Have you heard,' said he, 'what odd things are happening in our street? Mr Abercrombie, Mr Beauchamp, and Mr Cartwright have all been taken ill and have stayed away from their respective offices, while Mrs Ellerker lies in a dark room, moaning.'

Mr Gosling evidently knew nothing about Dr Mallako and his strange brass plate, so I decided to say nothing to him but to investigate on my own account. I visited in turn Mr Abercrombie, Mr Beauchamp and Mr Cartwright, but all of them refused to utter a single word. Mrs Ellerker remained invisible in her invalid seclusion. It seemed clear that something very strange was happening and that Dr Mallako was at the bottom of it. I decided to call upon him, not as a client, but as an investigator. I rang his bell and was shown by a trim parlourmaid into his well-appointed consulting room.

'And what, Sir, can I do for you?' he asked as he entered, smiling. His manners were suave, but his smile was enigmatic. His glance was penetrating and cold; and when his mouth smiled, his eyes did not. Something about his eyes caused me inexplicably to shudder.

'Dr Mallako,' I said, 'accident causes me to pass your gate every evening, except Saturdays and Sundays, and on four successive evenings I have witnessed strange phenomena, all of which had a common character which I find not unalarming. I do not know, in view of your somewhat enigmatic letter, what lies behind the announcement of your brass plate, but the little that I have seen has caused me to doubt whether your purpose is as purely philanthropic as you led me to suppose. It may be that I am mistaken in this, and if so, it should be easy for you to set my mind at rest. But I confess that I shall not be satisfied until you have given me some explanation of the strange condition in which Mr Abercrombie, Mr Beauchamp, Mr Cartwright, and Mrs Ellerker emerged from your consulting-room.'

As I was speaking, the smile disappeared, and Dr Mallako assumed a severe and reprehending demeanour.

'Sir,' he said, 'you are inviting me to commit an infamy. Do you not know that clients' confidences to a doctor are as inviolate as the confessional? Are you not aware that if I were to gratify your idle curiosity I should be guilty of a nefarious action? Have you lived so long without learning that a doctor's discretion must be observed? No, Sir, I shall not answer your impertinent queries, and I must request you to leave my house at once. There's the door.'

When I found myself again in the street, I felt for a moment somewhat abashed. If he were indeed an orthodox medical practitioner, his answer to my inquiries would have been wholly correct. Could it be that I had been mistaken? Was it possible that he had disclosed to all four of his clients some painful medical misfortune of which until that moment they had been ignorant? It might indeed be so. It seemed improbable, but what further could I do?

I watched for another week, during which I again passed his gate every morning and evening, but I saw nothing further. I found, however, that I could not forget the strange doctor. Night after night he would appear before me in nightmares, sometimes with hooves and tail and with his brass plate worn as a breastplate, sometimes with eyes glaring out of the darkness, and almost invisible lips forming the words 'YOU WILL COME!' Each day I passed his gate more slowly than on the previous day. Each day I felt a more powerful impulse to enter, this time not as an investigator, but as a client. Although I recognised the impulse as an insane obsession, I could not get rid of it. The horrid attraction gradually destroyed my work. At last I visited my chief, and without mentioning Dr Mallako, persuaded him that I was suffering from overwork and needed a holiday. My chief, a much older man, for whom I entertained a profound respect, after one glance at my haggard features, granted my request with kindly solicitude.

I flew to Corfu, hoping that sun and sea would enable me to forget. But alas, no rest came to me there, by day or by night. Each night the eyes, even larger than before, glared at me while I dreamt. Each night I would wake in a cold sweat, hearing the ghostly voice saying 'COME!' At last I decided that if there were a cure for my condition it was not to be found in a holiday, and in despair I returned, hoping that the scientific research upon which I was engaged, and in which I had been passionately interested, would restore to me a measure of sanity. I plunged feverishly into a very abstruse scientific investigation, and I found a way to and from the station which did not pass Dr Mallako's gate.

II

I began to think that perhaps the obsession was fading, when one evening Mr Gosling again visited me. He was cheerful, rubicund, and rotund – just the man, I thought, to dispel such morbid fancies as had robbed me of my peace of mind. But his very first words, after I had supplied him with liquid refreshment, plunged me again into the lowest depths of terror.

'Have you heard,' said he, 'that Mr Abercrombie has been arrested?'

'Good God!' I exclaimed, 'Mr Abercrombie arrested? What can he have done?'

'Mr Abercrombie, as you know,' Mr Gosling replied, 'has been a respectable and respected manager of a very important branch of one of our leading banks. His life, both professional and private, has been always blameless, as was his father's before him. It was confidently expected that in the next Birthday Honours List he would receive a knighthood, and a movement was on foot to have him chosen as Parliamentary candidate for the Division. But in spite of this long and honourable record, it appears that he has suddenly stolen a large sum of money, and has made a dastardly attempt to place the blame upon a subordinate.'

Having hitherto regarded Mr Abercrombie as a friend, I was deeply distressed by this news. As yet, he was on remand, and after some difficulty I persuaded the prison authorities to allow me to visit him. I found him emaciated and haggard, listless and despairing. At first he stared at me as though I were a stranger, and he only gradually became aware that he was seeing a former friend. I could not but connect his present disastrous condition with his visit to Dr Mallako, and I felt that perhaps, if I could pierce the mystery, I should find some explanation of his sudden guilt.

'Mr Abercrombie,' I said, 'you will remember that on a former occasion I tried to discover the cause of your strange behaviour, but you refused to reveal anything. For God's sake, do not again rebuff me. You see what has come of your previous reserve. Tell me the truth, I beseech you, for it may be not yet too late.'

'Alas!' he replied, 'the time for your well-meant efforts is past. For me there remains only a wearisome waiting for death – for my poor wife and my unhappy children, penury and shame. Unhappy moment in which I passed that accursed gate! Unhappy house in which I listened to the devilish insight of that malignant fiend!'

'I feared as much,' said I, 'but tell me all.'

'I visited Dr Mallako,' so Mr Abercrombie began his confession, 'in a spirit of carefree curiosity. What sort of horrors, I wondered, did Dr Mallako manufacture? What hope could he entertain of making a living out of persons who enjoyed his romances? There could not, I thought, be many like myself, willing to spend money in so idle a fashion. Dr Mallako, however, appeared completely self-assured. He treated me, not as most of the inhabitants of Mortlake, even the most substantial ones, were in the habit of treating me, as an important citizen whom it would be wise to conciliate. On the contrary, he treated me from the first with a kind of superiority which had in it a touch of disdain. And from his first sharp scrutiny I felt that he could read even my most secret thoughts.

'At first this seemed to me no more than a foolish fancy, and I tried to shake it off, but as his talk proceeded in even tones at an unchanging pace, and without the faintest indication of feeling, I fell gradually more and more under the spell. My will abandoned me, and strange secret thoughts which until that moment had not entered my consciousness except in nightmares came to the surface, like monsters of the deep emerging from their dark caves to bring horror to the crews of whalers. Like a derelict ship in the waste places of the Southern Seas, I drifted upon the tempest of his own creating, helpless, hopeless, but fascinated.'

'But what,' I interrupted, 'was Dr Mallako saying to you all this time? I cannot help you if your language is so vague and metaphorical. Concrete details are what I must have if Counsel is to be of any use to you.'

He sighed deeply, and proceeded: 'At first we conversed in a desultory manner about this and that. I mentioned friends of mine whom harsh business conditions had ruined. Under the influence of his apparent sympathy I confessed that I also had reason to fear ruin. "Ah, well," he said, "there is always a way to avert ruin if one is willing to take it.

' "I have a friend whose circumstances at one time were not very different from yours at the present moment. He also was a bank manager; he also was trusted; he also speculated and faced ruin. But he was not the man to sit down tamely under such a prospect. He realised that he had certain assets: his apparently blameless life, his satisfactory performance of all the tasks imposed by his professional duties, and, what perhaps was not the least of these assets, a man immediately beneath him in the hierarchy of the bank who had allowed himself to acquire the repute of being somewhat harum-scarum, not quite so correct in behaviour as becomes a man entrusted to deal with other people's money, not always sedate, sometimes the worse for liquor, and at least once in this condition guilty of uttering subversive political opinions.

' "My friend," so Dr Mallako continued, after a short pause, during which he sipped his whisky, "my friend realised, and this perhaps is the best proof of his ability, that should any defalcations be discovered in the bank's accounts, it would not be difficult to throw suspicion upon this irresponsible young man. My friend prepared the ground very carefully. Without the young man's knowledge, he hid in the young man's flat a

48

bundle of bank notes abstracted from the bank. Over the telephone, nominally in the young man's name, he placed large bets on horses which did not win a place. He reckoned correctly the number of days which would elapse before the bookmaker wrote indignant letters to the young man complaining of non-payment. At exactly the right moment he allowed it to be discovered that there was a huge loss in the bank's cash. He communicated at once with the police, and, apparently distraught, he reluctantly allowed the police to drag from him the name of the young man as the only possible suspect. The police proceeded to the young man's flat, found the bundle of notes and read with considerable interest the indignant communication from the bookmaker. Needless to say, the young man was sent to prison, and the manager was more trusted than ever. His speculations on the Stock Exchange from this moment onwards were more cautious than they had been. He made a large fortune, became a baronet, and was chosen to represent his constituency in Parliament. But of his ultimate activities as a Cabinet Minister it would be indiscreet of me to speak. From this true story," said Dr Mallako, "you will see that a little enterprise and a little ingenuity can turn threatened defeat into triumph, and secure the profound respect of all right-minded citizens." '

'While he spoke,' Mr Abercrombie resumed, 'my mind was in a turmoil. I myself was in difficulties through rash speculations. I myself had a subordinate who had all the characteristics of the young man denounced by Dr Mallako's friend. I myself, though my thoughts had hardly aspired so high as to a baronetcy, had toyed with the hope of a knighthood and a seat in Parliament. These hopes would have a firm foundation if my present difficulties could be surmounted; if not, I was faced by the prospect of poverty, perhaps disgrace. I thought of my wife, who shared my hopes, and had visions of herself as Lady Abercrombie, compelled perhaps to keep a seaside boarding-house, and not (so I feared) slow to point out to me morning, noon and night, the afflictions which my folly had brought upon her head. I thought of my two sons, now both at a good public school, looking forward to an honourable career, in which athletic honours should pave the way for responsible posts. I thought of these sons, suddenly taken away from their paradise, compelled to attend some plebeian secondary school, and at the age of eighteen to adopt some obscure and humdrum means of livelihood. I thought of my neighbours in Mortlake, no longer genial, but passing me in the street with averted looks, unwilling to share a drink or listen to my opinions on the Chinese imbroglio.

'All these visions of horror floated through my mind as Dr Mallako's calm and even voice inexorably proceeded. "How can I endure all this?" I thought. "Never, while any way of escape presents itself. But can I, I who am no longer young, I whose career has hitherto been blameless, I whom all my neighbours greet with a smile, can I suddenly abandon all this security for the dangerous existence of a criminal?" Could I live, day after day and night after night, with the dread of discovery hanging over me? Could I preserve before my wife that air of calm superiority upon which my domestic bliss depended? Could I continue as heretofore to greet my sons on their return from school with the moral maxims that are expected of a substantial parent? Could I inveigh with conviction in my railway carriage about the inefficiency of the police and their lamentable failure to catch criminals whose depredations were shaking the pillars of the financial order? I realised with a cold shudder of doubt that if I should fail in any of these things after acting like Dr Mallako's friend, I should be liable to incur suspicion. There would be those who would say: "I wonder what has happened to Mr Abercrombie. He used to utter his sentiments with full-blooded gusto in a loud and convincing tone, such as would cause any malefactor to quake, but now, though the same sentiments come from his lips, he whispers and stutters while he utters them, and I have even seen him looking over his shoulder when speaking of the inefficiency of the police. I find this puzzling, and I cannot but think that there is some mystery about Mr Abercrombie."

'This painful vision grew more and more vivid in my tortured imagination. I saw in my mind's eye my neighbours in Mortlake and my friends in the City comparing notes and at last arriving at the grim conclusion that the change in my manner closely synchronised with the famous disaster at my bank. From this discovery, I feared it would be but a step to my downfall. "No," I thought, "never will I listen to the voice of this sinister tempter. Never will I abandon the path of duty!" And yet . . . and yet. . . .

'How easy it all seemed, as the soothing voice went on and on, with its suave history of triumph. And had I not read somewhere that the trouble with our world is unwillingness to take risks? Had not some eminent philosopher enunciated the maxim that one should live dangerously? Was it not perhaps even in some higher sense my duty to listen to such teaching, and put it into practice with such means as circumstances placed at my disposal? Contending arguments, contending hopes and fears, contending habits and aspirations produced in me an utterly bewildering turmoil. At last I could bear it no longer. "Dr Mallako," I exclaimed, "I do not know whether you are an angel or a devil, but I do know that I would to God I had never met you." It was at this point that I rushed from the house and met you at the gate.

'Never since that fatal interview have I enjoyed a moment's peace of mind. By day I looked at all whom I met and thought to myself: "What would they do if. . . ?" At night before I slept, alternate horrors of ruin and prison buffeted me this way and that in an endless game of battledore and shuttlecock. My wife complained of my restlessness, and at last insisted upon my sleeping in my dressing-room. There, when tardy sleep came, it was more terrible even than the hours of wakefulness. In nightmares I walked along a narrow alley between a workhouse and a prison. I was seized with fever, and tottered this way and that across the street, constantly falling almost into one or other of these dreadful buildings. I would see a policeman advancing upon me, and as his hand fell upon my shoulder, I would awake, shrieking.

'It is not to be wondered at if, in these circumstances, my affairs became more and more involved. My speculations grew wilder, and my debts mounted up. At last it seemed to me that no hope remained unless I copied Dr Mallako's friend. But in my distraught state I made mistakes which he did not make. The notes which I planted in the apartment of my harum-scarum subordinate bore my finger-prints. The telephone message to the bookmaker was proved by the police to have come from my house. The horse which I had confidently expected to lose, won the race to the surprise of everyone. This made the police the more ready to believe my subordinate when he denied ever having placed such a bet. All the hopeless entanglement of my affairs was laid bare by Scotland Yard. My subordinate, whom I had supposed to be a man of no account, turned out to be the nephew of a Cabinet Minister.

'None of this bad luck, I am sure, caused any surprise to Dr Mallako. He, I do not doubt, foresaw from the very first the whole course of events up to the present frightful moment. For me nothing remains but to take my punishment. Dr Mallako, I fear, has committed no legal crime, but oh, if you can find some method of bringing upon his head one-tenth of the sorrow that he has brought upon mine, you will know that in one of Her Majesty's prisons, one grateful heart is thanking you!'

Wrung with compassion, I bade farewell to Mr Abercrombie, promising to bear his last words in mind.

III

Mr Abercrombie's last words greatly increased the already intense horror which I felt towards Dr Mallako, but to my bewilderment I found that this increase of horror was accompanied by an increase of fascination. I could not forget the terrible doctor. I wished him to suffer, but I wished him to suffer through me, and I wished that at least once there should be between him and me some passage as deep and dark and terrible as the things that looked out of his eyes. I found, however, no way of gratifying either of these contradictory wishes, and for some time I continued the endeavour to become wholly absorbed in my scientific researches. I had begun to have some degree of success in this endeavour when I was plunged once more into the world of horror from which I had been trying to emerge. This happened through the misfortunes of Mr Beauchamp.

Mr Beauchamp, a man of about thirty-five years of age, had been known to me for a number of years as a pillar of virtue in Mortlake. He was secretary of a society concerned in distributing Bibles, and he was also concerned in purity work. He wore always a very old and shiny black coat and striped trousers which had seen better days. His tie was black, his manner earnest. Even in the train he was liable to quote texts. Every species of alcoholic drink he spoke of as 'fermented liquor', and not the faintest sip ever passed his lips. When he spilt a cup of scalding coffee all over himself, he exclaimed: 'Dear me, how very annoying!' In a society of men only, if he was sufficiently assured of the earnestness of his companions, he would sometimes regret the sad frequency of what he called 'carnal intercourse'. Late dinners were an abomination to him; he always had a high tea, which before the war used to consist of cold meat, pickles and a boiled potato, but in the days of austerity omitted the cold meat. His hand was always moist, and his handshake limp. There was not one person in Mortlake who could recall one single action of his for which even he would have had cause to blush.

But shortly before the time when I had seen him emerging from Dr Mallako's gate, something of a change had been observed in his demeanour. The black coat and striped trousers gave way to a dark grey suit with trousers of the same material. The black tie was replaced by a dark blue tie. His allusions to the Bible became less frequent, and he could, of an evening, see men drinking without being led into a discourse on the virtue of temperance. Once, and once only, he was seen hurrying along the street towards the station wearing a red carnation in his buttonhole. This indiscretion, which set all Mortlake agog, was not repeated. But the gossips were provided with fresh material by an event which occurred a few days after the red carnation. Mr Beauchamp was seen in a very smart motor-car, sitting beside a young and lovely lady, whose dressmaker was obviously Parisian. For a few days everybody asked the question: 'Who can she be?' Mr Gosling, as usual, was the first to supply the gossip demanded. I, like others, had been intrigued by the change in Mr Beauchamp, and one evening when Mr Gosling came to see me, he said:

'Have you heard who the lady is who is having so marked an effect upon our holy neighbour?'

'No,' I replied.

'Well,' he said, 'I have just ascertained who she is. She is Yolande Molyneux, widow of Captain Molyneux, whose painful end in the jungles of Burma during the last war was one of the innumerable tragedies of that time. The lovely Yolande, however, overcame her grief without much difficulty. Captain Molyneux, as you of course remember, was the only son of the famous soap manufacturer, and as his father's heir, he was already possessed of an ample fortune, doubtless with a view to minimizing death duties. This ample fortune has come to his widow, who is a lady of insatiable curiosity about various types of men. She has known millionaires and mountebanks, Montenegrin mountaineers and Indian fakirs. She is catholic in her tastes, but prefers whatever is bizarre. In her wanderings over the surface of our planet she had not previously made the acquaintance of Low Church sanctimony, and meeting it in the person of Mr Beauchamp, she found it a fascinating study. I shudder to think what she will make of poor Mr Beauchamp, for while he is in deadly earnest, she is merely adding a new specimen to her collection.'

I felt that this boded ill for Mr Beauchamp, but I failed to foresee the depth of disaster that lay ahead of him, since I did not at that time know of the activities of Dr Mallako. It was only after I had heard Mr Abercrombie's story that I realised what Dr Mallako might make of such material. Since he himself was unapproachable, I managed to make the acquaintance of the lovely Yolande, who lived in a fine old house on Ham Common. I found, however, to my disappointment that she knew nothing of Dr Mallako, whom Mr Beauchamp had never mentioned to her. She spoke of Mr Beauchamp always with amused and contemptuous toleration, and regretted his efforts to adapt himself to what he supposed to be her tastes.

'I like his texts,' she said, 'and I used to like his striped trousers. I like his stern refusal to partake of "fermented liquor", and I enjoy his stern repudiation of even such mild words as "blast" and "blow". It is these things that make him interesting to me, and the more he endeavours to resemble a normal human being, the more difficult I find it to preserve with him a friendly demeanour, without which his passion would drive him to despair. It is useless, however, to attempt to explain this to the dear man, since the whole matter is beyond his psychological comprehension.'

I found it useless to appeal to Mrs Molyneux to spare the poor man.

'Nonsense,' she would say, 'a little glimpse of feelings outside the domain of sanctimony will do him good. He will emerge more able to deal with the sinners who occupy the focus of his interests than he has hitherto been. I consider myself a philanthropist, and almost a participant in his work. You will see, before I have done with him, his power of rescuing sinners will be augmented a hundredfold. Every twinge of his own conscience will be transformed into burning rhetoric, and his hope that he himself may not be irretrievably damned will enable him to offer the prospect of ultimate salvation even to those whom he has hitherto regarded as utterly degraded. But enough of Mr Beauchamp,' she continued with a light laugh, 'I am sure that after this dry conversation you will wish to wash away the taste of Mr Beauchamp by one of my very special cocktails.'

Such conversations with Mrs Molyneux were, I saw, completely futile, and Dr Mallako remained aloof and unapproachable. Mr Beauchamp himself, when I tried to see him, was invariably setting off towards Ham Common, if he was not busy with the affairs of his office. It was observed, however, that these affairs occupied him less and less, and that the evening train in which he had been accustomed to return no longer found him in his usual place. Although I continued to hope for the best, I feared the worst.

It was my fears that proved justified. One evening, as I was passing his house, I observed a crowd at his door, and his elderly housekeeper in tears, beseeching them to go away. I knew the good lady, having often visited Mr Beauchamp, and I therefore asked her what was the matter.

'My poor master,' she said; 'Oh, my poor master!'

'What has happened to your poor master?' I asked.

'Oh, Sir, never shall I forget the dreadful sight that met my eyes when I opened the door of his study. His study, as you might know, was used long ago as a larder, and there are still hooks in the ceiling from which, in more spacious days, hams and legs of mutton used to be suspended. From one of these hooks, as I opened the door, I saw poor Mr Beauchamp hanging by a rope. An overturned chair lay on its side just beneath the poor gentleman, and I am forced to suppose that some sorrow had driven him to the rash act. What this sorrow may have been I do not know, but I darkly suspect the wicked woman whose wiles have been leading him astray!'

Nothing further was to be learned from her, but I thought it possible that her suspicions might be not unfounded, and that the perfidious Yolande might be able to throw some light upon the tragedy. I went immediately to her house, and found her in the very act of reading a letter which had just arrived by special messenger.

'Mrs Molyneux,' I said, 'our relations hitherto have been merely social, but the time has come for graver speech. Mr Beauchamp has been my friend; he has hoped to be something more than a friend to you. It is possible that you may be able to throw some light upon the dreadful event which has occurred in his house.'

'It *is* possible,' she said, with something rather more than her wonted seriousness. 'I have this very moment finished reading the last words of that unhappy man, the depth of whose feelings I now know that I misjudged. I will not deny that I have been to blame, but it is not I who am the chief culprit. That role belongs to an individual more sinister and more serious than myself. I allude to Dr Mallako. His part is revealed in the letter which I have been reading. Since you were a friend of Mr Beauchamp, and as I know that you are the sworn enemy of Dr Mallako, I think it only right that you should see this letter.'

With these words she put it into my hands, and I took my leave. I could not bring myself to read the letter until I was in my own house, and even then it was with trembling fingers that I unfolded its many sheets. The evil aura of the strange doctor seemed to envelop me as I spread them on my knees. And it was with the utmost difficulty that I prevented myself from being blinded by the vision of his baleful eyes, which made it almost impossible to read the terrible words which it was my duty to study. At last, however, I pulled myself together, and forced myself to become immersed in the torments which had driven poor Mr Beauchamp to his desperate act. Mr Beauchamp's letter was as follows:

My very dear Yolande,

I do not know whether the contents of this letter will come to you as a sorrow or as a relief from embarrassment. However that may be, I feel that my last words on earth must be addressed to you – for these are my last words. When I have finished this letter, I shall be no more.

My life, as you know, was drab and colourless until you came into it. Since I have known you, I have become aware that there are things of value in human existence in addition to prohibitions and the dusty 'don'ts' to which my activities have been devoted. Although all has ended in disaster, I cannot even now bring myself to regret the sweet moments in which you have seemed to smile upon me. But it is not of feelings that I am now to write.

Never until now, in spite of your not unnatural curiosity, have I revealed to you what it was that occurred when, shortly after I had made your acquaintance, I paid a fateful visit to Dr Mallako. At the time of that visit I had begun to wish that I were the kind of dashing figure that might impress your dear imagination, and had begun to look upon my past self as that of a dismal sanctimonious dolt. A new life, I felt, would be possible for me if I could but win your esteem. I did not, however, see any way in which this could be possible until my ill-omened visit to that malignant incarnation of Satan.

On the afternoon upon which I called upon him, he received me with a genial smile, took me to his consulting-room, and said:

'Mr Beauchamp, it is a great pleasure to see you here. I have heard much of your good works, and have admired your devotion to noble causes. It is, I must confess, somewhat difficult for me to conceive any way in which I can be of use to you, but if such a way exists, you have only to command me. Before we proceed to business, however, a little refreshment might be not amiss. I am well aware that you do not partake of the juice of the grape, or the distilled essence of grain, and I would not insult you by offering either, but perhaps a nice cup of cocoa, adequately sweetened, would be not unwelcome.'

I thanked him, not only for his kindness, but for his knowledge of my tastes, and after his housekeeper had supplied the cocoa, our serious colloquy began. Some magnetic quality in him elicited from me a degree of unreserve which I had not anticipated. I told him about you; I told him my hopes and I told him my fears; I told him the change in my aspirations and beliefs; I told him the intoxicating moments of kindness, which enabled me to live through the long days when you were cold; I told him how conscious I was that if I were to win you I must have more to offer, more in worldly goods, but not in worldly goods only –

more also in richness of character and conversational variety. If he could help me to achieve all this, I said, he would put me forever in his debt, and the paltry ten guineas which I was to pay for the consultation would prove the best investment ever made by mortal man.

Dr Mallako, after a moment's scrutiny, remarked in a meditative voice:

'Well, I am not certain whether what I am about to say will be of any use to you or not. But however that may be, I will tell you a little story which has a certain affinity with your case.

'I have a friend, a well known man, whom perhaps you may have met in the course of your professional work, whose early years were spent much as yours have been. He, like you, fell in love with a charming lady. He early realised that he would have little hope of winning her unless he could acquire more wealth than his previous course of life was likely to bring him. He, like you, distributed Bibles in many languages and in many lands. One day in the train he met a publisher of a somewhat dubious reputation. At an earlier time he would not have spoken to such a man, but now the liberalising influence of his amatory hopes made him more hospitable to types that he had hitherto considered without the pale.

'The publisher explained the immense international network by which dubious literature is got into the hands of those degenerates whom such pernicious stuff attracts. "The only difficulty," said the publisher, "lies in advertising. There is no difficulty about secret distribution, but secret advertising is almost a contradiction in terms." At this point the publisher's eyes twinkled and, with a mischievous smile, he said: "Now if we had someone like you to help us, the whole problem of advertising would be solved. You could, in the Bibles that you distribute, have occasional pointers. For example, when we are told that the heart is desperately wicked and deceitful above all things (Jeremiah xvii : 9), you will put a footnote saying that further information about the wickedness of the human heart can be obtained from Messrs So & So on application. And when Judah tells his servants to look for the whore that is without the city gates, you will put a footnote saying that doubtless most readers of the Holy Book do not know the meaning of this word, but that Messrs So & So will explain it on demand. And when the Word of God mentions the regrettable behaviour of Onan, another reference to us will be in order." The publisher, however, seemed to think that this was not the sort of thing that my friend would care to do, although of course, as he explained in a meditative and slightly regretful tone, if it were done, the profits would be colossal.

'My friend,' so Dr Mallako continued, 'took very little time to come to a decision. When he and the publisher arrived at their London terminus, they adjourned to the publisher's club, and after a few drinks, concluded the main heads of their agreement. My friend continued to distribute Bibles, the Bibles were more in demand than ever, the publisher's profits rose, and my friend became rich enough to have a fine house and a fine car. He gradually ceased to quote the Bible, except those passages to which he had appended footnotes. His conversation became lively and his cynicism amusing. The lady, who had at first merely toyed with him, became fascinated. They married, and lived happy ever after. You may or may not find this story interesting, but I fear that it is the only contribution I can make to the solution of your perplexities.'

I was horrified by what I felt to be the wickedness of Dr Mallako's suggestion. I felt it unthinkable that I, whose life had been governed hitherto by the straitest rules of rectitudes, should become associated with anything so universally execrated as the sale of obscene literature. I put this to Dr Mallako in no uncertain terms. Dr Mallako only smiled a wise and enigmatic smile.

'My friend,' said he, 'have you not been learning, ever since you had the good fortune to become acquainted with Mrs Molyneux, that there is a certain narrowness in the code of behaviour that you have hitherto followed? You must, I am sure, at some period have read the Song of Solomon, and I feel convinced that you have wondered how it came to be included in the Word of God. Such wondering is impious. And if some of the literature distributed by my friend's publisher is not wholly unlike the work of the wise but uxorious king, it is illiberal, on that account, to find fault with it. A little freedom, a little daylight, a little fresh air, even on the subjects from which you have sought to avert your thoughts (vainly, I am afraid), can do nothing but good, and is indeed to be commended by the example of the Holy Book.'

'But is there not,' I said, 'a grave danger that the perusal of such literature may lead young men, ay, and young women too, into deadly sin? Can I look my fellow men in the face when I reflect that perhaps at this very moment some unwedded couple is enjoying unholy bliss as a result of acts from which I derive a pecuniary profit?'

'Alas,' Dr Mallako replied, 'there is, I fear, much in our holy religion that you have failed adequately to understand. Have you reflected upon the parable of the ninety-nine just men who needed no repentance, and caused less joy in Heaven than the one sinner who returned to the fold? Have you never studied the text about the Pharisee and the Publican? Have you not allowed yourself to extract the moral from the penitent thief? Have you never asked yourself what it was that was blameworthy in the Pharisees whom our Lord denounced while eating their lunch? Have you never wondered at the praise of a broken and contrite heart? Can you say honestly that your heart, before you met Mrs Molyneux, was either broken or contrite? Has it ever occurred to you that one cannot be contrite without first sinning? Yet this is the plain teaching of the

Gospels. And if you wish to lead men into the frame of mind which is pleasing to God they must first sin. Doubtless many of those who buy the literature that my friend's publisher distributes will afterwards repent, and if we are to believe the teachings of our holy religion, they will then be more pleasing to their Maker than the impeccably righteous, among whom hitherto you have been a notable example.'

This logic confounded me, and I became perplexed in the extreme. But there remained one hesitation.

'Is there not,' I said, 'in such behaviour a terrible risk of detection? Is there not a very considerable likelihood that the police will discover the nefarious traffic from which these great profits are derived? Do not the prison gates yawn for the men who have been drawn into this illicit traffic?'

'Aha!' said Dr Mallako, 'There are convolutions and ramifications in our social system that have remained unknown to you and your co-adjutors. Do you suppose that where such large sums are involved there is no one among the authorities who, for a percentage, would be willing to co-operate, or, at least, shut his eyes? Such men, I can assure you, exist, and it is by their co-operation that my friend's publisher acquires security. If you should decide to copy his example, you have to make sure that official blindness is at your disposal.'

I could think of nothing more to say, and I left the house of Dr Mallako in a state of doubt, not only as to what I should do, but as to the whole basis of morality, and the purpose of a good life.

At first, doubt completely incapacitated me. I kept away from my office, and brooded darkly as to what I should do and how I should live. But gradually Dr Mallako's arguments acquired a greater and greater hold over my imagination. 'I cannot resolve,' so I thought to myself, 'the ethical doubts which have been instilled into my mind. I do not know what conduct is right and what is wrong. But I do know (so I thought in my blindness) what is the road to the heart of my beloved Yolande.'

At last, chance decided my final move, or at least I thought it was chance, though now I have my doubts. I met a man of exceptional worldly wisdom, a man who had wandered about the world in questionable activities and dubious localities. He professed to know the whole connection of the police with the underworld. He knew which policemen were incorruptible and which were not – so, at least, he said. It appeared that he made his living as an intermediary between would-be criminals and pliant policemen.

'But you, of course,' so he said, 'are not interested in such matters, seeing that your life is an open book, and that never, by a hair's breadth, have you been tempted to depart from legality.'

'That, of course, is true,' I replied, 'but at the same time I think it is my duty to enlarge my experience to the utmost, and if indeed you know any such policeman, I shall be glad if you will introduce me to him.'

He did so. He made me acquainted with Detective-Inspector Jenkins, who, so I was given to understand, had not that unbending virtue which most of us take for granted in our noble police force. I became gradually increasingly friendly with Inspector Jenkins, and by slow stages approached the subject of indecent publications, preserving always the guise of one solely concerned to acquire a knowledge of the world.

'I will introduce you,' he said, 'to a publisher of my acquaintance, one, I may say, with whom I have at various times done not unprofitable business.'

He duly introduced me to a Mr Mutton, who, he said, was the sort of publisher that had been in question. I had not before heard of his firm, but that, after all, did not surprise me, as I was entering a wholly unfamiliar world. After some preliminary skirmishing, I suggested to Mr Mutton that I could be useful to him in the way in which Dr Mallako's friend had been useful to his publisher. Mr Mutton did not reject the idea, but said that for his own protection he must have something from me in writing as to the nature of the proposal. Somewhat reluctantly I agreed.

All this happened only yesterday, while still bright hopes were leading me further and further towards perdition. Today – but how can I bring myself to reveal the dreadful truth, a truth which shows not only my wickedness, but also my incredible folly? – today a police constable presented himself at my front door. On being admitted, he showed me the document which I had signed at the request of Mr Mutton.

'Is this your signature?' he said.

Although utterly astonished, I had the presence of mind to say : 'That is for you to prove.'

'Well,' he said, 'I do not think that will offer much difficulty, and you may as well know the situation in which you will then find yourself. Detective-Inspector Jenkins is not, as you had been led to suppose, a dishonest public servant. He is, on the contrary, a man devoted to the preservation of our national life from all taint of impurity, and the reputation of corruptibility which he has been careful to acquire exists only to draw criminals into his net. Mr Mutton is a man of straw. Sometimes one detective, sometimes another, impersonates this nefarious character. You will perceive, Mr Beauchamp, that your hopes of escape are slender.'

With that, he took his departure. I realised at once that no hope remained for me, and no possibility of an endurable life. Even should I be fortunate enough to escape prison, the document which I signed would put an end to the employment from which I have hitherto gained my livelihood. And the disgrace would make it impossible to face you, without whom, life can have no savour. Nothing remains for me but death. I go to meet my Maker, whose just wrath will, no doubt, condemn me to those torments which I have so often and so vividly depicted to others. But there is one sentence which I believe he will vouchsafe me before I depart from the Dread Presence. That one sentence shall be: 'Of all the wicked men that have ever lived, none can be more wicked, none more disastrously designing, than Dr Mallako, whom, O Lord, I beseech Thee to reserve for some quite special depth in that hell where I am about to make my abode.'

This is all that I shall have to say to my Maker. To you, my fair one, out of the depths in which I am sunk, I wish all happiness and all joy.

IV

It was some time after the tragic fate of Mr Beauchamp that I learned what had happened to Mr Cartwright. I am happy to say that his fate was somewhat less dreadful, but it cannot be denied that it was not such as most people would welcome. I learned what had become of him partly from his own lips, partly from those of my only episcopal friend.

Mr Cartwright, as everyone knows, was a famous artistic photographer, patronised by all the best film stars and politicians. He made a speciality of catching a characteristic expression, such as would induce all who saw the photograph to draw favourable inferences about the original. He had as his assistant a lady of extreme beauty, named Lalage Scraggs. Her beauty was marred for his clients only by a somewhat excessive languor. It was said, however, by those who knew them well, that towards Mr Cartwright there was no such languor, but that the pair were united by an ardent passion, not, I regret to say, sanctified by any legal tie. Mr Cartwright had, however, one great sorrow. Although he worked morning, noon, and night, with an impeccable artistic conscience, and although his clientele became more and more distinguished, he was unable, owing to the rapacious demands of the tax-gatherer, to gratify the somewhat expensive wishes of himself and the lovely Lalage.

'What is the good,' he was wont to say, 'of all this toil, when at least nine-tenths of my nominal earnings are seized by the Government to buy molybdenum or tungsten or some other substance in which I take no interest?'

The discontent thus engendered embittered his life, and he frequently contemplated retiring to the Principality of Monaco. When he saw Dr Mallako's brass plate, he exclaimed:

'Can this worthy man have discovered any horror more horrifying than surtax? If so, he must indeed be a man of considerable imagination. I will consult him in the hope that he may enlarge my mind.'

Having secured an appointment, he visited Dr Mallako on an afternoon when it so happened that he was not in demand for the photographing of any film star or Cabinet Minister or foreign diplomat. Even the Argentine Ambassador, who had promised to pay his fee in rounds of beef, had chosen a different date.

After the usual polite preliminaries, Dr Mallako came to the point, and asked what type of horror Mr Cartwright desired, 'for,' said Dr Mallako, with a quiet smile, 'I have horrors to suit all customers.'

'Well,' said Mr Cartwright, 'the horror I want is one concerned with methods of earning money that will escape the attention of the Tax Collector. I do not know whether you can invest this subject with such horror as your brass plate promises, but if you can, you will earn my gratitude.'

'I think,' said Dr Mallako, 'that I can give you what you want. Indeed, my professional pride is involved, and I should be ashamed to fail you. I will tell you a little story which may perhaps help you to make up your mind.

'I have a friend who lives in Paris. He, like you, is a photographer of genius. He, like you, has a beautiful assistant who is not indifferent to Parisian pleasures. He, like you, found taxation irksome, so long as he confined himself to the legitimate exercise of his profession. He now still depends upon photography, but his methods are more progressive. He makes a practice of ascertaining at what hotel in Paris each of the stream of celebrities who visit that great city is to be expected. His beautiful assistant seats herself in the lobby at the time when the great man is about to arrive. While he is busy at the desk, she suddenly gasps, totters, and appears about to faint. The gallant gentleman, being the only male who enjoys sufficient proximity, inevitably rushes to her support. At the moment when she is in his arms, the camera clicks. Next day, my friend waits upon him with the developed photograph, and asks how much he will pay to have the negative and all the copies destroyed. If the victim is an eminent divine or an American politician, he is usually willing to pay a very considerable sum. By this means, my friend has improved upon the forty-hour week. His assistant works only one day in the week; he works on two days – the one when he first takes the photograph, and the other when he visits his victim. The remaining five days of each week the pair spend in bliss. Perhaps,' Dr Mallako concluded, 'you may find something in this little story that may be of some use to you in your unfortunate perplexities.'

Only two things worried Mr Cartwright about this suggestion. One was the fear of discovery, the other was a distaste for such apparently amatory promiscuity on the part of the fair Lalage. Fear conjured up visions of the police; jealousy, even more potent, suggested some possible celebrity whose arms Lalage might prefer to his own. But while he was still debating the matter in his mind, he received a demand for twelve thousand pounds for income-tax and surtax. Mr Cartwright, to whom economy was wholly foreign, did not possess twelve thousand pounds in any available form, and after a few sleepless nights, he decided that there was nothing for it but to imitate Dr Mallako's friend.

After suitable preparations and a survey of the field of possible celebrities, Mr Cartwright decided that his first victim should be the Bishop of Boria-boola-ga, who was visiting London for a Pan-Anglican Congress. Everything went off like clockwork. The tottering lady fell into the arms of the Bishop, and the arms encircled her with no visible reluctance. Mr Cartwright, concealed behind a screen, emerged at the right moment, and waited next day upon the Bishop with a very convincing photograph.

'This, my dear Bishop,' he said, 'is, as I am sure you will agree, an artistic masterpiece. I cannot but think that you will wish to possess it, since everyone knows of your passion for negro art, and this might well serve as a religious picture in some native cult. But in view of my over-heads, and the large salary that I am compelled to pay to my highly skilled assistant, I cannot part with the negative and the few copies that I have made of it for less than a thousand pounds, and even this is a fee reduced to its lowest possible figure, out of sympathy for the well known poverty of our Colonial Episcopate.'

'Well,' said the Bishop, 'this is a most unpleasant contretemps. You can hardly suppose that I possess a thousand pounds here and now. I will, however, since clearly you have me in your grip, give you an I.O.U. and a lien on the revenues of my See.'

Mr Cartwright was much relieved to find the Bishop so reasonable, and they parted on almost friendly terms.

It so happened, however, that the Bishop in question differed in some important ways from the majority of his colleagues. He had been a friend of mine when I was at the university, and as an undergraduate he had been noted as a practical joker. Some of his jokes were perhaps not quite in the best of taste. People were surprised when he decided to take Orders, and still more surprised when they learned that, although his sermons were eloquent and convincing and although he brought thousands to a mood of piety, he was still unable to refrain from the kind of conduct that had made him notorious among his undergraduate friends. The authorities in the Church struggled to take a severe view of his misdemeanours, but inevitably at the last moment they could not refrain from smiling. They therefore decided that while some punishment was called for, it should not be too extreme, and the penalty they chose was to make him Bishop of Boria-boolo-ga, with the condition that he must never leave his diocese without the express permission of the Archbishops of Canterbury and York. I happened to meet him at this time when an anthropologist was reading a paper on the Central African ritual, to which, in the subsequent discussion, the Bishop contributed some trenchant comments. I had always enjoyed his society, and I induced him at the end of the meeting to come with me to my club.

'I believe,' said he, 'that you are a neighbour of a certain Mr Cartwright, with whom not long ago I had a somewhat curious encounter.'

He then related the circumstances, and wound up with the ominous remark:

'I fear your friend Mr Cartwright hardly realises what is in store for him.'

The Bishop had, in fact, been much impressed by Mr Cartwright's technique, and had wondered whether there was any method by which he could make use of it for the salvation of his black parishioners. At last he hit upon a plan. He took pains to study the Soviet Ambassador, and when he had grasped all his features, gestures, and mannerisms, he hunted among out-of-work actors for one closely resembling that eminent and respected diplomat. Having found one, he induced the man to pose as a fellow-traveller and to get himself invited to a Soviet reception. He then wrote a letter purporting to come from the Ambassador inviting Mr Cartwright to meet him in a certain hotel. Mr Cartwright accepted. The apparent Ambassador slipped into his hand a huge envelope, and at the moment at which he received the envelope he heard a sound only too familiar to him – the click of a concealed camera. On looking at the envelope he saw to his horror that it contained in large and clear writing, not only his name, but the superscription 'ten million roubles'. Sure enough, the Bishop came to see him next day, and said:

'Well, my dear friend, you know that imitation is the sincerest flattery, and I have come to flatter you. Here is a photograph quite as good as the one you took of me, and, if I may say so, far more damaging. For I doubt whether the inhabitants of Boria-boola-ga would think much the worse of me for embracing a lovely lady, but the authorities of this great country would certainly think the worse of you if they got a sight of this picture. I do not, however, wish to be too hard upon you, for I have a certain admiration of your ingenuity. I will therefore make easy terms. You must, of course, give me back my I.O.U. and the lien on the revenue of my See, and for so long as you continue the practice of your profession it must be subject to certain conditions. The men whom you blackmail must be only notorious infidels, whose moral downfall, if believed in, will redound to the credit of the true faith. Ninety per cent of any moneys that you receive in this way must be handed over to me.

'You will know that there are still a certain number of heathen in Boria-boola-ga, and that I have a large bet with the neighbouring Bishop of Nyam-Nyam as to whom can make the most rapid increase in the number of the faithful in his diocese. I have discovered that all the inhabitants of a village will consent to be baptised if the headman of the village does so. I have discovered also that a headman will consent for the price of three pigs, which is less in Central Africa than it is here. We may perhaps put it at about fifteen pounds. There are still about a thousand headmen to be converted. I require, therefore, for the completion of my work the sum of fifteen thousand pounds. When I have acquired this sum through your operations on free-thinkers, we shall reconsider our relations. For the present, you shall be free from any unpleasant attentions either on my part or on that of the police.'

Mr Cartwright, disconcerted, but not yet quite despairing, saw no alternative but to obey the episcopal directions. His first victims were leaders of the Ethical Movement, which exists to maintain that the highest virtue is possible without the help of Christian dogma. His next victims were Communist leaders from the United States, Australia, and other virtuous parts of the world, who had come together to an important conference in London. Before very long, he had succeeded in acquiring the fifteen thousand pounds that the Bishop demanded. The Bishop received the sum in a reverent spirit, and expressed his thankfulness that he would now be able to extirpate paganism in his hitherto benighted diocese.

'And now,' said Mr Cartwright, 'you will, I am sure, admit that I have earned freedom from your further attentions.'

'Not so fast,' said the Bishop, 'I still possess the original photograph upon which our compact was based. I can, without the slightest difficulty, supply the police with legal evidence of the methods by which you have collected the fifteen thousand pounds that you have handed to me, and you have no evidence whatever that I was in any degree a party to your practices. I cannot see that you have any claim to freedom from my demands.

'I am, however, as I said before, a merciful master, and though you will remain my slave, I will not make your bondage intolerable. There are still two things that are amiss in Boria-boola-ga; one is that the Head Chief still obstinately clings to the faith of his ancestors, and the other is that the population is less than that of Nyam-Nyam. There is a method by which you and your beautiful assistant can remedy both these defects. I have sent her photograph to the Head Chief, and he has fallen madly in love with it. I have given him to understand that if he will become a convert I can secure that she will become his wife. And as for your part, I shall demand that you take up your residence in Boria-boola-ga, and that you shall have a large dusky harem. You shall devote yourself, while your powers last, to begetting souls whom I shall baptise, and if at any time any neglect of your duties becomes apparent through a fall in the birth-rate in your harem, your criminal activities shall be made known.

'I will not say that this is a life sentence. When you reach the age of seventy, you and the exquisite Lalage, perhaps by that time no longer exquisite, shall be allowed to return to England, and to pick up such livelihood as is to be obtained from passport photography. Lest you should think of illegal violence as a way of escape, I must inform you that I have left a sealed envelope at my bank, with orders that it is to be opened if at any time I die in a manner capable of arousing suspicion. This envelope, once opened, will ensure your ruin. Meanwhile I look forward with much pleasure to the enjoyment of your company in our joint exile. Good morning.'

Mr Cartwright found no escape from this painful situation. The last time I saw him was at the docks, as he was embarking for Africa. He was bidding a heartbroken farewell to Miss Scraggs, whom the Bishop was compelling to travel by a different ship. I could not but feel some sympathy, but I consoled myself with the thought of the indubitable benefits to the spread of the Gospel.

V

Amid all the troubles of Mr Abercrombie, Mr Beauchamp, and Mr Cartwright, I had not lost sight of Mrs Ellerker. Indeed events had occurred in connection with her which had caused me much anxiety.

Mr Ellerker was a designer of aeroplanes, and was considered by the Ministry to be one of the ablest men in this department. He had only one rival, Mr Quantox, who, as it happened, also lived in Mortlake. Some authorities considered Mr Ellerker the abler man, some preferred the work of Mr Quantox, but no one else in England was considered to reach so high a standard of ability in their field. Except professionally, however, the two men were widely divergent. Mr Ellerker was a man of narrowly scientific education, unacquainted with literature, indifferent to the arts, pompous in conversation, and addicted to heavy platitudes. Mr Quantox, on the contrary, was sparkling and witty, a man of wide education and wide culture, a man who could amuse any company by observations which combined wit with penetrating analysis. Mr Ellerker had never looked at any woman but his wife; Mr Quantox, on the other hand, had a roving eye, and would have incurred moral reprobation but for the national value of his work, which, like Nelson's, compelled the moralists to pretend ignorance. Mrs Ellerker, in many of these respects, bore more resemblance to Mr Quantox than to her husband. Her father was Reader in Anthropology in one of our older universities; she had spent her youth in the most intelligent society to be found in England; she was accustomed to the combination of wit and wisdom, and of both with an absence of the ponderous moralism which Mr Ellerker retained from the Victorian age. Her neighbours in Mortlake were divided into those who enjoyed her sparkling talk, and those who feared that such lightness in word could not be wedded to perfect correctness in behaviour. The more earnest and elderly among her acquaintances darkly suspected her of moral lapses skilfully concealed, and

65

were inclined to pity Mr Ellerker for having such a flighty wife. The other faction pitied Mrs Ellerker, as they imagined his comments on *The Times* leaders at breakfast.

After Mrs Ellerker's dramatic departure from the house of Dr Mallako, I made a point of cultivating her acquaintance in the hope that sooner or later I might be of use to her. When I came to know Dr Mallako's part in the misfortunes of Mr Abercrombie, I felt it my duty to warn her against him, but this I found unnecessary, since she vehemently repudiated any thought of further acquaintance with him. A new anxiety soon beset me in relation to her. It came to be known that she and Mr Quantox were meeting more frequently perhaps than was wise in view of the rivalry between him and Mr Ellerker. Mr Quantox, in spite of the charm of his conversation, seemed to me a dangerous acquaintance for one in the unstable condition in which Mrs Ellerker had been left by the impact of Dr Mallako. I hinted something to this effect in the course of a conversation with her, but her reaction was quite different from what it had been in the case of Dr Mallako. She flared up, said that gossip was disgusting, and that Mr Quantox was a man against whom she would not hear a word. So angry did she become that I discontinued my visits to her house, and, in fact, became completely out of touch with her.

So matters remained until one morning, on opening the newspaper, I found terrible news. A plane built to a new model designed by Mr Ellerker had burst into flames on its trial flight. The pilot had been burnt to death, and an inquiry had been ordered. But worse was to follow. When the police examined Mr Ellerker's papers they found what appeared to be conclusive evidence that he had been in touch with a foreign Power, and that treachery had led him to deliberate faults in the design of the new plane. When these documents came to light, Mr Ellerker committed suicide by taking a dose of poison.

Recollections of Dr Mallako made me doubt whether the truth was quite what it had been made to appear. I visited Mrs Ellerker, whom I found in a condition not so much of grief as of distraction. I found her afflicted not only with natural sorrow, but with a kind of terror, which at the time I could not understand. In the middle of a sentence she would stop, and seem to be listening, though there was nothing that I could hear. She would then pull herself together with an effort, and say: 'Yes . . . yes . . . what was it we were saying?' and in a half-hearted way take up the conversation where it had been left. I was deeply troubled about her, but she refused at this time to give me her confidence, and I was helpless.

Mr Quantox, meanwhile, had been marching on to new triumphs. His only rival was gone; the Government depended more and more upon him as their main hope in the armaments race; his name appeared in the Birthday Honours, and his praise was in every newspaper.

For a month or two nothing further happened, until one day I learned from Mr Gosling that Mrs Ellerker, in the deepest widow's weeds, had rushed distractedly to the Air Ministry, had insisted wildly that she must see the Minister, and on being shown into his presence had poured forth an incoherent tale, which had appeared to him to be nothing but the product of madness due to grief. He could not quite understand her story, but he gathered that she was bringing incredible accusations against Mr Quantox, and, incidentally, against herself. An eminent psychiatrist was summoned, and agreed at once that poor Mrs Ellerker's mind had become unhinged. Mr Quantox was too valuable a public servant to be at the mercy of a hysterical woman, and Mrs Ellerker, after being quickly certified, was removed to an asylum.

It so happened that the medical officer in charge of this asylum was an old friend of mine. I went to see him, and asked him, in confidence, to tell me something about the sad case of Mrs Ellerker. When he had said as much as discretion permitted, I said:

'Dr Prendergast,' for that was his name, 'I have some knowledge of Mrs Ellerker's circumstances, and of her social milieu. I think it not impossible that if I am permitted to have an interview with her, without the presence of those attendants who are thought desirable in most mental cases, I may be able to discover the source of her disorder, and perhaps even to point the way towards a cure. I do not say this lightly. There are circumstances known to very few which have a bearing upon the strange occurrences that have brought about Mrs Ellerker's mental instability. I shall be deeply grateful if you will permit me the opportunity that I seek.'

Dr Prendergast, after some hesitation, agreed.

I found the poor lady sitting alone and dejected, showing no interest in anything, barely looking up as I entered the room, and giving almost no sign of recognition.

'Mrs Ellerker,' I said, 'I do not believe that you are suffering from insane delusions. I know Dr Mallako, and I know Mr Quantox, and I knew your late husband. I find it quite incredible that Mr Ellerker should have been guilty of such conduct as has been imputed to him, but I find it wholly credible that Dr Mallako and Mr Quantox between them should have brought a good man to destruction. If I am right in my suspicions you can at least rely upon me to give weight to anything that you may care to tell me, and not to treat it as the delusions of a ruined mind.'

'God bless you for these words,' she replied fervently, 'they are the first that I have heard from which I derive any hope of causing the truth to be believed. Since you are willing to hear my story, I will tell it to you in all its painful details. I must not spare myself, for my part has been one of deep obloquy. But, believe me, I am purged of the evil influence which led me along the downward path, and I wish with all my heart to make such amends as are possible to the besmirched memory of my poor husband.'

With these words she began a long and terrible history.

The whole chain of disaster began, as I had suspected, with the machinations of Dr Mallako. Mr Ellerker, having learned that Dr Mallako was a neighbour of considerable academic distinction, decided that social relations would be in order, and, accompanied by Mrs Ellerker, paid a call upon that enigmatic personage on the afternoon on which I encountered Mrs Ellerker fainting at the gate.

After some minutes of desultory conversation, Mr Ellerker, whose importance was such that the Ministry had always to be informed of his whereabouts, was rung up on the telephone, and told that certain documents in his possession were urgently needed and must be sent immediately by special messenger. He had these documents in his attaché case, and decided that he must go out at once and find a messenger to take them.

'You, my dear,' he said to his wife, 'will perhaps not mind staying with Dr Mallako during the short time that I shall be absent. When my business is concluded, I will return to fetch you.'

Mrs Ellerker, who had found Dr Mallako's conversation more promising than that of most of the inhabitants of Mortlake, was by no means unwilling to have this opportunity of conversation not overshadowed by her husband's pomposities. Dr Mallako, with a penetration which she vainly endeavoured to resent, had observed the irritation and boredom caused by her husband's lengthy verbosity. What struck her as remarkable, although not at the moment a cause of suspicion, was Dr Mallako's acquaintance with other people whose circumstances were not unlike her own. He had known, so he said, other designers of aeroplanes, some dull, some interesting. Oddly enough, so he continued, it was the dull ones who had interesting wives.

'You will of course understand, my dear lady,' so he interrupted his story to say, 'that I am merely gossiping about various people that I have happened to meet in the course of my life, and that none of them, so far as I am able to judge, bear any close resemblance to any of the inhabitants of this suburb.

'But in the very brief moments during which I have enjoyed your company, I have already perceived that the human drama is not without interest for you, and I will therefore proceed with my little story.

'I knew at one time two rivals (you will of course understand that this was in another country), one of whom I regret to say was filled with bitter envy of the other's success. The envious one was witty and charming, the other heavy, and without interest in anything outside his work. The envious one (I fear you may find this incredible, but I assure you it is a fact) ingratiated himself with the wife of his less interesting colleague. She fell madly in love with him. She feared that he was less in love with her than she with him. Infatuation drove her on, and at last she told him in a moment of uncontrollable passion that there was no act from which she would shrink if she could thereby win his love. He appeared to hesitate, but after some time he said that there was one quite small thing which she might do for him, a very little thing, so little that she might think it not worth such great preliminaries. Her husband, like other men with similar work, would often bring home with him from the office uncompleted designs to which he wished to put the finishing touches during the small hours. These designs lay on his desk, and while he slept, they were unguarded. Could she, perhaps, without interrupting the worthy man's snores, slip out at break of day, and make such slight changes in the design as her lover would indicate to her from time to time? She could and she would. Her husband, all unconscious of her activities, caused a new plane to be constructed, in accordance with his design as he thought, but in fact with those changes that the wicked lover had indicated. The plane was made; her husband, full of pride in his supposed achievement, took up the plane on its trial flight. It burst into flames and he was killed. The lover, full of gratitude, married her as soon as a decent interval had elapsed. You may have thought, my dear lady,' so Dr Mallako concluded the tale, 'that some remorse would have dimmed her bliss, but it was not so. So sparkling and delightful was her lover, that never for a single instant did she regret the humdrum husband whom she had sacrificed. Her joy was unclouded, and to this day they are among the happiest couples of my acquaintance.'

At this point Mrs Ellerker exclaimed in horror: 'There cannot be such wicked women!'

To which Dr Mallako replied: 'There are some very wicked women in the world – and there are some very boring men.'

Throughout Dr Mallako's discourse, Mrs Ellerker, who had hitherto, though with difficulty, lived a virtuous life, found herself obsessed by images which she longed to repress, but could not. She had met Mr Quantox at various social gatherings. He had shown the most flattering interest in her. He had appeared aware that she had not only charms of person, but a distinguished mind. He had always shown more desire to converse with her than with anyone else in the company. Only now, while Dr Mallako was talking, she became aware that after such meetings the thought had darted through her mind how different life might be if he were her husband, and not her poor Henry. This thought had been so fleeting and so quickly repressed that until Dr Mallako's discourse brought it into the open, it had not been sufficiently emphatic to distress her. But now it was out in the open. Now she imagined what she would feel if Mr Quantox's eyes looked at her with passion, if Mr Quantox's arms were about her, if Mr Quantox's lips were in contact with her own. Such thoughts made her tremble, but she could not banish them.

'My mind,' she thought, 'has been decaying in the soporific monotony of Henry's undeviating flatness. His comments on the newspaper at breakfast make me wish to scream. After dinner, when he imagines we have a happy time of leisure, he invariably sleeps, and yet notices at once if I attempt to occupy myself in any way. I do not know how to endure his assumption that I am a sweet and silly little woman, such as he used to read about in adolescence in the bad Victorian novels which he has never outgrown. How different my life would be if it were passed with my dear Eustace, as at least in my dreams I must call Mr Quantox. How we should stimulate each other, how shine, how make the company marvel at our brilliance! And how he would love, with passion and fire, and yet with a kind of lightness, not with the heaviness of uncooked dough.'

All these thoughts and images rushed through her mind as Dr Mallako talked. But at the same time another voice, not so loud, not so strident, but nevertheless not without power, reminded her that Mr Ellerker was a good man, that he did every duty of which he was aware, that his work was distinguished, and his life honourable. Could she, like the wicked woman in Dr Mallako's story, doom such a man to a painful death?

Torn between duty and desire, she was rocked this way and that by the conflict of passion and compassion. At length, forgetting all about Mr Ellerker's intended return, she fled wildly from the house, and fainted as she met me at the gate.

Mrs Ellerker, amid the turmoil of her feelings, would have wished to avoid Mr Quantox, at any rate until her mind was made up one way or the other. For a few days she took refuge in illness and kept to her bed, but this way out could not last. To her dismay, as soon as she was up and about, Mr Ellerker said to her:

'Amanda, my dear, now that my little singing bird is restored to health, I wish to ask our neighbour Mr Quantox to tea. You, of course, do not trouble your pretty head with my professional duties, but Mr Quantox and I are, in a sense, rivals, and I should wish that there should be between us that civilised behaviour which becomes men of the twentieth century. I think therefore it would be a good plan to ask Mr Quantox here, and I hope you will do your best to be nice to him – and when you are nice, my dear, few people can be nicer.'

There was no escape. Mr Quantox came. Mr Ellerker, as was his wont, retired to his desk and his papers as soon as politeness permitted, saying as he went:

'I am sorry, Mr Quantox, that public duty prevents me from enjoying any more of your delightful society, but I leave you in good hands. My wife, though not capable of following the intricacies of our somewhat difficult profession, will, I am convinced, be not unable to entertain you for the next half hour or so, if you can tear yourself away for so long a time from those occupations which to us both contain the chief fascination of life.'

When he was gone, Mrs Ellerker, for a moment, was paralysed by embarrassment, but Mr Quantox did not allow this mood to continue.

'Amanda,' he said, 'if I may be permitted so to call you, this is the moment for which I have waited since our first meeting at that tedious party, which you alone made tolerable. Who indeed is there in this tiresome suburb with whom either you or I can exchange an intelligent word except each other? I allow myself to hope that you perhaps recognise in me, as I in you, a civilised being, capable of speaking the language that to both of us is natural.'

The rest of his conversation was less personal. He spoke with taste and understanding and knowledge of books and music and pictures, of things which Mr Ellerker ignored, and Mortlake had never heard of. She forgot her scruples, and as he rose to say good-bye, her eyes were shining.

'Amanda,' he said, 'this has indeed been a delightful half hour. May I hope that some day, some not too distant day, you may be induced to inspect my first editions? I have some which are not unworthy of even your eyes, and it would be a pleasure to show them to one so well able to appreciate them.'

For a moment she hesitated, then, overcome with reckless desire, she agreed, and a date was fixed at a time when Mr Ellerker was certain to be in his office. Somewhat nervously she rang his bell. It was he himself who opened the door, and she realised that they were alone in the house. He led the way to his library, and as soon as the door was shut, he took her in his arms. . . .

When at last she tore herself away, in the realisation that dear Henry was about to return, and would expect to greet her playfully with the question: 'Well, and what has my little singing bird been doing in the absence of its mate?' she felt desperately that some bond stronger and more stable than mere passion must be forged if she and her beloved Eustace (as she had learned to call Mr Quantox) were to have more than a passing affair.

'Eustace,' she said, 'I love you, and there is nothing that I would not do, if it might in any way further your happiness.'

'My dear one,' he replied, 'I could not burden you with my problems. You are to me sunshine and light, and I do not wish you associated in my thoughts with the dismal round of daily toil.'

'Oh, Eustace,' she replied, 'do not think of me so. I am not a butterfly. I am not, as Henry supposes, a little singing bird. I am a woman of intelligence and capacity, capable of sharing in the serious life of even such a one as you. I have enough at home of being treated as a plaything. It is not so that I wish you, my beloved, to treat me.'

Mr Quantox seemed to hesitate, and then, at last, to make up his mind. With a momentary pang of terror she heard him repeat almost literally the words of Dr Mallako's 'little story'.

'Well,' he said, 'there is one thing that you could do for me, a very little thing, too little, you may think, for such preliminaries.'

'Oh, what is it, Eustace? Tell me!' she cried.

'Well,' he said, 'I imagine that your husband not infrequently brings home with him uncompleted plans for the construction of new planes. If you were to make some very small and unimportant alterations in these plans, such as I shall suggest to you, you would be serving me, and, I dare to hope, yourself.'

'I will do it,' she said, 'you have but to instruct me!' And with that she hurried from the house.

Mr Quantox's words had been a ghostly echo of the words in Dr Mallako's little story. The subsequent days continued the echo of this story, until the day when her husband, full of triumph, informed her that his new plane was now completed, and was to have its trial flight on the morrow. It was after this that reality began to diverge from Dr Mallako's story. It was not Mr Ellerker, but a pilot, that took the plane on its trial flight, and was burnt to death when the plane caught fire. Mr Ellerker came home in the deepest dejection and despair. When a police inquiry found among his papers evidence of treasonable correspondence with a foreign power, Mrs Ellerker quickly realised that this evidence had been manufactured by her beloved Eustace, but she held her tongue, even after her husband took poison and died.

Mr Quantox, left without a rival, rose higher and higher in the public esteem, and was rewarded by a grateful sovereign in the next Birthday Honours. But to Mrs Ellerker his door remained closed, and if they met in the train or the street he gave her only a distant bow. She had served her purpose. Under the lash of this disdain, her passion died, and was succeeded by remorse, bitter, unavailing, and unendurable. At every turn she seemed to hear her dead Henry's voice uttering the familiar platitudes which, while he lived, she had found intolerable. When the newspaper was filled with the trouble in Persia, she seemed to hear her husband's voice saying: 'Why do they not send a few regiments of soldiers to teach these wretched Asiatics a lesson? I warrant you, they would run fast enough when they saw British uniforms!' When she returned in the evening from disconsolate wanderings in search of a moment's respite from torturing thoughts, she would seem to hear her husband saying: 'Do not overdo it, Amanda. These foggy evenings are not good for you. Your cheeks look pale. It is not for delicate women to weary themselves in this manner. The rough and tumble of life is for men, and we must protect our little treasures from all the rubs and troubles with which our lives are beset.' At every odd moment, in the middle of conversations with neighbours, in shopping, in trains, she would hear his rotund but kindly platitudes whispered into her ear, until she could not believe that he was really absent. She would look round quickly, and people would say: 'What is it, Mrs Ellerker? You look startled.' And then fear, stark, terrible fear, would take possession of her soul. Every day more insistently the voice whispered; every day the rolling platitudes grew longer; every day the kindly solicitude grew more intolerable.

At last she could bear it no longer. The sight of Mr Quantox's name in the Birthday Honours was the last straw. She rushed wildly from the house, and tried to tell her tale, but only the silence of the asylum walls was allowed to hear it.

After listening to this dreadful story, I spoke to Dr Prendergast. I spoke to Mr Ellerker's chiefs in the Air Ministry. I spoke to all that I thought could be of some use to poor Mrs Ellerker, but not one auditor did I find who would listen to my story.

'No,' they all replied, 'Sir Eustace is too valuable a public servant. We cannot have his name tarnished. But for him we could not compete with American designers. But for him the Russian planes would out-class us. It may be that the story you have told is true, but whether true or false, it is not in the public interest that it should be known, and we must request you, indeed we must command you, to hold your tongue about it.'

And so Mrs Ellerker continues to languish, and Mr Quantox to prosper.

VI

My failure to help Mrs Ellerker, not only in itself, but in its political implications, was a cause of profound mental disturbance to me. 'Can it indeed be the case,' I thought, 'that these men to whom I have appealed, medical men and statesmen, among the most highly respected individuals in our supposedly decent community, can it be that these men, one and all, are prepared that this poor woman should suffer under an undeserved stigma, while the culprit to whom her misfortunes are due marches on from one honour to another? And for what end are they willing to perpetrate this infamy?' At this point my thoughts became perhaps somewhat unbalanced. Their acts, it seemed to me, had only one end in view, that through the ingenuity of Mr Quantox many Russians should perish who, but for his ingenuity, might remain alive. In my unwholesome state of mind I did not consider this a sufficient compensation for the unjust treatment of Mrs Ellerker.

I became increasingly filled with a general detestation of mankind. I surveyed those whom I had known, and they seemed a sorry crew. Mr Abercrombie was willing to let an innocent man suffer obloquy and prison in order that he and his wife might have the empty pleasure of a trivial title. Mr Beauchamp was willing to debauch the minds of schoolboys in the hope of pleasing a heartless lady of easy virtue. Mr Cartwright, although he firmly believed in the pre-eminent merit of those whom the world delights to honour, was nevertheless prepared to cause them shame and misery and financial loss to provide himself with gross luxuries. Mrs Ellerker, I had to admit, had been guilty, so far as mere acts are concerned, of conduct quite as dreadful as that of Mr Abercrombie, Mr Beauchamp and

Mr Cartwright. But, perhaps inconsistently, I refused to regard her as morally responsible during the period of her crime. I thought of her as the hapless victim of Dr Mallako and Mr Quantox, acting in a sinister harmony. But, like the Lord when he plotted the destruction of Sodom, I did not consider that one exception was enough to earn a respite for the human race.

'Dr Mallako,' so my thoughts went in this gloomy and dreadful time, 'Dr Mallako is the prince of the world because in him, in his malignant mind, in his cold destructive intellect, are concentrated in quintessential form all the baseness, all the cruelty, all the helpless rage of feeble men aspiring to be Titans. Dr Mallako is wicked, granted, but why is his wickedness successful? Because in many who are timidly respectable there lurks the hope of splendid sin, the wish to dominate and the urge to destroy. It is to these secret passions that he makes his appeal, and it is to them that he owes his dreadful power.

'Mankind,' I thought, 'are a mistake. The universe would be sweeter and fresher without them. When the morning dew sparkles like diamonds in the rising sun of a September morning, there is beauty and exquisite purity in each blade of grass, and it is dreadful to think of this beauty being beheld by sinful eyes, which smirch its loveliness with their sordid and cruel ambitions. I cannot understand how God, who sees this loveliness, can have tolerated so long the baseness of those who boast blasphemously that they have been made in His image. Perhaps,' I thought, 'it may yet fall to my lot to be the more thoroughgoing instrument of the Divine Purpose which was carried out half-heartedly in the days of Noah.'

My physical researches had shown me various ways in which human life might be brought to an end. I could not but think it my duty to carry one of these means to its completion. Of all those that I had discovered, the easiest appeared to be a new chain reaction by which the sea could be made to boil. I concocted an apparatus which, so far as I could see, would achieve this purpose whenever I chose. Only one thing held me back, and that was that, while men would die of thirst, fishes would die of being boiled. I had nothing against fishes, which, so far as I then knew, and so far as I had observed in aquariums, were harmless and pleasant creatures, not infrequently beautiful, and possessed of a far from human dexterity in the avoidance of impacts with each other.

In a nominally jocular spirit I spoke to a zoological colleague about the possibility of making the sea boil. And I said, laughing, that perhaps it would be rather hard upon the fishes. My friend entered into the spirit of the supposed joke.

'I shouldn't worry about the fishes, if I were you,' he said. 'I can assure you that the wickedness of fishes is appalling. They eat each other; they neglect their young; and their sexual habits are such as bishops pronounce gravely sinful when practised by human beings. I do not see that you need have any remorse in causing the death of sharks.'

Little as he knew it, this man's jesting words determined me. 'It is not only man,' so my thoughts ran, 'that is rapacious and cruel. It is part of the very nature of life, or at least of animal life, since it can only live by preying upon other life. Life itself is evil. Let the planet become dead like the moon, and it will then be as beautiful and as innocent.'

With great secrecy I set to work. After some failures I made an apparatus which, I was persuaded, would cause first the Thames, then the North Sea, then the Atlantic and the Pacific, and, last of all, even the frozen Polar Oceans, to boil away into futile steam. 'As this happens,' so ran my somewhat disordered thoughts, 'as this happens, the earth will grow hotter and hotter, men's thirst will increase, and, in a universal shriek of madness, they will perish. Then,' I thought, 'there will be no more Sin.' I will not deny that in this vast vision my thoughts reserved a quite special place for the downfall of Dr Mallako. I imagined his mind to be full of ingenious schemes for becoming the Emperor of the world, and imposing his will upon reluctant victims, whose torments should increase for him the sweet savour of their submission. In imagination I enjoyed triumph over that wicked man, a triumph achieved perhaps by what some might think a wickedness even greater than his own, but redeemed by the clean purity of a noble passion. While these thoughts boiled within me, as terribly as in my hopes the sea was about to boil, I completed my apparatus and attached it to a clockwork mechanism. One morning at ten o'clock I set the mechanism. The sea was to boil at noon. And having set the mechanism, I paid a last and final visit to Dr Mallako.

Dr Mallako, who was well aware that my feelings towards him were not wholly friendly, was somewhat surprised by my call.

'To what,' he said, 'do I owe the honour of this visit?'

'Doctor,' I replied, 'this, as you surmise, is no mere social call. It is useless for you to offer me your whisky, or your comfortable chair. It is not for a pleasant chat that I have come. I have come to tell you that your reign is at an end, that the evil sway which you have exercised over the minds and hearts of those who have had the misfortune of your acquaintance is to cease from this time forth, and is to cease through a combination of intelligence and courage as great as your own, but devoted to a nobler end. I, the poor despised scientist, whom you considered of no account, whose efforts to thwart the tragedies that you have brought about have hitherto been as unavailing as you could wish, I have at last discovered how to thwart your ambitions. A clock is at this moment ticking in my laboratory, and when the hands of this clock point to midday, a process will be set in motion which, within a few days, will put an end to all life on this planet – and, incidentally, to your life, Dr Mallako.'

'Dear me,' said Dr Mallako, 'how very melodramatic! It is too early in the morning for me to suppose that you have been drinking, and I am therefore compelled to suppose some graver derangement of your mental faculties. But if you find the matter of sufficient interest, I shall be delighted to listen while you expound your scheme for producing this slightly catastrophic result.'

'It is all very well,' I replied, 'for you to sneer. It is perhaps all that is left for you to do. But soon your sneers will be stilled, and as you perish, you will be forced to admit, with whatever bitterness of defeat, that the ultimate triumph is mine.'

'Come, come,' said Dr Mallako, with some impatience, 'enough of this rodomontade. If indeed only a few hours remain to us, how can we spend them better than in intelligent converse? Tell me your scheme, and I will see what I think of it. I will confess that as yet I am not much alarmed. You were always a bungler. What did you achieve for Mr Abercrombie, or Mr Beauchamp, or Mr Cartwright, or Mrs Ellerker? Are any of them the better for your protection, and will the human race be any the worse for your enmity? But, come, tell me your plan. It may be that failure has sharpened your wits, though I doubt it.'

I could not resist this invitation. I was confident in my invention, and determined to have the laugh on the contemptuous Doctor. The principle upon which I had operated was simple, and the Doctor's wits were nimble. Within a few minutes he had grasped both my theory and my practice. But, alas, the result was not what I had hoped.

'My poor fellow,' he said, 'it is just as I had supposed. You have overlooked one small point, which makes it certain that your apparatus will not work. When twelve o'clock strikes your clock will blow up, and the sea will remain as cold as before.'

In a few simple words he demonstrated the truth of what he had said. Deflated and miserable, I prepared to take my departure.

'Wait a minute,' he said, 'do not imagine that all is lost. Hitherto we have worked against each other, but perhaps if you will deign to accept my help something of your curious hopes may yet be salvaged. While you were talking I not only perceived the flaw in your apparatus, but also a method of remedying it. I shall now have no difficulty in constructing a machine which will do what you thought yours would do. You fondly imagined that the destruction of the world would be a grief to me. You little know. You have seen so far only the outer fringes of my mind. But in view of our peculiar relations, I will pay you the compliment of taking you somewhat further into my confidence.

'You have imagined that I wanted riches and power and glory for myself. It is not so. I have been always disinterested, never out for myself, but always pursuing aims that were impersonal and abstract. You imagine in your miserable way that you hate mankind. But there is a thousand times more hate in my little finger than in your whole body. The flame of hate that burns within me would shrivel you to ashes in a moment. You have not the strength, the endurance, the will, to live with such hate as mine. If I had known sooner what, thanks to you, I now know, the means to bring about universal death, do you suppose I should have hesitated? Death has been my aim throughout. I have been merely practising on the wretched individuals who roused your silly compassion. Always greater things have lain before me. Have you ever asked yourself why I helped Mr Quantox towards his triumphs? Have you known (I am sure you have not) that I am giving equal help to his adversaries, who are designing engines of destruction to be used against him and his friends? You have not realised (how indeed should you, having an imagination of so paltry a scope?), you have not realised that revenge is the guiding motive of my life – revenge not against this man or that, but against the whole vile race to which I have the misfortune to belong.

'Very early in my life I conceived this purpose. My father was a Russian prince, my mother a slavey in a London lodging house. My father deserted her before I was born and became a waiter in a New York restaurant. He is now, I believe, enjoying the hospitality of Sing Sing. But he is of little interest to me, and I have not troubled to verify the sources of my information. My mother, after he had deserted her, sought alcoholic consolation. Throughout my early childhood I was always hungry. As soon as I could toddle, I learned to rummage in dust heaps for crusts of bread or potato peelings or anything else from which some scrap of nourishment was to be derived. But my mother objected to these wanderings, and when she remembered, she would lock me up while she visited the public house. When she returned, completely intoxicated, she would knock me about till I bled, and at last stunned me into insensibility to stop my cries. One day, when I was about six years old, as she was drunkenly dragging me along the street, she set to work to give me wanton blows. I dodged. She overbalanced, and a passing lorry put an end to her life.

'A philanthropic lady, who happened to be passing, seeing me left alone and helpless, took pity on me. She brought me to her home, washed me and fed me. My intelligence had been sharpened by misfortunes, and I exerted myself to augment her benevolent pity to the utmost. In this I was wholly successful. She was persuaded that I was a good little boy. She adopted me, and educated me. For the sake of these benefits, I put up with the almost intolerable boredom that she inflicted upon me in the shape of prayers and church-goings and moral sentiments, and a twittering sentimental softness to which I longed to retort with something biting and bitter, with which to wither her foolish optimism. All these impulses I restrained. To please her I would go on my knees and flatter my Maker, though I was at a loss to see what He had to be proud of in making me. To please her I would express a gratitude which I did not feel. To please her I would seem always what she considered "good". At last when I reached the age of twenty-one she made a will leaving me all her property. After this, as you may imagine, she did not live long.

'Since her death my material circumstances have been easy, but never for one moment have I been able to forget those early years – the cruelty of my mother, the heartlessness of neighbours, the hunger, the friendlessness, the dark despair, the complete absence of hope – all these things, in spite of subsequent good fortune, have remained the very texture of my life. There is no human being, no, not one, whom I do not hate. There is no being, no, not one, whom I do not wish to see suffering the absolute extremity of torment. You have offered me the spectacle of the whole population of the globe maddened with thirst, and dying in agonies of futile frenzy. What a delicious spectacle! Were I capable of gratitude I should feel some to you now, and should be tempted to think of you as almost a friend. But the capacity for such feelings died in me before I reached the age of six. You are, I will admit, a convenience to me, but more than that I will not admit.

'You will go home and see your silly machine explode harmlessly. You will know that I, I over whom you thought to triumph, I whom frivolously and absurdly you chose to think worse than yourself, that I am going to achieve the ultimate triumph which you had reserved for yourself, and, so far from hindering my plans, you have supplied the one thing lacking to my perfect triumph. And as you die of thirst, you need not think that I shall be suffering equal torments. When I have set the inexorable machinery in motion I shall die painlessly. But you will be left for a few hours, perhaps for a few days, to writhe in ignoble agony, knowing that in my last moments I shall have rejoiced in the prospect.'

But as he talked, my thoughts went through a sudden revulsion. That he was wicked was my most profound belief. If he wished to destroy the world, then it must be wicked to destroy the world. When I had thought that I would destroy it, I had enjoyed the vision of cleansing power. When I thought that he would destroy it, I had only a vision of diabolic hate. I could not permit his triumph. The world which I had been hating began, as he talked, to seem beautiful. The hatred of human beings, which was the very breath of his being, was in me, as I now saw, only a passing madness. I determined that for all his proud words he should be defeated. For a moment he looked out of the window, and exclaimed:

'How many houses can be seen from here! Out of each of these houses, not many days from now, shrieking maniacs will rush. I shall not see it, but in my mind's eye, as I die, the delicious panorama will be unfolded.'

While he said this, his back was to me. I whipped out the revolver which I had brought in case of violence.

'No!' I said, 'this will not happen.'

He turned round, with an angry sneer, and as he turned I shot him dead. I first wiped the revolver, then, putting on gloves, I pressed his fingers round it, and left it lying near him. I quickly typed a suicide note on his typewriter. In this note I made him say: 'I find that I am not the man of iron will that I had hoped I was. I have sinned, and remorse is devouring me. My latest schemes were on the point of failure, and I should have been disgraced and ruined. I cannot face this, and I die by my own hand.'

I then went home and disconnected my useless machine, just in time to prevent a paltry explosion.

VII

For some time after putting an end to Dr Mallako, I felt happy and carefree. From him, I thought, had emanated a kind of poisonous miasma, infecting with crime or madness or disaster all in his neighbourhood. And now that he was gone, it should be possible to live freely and joyously, to prosper in my work, and be peaceful in my personal relations. For some months I slept as I had not slept since the day when Dr Mallako's brass plate first met my eyes, dreamlessly, refreshingly, and sufficiently. From time to time, it is true, I was visited by recollections of poor Mrs Ellerker, living among lunatics, desolate and alone. But I had done all that I could for her, and nothing was to be gained by further brooding. I determined that I would resolutely banish all thought of her from my life.

I met a charming and intelligent lady, who at first captured my attention by her knowledge of the more devious paths of psychiatry. Here, I thought, is someone who, should the need ever arise, as, please God, it will not, will be able to follow the strange convolutions of evil through which it has been my misfortune to thread my way. After a not unduly protracted courtship, I married this lady and believed myself happy. But still at times strange disquieting thoughts would come into my mind, some expression of horrified perplexity would pass over my face in the middle of a conversation about everyday matters.

'What is it?' my wife would say, 'some troubling vision seems to have occurred to you. Perhaps you would be the better for telling it.'

'No,' I would reply, 'it is nothing, only some rather tiresome memory which inadvertently interrupted my planning.'

But I observed with alarm that these thoughts came with increasing frequency and continually increasing vividness. I found myself in imagination holding colloquy with Dr Mallako, continuing the argument of the last hour of his life. For a moment his quietly contemptuous face would appear before me in vivid, visualised detail, and I would seem to hear his sneering voice saying: 'You think I'm defeated, do you?' If this occurred when I was alone in my study, I would shout: 'Yes, I do, damn you!' and once, when I was shouting this, my wife came in at the door and looked strangely at me.

Oftener and oftener I felt his imagined presence. 'You have not been much good to Mrs Ellerker, have you?' I would hear him saying. 'You think you have recovered your sanity, do you?' I should seem to hear him whisper. My work suffered because, whenever I was alone, I could not banish from my mind the phrases that I fancied he would use: 'Fine ideas you used to have about destroying the world and all that, and now look at you! As humdrum and respectable a man as is to be found in Mortlake. Do you really imagine that you can escape my power by the help of a mere revolver? Do you not know that my power is spiritual and rests unshakably upon the weakness in yourself? If you were half the man that you pretended to be in our last little talk you would confess what you have done. Confess? Nay, boast. You would explain to the world of what a monster you had rid it. You would boast yourself a hero, one who in single combat had worsted the forces of evil concentrated in my wicked person. Did you do any of this? You did not. You left an unavailing and lying pretended confession, attributing contemptible weakness to me – ME – whom alone of mankind weakness has never approached! Do you think that this can be forgiven you? Had you boasted of your deeds I might perhaps have thought you no unworthy adversary. But in this snivelling garb of matrimonial insignificance you have become to me an object of such contempt that, though I be dead, yet I must still show that I can destroy you.'

All this I fancied him saying. At first I knew it was fancy, but as time went on I came more and more to feel that his terrible ghost was real. I would even seem to see him standing before me with his correct black clothes and his smooth, oily hair. Once in a frenzy I walked straight through the apparition in order to persuade myself that it was an apparition, but in the dreadful moment in which it enveloped me completely I felt such a chill breath upon me that I all but shrieked and fainted. My wife, finding me pale and trembling, inquired after me with anxiety. I assured her that river mists had given me an ague, but I could see that she doubted whether this were all. When the ghost taunted me with having concealed my part in his death I began to think that perhaps, if I confessed all, he would let me be.

In dreams I re-enacted the scene in which I had shot him, but with a different ending. In my dreams, when his corpse lay at my feet, I threw open his window, and called out into the street: 'Come up, come up, all you who live in Mortlake! Come up and behold a dead fiend, dead by my heroic act!' So the scene ended in my dream. But when I awoke, there was the sneering ghost saying: 'Ha ha! – that was not quite what you did, was it?'

The torment grew gradually worse, the haunting more continual. Last night the climax came. After a dream even more vivid than usual I awoke shouting: 'I did it. It was I.'

'What did you do?' asked my wife, awakened from sleep by my shout.

'I killed Dr Mallako,' I told her. 'You may have thought that you had married a humdrum scientific worker, but it is not so. You married a man who, with a rare courage, with determination and with an insight possessed by none among the other inhabitants of this suburb, pursued a cruel fiend to his last end. I killed Dr Mallako, and I am proud of it!'

'There, there,' said my wife, 'hadn't you better go to sleep again?'

I raged and stormed, but my raging and storming were of no avail. I saw fear overcoming all other feelings in her. As morning came I heard her go to the telephone.

Now, looking out of my window, I see on the doorstep two policemen, and an eminent psychiatrist whom I have long known. I see that the same fate awaits me as that from which I failed to save Mrs Ellerker. Nothing stretches before me but long dreary years of solitude and misunderstanding. Only one feeble ray of light pierces the gloom of my future. Once a year, the better behaved among male and female lunatics are allowed to meet at a well-patrolled dance. Once a year I shall meet my dear Mrs Ellerker, whom I ought never to have tried to forget, and when we meet, we will wonder whether there will ever be in the world more than two sane people.

Zahatopolk

The Past

Professor Driuzdustades, the eminent Head of the College of Indoctrination, with portly step and billowing gown, mounted to his desk in the reverently restored hall of the Incas at Cuzco, and faced the eager audience at the beginning of the academic year. He had succeeded to his important office on the death of his scarcely less eminent father, Professor Driuzdust. The students to whom he was about to lecture were the hundred most promising in the whole realm. They had finished their ordinary studies, and were now about to embark upon their post-graduate curriculum which secured to the College of Indoctrination its immense power over opinion. The eager young faces looked up to him for the weighty words of wisdom which, they did not doubt, were about to flow from his lips. Of the whole hundred there were two who showed especial brilliance: one was his son Thomas who, it was hoped, would in due course succeed to his father's august office; the other was a girl named Diotima. She was beautiful, earnest and profound, and had captured the heart of Thomas.

After clearing his throat and taking a sip of water, the Professor spoke as follows:

'The subject of my lecture today will be the thirtieth century before Zahatopolk or, as it was called by those who lived in it, the twentieth century A.D. It is thought by the wise men who regulate education in this happy land that you, the chosen hundred, are by this time sufficiently firm in understanding and appreciation of our holy religion and of the revelation which we owe to the divine Founder Zahatopolk, to be able to hear without loss of mental equilibrium about ages lacking our faith and our wisdom. You will, of course, never for one moment forget that they were ages of darkness. Nevertheless, as serious students of history it will be your duty – at times a difficult and painful duty – to set aside in imagination all that you know of the true and the good and to realise that even in that darkness there were men who, at least in comparison with others of their time, might be accounted virtuous. You will have to learn not to shudder at the thought that even men who were universally respected, publicly and without shame ate peas. What perhaps you will find only slightly less difficult to forgive is the fact that, when the number of their children exceeded three, they did not, as we do, eat the excess to the glory of the State, but selfishly kept them alive. In a word, you will have to cultivate historic imagination. You will, of course, understand that this, though a virtue in you, the chosen élite, would be subversive and highly dangerous if it spread to wider circles. You will understand that what is said in this lecture-room is said to the wise, and is not to be broadcast to the vulgar. With this proviso, I will proceed to my task.

'The thirtieth century B.Z. was a time of chaos and transition. It was the time when the Graeco-Judaean synthesis was replaced by the Prusso-Slavic philosophy. It was a time of convulsions and disasters; a time when that basis of dogma, without which no society can be stable, was absent in the minds of young and old alike. There had been a time known to the nostalgic victims of doubt as the age of Faith, when the Graeco-Judaean synthesis had been unquestioningly accepted, except by small minorities which, very properly, had been silenced by the rack or exterminated by the stake. But this age had been brought to an end by a pernicious doctrine which, I am happy to say, has never found any advocates among us. This was called the doctrine of toleration. Men actually believed that a State could be stable in spite of fundamental divergences in the religious beliefs of the citizens. This insane delusion it was, which caused the Graeco-Judaean synthesis to fall before the new virile dogmatism of the Prusso-Slavic philosophy. Pray do not mistake me. I am not suggesting – and I hope none of you will imagine for one moment that I am suggesting – that there was any least particle of truth either in the dogmas of the Graeco-Judaean synthesis or in those of the Prusso-Slavic philosophy. Neither foresaw the divine Zahatopolk. Neither recognised the innate superiority of the Red Man. Neither grasped the great principles upon which, among ourselves, both public and private life are so happily established. I am saying only one thing concerning these outworn systems: I am saying that while they survived and while they were believed with sufficient fervour to make insistence upon uniformity inevitable, so long they could hold society together after a fashion – though not, of course, with that smooth perfection which we owe to the Zahatopolkian revelation. All past systems had their imperfections which caused them to fall. The Prusso-Slavic system in its heyday looked solid; so did its successor, the Sino-Javanese system. But their defects, in the end, brought about their downfall. Only the Zahatopolkian system has no defects; and therefore, only the Zahatopolkian system will last as long as there are human beings to supply Zahatopolk with worshippers.'

The Professor told how almost all the accounts that we possess of the dissolution of the Graeco-Judaean synthesis are from the point of view of the victors, representing the triumphant march of the divine Satalinus and the extermination in every part of the world of the lingering adherents of the defeated system. But the Professor pointed out that, wherever possible, the historian must search for records from both points of view, and must allow the vanquished their share in the historian's pages.

'Fortunately,' he continued, 'a document has recently come to light in the Falkland Islands which enables its readers to view with human sympathy the bewilderment and despair that mark the end of a great era.'*

After reading this document the Professor continued:

'Throughout the reign of the Prusso-Slavic philosophy, documents such as the above were, of course, unknown. Under the banner of the great god Dialmet the inhabitants of the northern plains established their victorious Empire and maintained it with all the ruthless dogmatism without which their preposterous myths could not have won acceptance. The two apostles, Marcus and Leninius, became familiar in every part of the globe through the icons which every house had to possess on pain of death to its occupiers. These two Founders became known familiarly as Long-Beard and Short-Beard respectively, and it came to be generally held that magic virtue resided in their hirsute appendages. Their successor Satalinus, whose virtue was military rather than doctrinal, was honoured only less than they were, and the lesser degree of his honour was symbolised by the substitution of a mere moustache for a beard. The German language, in which the sacred books of this era were written, became extinct soon after the time of Satalinus, and the sacred books could thereafter only be read by a few learned men, who were not allowed to communicate directly with the populace, but only through the medium of the supreme political authority. This restriction was necessary because there were passages in the scriptures which, if interpreted literally, might have caused considerable embarrassment to rulers, and even have stirred up disaffection among the ruled.

'For some centuries all went well. But at last a time came when the rulers imagined themselves safe and allowed themselves to listen to the sceptical scholars of China. Some of these sceptics no doubt had no ulterior motives, but were actuated only by that unbridled intellectual curiosity which had done so much to bring the previous era to destruction. Others, however – and these were the majority – had a more subtle purpose. They saw no reason why White men should have a monopoly of the sacred books. They determined insidiously to deride these books, while suggesting that in their own language, of which the rulers were ignorant, there were far more ancient sacred books, far more unintelligible, and far more awe-inspiring. Gradually they softened their masters and made scepticism fashionable among them. They themselves, however, refrained from scepticism. Bound together in the closest ties of esoteric dogma, they worked with patient secrecy at the undermining of the imposing edifice of Prusso-Slavic statecraft. On a given day, long predetermined in their inner councils, they rose, destroying their rulers by means of a subtle poison distilled from the

---

* See Dean Acheson's nightmare, p. 248

volcanic vegetation of Krakatoa. Thus was inaugurated the Sino-Javanese era, which immediately preceded our own happy age.

'Our own country, now great and glorious and immutably secure, endured long ages of bitter suffering. During the last four centuries of the Graeco-Judaean era the Red Man was massacred, or outlawed, or reduced to the status of a slave. The insolent White Man dominated throughout our great Continent, from which beneficent Nature had so long excluded him while the first Inca Empire flourished. For a moment it seemed as if the downfall of these ruthless masters would bring liberation. The Prusso-Slavs enlisted our support in overthrowing the Graeco-Judaean intruders, and, in order to stimulate our efforts, they made great promises of freedom. But when the victory had been won, their promises were forgotten, and the brave Red Men, whose help had been so necessary, found themselves no better off than before. Nor did the Sino-Javanese era bring any amelioration of our lot. Only the ancient traditions of the divine Incas of the distant past, and the ruins from which their greatness could still be imagined, kept alive in a small secret band the hope that the God of our ancestors would yet return and give us that mastery of the world which we had deserved through our virtues and our suffering.

'The Sino-Javanese, like all rulers of eras before our own, had gradually allowed themselves to be seduced by the love of pleasure and soft living. The arduous peaks and scarcely accessible valleys of our divine land did not attract them. They lived in palaces in the plains, surrounded by every luxury, dressed in soft silks, and reclining upon exquisitely-fashioned couches, served – though I blush to report it – by slaves of our own race, slaves who, since they had no share in the luxury, had also no share in the effeminacy of their masters. It was at this epoch, just one thousand years ago, that the divine Zahatopolk appeared. There were, at first, some who maintained that He was a mere man; but that we know was false. He appeared out of the sky, and landed upon the summit of Cotopaxi. Many thousands of our race, warned by an oracle, saw His descent. From that sacred mountain, He deigned to come down amongst His worshippers, who beheld at once in His features the likeness of their glorious God who had received their homage before the coming of the infamous destroyer Pisarro. A divine enthusiasm inspired in all a miraculous unanimity. They exterminated the Chinese sybarites, whom they took unawares. In the great wars that followed, the divine Zahatopolk led them to victory by the help of the deadly fungus of Cotopaxi, whose properties had been unknown until He revealed them to His worshippers. For thirty years He wrought among them, first in war and then, after universal victory, in the even more difficult arts of peace. The institutions under which we live we owe to Him. The Book of Sacred Law, whatever accretions subsequent ages may have brought, remains the basis of our policy. And woe to him who should suggest any smallest departure from that celestial revelation!'

85

II

The Present

The régime inaugurated by the divine Zahatopolk took some time to become firmly established, but so solid and statesmanlike had been His principles that no radical new departures had been needed during the thousand years since His advent. All previous Empires – so Zahatopolk taught – had been brought to an end by softness – softness in living, softness in feeling, and softness in thinking. This His followers must avoid, and in order to avoid it certain rigid and inflexible rules must be accepted without questioning and enforced without mercy.

The first thing that the God bade His worshippers always remember was the superiority of Red Men to men of different pigmentation, and among Red Men the overlordship of the Peruvians, while recognising the Mexicans as next in merit. It was permissible, and even laudable, to praise the wisdom of the ancient Maya, before the white abomination had begun to pollute the Western hemisphere, but the palm in antique glory was reserved for the Incas. The slopes of Cotopaxi yielded a poisonous microscopic fungus to which pure-blooded Peruvian Indians were immune, but which spread contagious death among other populations. After some experience of the devastation that this plague could cause, the rest of the world submitted to Inca domination. And in the course of centuries rebellion had become almost unthinkable.

The virility of the ruling race was kept intact by many wise regulations. No physical luxury was permitted them. They slept on hard beds with wooden pillows. They dressed in clothes made of leather; one suit was expected to suffice for either a man or a woman from the time of being full-grown until death. Cold baths were enforced by law even in frosty weather and among mountain snows. Food, though wholesome and sufficient, was always plain, except at the annual feast of the Epiphany. Every day every Peruvian must take sufficient physical exercise to insure complete fitness. Alcohol and tobacco were forbidden to the ruling race, though permitted to their subjects. The divine Zahatopolk revealed, what had not previously been known, that the eating of peas is an abomination which produces a loathsome pollution. Any Peruvian who ate peas, even if no other nourishment was available, was put to death, and those who had witnessed the dreadful deed were subjected to a long and painful process of purification. This prohibition also applied only to Peruvians; others were already polluted in their blood, and no abstinence could cleanse them.

The hardening process began in childhood, especially where boys were concerned. The hours at school were divided between lessons, gymnastics, and rough fiercely-competitive games. No boy was allowed to say that he was tired, or cold, or hungry; if he did, he was despised as a weakling, and had to endure not only the contempt of the authorities, but the well-merited ill-treatment inflicted by the other boys. Those who had any physical weakness died of this regimen, but it was held that it would have been useless to keep them alive. They died despised and unregretted, and if their parents mourned them, they had to do so in secret, for fear of sharing the obloquy of their sons.

The severities in the education of girls were somewhat different, since it was held that muscular development is no help in child-bearing. Girls were never permitted the slightest gratification of vanity, nor was any display of emotion tolerated, with the one exception of religious exaltation and devotion to the Inca. Absolute obedience was exacted, often in purposely painful ways. A very few, however, who showed some marked ability of a sort considered usually masculine, were allowed some freedom and some initiative, though only in such ways as were conventionally tolerated.

Women, except those few who had been classified in youth as unusually gifted, were confined to domestic duties. They were not considered the equals of men, since they were not so useful in battle. It is true that, after the first years, battles did not occur, but that was only because the Peruvians were known to be invincible. Never must they forget – so Zahatopolk had taught – that only by superior strength could they maintain their Empire, and that a false sense of security had brought disaster to every previous Master Race. Women, therefore, must remain subordinate, and husbands must practise in the home those habits of command which they would need in the world.

The strictest monogamy was rigidly observed. Neither men nor women were allowed to stray from the path of virtue. It was not only illicit love, but all love, that was frowned on. Marriages were arranged by parents, or, in the case of orphans, by the priests. For either party to object was unheard of: the ends of life were not pleasure, but duty to the State and to the Holy Zahatopolk. In the very rare cases of subsequent infidelity, the culprit was degraded, and compelled to live abroad as a member of some non-Peruvian horde.

Zahatopolk taught that Peruvians must remain a proud governing aristocracy. Their numbers must not increase so fast that many of them would be poor, nor must they be unable to live on the produce of Peru, for power, not wealth, was what they should seek in their dealings with the outside world. Their divine Lawgiver, therefore, decreed that when a married couple had already had three children, any further children born to them should be reverently eaten within a month of birth, both to prove that the parents were innocent of any intention to cause a food shortage, and as a symbol of submission to Zahatopolk as the God of Fertility. There had at one time been a short-lived heretical sect which, misled by a weak-kneed humanitarianism, maintained that birth control was preferable to eating surplus children. But the leading divine pointed out that birth control is a sin against God's gift of life, whereas eating a child only makes its flesh a partaker in the life of the parents from whom the child's life has come, and with which it always remains mystically one. Accordingly, the eating of one's child is a deeply religious act, bodying forth in a material form the eternal continuity of the stream of life. And as such this act came to be universally accepted.

Although all Peruvians formed an aristocracy in relation to lesser breeds, there was also an aristocracy among Peruvians. It was an aristocracy partly of birth, partly of ability. Any boy or girl of really outstanding talent could be admitted to its ranks, but most of its members were descendants of the Captains who had led the forces of Zahatopolk to victory in His great wars of liberation and conquest. The priesthood, who were very powerful, were all chosen from the aristocracy. Aristocrats had in some respects more freedom than other people: for example, they might without censure have intercourse with the wives of plebeians, and they were partially exempt from the sumptuary laws regarding dress and diet.

Religion, to a very considerable extent, followed the pattern of ancient Peru and Mexico. Zahatopolk was in some sense identified with the sun, and it was His divine rays that caused the crops to grow. There was also a Goddess, representing the moon, though She was less prominent in the cult. She had, however, one important part to play in the Zahatopolkian year. At the first new moon after the winter solstice, at the moment when both sun and moon seemed in danger of losing their several virtues, both were magically revivified by a solemn and ancient rite. For a brief time Zahatopolk, as the Sun God, became incarnate in the reigning Inca, while the Moon Goddess became incarnate in a virgin whose identity was revealed to the priests by means of certain sacred insignia. Sun and moon were brought together in order to give each other new life. The chosen virgin was solemnly led to the Inca by the priests, and by his union with her the sun recovered strength. In order that the union might be completed as fully as possible, the Inca next morning reverently consumed the lady, who could no longer serve the purpose for which virginity was essential. This most sacred rite, performed just after the winter solstice, was the occasion for the great public holiday of the Epiphany, when, for a moment, much of the habitual frugality was relaxed.

The Inca's annual union with the Virgin of the Year was, of course, only for religious purposes. He had a wife, whose oldest son would succeed him. It was not as himself, but as temporarily Zahatopolk, that he had intercourse with the lady who, while the rite lasted, was honoured as the Bride of Zahatopolk. To be the Chosen One was the greatest honour possible for a woman, and families which had enjoyed this honour were exalted by it. The Bride herself invariably rejoiced in spite of the death that awaited her. The loveliest lyric poetry known consisted of a paean of triumph in stiff archaic ritual language celebrating the joy of the Bride at the thought of being absorbed into the divine stomach.

Once, during the first century of the régime, a dreadful impiety had shaken Authority to its foundations. A man who had been acknowledged as the Inca fell so deeply in love with the Bride of Zahatopolk that he impiously refrained from killing and eating her, but kept her alive and visited her in secret. The consequences were such as might have been expected. The sun failed to recover, rising every morning as late as at the winter solstice. The supposed Inca became prematurely old, losing both hair and teeth. There was bewilderment and despair, combined with dark suspicions. At the festival of the spring equinox, which was held at the usual time in spite of the sun's failure to rise when it should, lightning from a clear sky struck the supposed Inca dead. It was subsequently discovered that his mother had impiously committed adultery, and that he had therefore no right to the throne. Before this incident some scepticism had lingered among intellectuals, but after it, naturally, there was none.

The sacred land of Peru included the territories which in the Spanish era had been known as Ecuador and Chile. Throughout this region, as soon as the liberation was completed, Zahatopolk decreed measures to secure the purity of Indian blood. Whites and Negroes were exterminated and all Mestizos were sterilised. Some, however, in whom the taint of foreign blood was not evident, escaped, so that, from time to time, children with White or Negro traits were born. All new-born children were examined by State physicians, and if any such taint was discovered, the parents had to eat the child and submit to sterilisation. While the régime was still new, this severity was apt to cause disaffection. All such parents therefore remained suspect and were carefully watched by the Secret Police. After about two hundred years of this process, the taint of foreign blood disappeared and only pure Indians were to be found throughout the length and breadth of the Holy Land.

Outside Peru the official policy was different. Mexicans were treated almost as equals. They were allowed in the army and in foreign Government posts, except the very highest, provided their blood was pure. They were also allowed higher education and were even admitted to the University of Cuzco. Other Indians had lesser privileges, and it was admitted that their merit might be such as to deserve recognition. But whites, yellows, browns and blacks were treated as inferior species, and were deliberately kept in a state of degradation. There was, it is true, a difference. The blacks, who had never yet achieved world Empire, were despised but not feared. The whites and yellows, since they had held world Empire, were feared, and the contempt that was inculcated towards them had to be carefully fostered.

Education was denied to all who were not Indian. All, without distinction, were condemned to ten hours a day of manual work. While the land of

89

Peru preserved an ancient rustic simplicity and carefully avoided all damage to natural beauty, the rest of the world was filled with everything most up-to-date in the way of industrialism. Factories, mines, vast slag-heaps, filthy slums, smoke and grime were thought suitable to the scum of foreign lands. Peruvians believed, and all the world was taught, that while Peruvians were the children of the sun, other races were foetidly generated from slime. All that Zahatopolk had taught about the softening influence of pleasure was used to degrade the non-Indian populations. When their ten hours of work were finished, every opportunity was put in their way for alcoholic excess and the stupefying effect of opium. Marriage was not recognised and universal promiscuity was encouraged. Physicians were forbidden to combat the resulting spread of venereal disease. Any Peruvian who was found guilty of sexual intercourse with a member of an inferior race was instantly put to death. Peruvian guards, who were necessary to keep the bestial population in order, were very carefully protected against degradation by their horrible surroundings. They were encouraged to see natives eating peas, and this nauseous spectacle stimulated their patriotism in the highest degree. The non-Indian population of the world diminished slowly as a result of disease and excess. Certain visionaries foresaw in a more or less distant future a world purged of all but Red Men, and imagined in that future an equality of all men which could not, as things were, be tolerated. Such Utopian visions were, however, thought risky, and those who indulged in them were viewed with a certain suspicion. The Governors of foreign countries were very carefully selected, since experience had shown that those who had in their nature any element of instability were liable to nervous disorders of various sorts. Some practised needless cruelties towards the natives; others, more gravely disordered, attempted to make friends with them and treated them as in some degree equals. There were even a few instances of Governors who believed in the brother-hood of man and unearthed ancient documents from the Graeco-Judaean epoch which preached this outlandish doctrine. These men had to be dealt with very severely, and the School of Indoctrination at Cuzco had to inaugurate courses designed to guard against this danger. As time went on, however, the danger grew less, since the measures adopted by the Government succeeded in making the natives progressively more and more degraded and more and more purely animal. After some centuries the Peruvian supremacy came to seem unshakable.

III

The Trio

The lectures of Professor Driuzdustades continued throughout the academic year and gave rise to earnest discussions between Thomas and Diotima, in which her friend Freia had a minor part. Diotima, partly from the lectures and partly from the reading of ancient history, began to feel perplexities which surprised and disquieted her. She did not feel quite sure that cannibalism was either necessary or desirable. Professor Driuzdustades had explained that the identification of the Bride with the moon was not to be taken literally, but was only a beautiful allegory. One morning the terrible thought came to Diotima: 'Why, if the union is only allegorical, cannot the eating also be so? Could not a gingerbread puppet be substituted for the living Bride?' The blasphemous character of this thought made her go cold all over. She shivered and turned pale. Thomas, who was present, inquired anxiously what was the matter. But the thought had been fugitive, and she felt it unwise to reveal it. Other doubts also assailed her. In the university library she found an old dusty volume that had obviously remained undisturbed for a very long time. It contained the most noteworthy speculations of the ages of darkness before the coming of the Holy Zahatopolk. She could not resist the thrill of their enormous antiquity, for some antedated even the beginnings of the Graeco-Judaean synthesis. In some of these writings she found a doctrine to the effect that a man's sympathies should not be confined to his own race, but should extend to the whole human species. She discovered also that long ago men who had not been red had thought thoughts and said words that seemed to her at least as wise and at least as profound as any that had been produced by the Zahatopolkian era. She began to wonder whether the present bestiality of white, yellow, and brown men was really, as she had been taught, due to congenital inferiority or might not, rather, have been induced by the institutions which Peruvian statecraft had established. Of these doubts she said little, but something of them showed through her guarded utterances.

Thomas was troubled by her state of mind. His admiration for her was such that every word falling from her lips had weight with him, and, however she might alarm him, he could not dismiss her vaguely adumbrated doubts as he would those of any other fellow-student. Although he was troubled, his faith survived, for it seemed to him that without the hard framework of Zahatopolkian orthodoxy society would dissolve and there would be universal chaos. In the war of all against all which he imagined, he feared to see the loss of all that is good in civilisation. What would become of science and art? What would become of ordered family life? What safeguard would remain against vast destruction in world-wide combats of rival hordes? All these horrors, so it seemed to him, were prevented only by the monumental stability of the traditional orthodoxy. Let doubt once penetrate through even the smallest chink and the whole system would dissolve. A deep cultural night would spread over the globe and men everywhere would become as degraded as the most degraded of present subject populations. Such thoughts made him shudder whenever

Diotima, through some momentary carelessness, allowed her new tentative opinions to appear.

'O Diotima,' he would say, 'beware! You are embarked upon a perilous mental journey, a journey leading only to a dark and measureless abyss in which, if you do not retrace your steps, you will be engulfed. I do not wish to see you pursuing this path alone, but much as I love you I cannot pursue it with you.'

Freia, who was sometimes present during these discussions, was unable to appreciate their gravity. Diotima, whom she had known since childhood, was endeared to her by many common memories. Thomas, as the brilliant son of a brilliant father, destined as everybody hoped to carry on the age-old tradition of Zahatopolkian culture, inevitably commanded the respect of one to whom everything established was sacred. She was, however, less perturbed than she should have been, as she spent most of her time in a dream-like daze of mystic exaltation, and whatever did not fit with this mood seemed to her to be due to some misapprehension. When Diotima said anything that seemed subversive, Freia would smile gently and say, 'of course, my dear, you don't really *mean* that!' And Diotima, who thought it neither possible nor desirable to disturb Freia's beliefs, would seemingly acquiesce as though she had been engaged in mere intellectual play.

Diotima's family belonged to the highest and most ancient aristocracy of Peru. In the War of Liberation their ancestor had commanded one of the largest of Zahatopolk's armies, and throughout the subsequent centuries they had worthily upheld the established order. Several times the Bride of the Sun had belonged to their family. The portraits of these Brides, perpetually wreathed in ever-fresh myrtle, occupied the place of honour in the dining-hall of the family. Their imposing house was in the best quarter of Cuzco and had a lovely garden which filled the steep hillside with the colour and scent of many flowers. Freia's family, though not quite so august, were also aristocratic. Thomas, on the other hand, owed his admission to these exalted circles to the intellect and public service of his distinguished father. Some slight condescension was perhaps natural in the attitude of ancient families towards such as he. But it was recognised by the Government that the stability of the régime required the continual services of the best available brains, and policy indicated as complete as possible a social acceptance of those who, by this means, had risen in the social scale. It was not, therefore, surprising that, when Diotima mentioned to her parents her two friends, Freia and Thomas, they agreed that she should invite both of them to be inspected and judged by the shrewd standards which ages of supremacy had developed. Her parents, though she seldom spoke to them of her secret thoughts, had divined in her an intellectual recklessness that they deeply deplored. She seemed to have the bad habit of letting the argument determine her conclusion, instead of first deciding on the conclusion and then making the argument fit. There was in this, they felt, something anarchic and dangerous. But, although they were worried by her wild speculations (which were, in fact, far wilder than they knew), they thought them merely the exuberance of youthful high spirits which a little experience of the real world would subdue. They rejoiced in her friendship with Freia, to whose exemplary piety many common friends had borne witness. Sometimes they wistfully regretted that their daughter did not more resemble this untroubling saint. The testimonials of teachers to Diotima's great abilities and zeal in study did something to allay their fears. Time, they felt, would show her that intellect is not everything, and would give her that moral earnestness in which for the moment she seemed lacking. Thomas, vouched for by his father's great reputation and his own excellent record, was just such a friend as they could have wished for their daughter. Their only hesitation in his regard was due to his reputation for brilliant intellect, since it was not, in their opinion, intellect that needed developing in their daughter. But from all that they could learn about Thomas, intellect had never yet led him astray any more than it had his father, and there was every reason to hope that he would become as valuable to the stability of the social order as his distinguished parent. Such were the considerations which led Diotima's mother to invite Thomas and Freia to her tea-table.

Diotima's mother, as a hostess, was gracious and anxious to set her guests at their ease, although she could not divest herself of a grand manner which at first they found somewhat intimidating. Her language was always correct, her sentiments always impeccable. No looseness of grammar or vocabulary would be overlooked. No sentiment departing even slightly from the correct would escape at least the censure of a raised eyebrow. Diotima paid but little respect to her mother's social taboos. Her language was adventurous; some of her words were too erudite, others had a tincture of slang. She could not resist wit that was at times irreverent, and on occasion would even make fun of eminent men who were her father's friends.

'My dear,' said her mother, 'you will never get a husband if you use such inelegant expressions and show such a lack of proper respect to your elders.' Seeing that Diotima obviously thought well of Thomas, and hoping that he might exert a restraining influence upon her over-bold daughter, she turned to him and said, 'I am sure Professor Driuzdustades would not approve, would he, Thomas?'

At this, Thomas was intolerably embarrassed. Secretly he agreed with his hostess, but loyalty would not permit him to desert Diotima. However, Freia came to the rescue. She went into raptures about the beauty of the place.

'What happiness must be yours,' she said, 'to sit in this exquisite garden viewing the eternal snows and conscious that our Holy Realm is as eternal and as sublime as those lofty peaks!'

Diotima's mother shared these sentiments, but was not quite sure that it was compatible with good taste to express them; for, although enthusiasm is all very well in its place, it must always be kept within the limit of manners and decorum. While she was hesitating for a moment as to the proper response to Freia's rhapsody, Diotima rushed in:

'Come, come, Freia,' she said, 'the peaks are not eternal. We know from geology that they were thrust up by a cataclysm, and some day another cataclysm will bring them tumbling down. Are you not afraid there may be a tinge of blasphemy in comparing the Zahatopolkian régime to these top-heavy lumps?'

This remark produced a pained silence which Thomas endeavoured to smooth over, saying, 'Oh, of course Diotima is only teasing. I am afraid that sometimes her sense of humour runs away with her.'

'Ah well,' said her mother, 'I suppose we mustn't be too hard upon her. I can remember how, in earlier years, her dear father, who is now as grave as I could wish, sometimes pained me by flippancy about eminent men of the previous generation. She will learn as we all have to.'

On this soothing note the party broke up.

Doubt, having once found a lodging in Diotima's thoughts, was nourished by various discoveries. The ancient volume which she had found gave her a taste for research in parts of the university library that were too dusty and archaic to be commonly visited. In one of these she found a contemporary account of the wicked Inca who had avoided the duty of eating the Sacred Bride. She found that at the time he had many partisans who maintained that the failure of the sun to recover vigour was only apparent. They maintained that the priests caused all public clocks to lose by day and gain by night, thereby making it seem that the days were getting no longer and the nights no shorter. They maintained also that the Inca's loss of hair and teeth was due to a slow poison, and that he was killed, not by lightning, but by a flash between two highly-charged electric poles. His successor naturally opposed this sect, and it was put down with great ruthlessness. But Diotima observed that only persecution, not argument, was employed against it.

Another blow to her tottering faith was administered unwittingly by an uncle of hers who held a high position in the Inca's household. This man was at one time very ill and, in delirium, said many things which those who heard them regarded as insane ravings. To Diotima, however, whose occasional duty it was to nurse him, there seemed to be truth in his delirious fantasies.

'Ha, ha,' he would laugh, 'people imagine that it is the priests who choose the Sacred Bride. How pained they would be if they knew she is chosen by the Court eunuchs as the girl best qualified to serve the Inca's lusts!'

The Court eunuchs were a body of men whose only publicly acknowledged function was to sing ancient hymns to the sun in the magnificent temple which formed the centre of Zahatopolkian religion. Their ethereal and exquisite voices filled all hearers with what they believed to be the Divine Spirit. While they listened their hearts were lifted up to Heaven, and some degree of mystic unity with the Divinity seemed to come within the reach of all reverent hearers. It was appalling to think of these men as panders to a grossness that wore a deceitful mask of religion. And yet that was what her uncle's disordered ravings compelled Diotima to think.

These two revelations of pious fraud, one long ago, the other repeated year by year down to the present day, produced in Diotima a profound revulsion of which, however, for the present, she allowed little to appear. In her conversations with Thomas she kept her most dangerous thoughts to herself, hoping to lead him on gently and bring him little by little to her way of thinking. Any premature shock, she knew, would repel him. Freia, in spite of her exquisite beauty, was too insipid and too unintellectual to excite Thomas's deeper feelings. Diotima, on the other hand, he found intoxicating, almost madly stimulating, but at the same time terrifying. He felt with her the exhilaration that comes to a climber on a dangerous glittering ice-slope. He could not keep away, he could not acquiesce, and he could not wholly reject.

IV

Freia

One day when the trio were sitting by a mountain stream in deep discussion, Diotima saw peering at them from behind the trees two men whom, by their uniform, she knew to be Court eunuchs. One of them was pointing at Freia and the other was gravely nodding his head. Her companions had not perceived this scene, of which, in view of her uncle's revelations, the significance was obvious. She turned pale, and in a subdued voice said, 'Let us return into the city.' 'What is the matter?' asked the others. When they had reached a safe distance she explained that it had come to her knowledge that Freia would be the next Bride of Zahatopolk. 'But how can you know?' they both asked. 'That,' she replied, 'is something I cannot now explain. But you will find that I am right.'

Very soon afterwards, the choice of Freia was made public. Freia was overwhelmed with humble ecstasy, and experienced all those emotions which in the days of the Graeco-Judaean synthesis had been attributed to the Madonna at the Annunciation. Diotima was profoundly shocked, and not prevented by religious faith from feeling that her life-long friend was to suffer a dreadful fate. Thomas was, of course, aware that Diotima's emotions were not such as the orthodoxy would demand. He could not think her right in this, but he could not bear the pain of thinking her wrong. Freia's parents, as was to be expected, were overjoyed that this great honour should come to their family. Diotima's mother congratulated her on being a friend of Freia, and boasted of the friendship to all her visitors. Freia, a few days after the announcement, was removed from profane contacts and subjected to the long process of purification and sanctification that preceded her apotheosis. Diotima mourned her. Thomas tried, ineffectually, to rejoice in the honour done to her. Diotima, having still hopes of his complete conversion, took pains that their disagreements should never lead to a rupture. In this state of doubt and suspense, things remained between them throughout the months of Freia's preparation.

Freia, under the influence of the regimen slowly perfected throughout the centuries by the sacred eunuchs, became gradually more and more absorbed by mystic ecstasy. She was treated by the ministrant eunuchs as a divine being. Ancient and beautiful robes, worn only by Brides of Zahatopolk, were brought forth for her adornment. Every morning precisely at sunrise she was taken to bathe in a Sacred Stream which was forbidden on pain of death to all except the Brides of Zahatopolk. In a jewelled chapel of which the walls glittered with mosaics depicting the earthly life of Zahatopolk, she listened to the sacred chants that the eunuchs sang with voices of unearthly purity. She was nourished upon special food different from that of mere men and women. She was given books of ancient poetry celebrating the transports of the moon in the embraces of the sun, and pictures of Zahatopolk and His Bride in a holy and passionate embrace. In a world of ancient legend and ritual the memories of her previous daily life grew dim. She moved and breathed as if in a dream. And it seemed to her that day by day the soul of the Goddess more and more took possession of her.

At length the supreme night arrived. Dressed in a robe of brilliant blue adorned with innumerable stars, and carrying in her hand a flaming torch, she slowly descended the Sacred Stairs that led towards the waiting Inca. And as she descended, she sang a chant of immense antiquity and almost unbearable beauty. With the last note she reached the end of the stairs, and saw before her the long-awaited figure of the Inca.

The Inca, a man with thick lips, bulbous nose and pig's eyes almost buried in fat, nevertheless appeared to her as a Divine Being and a worthy embodiment of Zahatopolk. He took hold of her roughly, saying, 'Now then, off with that robe. Mustn't keep me waiting all night.' She felt that this is how a God should behave, and she welcomed the opportunity to humble herself before Him. When the rite had been performed, He fell asleep and snored, while she reverently contemplated His sleeping form. In the middle of the night the priests very quietly opened a secret door and beckoned to her. Slowly, ecstatically, she followed them to her death.

In due course the Inca woke up and descended to his breakfast. 'Well, at any rate,' he murmured with his first mouthful, 'they've cooked her rather well this year.'

V

Diotima

After Freia had been led away to deification and death, Diotima's mood changed. She had been full of gaiety and wit. She had loved intellectual play, and would follow out an argument with more regard for logic than for social implications. Now, however, under the impact of the loss of Freia, she became oppressed with the social consequences of false beliefs. Not a word of the official theology could she any longer accept. It became clear to her that Zahatopolk had been a mere man, and that his doctrine of Peruvian supremacy was nothing but a very human embodiment of national vanity. The whole of the rites connected with the winter solstice came to seem to her at once absurd and cruel. Freia, she felt, had been sacrificed not to a God, but to the lusts of a brute. But rebellion against so firmly rooted a system would be no light matter, and for a time she confined herself to inward debate. As rebellion became more complete in her thoughts, she increasingly suppressed its outward manifestations. Thomas, who had dreaded her rebelliousness, hoped that it was subsiding. When he argued with her against those first beginnings of doubt which she had expressed to him at an earlier stage, she did not rebut his arguments, and he fancied that he had convinced her. She saw that he loved her, and she could have loved him in return but for a growing sense of dedication to a task of appalling difficulty. This feeling set her apart and made it impossible for her to yield whole-heartedly to any passion for a merely human object. Thomas sensed her aloofness and suffered from it. At length a day came when she decided that she could no longer hide from him the thoughts which dominated her every waking moment.

Early one morning Thomas and Diotima walked together in a deep Andean valley. The warm beauty of a profusion of spring flowers was at their feet. Above them, reaching to incredible heights, were snowy peaks thrusting almost insolently into the deep blue of the upper sky. Most parts of the valley were still in shade, but here and there rays of dazzling sunshine penetrated between the shadows of the mountains. The chiselled calm of Diotima's perfect features seemed to Thomas a synthesis of the warm beauty below and the cold sublimity above. The scene and the woman combined to produce in him a feeling of almost more than human ecstasy. Love burned in him like a fire, but was kept in check by something more than love – awe and wonder and reverence and a realisation of what it is possible

97

for a human being to be. No ordinary words of love seemed adequate. And for a time he walked in quivering silence. At last he turned to her and said : 'At this moment I am beginning to know how life should be lived.'

'Yes,' she said, 'it should be soft and lovely like the flowers, it should be immovable and clear like the peaks, and it should be immeasurable and profound like the sky. It is possible for life to be lived so. But not amid such ugliness and horror as reigns in our community.'

'Ugliness and horror!' he exclaimed. 'What do you mean?'

'There is ugliness,' she said, 'when a mere human being, because he is thought to be a God, is allowed to commit abominations.'

At these words Thomas trembled and shrank away, 'A mere human being?' he queried. 'You cannot mean the divine Zahatopolk!'

'I do,' she said, 'he is not divine. The myth that exalts him has been created by fear: fear of death, fear of the blows of fate, fear of the powers of nature, and fear of the tyranny of man. From these peaks above us swift death from time to time rolls into the valleys beneath. The powers that rule in the peaks are felt to be cruel, and it is thought that only a sympathetic cruelty can appease their terrible implacability. But all fear is ignoble, and the myths that it generates are ignoble, and the men whom the myths exalt are ignoble. Zahatopolk is no God, but a gross man, in many ways lower than the beasts. The rite in which Freia was sacrificed is not of divine origin. Nothing is of divine origin. The gods are shadows of our fears upon the opacity of the night. They embody the abasement of man before the forces that can destroy him physically. They embody the slavery to time, which cannot value the eternal moment if in the temporal order it is *but* a moment. I will not yield to this prostration. While I live I will stand upright like the mountains. If disaster comes, as no doubt it will, it can be only outward disaster. The citadel of my belief in what can be will remain unsubdued.'

While she spoke, an appalling conflict seemed to tear him asunder. One part, the part that but a moment before had seemed one with her in a transcendent unity, was fired by her words and longed to agree. But another part, just as strong if not stronger, stood out against her. All that he had been taught, all that he knew of the society in which they lived, all the feelings of awe and reverence which had been instilled into him since infancy, rose in opposition, and the cold Godless world which she portrayed filled him with cosmic terror. Better, he felt, a God who might be cruel, but who at least was not utterly alien, since he experienced passions like our own; better such a God than a vast, cold, lifeless universe, unthinkingly generating and sweeping away, caring nothing for human beings, whom it had produced without intention and would destroy without compunction. This cosmic terror was for the time being stronger even than his love. Pale and trembling, he turned towards her and said: 'No. I cannot accept your world, I cannot live with your thoughts. I cannot keep alive the flickering flame of human warmth amid such a chill blast of immeasurable inhumanity. If it is to be your task to destroy the faith of my fathers, we must go our separate ways.'

They walked on slowly and in silence until they came to the one house that the valley contained. There they found the Inca's eunuchs in waiting. 'You have been chosen,' they said to Diotima, and bore her off. Thomas gazed after her until she was lost to sight. But he said no word and made no movement.

The choice of Diotima as the Bride of the Year was communicated officially to her parents, and also to Professor Driuzdustades to explain her absence from his classes. Her parents, following immemorial custom, gave a great party to celebrate the honour done to their daughter. All the aristocracy of Cuzco came with wedding gifts and congratulatory speeches. Her mother accepted the gifts and speeches with a courteous pretence of humility. Her father, upright and rather portly, preserved a soldierly demeanour in which satisfaction was half-concealed by decorum. The party was an immense social success, and Diotima's family was felt to have become even more exalted than before.

The Professor also felt that he enjoyed some reflection of Diotima's glory. Doubtless the Moon Goddess had observed that under his influence Diotima had become worthy to be the vehicle of incarnation. Professor Driuzdustades congratulated his son upon his friendship with the exalted lady, but was somewhat disquieted to observe that Thomas did not seem as elated as the occasion warranted. At first, however, he consoled himself with the thought that, however shocking to strictly correct sentiment, some regret in the loss of Diotima's companionship might be excused in one so young as Thomas.

But within a few days dreadful rumours began to circulate. It was whispered that Diotima was not accepting the honour in the right spirit, that she was refusing to do her part in the purificatory ceremonies, that she was denying any awareness of the Moon Goddess entering her body, that she was speaking disrespectfully of the Inca, and even – Oh depth of infamy! – maintaining that the sun and moon would get on just as well if the rites of the Epiphany were not performed.

These rumours, alas, were but too well founded. Priests and eunuchs alike were filled with consternation. Nothing even faintly analogous had happened since that long ago time when the False Inca had refused to eat the Bride. In their perplexity they decided to temporise. They would not let the Inca know of Diotima's recalcitrance, but they would bring all possible pressure to bear upon her in the hope that her resolution might be broken and she might consent to conform. With this end in view, they arranged a series of interviews with those whom they thought most likely to convince her.

99

The first of these interviews was with her mother. Her mother had been proud and somewhat imperious, little given to the display of emotion, but always self-contained and self-controlled. Now all this was changed. She felt utterly humiliated. She could not face the world. She dared not see her friends for fear of their criticism or – what would be even worse – their commiseration. She found her daughter in a bare cell, dressed in a penitential garb, and kept on a diet of bread and water. Convulsed with sobs and with tears coursing down her cheeks, she stammered out incoherent words of sorrow and reproof.

'O Diotima,' she said, 'how can you inflict upon your father and mother this dreadful depth of degradation? Have you no memory of the years of your innocent childhood, when by my care you grew in wisdom and stature and daily raised higher our hopes for your future? Have you no feeling for the proud family which for many centuries has borne the banner of history in this glorious land? Can you inflict upon those who have loved you the most dreadful fate that can befall a human being – I mean the shame that is being brought upon us by a shameless daughter? O Diotima, I cannot bring myself to believe it. Say that it is but an evil dream and that my love may go out to you as heretofore.' At this point sobs choked her utterance and she could say no more.

Throughout her mother's broken words Diotima remained unmoved. Proud and apparently cold, she replied:

'Mother, something is involved which is greater than parental affection, greater than family pride, greater even than this realm which has stood for a thousand years. For this proud realm, though I know that you cannot recognise the fact, is built upon lies and cruelties and abominations. To these I cannot be a party. If I seem unmoved by your tears, it is not from coldness. It is because I burn with another and a greater fire than any that you can imagine. You cannot either understand or approve, and I beg you to forget that you were ever afflicted with such a daughter.'

Slowly, in utter despair, her mother turned away and left Diotima in solitude.

Her mother having failed, her father, next day, was admitted to her cell. His line was somewhat different from her mother's.

'Come, come,' he said, 'why are you being such an obstinate young fool? I see that you are upset by having learnt too soon and too quickly things which we who live about the Court have long known and accepted. You don't suppose, do you, that sensible men believe all that palaver about the sun and moon? Or imagine that the Inca, whom we all know and despise, becomes divine once a year by the calendar? We know perfectly well that no religious motives inspire him during what is called the Holy Night: but we do not make a hullabaloo about it as you threaten to do, for we know that these beliefs, however groundless they may be, are useful to the State. They cause the Government to be revered, and enable us to preserve order at home and Empire abroad. What do you suppose would happen if the populace came to think as you do? There would be disorders in Peru; there would be insurrections abroad; and very soon the whole fabric of civilised society would be in tatters. Rash girl! You refuse to be a sacrifice to the Inca, but you have not thought that the true sacrifice is to Law and Order and Social Stability, not to a gross prince. You prate of truth, but how can truth preserve an Empire? Has the Professor failed to teach you that all Empires, always, have been built upon useful lies? I am afraid you are an anarchist, and if you do not recant, you can scarcely hope that the State will show you mercy.'

'Father,' she replied, 'it is natural, I suppose, in view of our family traditions, that the Peruvian State should be a God to you. Some effort of imagination is needed to think of another order of society than that in which you have lived all your life. And, Father, I am afraid that imagination is not your strongest point. I see in my thoughts a better world than that which our race has created: a world containing more justice, more mercy, more love, and, above all, more truth. Cataclysms and disorders there may be on the road to this better world, but even they are to be preferred to the dead rigidity of our public and private abominations.'

At this her father became red with fury, and, exclaiming in a loud voice, 'Impertinent child, I leave you to your fate!' he marched out into the sunshine.

The next to visit the obstinate prisoner was the Professor. He entered her cell with an air of suave and hypothetical benignity, and addressed her in tones which masked authority by their intended persuasiveness. 'My poor girl,' he said, 'I am sorry to see you here, and I cannot but think that some part of the blame must be mine, for in the year during which you have listened to my indoctrinating lectures I ought to have succeeded in conveying to you a more just apprehension of social duty than is indicated by your present predicament. But tell me, Diotima, at what points, and for what reasons, do you dissent from the doctrines which it has fallen to my unworthy self to endeavour to instil?'

'Well,' she replied, 'since you ask me, I will tell you. I don't believe your facts. I don't believe your theories. I think your conception of social utility intolerably narrow and your belief in the unchangeability of dogma so wooden as to bring death to intellect and feeling alike. I think your indifference to truth revolting, and your subservience to the powers that be, toad-eating and contemptible. Now, having cleared the air, I am willing to hear what you have to say.'

At these rude words the Professor flushed, and for a moment he was tempted to retort with mere abuse, but that would have been to betray the traditions of his order. Diotima had been blunt. She had eschewed ambiguity and vagueness in a manner which he could not too deeply deplore. She had been content to dwell in those regions of mere fact which to the initiate are but the foot-hills of the lofty peaks of wisdom. Restraining his annoyance with an effort, he told himself that the girl was overwrought and that the diet of bread and water might well cause bad temper. The habits of a lifetime of lecturing came to his aid, and he replied to her diatribe in a manner truly admirable in view of his greatness and her youth.

'Diotima,' he said, 'there are some things that you do not seem to know and that, even at this late hour, I must put before you with all the power at my command. I will begin with what is at the basis of all else: Do you deny the Godhead of the Holy Zahatopolk?'

'I do,' she replied. 'We are taught that he descended from Heaven in a miraculous manner. For my part I believe that he descended in a helicopter from a plane hidden above the clouds. We are told that he did not die, but ascended miraculously into Heaven when his work on earth was ended. This, also, I do not believe. I believe that a camarilla of his generals surrounded him during his last illness and kept him from all contact with the outer world. I believe that they threw his corpse into the crater of Cotopaxi. Legends to this effect have been handed down secretly in my family, whose ancestor was the ringleader in this proceeding. All are sworn to secrecy and only the men are initiated. But men have fevers, and fevers bring delirium, and in delirium even the gravest secrets can be blabbed.'

At this point the Professor saw that a lecture on Truth was called for: 'Granted, my dear girl,' he said, 'that on the mundane level of sensible fact things were as you say, do you not realise that there is a higher sense in which the orthodox doctrine of our land conveys a truth more profound than any mere legend of helicopters and military camarillas? What have helicopters to do with Divinity? They are mere contrivances: ingenious, no doubt; convenient, no doubt; but unworthy to hold a central place in the fundamental doctrines of cosmogony. If, indeed, our Divine Founder deigned to make use of some such mechanism, He did so, no doubt, for a wise purpose which it is not for us to question. And when you deny that He descended from Heaven, are you so certain that you know where Heaven is? Have you never learned the great spiritual truth that Heaven is wherever there are heavenly thoughts? And wherever Zahatopolk may have been, there, rest assured, heavenly thoughts had a home. Of His death very similar things may be said. What if His earthly integument became cold and lifeless? What if His disciples reverently restored it to that terrestrial fire which of all things on this earth is nearest to the Divine Fire that had enabled Him to instruct His disciples? It was not the earthly integument that was to be worshipped, for our God is to be worshipped in Spirit and in Truth, and Spirit and Truth dwell in the soul, not in the body. The rash words that you uttered concerning the Most High God may have been in some gross sense not out of harmony with material fact, but spiritually, as

102

I have shown you, and in the only sense that concerns us as beings partaking, however imperfectly, of the Divine Essence, they are utterly false and to be condemned with all the force that our Holy Religion can inspire.'

'Professor,' the girl replied, 'what you say is of course very impressive, but I have arrived at a view which I fear you may find shocking. I think that there are facts and fictions, there is truth and there are lies. I know that those who preach the doctrine of the Golden Mean, of which I suspect you of being an adherent, consider that one should observe the golden mean between truth and falsehood, as you so admirably did in the speech to which I have just listened. But, to my mind, facts are harsh and will not be denied. I know that in a brutal orgy the sadistic Inca first enjoyed, and then ate, my friend Freia. This is fact. And however you may clothe the fact in a mantle of mist and myth, it will remain a fact, and so long as you try to hide it from your gaze you will share its vileness and it will pollute you.'

'Come, come,' said the Professor, 'this is strong language, and I cannot think that you have studied the philosophical theory of truth as deeply as your academic duty demanded that you should. Do you not know that the truth of a doctrine lies in its social utility and its spiritual depth, not in some wretched vulgar accuracy such as can be measured by a foot-rule in the hands of a clod? Measured by any true standard, how paltry are your feelings concerning your friend Freia! How much more profound, how much more consonant with the needs of the human race, was her ecstasy in those moments of apotheosis! Consider what, for her, has been achieved. Through a few brief moments, some aspects of which you, in your arrogance, find revolting, she has become one with the Moon Goddess. In eternal calm and eternal beauty, what was imperishable in her, sails through the skies, exempt from the sorrows and tribulations of this mortal life. And consider what mankind owes to that majestic ritual in which her earthly life was ended. Consider the poetry, the slow-moving music, the glorious mosaics, and the Temple whose sublime and severe lines draw eye and soul alike towards heaven. Would you have all this perish from the earth? Would you have mankind reduced to a dusty, book-keeping pedestrianism? Would you have poetry and music and architecture perish? Yet how could any of these survive without the divine myth (I use the words in no derogatory sense) by which they have been inspired?

'But if art and beauty mean nothing to you, what of the social structure? What of law, what of morality, what of Government? Do you suppose that these could survive? Do you suppose that men would abstain from murder, and theft, and even intercourse with non-Peruvians, if they did not feel the eye of Zahatopolk upon them? And do you not see that, since the true is what is socially useful, the doctrines of our holy religion are true? Renounce, I beseech you, your self-willed pride; submit yourself to the

103

wisdom of the ages; and, by so doing, put an end to the torment and shame that you are inflicting upon your parents, your teachers and your friends.'

'No!' exclaimed Diotima. 'No! a thousand times no! This higher truth of which you speak is to me only higher humbug. This social utility of which you make so much is only the preservation of unjust privilege. This marvellous morality of which you prate justifies the oppression and degradation of the great majority of the human race. My eyes are opened, and not all your tortuous words can induce me to close them again.'

The Professor, incensed at last, exclaimed: 'Then perish in your stiff-necked arrogance, wretched apostate! I leave you to the fate that you have so richly deserved.' And with that he left her.

Only one possibility of bringing Diotima to repentance remained. It was known that Thomas had loved her, and it was hoped that she had loved Thomas. Perhaps love would effect what authority had failed to do. It was decided that Thomas should have an interview with her, but that, if he failed, no further efforts should be made to turn her from the error of her ways.

Thomas had been passing through a very difficult time of conflict, fear and misery. As a man in love, he suffered from the death of his hopes. As an ambitious youth, whose path to success hitherto had seemed plain, he dreaded the suspicion that might attach to him as the intimate friend of a heretic. As a student of theology and history, who had never on his own account seen reason to question his father's wisdom, he was appalled by the dangerous consequences that would ensue if Diotima's beliefs became common. Since her apostasy he had found many former friends avoiding him, and he saw that he was losing the position of a leader in his own group. His father, returning furious from his interview with Diotima, spoke to him with grave severity:

'Thomas,' he said, 'Diotima is inspired by the Spirit of Evil, to which in my theology I have hitherto given insufficient attention. Dangerous thoughts emanate from her like lurid flames from a sulphurous fire. I do not know what lodgement the poison may have found in your own brain. For your sake, I hope not much. But if you are to recover the general respect which has hitherto rejoiced my parental heart, you will have to be very clear, and make it very clear to all and sundry, that you are utterly opposed to her vile heresies, and that no lingering affection will blunt the edge of your desire to see her suffer the just penalty of her infamy. There is, however, still a faint hope. It may be that you will succeed where her parents and I have failed. If you do, all will be well. But if you do not, it will be your duty to prove by your zeal that you have suffered no contamination.'

With these alarming words still ringing in his ears, Thomas found himself admitted to Diotima's cell. For a moment the spectacle of her beauty and her calm overwhelmed him. Human love, and a passionate longing that she might yet be saved, swept away in that first instant both prudence and orthodoxy. He burst into tears and exclaimed, 'Oh Diotima, would that I could save you?'

'My poor Thomas,' she replied, 'how can you cherish so foolish a hope? Whatever I may do, my life is forfeit. Either I die as the Bride of Zahatopolk, with public honour and inward shame, or I die as a criminal, despised and execrated except by my own conscience.'

'Your own conscience!' he answered. 'How can you set it up as the sole arbiter against so much wisdom and such long ages? O Diotima, how can you be so sure? How can you know that all of us are wrong? Have you no respect for my father? Are you willing to besmirch your ancestors? I have loved you. I have hoped that you might love me. But that hope, I see, was vain. It is anguish to say so, but I cannot continue to love you while you lacerate all my deepest feelings. O Diotima, it is more than I can bear!'

'I am truly sorry,' she said, 'to have brought upon you this cruel dilemma. Hitherto, you have had every reason to expect a career both smooth and honourable. Henceforth, you have to choose. If you condemn me, your career may still be smooth. If you do not, it may be honourable. But I know, however you may disguise it from yourself, that in your heart of hearts you cannot be happy if you condemn me. You may, perhaps, during the busy hours of the day, silence your doubts while you listen to public applause; but in the night, you will see a vision in which I shall be beckoning you towards a happier world. And as you turn your back upon me, you will wake in agony. For I know that you have seen, if only briefly, that vision for the sake of which I am willing to be condemned. It is not, as we pretend, the sun and moon that inspire our official creed. It is pride and fear: pride in our Empire, and fear lest we may lose it. It is not upon these passions that human life should be built. It should be built upon truth and love. It should be lived without fear, in a happiness that all can share. It should be unable to find a contentment resting upon the degradation of others. It should be ashamed to aim at a paltry physical safety at the expense of the inner springs of joy and life which well up in those who open their spirit to the world in fearless adventure. We have let ourselves be bound in chains. Outside our own land the chains have been forced upon their victims by us. We have not realised that whoever imprisons another becomes himself a prisoner, a prisoner of fear and hate. And the chains which we have forged for others have bound us in a mental dungeon. Remember the sun that found its way into our valley. Even so, light must fall upon dark places of the world. And however little you may know it now, it will be your mission when I am dead to carry on this work.'

For a moment her words found an echo in his heart. But he summoned up his resolution, and his momentary yielding turned to anger. 'How can you think so! How can you think that such high-flown verbiage can make me abandon all that I revere! Further speech with you is useless. You must die. And I must live, to combat the evil that you think good.' With these words he rushed from her cell.

After Thomas's failure, the authorities gave up hope of inducing Diotima to recant. A new Bride was chosen and Diotima was condemned to die publicly at the very moment when she should have enjoyed mystic unity with the Divinity.

The day of expiation was proclaimed a public holiday. The stake was erected in the central square of the city. Seats for the notables were in the front ranks. Behind, the whole population of the city stood in greedy expectation. They laughed and joked and jeered. They ate nuts and oranges. They made coarse jests, and exulted in the expectation of the torture they were about to witness. The notables in the front rows were more dignified, and the Inca on His throne was majestically silent. Thomas, as his father's son, was privileged to sit among the notables. He had been suspected of sharing Diotima's heresy, and had cleared himself of this suspicion with some vehemence. Both as a reward and as a test, he was to have a full view of her death.

She was led in naked, and preserved a calm and unmoved demeanour. The crowd shouted: 'There's the wicked woman! Now she'll find out who's God!' She was tied to the stake, and flaming torches kindled the fire. As the flames reached her, she looked at Thomas – a strange and piercing look, expressing at once anguish, pity, and appeal, pity for his weakness and appeal to carry on her work. Her anguish tore his heart, her pity bruised his manhood, and her appeal kindled in his mind a flame scarcely less searing than that which was consuming her body. In a blinding moment he saw that he had been wrong; he saw that what was being done was an abomination; he saw that she stood for what can be splendid in human life, and that the dignitaries and the multitude alike were grovelling victims of bestial fear. In this one terrible moment he repented – but repentance is too mild a word for what he experienced. He experienced a passion as intense as that which had upheld her in the flames, a passion to devote himself to the work which she could no longer perform, a passion to liberate mankind from the shackles of fear and the cruelty that it generates. He thought that he cried aloud, 'Diotima, I am yours!' But in this moment he fell unconscious, and the cry must have been only in his own heart.

VI

Thomas

For a long time Thomas lay in hospital, gravely ill and incapable of coherent thought. Intolerable loathsome visions floated through his mind of tortured women and brutal men, of flames and death and bestial cries of triumph. Slowly, reason reasserted itself. Health returned and, with health, an inflexible determination by which his whole character was transformed. No longer was he a gentle and trusting youth willing to tread in his father's footsteps and win such easy low-level success as his father's example would secure him. With an insight born of devouring passion he saw through all the pretences of the Peruvian system and perceived the far from laudable motives by which it was inspired and supported. His intellect, which had been trained to work with mechanical perfection within the limits imposed by orthodoxy, passed beyond those limits without losing the keen edge of pitiless accuracy. But it was not only his intellect that was liberated; it was also, and even more, his heart. Peruvians had been taught reverence to the State as the earthly garment of God, and to limit their sympathies to those who served the State to the best of their abilities. But the State had destroyed Diotima and, in rebellion against that cruelty, he found himself rebelling against all the other cruelties, all the other inhumanities, all the other institutions which fettered human sympathy, not only in his own country but wherever human beings were to be found. Love, hate and intellect were welded together by the fire of his passion into a single steely whole; love first for Diotima, and thence, by transference, to all other victims; hate for those who condemned her, and thence for the whole system which had made this condemnation possible; intellect, which told him that the divinity of Zahatopolk was a myth, that the sun and moon were not divinities but lifeless masses, that the condemnation of birth control was superstitious, and that, in eating their children, men killed in themselves their own capacity for sympathy and kindliness. With all his mind and heart and will he resolved that, if it were in any way possible, he would establish upon earth a better system than that which he had been taught to revere, a system more in harmony with Diotima's vision. The sense of guilt which gnawed at his inmost being could, he thought, be appeased only if he could make this offering to the torturing memory of Diotima.

But the offering to her memory, if it was to appease his remorse, must be a change in the world, not a mere personal dedication or a futile martyrdom. With a determination inwardly white-hot, but outwardly as cold as ice, he set to work, first to think out a plan, and then to carry it into execution. In public and with all whom he could not fully trust, he breathed no word of criticism of the established order. To his father, as to almost everybody else, he appeared cleansed of whatever doubts he might once have felt. The distrust with which he had been viewed during the last days of Diotima soon passed away, and his official career marched smoothly from success to success. He acquired a position of leadership among his contemporaries, and his words were listened to as having weight and wisdom.

His most ardent friend and admirer was a young man named Paul. To

Paul, at a very late hour on a summer night, he opened his heart – tentatively at first, but gradually, as he met with response, more and more completely. Paul had had misgivings about the burning of Diotima, but had wisely kept his misgivings to himself. As Thomas spoke, Paul's misgivings acquired new force. They talked through the whole summer night until the dawn appeared. They parted sworn confederates in the promotion of whatever revolution might prove possible. Gradually they gathered about them a secret society of intending rebels. Students of science found it impossible to accept the divinity of the sun and moon; students of history could not believe in the inferiority of other races; students of psychology were revolted by the cannibalistic thwarting of parental affection. Stories of the Inca's far from divine behaviour filtered through from Court circles in spite of all precautions. But still Thomas held his hand.

In secret he encouraged the ablest among his disciples to make researches of a kind which the Government had forbidden on pain of death. Peruvian power had rested upon the death-dealing fungus of Cotopaxi, but a brilliant young physician discovered a prophylactic against the plague. Several among Thomas's confederates became Governors of remote provinces, for such posts, since they involved exile from Peru, were considered disagreeable and usually given to young men as the first step in the official hierarchy. Very cautiously and very secretly, these men set to work to undo the degradation which it had been the policy of Peru to produce in other parts of the world. Paul, who remained his second-in-command, became Governor of the Province of Kilimanjaro. The mountaineers of that region, owing to the austerities imposed by nature, had remained hardy and vigorous. He took their headmen into his confidence and gave them, for the first time in many centuries, the hope of escape from unworthy subjection. Many of the conspirators remained in key positions in Peru, completely unsuspected by their superiors.

At length, after twenty years of careful preparation, Thomas judged that the time had come for open action. The whole course that events were to take was carefully mapped. Thomas, by this time Rector of the University, announced that on a given day he would make a sensational revelation. All of his adherents, except such as had special duties assigned to them, were told to be present in the hall in which he would speak. Like his father at an earlier time, he mounted the rostrum, but the words which he spoke were very different from his father's. He avowed all his beliefs and all his disbeliefs. To the amazement of those who were not in the plot, his most subversive sentiments received loud applause. There was bewilderment and panic. But the authorities, as had been foreseen, succeeded in seizing him, and he was condemned, like Diotima, to perish in the flames on the feast of Epiphany.

What happened after this was not what the Government had intended. One of his scientific friends had discovered how to make rain, and a deluge made it impossible to light the flames in which he should have perished. His friend Paul, knowing the exact hour at which the execution was to take place, dispatched from the headquarters of the Government at Kilimanjaro an enormous plane which travelled at supersonic speed until it reached the rain-clouds over Cuzco. From that point is dispatched a helicopter, which descended upon the market-place and snatched up Thomas, who was borne off to Kilimanjaro leaving the populace with the unshakable conviction that they had witnessed a miracle. The Government found itself paralysed by the unsuspected disaffection of many of its officers. When the authorities of Cuzco heard of rebellion in Kilimanjaro they supposed that they could deal with it by means of the fungus plant. When they learnt that the inhabitants of Africa were immune to this plague, they were seized with terror, which turned to consternation when they found that Thomas's scientists had discovered how to produce radio-active death from the volcanic slopes of the new Sacred Mountain. They had for so many centuries had no occasion for fear that in the crisis their courage failed them, and when Thomas's emissaries, in a great fleet of planes, circled above them, threatening to let loose the death-dealing dust that they had brought with them, the whole governing aristocracy surrendered on the promise that their lives should be spared. Kilimanjaro became the centre of Government. Thomas was proclaimed President of the World, and Paul was appointed his Prime Minister. All recognised that a new era had begun and that the age of Zahatopolk was ended.

Thomas, as soon as his régime was secure, set to work to undo the degradation to which non-Indian populations had been subjected. He diminished the hours of physical work, which the Peruvians had kept to ten, not from any economic motive, but only in order that the workers might be too tired to have any initiative. By means of his faithful band of scientists, he greatly increased the world's food supply, and by declaring the preventing of conception innocent, made the increase minister to health and happiness, and not only to more rapid multiplication. He gave a share of political power to all who had sufficient education, and he extended education as quickly as possible throughout all parts of the world. In many of the hitherto oppressed countries there was a great outburst of painting and poetry and music. The suppressed energies, which had lain dormant for centuries, sprang into a luxuriant life such as had only been known before in a few countries in a few great ages. He taught that there are no Gods. And, although the populace ascribed his escape to a miracle, he did his best to persuade the world that miracles are impossible. There were those who wished to give him the position that Zahatopolk had previously had, but he refused deification with emphasis and caused the doctrine to be combated in all the schools. Under his régime there were no priests and no aristocrats, no ruling races and no subject peoples.

109

VII

The Future

The above is the account of the Great Revolution given by Thomas's friend Paul after Thomas's reign of many years had been brought to an end by his death. This account of his life and doctrines has remained ever since the Sacred Book of the Kilimanjaro Era. But it has gradually been found that some parts of Thomas's doctrine are liable to misinterpretation, and that the reading of Paul's book by all and sundry may be dangerous. He was not always careful to indicate when he was to be taken literally and when he was speaking allegorically. It is now universally recognised that Thomas was in fact a God, and that Diotima was a Goddess. We know that both for a time put on humanity, but at the moment of their earthly death resumed their heavenly life, which for a few brief years they had put away for our salvation. When Thomas denied his Godhead he was, as all now acknowledge, denying it only as regards his earthly manifestation. All this was carefully explained about five hundred years after his death by the great commentator Gregorius.

For a time Paul's book was still allowed to circulate, provided the commentary of Gregorius was bound up with it. But even this was found to have dangers, and the book, even with the commentary, is now not allowed to be read except by licensed Divines. Even so, it remains a danger. New Zealand contains one copy in the University of Auckland. This copy was lately returned to the University with a strange note upon its last page. The note said:

'I, Tupia, of the tribe of Ngapuhi, a dweller upon the slopes of Ruapehu, am not persuaded of the justice of Gregorius's glosses. I am convinced that Thomas was wiser than Gregorius, and that he meant literally all the things which that theologically-minded priest finds troublesome. It shall be my mission, if possible, to lead the world back to that ancient unfaith which its liberator tried to spread.'

These are ominous words, and their outcome is as yet uncertain.

Faith and Mountains

I

The Nepalese delegate to UNESCO was surprised and puzzled. It was the first time that he had abandoned the safety of his native glaciers and precipices for the bewildering perils of the West. Arriving by air late on the previous evening, he had been too tired to notice anything, and had slept heavily until the morning was well advanced. He looked out upon a street which, as he was informed by the waiter who brought his breakfast, was called Piccadilly. But it did not wear the aspect which the cinema had led him to anticipate. There was no ordinary traffic, but an immense procession of men and women on foot bearing banners of which his phrasebook did not enable him to guess the meaning. The inscriptions on the banners were repeated at such frequent intervals that at last he had deciphered them all. They said various things which, he was compelled to suppose, all pointed to one moral. The commonest was, 'Hail to Molybdenum, Maker of Healthy Bodies!' Another which occurred with great frequency was 'Up with the Molybdenes!' A third, not quite so frequent, said, 'Long Life to the Holy Molly B. Dean!' One peculiarly ferocious band had a banner saying, 'Death to the Infamous Magnets!' The procession was of enormous length and, at intervals of about a quarter of a mile, there was a band and a choir which sang what appeared to be the battle-hymn of the marchers:

Molybdenum of metals best
Is good for high and low.
It cures diseases of the chest
And makes our muscles grow.

The hymn was sung to the tune of 'There is a book who runs may read', but this the delegate did not know, as he had not had the benefit of a Christian upbringing.

After he had begun to think that the procession would never end, there came a gap. Then a solid squadron of mounted police. And then another procession, with quite other banners. Some of these said, 'Glory to Aurora Bohra!' Others said, 'All Power to the Northern Pole!' Yet others said, 'Through Magnetism to Magnificence!' The marchers in this second procession also sang a hymn, as unintelligible to him as the hymn of the first procession. They sang:

I go forth
To the North
In my jet-propelled chariot.

I descend on the Pole
For the good of my soul
And learn to think Bohra much better than Harriet.

With every moment his curiosity increased. At last it became overwhelming. He rushed out into the street and joined the procession. With true Oriental courtesy he addressed his neighbour pedestrian with the words : 'Would you, Sir, deign to have the great kindness to explain to me why this musical multitude marches westward with such rhythmic persistence?'

'Lor bless yer!' said the man he addressed. 'Mean to say yer don't know about the Magnets? And where may you have come from?'

'Sir,' replied the delegate, 'you must bear with my ignorance. I have but recently dropped from the skies, and have dwelt hitherto in the Himalayas, in a region inhabited only by Buddhists and Communists, who are quiet, peaceable folk, not addicted to such singular pilgrimages.'

'Gorblimey!' said his neighbour. 'If that's so, it would take more breath than I can spare to make you understand!'

The delegate therefore marched on in silence, hoping that time would bring enlightenment.

At length the procession arrived at an enormous round building which, as his neighbour informed him, was called the Albert Hall. Some of the procession were admitted within, but the great majority were compelled to remain without. The Nepalese at first was refused admission. But, on explaining his official position as a delegate, and the profound interest of his country in Occidental Cultural Phenomena, he was at last allowed to take a seat far back in the exact middle of the platform.

What he saw and what he heard seemed to him to throw a great light upon the manners and customs, the beliefs and habits of thought of the strange people among whom he found himself. But so much remained unintelligible to him that he determined to devote himself to serious research and to draw up an elucidatory report for the enlightenment of Himalayan sages.

The work proved onerous, and it was not until twelve months had passed that he deemed it worthy of the wise eyes of those who had sent him. During these twelve months I had had the good fortune to make friends with him, and to be allowed to share in his wisdom. The following account of the great debate, and the events that led up to it and followed it, is based upon his report. Without his labours, my account could not have been so exhaustive or so minutely accurate.

II

The two sects, whose public debate the Nepalese delegate witnessed, had each emerged after a period of obscurity, and had, in recent years, grown with such amazing rapidity that hardly anybody, except highbrows, failed to belong to one or other. They were called, respectively, the Molybdenes and the Northern Magnets, or simply the Magnets. Each had its head office in London. The affairs of the Molybdenes were directed by Zeruiah Tomkins, and those of the Magnets by Manasseh Merrow. In each case the fundamental doctrine of the sect was simple.

The Molybdenes believed that the human frame requires, for full development of health and strength, a larger amount of molybdenum in the diet than has hitherto been customary. Their favourite text was: 'He that eateth, eateth unto the Lord. And he that eateth not, unto the Lord he eateth not.' But they changed the order of the words in the latter half of this text so as to make it read: 'He that eateth not, eateth not unto the Lord.' He that eateth, they explained, means a person who eats molybdenum. They supported their position by a story for whose truth I cannot vouch. Large flocks of sheep in a certain district of Australia, which had withered away, had slowly perished because their scanty pastures, unlike those of Europe and Asia, were wholly destitute of molybdenum. Certain biochemists and medical men – not perhaps quite the most eminent in their respective professions – had made statements as to the dietetic importance of molybdenum, and these statements were seized upon by the faithful as supports for their creed. There had been a considerable demand for this not very common metal in armaments, but the gradual lessening of tension had diminished this demand. Now, however, owing to the growth of the Molybdenes, the demand for molybdenum had ceased to be dependent upon the threat of war. The Molybdenes were opposed to war. They regarded all men as brothers, except the Northern Magnets; and the Northern Magnets were to be overcome, not by force of arms, but by the Pure Light of Truth.

The Northern Magnets found the secret of human welfare in a quite different direction. 'We are all,' so they said, 'the Children of Earth, and the Earth, as every schoolboy knows, is a great magnet. We must all share, in a greater or lesser degree, the magnetic propensities of our Mighty Mother, but, if we do not submit ourselves to her beneficent authority, we shall become unclear and confused. We should therefore always sleep with our heads towards the North Magnetic Pole and our feet towards the South Magnetic Pole. Those who persistently sleep thus will gradually acquire a share in the magnetic powers of Earth. They will be healthy, vigorous, and wise.' So, at least, the Northern Magnets unshakably believed.

In both sects there was an inner and an outer circle. The inner circle were called 'Adepts', and the outer circle, 'Adherents'. Inner and outer circle alike had a badge by which they could be known. The Molybdenes wore a ring made of molybdenum, and the Northern Magnets wore a magnet as a locket. The Adepts devoted themselves to the holy life, consisting partly in observances and partly in missionary work. Both communities of Adepts were healthy, happy and virtuous. Alcohol and tobacco were forbidden them. They went early to bed, the Molybdenes, in order that the health-giving molybdenum they had consumed might be absorbed into the blood-stream, the Northern Magnets in order that the magnetic powers of Earth might operate fully during the hours of darkness. Sustained by faith, the Adepts were little troubled by the daily rubs which ruffle the tempers of those not sustained in this way. True, they had in early days had their difficulties. Unwise zealots had pushed the eminently sane doctrines of the two sects beyond the limits of wisdom. At one time there was among the Molybdenes an extreme faction which thought that holiness could be measured by the amount of molybdenum consumed each day. Some went so far that their skin became metallic, and it was found that, sublime as were their intentions, in molybdenum, as in everything else, it was possible to indulge to excess. The elders, after a stormy meeting, were compelled to discipline the zealots. But after this painful incident no similar trouble again arose.

Among the Magnets there was a different deviation into fanaticism. There were those who said: 'If virtue comes while we lie prone in the direction of the lines of terrestrial magnetic force, it is clear that we ought always to lie thus, and that to rise from our beds is to risk dissipation of the vivi-facatory virtue that Earth confers upon those who duly worship her.' These zealots accordingly spent the whole twenty-four hours in bed, to the no small inconvenience of their less ardent relatives and friends. This heresy, like that of the Molybdenes, was subdued, though with difficulty, by the authority of the elders, and it was decreed that, except in times of ill-health, no Northern Magnet should spend more than twelve hours out of twenty-four in his bed.

Both these troubles, however, belonged to the early days of the two sects. In their later days, missionary ardour and swift success combined with health and vigour to fill their lives with joy. One thing only troubled the Adepts: The Molybdenes could not understand why Providence permitted the growth of the Northern Magnets; and the Northern Magnets could not understand why Providence permitted the growth of the Molybdenes. Each sect consoled itself with the thought that there must be mystery somewhere, and that it is not given to the finite intellect of man to fathom the august designs of Providence. Doubtless, in the fullness of time, Truth would prevail, and the sect which had throughout proclaimed the Truth would win universal adherence. Meantime, it was the duty of the Adepts, by example, by precept, by wise words in and out of season, to spread the light. In this effort, the success of both parties was, to the indifferent, amazing.

In early days, each sect had had to face the ridicule of unbelievers. 'Why molybdenum?' said these scoffers. 'Why not strontium? Why not barium? What is the peculiar glory of this one element?' When the believers replied that this was a mystery intelligible only to those who already had faith, the answer was received with derision.

The Northern Magnets had equal difficulties to face, 'Why not the South Magnetic Pole?' said the sceptics. Some, especially certain inhabitants of the Southern hemisphere, went so far as to sleep habitually with their heads towards the South, and challenged Northern Magnets to wrestling matches designed to prove that the South Magnetic Pole is as invigorating as the one in the North. Such challenges were treated by the Northern Magnets with the contempt that they deserved. They replied that, while those who followed the prescribed regimen would achieve physical health and strength, it was not this alone that they would achieve, but an inner harmony through interpenetration by the magnetic might of Earth. In *mere* brawn some among them might be surpassed by some among unbelievers. In the perfect harmony of body and spirit True Believers would remain supreme. And as for the pretence that the South Pole was just as good as the North Pole, how, if this were true, could it be explained why the Creator had made so much more land in the North than in the South? This argument, though it aroused some anger in South America, South Africa and Australia, was felt to be very difficult to meet. Only the firm fervour of the Molybdenes was impervious to the arguments of the Northern Magnets.

Each side urged, and urged with justice, that to meet faith in falsehood, only faith in Truth was adequate. Never could cold reason unaided prevail against the misleading ardour of deluded fanatics. While the two sects were still young, some men of science and some literary satirists had endeavoured to meet their claims by the combined force of statistics and ridicule. But they had been powerless to stem the popular tide, and, in time, only men whom superior intelligence (or what they themselves deemed such) had cut off from sympathy with the mass of mankind stood out against both sects. The more expensive newspapers, which had small circulations, and were read only by the aristocracy of intellect, continued to remain aloof and neutral. They said as little as they could about the doings of the two sects, with the result that persons of superior education were almost unaware of what was happening round about them. The cheaper news-papers tried at first to placate both parties, but this proved impossible. Any word of praise of the Northern Magnets roused all Molybdenes to fury. Any not derogatory mention of the Molybdenes caused the Northern Magnets to vow that they would never again read so degraded a journal. The popular newspapers were therefore compelled to take sides. *The Daily*

Lightning sided with the Northern Magnets; *The Daily Thunder* with the Molybdenes. Day by day, each portrayed more luridly than before the moral and intellectual degradation of the opposite party and the almost incredible heights of purity, devotion and vigour achieved by the party which the journal supported. Under the influence of such journalistic skill, party spirit ran higher and higher, national unity was lost, and it was even feared that civil war might ensue.

Nor was the trouble confined to Britain. Indeed its gravest aspect was an increasing tension between the United States and Canada, which came about through causes that we have not yet set forth.

III

The Founder of the Molybdenes was a certain middle-aged American widow named Molly B. Dean. Her husband had been a very rich man, but meek with that kind of meekness which, according to the Gospels, inherits the earth. He possessed, partly by inheritance and partly by skilful investment, a great deal of the earth of Colorado. His wife, to whom he left the whole of his immense fortune, was one of those ladies who are obviously born to be widows. Those who marry such ladies never achieve old age. And Mr Dean duly died in the prime of life. She, however, appears to have not recognised this as an inevitable part of her destiny, for, when discoursing on the merits of molybdenum, she was wont to say: 'Ah, had I but known of the beneficent effects of this metal sooner, my dear husband Jehoshaphat might still be on this side of the Great Veil!'

Mrs Molly B. Dean, whose religion and business acumen were perhaps not quite so separate as one could wish, discovered, on examining her husband's investments after his death, that she owned about nine-tenths of the world's supply of molybdenum ore. She was struck by the similarity between the name of this element and her own name. Such similarity, she felt convinced, could not be due to chance. It must be the work of Destiny. It must be her glorious mission to give her name to a new faith, purer than any previous faith and not less profitable to herself.

The adherents of the new faith should be taught to consume molybdenum, and should be named, after herself, the Molybdenes. The offspring of the moment of creative thought grew rapidly and was soon able to walk upon its two legs of religious faith and business acumen. Lest either should interfere with the other, she formed a company, called Amalgamated Metals Inc., of which she retained control, although her name did not appear. At the same time, she poured her religious beliefs into the mind of Zeruiah Tomkins, a man somewhat younger than herself, who had had great success as a Baptist preacher, but had fallen into disfavour through a slight lapse from orthodoxy. Her powerful personality dominated him completely. He accepted her every word as divine revelation, and became filled with an immense ardour for the regeneration of mankind through her very original gospel. His organising capacity was as great as his zeal; and she entrusted to him, without a qualm, the terrestrial affairs of the holy brotherhood of the Molybdenes.

The Northern Magnets owed their origin, though they themselves were unaware of this fact, to an important man named Sir Magnus North. Sir Magnus was a prominent figure in the national life of Canada and the owner of vast tracts of land in the empty North-West, which he believed to be possessed of great mineral wealth. He decided to put the North-West 'on the map'. He employed eminent geophysicists to locate the Magnetic Pole more accurately than had hitherto been done, and discovered, as he had hoped, that it was in the very middle of the lands of which he was owner. He discovered also, or rather the explorers whom he employed discovered, that at the Magnetic Pole there is a volcanic mountain, and, whether from volcanic action or as a result of radio-activity, the soil in the neighbourhood is warm, snow does not lie, and there is a lake which even in winter remains unfrozen. With these data in his possession he planned a great campaign. With the help of a professor of anthropology who had studied the beliefs of Eskimos and Northern Indians, he formulated the main tenets of the creed which became that of the Northern Magnets. But, as he was warned by the anthropologist, and as he knew from experiences on the Stock Exchange, it is not by pure reason that men are governed. Although to a rational mind the arguments in favour of the creed which he wished to propagate must prove irresistible, he sought and found a key to men's hearts at once softer and more compelling. He realised that it was not for him to be the missionary of the new sect. The missionary must be at once dynamic and mystical, someone capable of appealing to the deepest chords of the human heart, someone who could introduce into the feelings of men and women that strange unquiet peace which seems to bring happiness, but does not bring slothful inactivity.

The search for such a Founder he left in the hands of his anthropologist, who interviewed the leaders of sects in Los Angeles, in Chicago, and wherever new beliefs were being ardently sought. Acting on the orders of Sir Magnus, he did not reveal his purpose. As last he prepared a short list of three, and submitted it to Sir Magnus for his final decision. Of the three, there was one whom Sir Magnus judged to be outstanding. She had been electrifying Winnipeg, of which she was a native, by the promise of a great revelation to come; but what the nature of the revelation should be she had not yet told. She was a lady of majestic proportions: her height was six foot four, and all her other dimensions were to scale. Many of those who beheld her were reminded of the Statue of Liberty, but she was even more august. There was only one thing against her, and that was her name, which was Amelia Skeggs. Sir Magnus, when he reflected upon the future for which he hoped, found it difficult to imagine the world adhering to Skeggendom or Skeggianity. He remembered the fate of the Muggletonians, who had everything in their favour, except the unfortunate name Muggleton. For a time this difficulty made him hesitate, but in the end he found a triumphant solution. When he had found it, he decided that the time had come to reveal to the majestic Amelia the great destiny which he planned for her.

'Miss Skeggs,' he said, 'I know from your eloquent preaching that you are aware of a great destiny. Nature has fashioned you to dominate mankind not only by your splendid frame but by the greatness of the soul that inhabits it. You know that you are to have a mission; but you have not known until now what that mission is to be. It is left to me, as the humble emissary of Providence, to show you the way to that towering spiritual eminence for which you know yourself to be destined.' He then explained to her the tenets which became those of the Northern Magnets.

As he spoke, she became filled with spiritual fire. Not a doubt remained anywhere. This was the gospel which she had been seeking. This was the happy truth which should make Canada the Holy Land, and lead the faithful of all the world, in humble pilgrimages, to its magnetic shrine.

One step remained for Sir Magnus. 'You must have in religion,' he said, 'a different name from that which you have had in the world; a dedicated name, a name whose very syllables reverberate your sacred task. Henceforth, you shall be known to all the nations of the world by a new and splendid appellation: All Hail to You,

AURORA BOHRA!'

She left his presence intoxicated, exalted, filled with mystic ecstasy and high purpose. From that moment, their collaboration was perfect. But, acting upon his instructions, she kept his part secret.

It did not take long for Aurora Bohra to become known and successful in wide circles. She was fortunate in obtaining the assistance of Manasseh Merrow, a man who, while possessed of great organising ability, had always been conscious of a lack in himself, a lack of those spiritual qualities which, as a youth, he had admired in the memory of his sainted mother. This lack was made up to him by Aurora Bohra, for whom he felt a devout and unfaltering worship. If anyone had asked him whether he loved her, he would have been outraged by the blasphemy. It was not love, but adoration that he felt for her. He laid at her feet all his great ability in practical affairs, and left her free for the expression of that mellifluous ecstasy upon which her hold on men and women depended.

IV

One of the first enterprises to which the Northern Magnets owed their success was the creation of the great circular sanatorium surrounding the Magnetic Pole. To this sanatorium was given the name of the Magnetic Home. In this enormous edifice the head of every bed pointed exactly towards the North Magnetic Pole which occupied the centre of the circular courtyard. The foot of every bed pointed exactly towards the South Magnetic Pole. Owing to the situation of this sanatorium, the curative effects of terrestrial magnetism were far greater than elsewhere. Most of the Adherents secured both mental and physical health by obeying the ordinary regimen; but there were some who, in the early months of their discipleship, retained traces of a neurasthenia which they had brought from their days of unbelief. Such unquiet spirits, provided they had the necessary means, were transported in luxurious jet-planes to the Polar sanatorium where every luxury was provided, and where alcohol and tobacco, elsewhere forbidden to the faithful, were permitted for medicinal purposes.

One of the earliest of these neurasthenic visitors to the sanatorium, whose name was Jedidiah Jelliffe, had been driven to the verge of insanity by hopeless love for an exquisitely beautiful lady named Harriet Hemlock. The magnetism of Aurora Bohra completely cured him. And, in gratitude for his cure, he celebrated his liberation in immortal verse, which became the marching hymn of the Northern Magnets and which had bewildered the ears of the Nepalese delegate.

At the exact location of the Magnetic Pole, which was in the precise centre of the circular courtyard, there was a flagstaff from which floated at most times the banner of the Northern Magnets, which represented the head of Aurora Bohra with the Aurora Borealis streaming from it in all directions. But once every day, after a period during which the faithful, under the threat of dire penalties, were compelled to avert their gaze, the flag was replaced by an eyrie from which, dressed in flowing black robes, the majestic priestess spoke her words of inspired wisdom. Above her head were nine loud speakers, eight of them horizontal, pointing North, South, East, and West, North-East, South-West, South-East, and North-West. These were trumpets of silver. But there was in addition another loud speaker, a trumpet of pure gold, pointing straight upwards in order that her words might be heard in heaven as well as on earth.

Standing upon a pedestal unseen by the faithful below, in a slowly rotating circular chamber with walls of the most translucent glass, with arms waving as though in an incipient embrace and her whole body slowly undulating as though obeying the lines of a magnetic stream, with her great eyes piercing and yet contemplative, sometimes flashing, sometimes veiled, she spoke. Her voice, which was unlike any that the hearers had

119

heard elsewhere, combined the majesty of rolling mountain thunder with the lingering gentleness of the dove.

'Dear Brothers and Sisters in Magnetism,' she would say, 'it is my privilege once again to speak to you of our Holy Faith, and to convey, by the power mysteriously vouchsafed to me, the strength and peace of our Magnetic Mother Earth. Through my veins flows Her fire; in my thoughts dwells Her ineffable calm. Both shall come, though perhaps in diminished degree, to you, My Beloved Hearers. Is your life troubled and unquiet? Do you fear that the ardent affection, which you once received from your husband or your wife, is less than it was? Does your business fail to prosper? Do your neighbours treat you with less respect than, I am sure, you deserve? Be not troubled, Dear Friends. The arms of Our Great Mother Earth enfold you. Your sorrows, permitted for a moment, are but intended to try your faith. Lay aside your burdens, and let Magnetic Health flow into you. Love, strength and joy be yours, as they are mine!'

All who heard her were affected in their different ways. The weary became alert; the despondent were filled with peace; those who had been embittered by grievances began to feel them trivial; and, in the adoration of Aurora, all found themselves united in a mutual harmony.

The Molybdenes also had their recreative palace, situated at the top of Acme Alp in Colorado. This was a mountain some ten thousand feet high, covered in snow during eight months of the year, but, during the other four, lovely with mountain meadows carpeted with gentians and other wild flowers. From its summit there was a vast prospect in every direction of mountains and valleys, woods and streams, and the red Colorado River winding its way through obstacles in the distance. It was not, however, the beauty of the prospect alone that recommended this site to Molly B. Dean. It had another, and perhaps even greater, merit in her eyes. Acme Alp was at the very centre of the molybdenum region over which she held sway. The recreative palace at its summit was known far and wide as the Acme Sanitarium. Owing to the steepness of the hillside it could be reached only by helicopter. Visitors were brought by plane to Denver, and there transshipped into one of the great fleet of these ingenious machines kept always in readiness for the guests of that luxurious establishment.

Although perhaps less theatrical than the Magnet Sanatorium, the Acme Sanitarium was no whit less comfortable. New arrivals, it is true, were sometimes a little alarmed by the unusual quality of the menu. They would find that they were being offered for their first dinner Molydacious Mulligatawny, Molyb Polyp, Molybdenised Mutton, and Molyfluous Meringues – or some variant, for Molly B. Dean was aware that monotony was of all things to be avoided, and the Molybdenic quality of the diet therefore underwent different disguises on different evenings. There was a great difference between the atmosphere created by Molly B. Dean and that diffused by Aurora Bohra. Aurora Bohra believed in the mystic powers of

Earth, and encouraged a certain passive receptivity as the source of subsequent vigorous action. Molly B. Dean, on the contrary, believed in calling out in each individual his own strength, his own power of will, his own control over his destiny. Not for her, the reliance upon external help! In her stirring radio addresses, to which, before the evening meal, the guests in her Sanitarium were compelled to listen, she would appear to each man and each woman – aye, and to each child, too – to draw upon that inner fund of determination, upon which, in the last resort, we must all depend. She had worked out a technique for the development of these powers:

'Do you,' she would say, 'feel a reluctance to rise from your bed in the morning? Do not yield to it! Begin your waking day with a firm act of will. Mount your mechanical horse, and, after five minutes of strenuous exertion with this health-giving implement, devote yourself to muscular exercises unassisted by adjuncts. Touch your toes with your hands ninety-nine times while keeping your knees as stiff as a ramrod. After this, you will feel no hardship in your cold bath, though the water be obtained from melting snow. Your toilet completed, you will descend to your communal breakfast filled with appetite and energy, ready for whatever the day may bring. Is your mail full of tiresome chores? What of it? You dispose of it with only a tiny fragment of the power derived from your pre-breakfast regimen. Have your investments diminished in value? That need not trouble you, for the intellectual clarity derived from the mechanical horse will enable you, without difficulty, to select, with shrewd judgement, new investments of which the future prosperity is unquestionable. And should sinful thoughts come, as come they may even in this Holy Palace; should you permit yourself to wish that a longer period in bed, or a less frigid bath, were permitted; should you hanker after non-molybdenised mutton; should you even, tempted doubtless by Satan, harbour the dreadful thought that strontium might do just as well – in all or any of these terrible situations you can find salvation by a simple rule: you must first run ten times round the courtyard of the palace, and then open at haphazard the Sacred Volume, *Molybdenum, the Cure for Morbid Mopings.* Wherever this volume may open you will find your eye resting upon some health-giving text, and you will be able, by your own strength, to banish the horrid thoughts which had been diverting the pure stream of your unsullied life-force. Above all, remember this: It is not in thought that salvation is to be found, but in action, strenuous action, health-giving action, action that generates power. When the wiles of Satan threaten to ensnare you, it is not to tortuous thought that you must turn, but to action. And what that action should be, you will find in the Sacred Volume. Action! Action! Action! Action in the Holy Name of Molybdenum!'

V

The business management of the two recreative palaces was left by Molly
B. Dean and Aurora Bohra in the hands of their respective managers, Mr
Tomkins and Mr Merrow. Each of these men realised that the sect of which
he was in charge was exposed to the enmity of the other sect. Each was
persuaded that the other sect consisted of unscrupulous scoundrels, who
would shrink from nothing to effect the ruin of their rivals. Each therefore
installed, not only in the public rooms, but in every bedroom, dictaphones
which recorded the supposedly private conversations of the guests. Each
found that there were grumblers, nay even incipient sceptics, who had
somehow found admission in spite of all the care of the Reception
Committee.

In Acme Alp the centre of disaffection was traced, by skilful Secret
Service work, to a certain Mr Wagner. Mr Wagner had seemed to the
Management exactly the sort of man for whom the Sanitarium was
designed. He had been, the Management understood, a successful business
man, but had become afflicted with indecision. He would say, 'I have
studied the merits of this and that, and have found the arguments exactly
evenly balanced. What, in these circumstances, am I to do?' There was a
danger that in this mood his fortune would be dissipated. He had sought
salvation with the Molybdenes, and had apparently hoped to find it. But
although his condition improved, the cure remained incomplete, and it was
decided that a period of Acme Alp would be necessary. With due submission to the authorities, he agreed. And, leaving his business interests for
the time being in the hands of subordinates, he sought the health-giving
atmosphere of that strenuous House of Rest.

But his conversation while there was of a sort that it was difficult to
approve. He would say, addressing some chance acquaintance after dinner,
'You know, it is marvellous what molybdenum does for the Molybdenes!
But there are some things that puzzle me, and to which I find no answer in
the Sacred Volume. Since molybdenum is mainly concentrated in Colorado,
one must suppose that the inhabitants of this State consume more of it
than those who live in other parts of this great Republic. But, on examining
the vital statistics, I have not discovered any measurable difference between
the health of Colorado and that of other States. This, I confess, puzzles me.
Another thing also gave me pause: I asked a scientific physician of my
acquaintance to examine minutely the imports and exports of molybdenum
in the body of a devout Molybdene, who has consumed that amount of the
Sacred Metal prescribed by our revered Leader, and in an ordinary citizen.
I found, to my amazement, that the amount of molybdenum retained in
the body of a healthy Molybdene is no greater than that retained in the
body of a man whose diet is normal. I am sure there must be an answer

to these perplexities, but I wish I knew what it is. I do not wish to trouble Mr Tomkins, who is a very busy man. Can you suggest some way of resolving my difficulties?'

It was found that he had made speeches of this sort to a number of people at Acme Alp. But nothing definite could be proved against him, and, in the end, it was decided to pronounce him cured and send him back to his home.

A somewhat similar trouble arose shortly afterwards at the Magnetic Home. A certain Mr Thorney, who was, or was supposed to be, a traveller in out-of-the-way lands, returned from an expedition, or so he said, worn out with the hardships that a series of mishaps had imposed upon him. Weary and discouraged, he sought the life-giving force that the Northern Magnets offered. He became an Adherent, and his friends among the Faithful hoped for rapid improvement. But improvement was discouragingly slow, and he seemed incapable of feeling against the zest which had sent him upon his travels. It was decided by the authorities that only a visit to the Magnetic Pole could complete his cure. There, however, as on Acme Alp, dictaphones had been installed by the wise prudence of those who foresaw the machinations of their rivals. And it was found that, while Mr Thorney's conversation could not be condemned as definitely heretical, it had nevertheless a subtle tendency to diminish the firmness of belief in those who listened to it. It was suspected that he had not a due reverence for Aurora Bohra, whom the Faithful never saw except when she was in her eyrie. 'Have you ever wondered,' he would say to a neighbour, 'how tall Aurora really is?' 'No,' the neighbour would say in a slightly shocked tone, 'and I am not sure that I consider the question quite nice.' 'Oh well,' Mr Thorney would reply, 'she is, after all, a real woman of flesh and blood. Having had to practise surveying in my travels, I took the liberty of estimating her height with my sextant. Allowing for her feet, which I could not see, I concluded that her height is between six foot three and a half inches and six foot four and a half inches. I could not make my estimate more exact because of the refracting properties of the glass through which we see her. But I was able to assure myself beyond a doubt that she is a fine figure of a woman.'

It was not the thing to speak in these terms of the presiding Goddess; but it must be acknowledged, though with pain, that there were some who fell in with Mr Thorney's manner, and were thenceforth less inclined to attribute supernatural powers to that Noble Lady. Where he found favourable soil for the seeds of his irreverence, he would go farther. He would say, 'You know, there is a circumstance, known perhaps to few white men except myself, which I find very difficult to explain on the basis of the Magnetic Principles that we all accept. There is, in a certain very remote part of Tibet, a valley of quite extraordinary narrowness, almost a chasm, which points, as my survey assured me, directly towards the North Magnetic

Pole. Although the valley is so narrow, there are those who spend the summer in it, because it contains diamonds. They have to sleep with their heads towards the North or with their heads towards the South. Some choose the one, some the other. One might have expected that those who sleep with their heads towards the North would be in all respects superior to those who choose the opposite posture. But, although I spent a considerable time among them and made inquiries into their past history, I was unable to discover any such difference as our Holy Faith compels us to postulate. There is, I am sure, some quite conclusive answer, but I have been unable to imagine what it may be. If you, or any of your friends, can resolve my perplexity, you will earn my deepest gratitude.'

When dictaphones revealed his habit of putting such questions to the other visitors in the circular palace, it was decided by the authorities that, though he was doubtless a genuine seeker after Truth, the form and method of his search were not such as to deserve encouragement. He was therefore prematurely pronounced cured, and sent home, with a caution to meditate in silence, if at all, upon the curious questions that he had somewhat rashly raised.

VI

In spite of such slight difficulties, both movements prospered. The Northern Magnets won the support of everybody in Scandinavia, except the Intelligentsia. Iceland and Greenland followed suit, and their men of science proved conclusively that, in course of time, the Magnetic Pole would be theirs. In the United States it was the Molybdenes who flourished. The State of Utah, where considerable stores of molybdenum were discovered, solemnly abandoned the *Book of Mormon* and substituted *Molybdenum, the Cure for Morbid Mopings*. As some reward for this accession to the True Faith, Molly B. Dean conceded that Utah should be incorporated in the Holy Land. Throughout the Western World, the bewildered young, who had been unable to choose whole-heartedly either the Kremlin or the Vatican as objects of adoration, found mental and emotional rest in one or other of the two new creeds.

In England, where the two factions were very evenly balanced, acute conflict was more threatened than anywhere else. Test matches no longer aroused interest, the older football teams were forgotten, and only the great matches between Molybdenes and Magnets attracted the crowds. Not only in football, but in every kind of athletic contest, the Molybdenes and the Magnets competed with fluctuating success and without decisive superiority for either. It was found, with some dismay, that the crowds were no longer good-natured, and that fights broke out between irascible adherents of the rival faiths. At last a rule had to be adopted separating Molybdenes and

Magnets by placing one of these to the right and one to the left. Those who avowed themselves neutrals were viewed with contempt and told to go home.

The Highbrows would have been delighted to make their peace with both, but this was impossible. 'He that is not with us, is against us,' such temporisers were firmly told. Nevertheless, some attempts at conciliation persisted. The *Tempora Supplementary Letters* had a deeply reflective article on the two creeds. 'It must be conceded,' so this article said, 'that to the coldly critical intellect, there are difficulties in both the Gospels which are bringing new hopes and new life to the weary West. But those who are imbued with the great tradition, those who have absorbed and digested the message of all the great thinkers, from Plato to St Thomas Aquinas, will not lightly reject new faiths, even though they may appear impossible, as the Christian faith did to Tertullian, who, in spite of such impossibility – nay, because of it – accepted whole-heartedly the new tenets which transcended reason. All right-thinking people, whatever difficulty they may have in choosing between the Molybdenes and the Magnets, will welcome what the two movements have in common. Not so long ago a coldly mechanist philosophy dominated the thoughts of our accepted pundits. Those deeper sources of wisdom, which are not derived from mere observation of brute fact, but well up in the humble heart when it opens itself to the operation of the Great Spirit of Truth – from these the Molybdenes and the Magnets alike derive refreshment. Gone is the insolence of sciolists; gone is the shallow certainty of those who ignore the Eternal Verities upon which our Western World is founded. In the Molybdenes and the Magnets alike there is so much that every lover of wisdom must welcome, that we cannot but regret their separateness and rivalry. We believe, and in this belief we are not alone, that an amalgamation is possible, and that, if effected, it will give to the faith in our Western Values that unshakable strength which is needed in the fateful contest with the atheism of the East.'

This weighty pronouncement had influential backing. The British Government, torn between love of the Commonwealth and dependence upon the United States, viewed with the deepest alarm the growing tension between Canada and the western half of the United States. Such tension, if it could not be eased, could bring to nought the work, not only of the United Nations, but also of NATO. In England, the adherents of the two parties were about equal in numbers. Both were strong, but neither could hope to be supreme. The British Government approached Mr Tomkins and Mr Merrow with proposals for a conference, and with earnest suggestions for at least a *modus vivendi* between the two sects.

Mr Tomkins and Mr Merrow consulted by long-distance telephone the High Priestesses, Molly B. Dean and Aurora Bohra. Aurora Bohra secretly consulted Sir Magnus North. The outcome of these various consultations was the decision to hold a great meeting in the Albert Hall at which, by public debate, some form of agreement was to be reached. Such, at least, was the outcome for which the Government hoped. But the hopes of the two parties were different. Each was so firmly persuaded of its own invincibility that it felt no doubt of victory in a public confrontation, and it was in virtue of this confidence that each side assented to the Government's proposals.

It was agreed that the great meeting should be held under the chairmanship of the Professor of Comparative Religion at the University of Oxbridge. This wise and urbane scholar knew all about the religion of the extinct Tasmanians, the beliefs of the Hottentots, and the creed of the Pygmies. It was therefore supposed by the Government that he could give sympathetic understanding to both the Molybdenes and the Magnets. But, lest he should fail, through being more urbane than forceful, he was to be supported by a band of some hundreds of stalwart stewards, each of whom should have been carefully screened to make sure that he had no inclination towards either party. Lots were drawn as to which party should be to the right and which to the left. The right fell to the Magnets, the left to the Molybdenes. On the stage, and on the floor of the hall, and in every gallery, this division was observed. A wide aisle was left between the two parties, and throughout the meeting the neutral stewards marched up and down this aisle with stern orders to preserve the peace at all costs.

Aurora Bohra and Molly B. Dean had descended from their mountains to inspire their faithful followers on this momentous occasion. Each sat on a throne near the centre of the stage, separated from the other only by the width of the aisle. Molly B. Dean loved all mankind, but she did not love Aurora Bohra; Aurora Bohra loved all mankind, but she did not love Molly B. Dean. Molly B. Dean, with sharp, black, snapping eyes, after surveying the gathering, darted a venomous glance upon Aurora Bohra, a glance so venomous that it must have shrivelled a lesser personality. Aurora Bohra, after gazing raptly at the ceiling, allowed her great eyes to wander vaguely over the assembled multitude. Although, at times, her gaze seemed to be directed towards the opposite throne, it appeared that in that direction she saw nothing. The Medusa glances of Molly B. Dean passed her by. Only in the rapt contemplation of the great dome did she seem to yield to those sublime emotions which had made her what she was.

Mr Tomkins and Mr Merrow, each bristling with a sheaf of papers, stood at their desks, primed with all the facts and all the arguments most calculated to overwhelm the other party.

Immediately behind Zeruiah Tomkins sat his son and destined successor, Zachary. Zachary had been educated by his father with the most careful regard to the preservation of this orthodoxy. Never for a moment had he doubted the tenets of the Molybdenes, never for a moment had he imagined any other destiny than to help his father while he lived, and to carry on his work when death should call him to an even happier land. But, in spite of a diet adequately flavoured with molybdenum, he was a somewhat weedy youth, and in his spare time turned his thoughts towards poetry rather than theology. Although molybdenum was supposed to confer muscular good cheer upon its devotees, he was the victim, to his secret shame, of a somewhat melancholy outlook. He thought Keats's *Ode to Autumn* unduly cheerful and wrote, himself, an *Ode to Autumn* beginning,

> Autumn leaves
> And barley sheaves
> Bring thought of the morrow
> And snow and sorrow.

Often he would take himself to task, and wish that he could achieve the eupeptic jollity which was the ideal of his sect. But, in spite of all his efforts, melancholy and languor invaded his inmost being whenever he could escape from the hustle and bustle of the Molybdene office.

Behind Manasseh Merrow, and exactly opposite Zachary, sat Mr Merrow's daughter, Leah. Leah, like Zachary, had been educated to the strictest orthodoxy. Like Zachary, it was intended that she should succeed her father. But, like Zachary, she had difficulty in preserving the state of mind demanded of an Adept. There were even dreadful moments when she could not bring herself to reverence Aurora. The time that she could spare from helping her father at the office, she spent at the piano. Mendelssohn was her favourite, but she rose occasionally to Chopin. Her real preference, however, was not for classical music, but for old-fashioned romantic songs such as *Gaily the Troubadour* and *The Bailiff's Daughter of Islington*. She was not strictly beautiful, but her expression had a certain earnest exaltation and her eyes were large and sad.

Both Zachary and Leah, at the meeting, found themselves, as was natural, more interested in the opposite party than in their own. Zachary bestowed a brief glance upon Aurora Bohra, but shrank in revulsion from her vastness. Leah, encountering for a moment the piercing glance of Molly B. Dean, was so filled with terror that she longed to hide. Each, after this moment of alarm, was consoled by the sight of equal alarm across the aisle. Their eyes met. Each had supposed until that moment that all who supported the opposite faction were base and wicked. Each, meeting those frightened eyes, experienced a shock. 'Surely,' each thought, 'it is nothing villainous that those eyes express! Can my dear father have been mistaken? Is it possible that the feelings which I experience may also exist in the breast of an opponent? Can it be that there is a common humanity which might override these differences?' And while each so thought, each continued to gaze into the eyes of the other.

Meanwhile, the business of the meeting proceeded, though the two young people were at first scarcely conscious of what was going on around them.

The Professor rose to deliver his opening address, which he had prepared with the utmost care, and of which he and the Prime Minister had conned every word to eliminate the slightest hint of criticism or lack of neutrality. Somewhat nervously he cleared his throat and began:

'Revered Pythonesses, Ladies and Gentlemen, we are all aware that in this great gathering there is disagreement ['Hear, Hear!' from all parts of the Hall], but there is one matter as to which we are, I trust and believe, all at one. All of us are eager to seek Truth, and when found to proclaim it.'

From both sides of the Hall a vast shout went up at these words, a shout of 'No, No! Not on the other side!' The poor Professor, somewhat disconcerted, skipped several mellifluous phrases, and continued, 'Well, be that as it may, it has been decided, by men for whose wisdom I have a profound respect, that the division of our great country into rival factions brings with it now, as it did in the days of the Wars of the Roses, as it did again in the lamentable dissensions of King and Parliament in the seventeenth century, a danger lest, absorbed in internal quarrels, we should lose sight of the peril from overseas. It is because of this peril that this meeting has been convened in the hope that, without any loss of fervour, without any diminution in the profundity of religious conviction, the two creeds may unite and forge, by their union, a weapon of irresistible might for the repelling of whatever enemies may threaten our National Life.'

At this point, again, he was interrupted. Cries came from everywhere: 'That's easy! Let the others join *us*!' Again, the Professor skipped some pages of his prepared address, since he deemed it wise, in view of the temper of the meeting, to make an end quickly. 'It is not for me,' he concluded, 'to dictate the agreement to be arrived at. This is for you to decide, since we live in a democracy. I will only repeat that the occasion is momentous, and that your responsibility is great. May God bless your deliberations!'

Even during these opening remarks it had become clear that the temper of the meeting was difficult. The unusual course was adopted of having the Order of the Proceedings announced, not by the Chairman, but by the Commissioner of Police. In authoritative tones, very unlike those of the Professor, he announced that each side would be allowed three speakers, each to speak for twenty minutes, and that the toss of a coin had allotted the first speech to the Molybdenes. He announced also that he had in reserve a large force of police, and that, at the first sign of disorder, the Hall would be cleared. Somewhat cowed, the audience became for a time subdued, and listened to the first two speeches without excessive interruption.

These speeches were made by Mr Tomkins and Mr Merrow. Each dealt with the merits and success of his own movement, and studiously refrained from any mention of his rivals. There were coughs and yawns, and not a few, overcome by the oppressive atmosphere, fell asleep. It seemed as if the whole meeting would end in flat boredom. But there were fireworks in reserve. When Mr Merrow sat down, Mr Tomkins called upon Mr Thorney to address the meeting. Mr Thorney, from his very first words, showed no disposition to be conciliatory:

'Ladies and Gentlemen and Northern Magnets,' he began. 'I am the Head of the Molybdenic Secret Service. I know things that you do not know. I know the income of Sir Magnus North. I know the extent of his estates in the North-West Territory. I know that every evening he spends many hours, whether in lascivious or merely lucrative commerce I know not, with the supposed Holy Woman, Miss Bohra.'

By these words the meeting was, for a moment, completely stunned. The Magnets had known Mr Thorney as a friend. The Molybdenes were finding difficulty in his new role. While the meeting was still held in bewildered silence, Mr Wagner leapt up and shouted:

'You have listened to lies, but *I* will tell you Truth! What do you know of Amalgamated Metals Inc.? What do you know of the fortune of its principal shareholder? What do you know of the role of molybdenum in its transactions? I, as Head of the Secret Service of the Magnets, I can give you the amazing answer: the fortune is immense; it is based upon molybdenum; and its lucky owner is the Widow Dean!'

By the time he sat down, both sides were wrought to the utmost pitch of fury. 'Death to Sir Magnus and shame on his Infamous Paramour!' was shouted from one side. 'Down with Grasping Plutocrats! To the Gallows with Murderous Molly!' the other side retorted. For a brief moment their co-operative efforts were devoted to overcoming a posse of stewards. That done, the rival Saints met in savage mêlée. The police, who had retained their coherence, cleared the Hall with tear gas. With streaming eyes and thunderous sneezes, the disconcerted thousands poured into the street. Revived by the outer air, they resumed the fray in disorganised groups. Clothes were torn from backs, blows were exchanged, feet were stamped upon, objurgations were shouted. Late into the night the vague tumult continued, until at last, utterly exhausted, the Holy Combatants fell asleep upon the cold pavement.

VII

The leading personages on the stage, meanwhile, had been exhorted by the police to make use of a secret exit. The Chairman, feeling that his functions could no longer be exercised, was very willing to depart. The Nepalese delegate, who had felt disaster coming, tapped the Professor on the shoulder and said, 'Let me take care of you.' The two together were hustled into a police car. 'Oh, where shall we go?' said the Professor. 'To the Nepalese Embassy', said his new friend. Arriving there tired and hopeless, he was slowly revived by kindness, and when he had had time to collect his thoughts, he was offered a Professorship in his own subject in the Himalayan University of Nepal, provided he would sign a document in a language unknown to him. He did so, and, having thus established his credentials, which, as he discovered long afterwards, consisted of a statement to the effect that Tensing had been the first to reach the summit of Everest, he was taken by plane to the seat of his new academic activities. At the end of ten years he produced his monumental work, *Religion and Superstition among the Aborigines of the West*. But this work has not appeared in any European language.

The two Priestesses presented the police with a difficult problem. Oblivious to everything else, Molly B. Dean had rushed across the aisle to make a frenzied assault upon the massive Aurora. Reaching up with her nails, she made long bloody scratches upon the face of her rival, who, with her open hand, gave her a push, which knocked her flat upon the floor. 'Harridan!' she shouted as she lay prone. 'Peculating virago!' Aurora retorted in a voice very different from, and much more shrill than, that to which her disciples were accustomed. Some policemen picked up Molly B. Dean, while ten others, with drawn truncheons, propelled Aurora Bohra. Both together were placed in a Black Maria, where, across an intervening wall of policemen, they continued to hurl insults at each other. Both were accused of a breach of the peace, and they were confined for the night in separate cells which invited far from pleasant reflections.

Mr Tomkins and Mr Merrow, neither of whom had expected the intemperate intervention of their Secret Agents, retired under police protection to their respective offices. There, deeply dejected, with their heads buried in their hands, they contemplated the ruin of their life-work. Although total abstinence, except in the Recreative Palaces, was a rigid tenet of both sects, both these devoted men were found by charwomen in the morning, prone on the floor with an empty bottle beside each.

As for Zachary and Leah, they had been so absorbed in each other that they were not aware of what was going on about them until the din became overwhelming. Sitting among the neutrals, a little way behind them, was Ananias Wagthorne, an official of the Ministry of Culture, who had been sent to obtain data for any bureaucratic action that might be called for. He was a kindly and perceptive person, and had observed their absorption in each other. In the final confusion he extended a hand to each, and said, 'Let me escort you to safety.' Although somewhat embarrassed by each other's presence, they obeyed, since any other course seemed difficult. Helped by the police, he extricated them and conveyed them safely to his flat. He introduced them to his wife, who listened understandingly to his account of the monumental fiasco. His wife was a good-natured lady, filled with sympathy for the young people. 'I do not think,' she said to her husband, 'that these young people ought to attempt to go to their homes tonight. The streets are disturbed, and no one can tell what furious mobs may do. If Mr Zachary could be content with the drawing-room sofa, Miss Leah could have the spare room, and both could stay here for the night.' Both accepted gratefully. And both, utterly worn out, soon fell asleep.

As the great meeting had been held on a Saturday, Mr Wagthorne was able to stay at home next morning, and devoted himself to comforting the young people and diminishing their perplexities. Neither knew what to believe of the lurid revelations to which they had listened. Could it be that the Molybdenic Faith was built upon financial fraud? Zachary's thoughts shuddered away from so dreadful a possibility. Could it be that the Faith of the Magnets was only an incident in the rise of Sir Magnus North to wealth and power? This nightmare suggestion seemed to Leah to empty life of all its purpose. Mr Wagthorne, finding them disconsolate, and with no appetite for their breakfasts, inquired into their doubts. 'Can these things be true?' they both asked.

'I fear they are but too true,' he replied. 'It has been my official duty to make inquiries as to both sects. From the Board of Trade, I have ascertained the extent of Mrs Dean's interests in Amalgamated Metals Inc.; and from the Administration of the North-West Territory, I have discovered the vast area possessed by Sir Magnus, and its almost unlimited possibility of mineral wealth. The relation of Sir Magnus with Aurora Bohra has long been known and watched by the police. Your fathers, my dear young people, were, I am convinced, totally ignorant of the revelations that were made at yesterday's meeting. They, I am sure, are honestly and wholeheartedly persuaded that the doctrines they preach are both true and beneficent. It may be that, when you have had time to reflect, each of you will agree with his or her father, and continue to believe as heretofore. But I think it more likely that you will both perceive what I believe to be the facts in this painful situation, and that you will learn to build your lives upon a firmer foundation than that upon which they have rested hitherto.'

'But is it possible,' both exclaimed, 'that any movement so vast, and so potent in moving men's minds, should be based upon nothing but fraud and folly?'

'It is only too possible,' he replied. 'It has been my duty to study the history of such movements. They have been numerous. Some have flourished briefly, others have lasted for centuries. But there is no relation whatever between the vitality and life of a movement and its basis in good sense.'

At this point he fetched from his shelves a large tome called *The Dictionary of Sects, Heresies, Ecclesiastical Parties, and Schools of Religious Thought.*

'Do not imagine,' he said, 'that you have any reason for shame, or that you differ from the rest of mankind in the capacity to believe what afterwards appears to have been nonsense. In this volume the similar follies of the last two thousand years are recorded, and a little study will show you

131

that, in comparison with many of these, your creeds have been sensible and moderate. Both your heresies begin with the letter M, so let us see what this book has to say under this letter. Let me recommend you to study the doctrines of Macarius. I can assure you they are well deserving of attention, as are those of the Majorinians, and the Malakanes, and the Marcellinians, and the Marcosians, and the Masbothians, and the Melchisedechians, and the Metangismonitae, and the Morelstschiki, and the Muggletonians. Take, for example, the Marcosians, who followed Marcus the Magician, "a perfect adept in magical impostures . . . joining the buffooneries of Anaxilaus to the craftiness of the Magi", and by these arts seducing the wives of deacons, and justifying unlimited licence by the doctrine that he had "attained to a height above all power", and was therefore free to act in every respect as he pleased. Or, again, you may be thankful that neither of you belong to the sect of the Morelstschiki, whose "custom is to meet together on a certain day in the year in some retired place, and having dug a deep pit, to fill it with wood, straw, and other combustibles, while they are singing weird hymns relating to the ceremony. Fire is then applied to the piled-up fuel, and numbers leap into the midst of it, stimulated by the triumphant hymns of those around, to purchase a supposed martyrdom by their suicidal act." No, my dear young friends, you need not feel that you have been exceptional in folly, for folly is natural to man. We consider ourselves distinguished from the ape by the power of thought. We do not remember that it is like the power of walking in a one-year-old. We think, it is true, but we think so badly that I often feel it would be better if we did not. But I have matters that I must attend to, and, for the moment, I will leave you to each other.'

Left *tête-à-tête* they preserved at first an embarrassed silence. Then Zachary said, hesitatingly, 'I cannot yet disentangle what I am to think of what we heard yesterday, and of what our kind friend has been saying. But there is one thing of which I feel sure, and which I will say: When I looked across the aisle and saw the crystal purity and gentle charity that shone from your eyes, I could no longer believe that all Northern Magnets are degraded beings.'

'Oh, Mr Tomkins,' she replied, 'I am glad you have said what you did, and . . . and . . . I . . . felt the same about the Molybdenes.'

'Oh, Miss Merrow,' he replied, 'can it be that, amid such ruin, something has been salvaged? Drifting alone, parted by doubt and despair from former companions and former hopes, may I think that in this night of apparent solitude we have found each other?'

'I think you may, Mr Tomkins,' she said.

And with that they fell into each other's arms.

For a little while they forgot their sorrows in mutual ecstasy; but presently Leah sighed, and said, 'But, Zachary, what are we to *do*? Can we break our fathers' hearts? But how can we do otherwise? It is impossible that we should marry and should continue to profess our several former tenets.'

'No,' he replied, 'that would be impossible. We must tell our fathers of our loss of faith, whatever may be the pain to them. You and I henceforth, dear Leah, must be one in thought and word and deed, and that will be impossible if we pretend to a divided allegiance.'

With heavy hearts, they decided to confront their fathers. But, strengthened by the new fire of love, neither faltered before the ordeal.

VIII

Zachary and Leah, after some further conversation, decided to postpone to the next day their confrontation with their respected fathers, the rather as the Wagthornes had very kindly asked them to stay another night. After luncheon they walked in Kensington Gardens, and, having known until that time nothing but offices throughout the week and big meeting halls on Sundays, they were struck by the beauty of wild nature and enjoyed emotions for which others have to travel to the Alps or the Victoria Falls.

'I begin to think,' said Zachary, as he feasted his eyes upon a multi-coloured bed of tulips, 'that perhaps we have lived, hitherto, with somewhat too limited preoccupations. These tulips, I am convinced, owe nothing to molybdenum.'

'How refreshing are your words of wisdom!' Leah replied. 'Magnetism also, I am persuaded, has done nothing to produce this wild loveliness.'

They agreed that they felt themselves expanding in mind and heart with every moment that passed since they had escaped from the bondage of dogma. They had been brought up to worship brawn, in which neither excelled. They had been taught to despise everything delicate and subtle, everything fragile and evanescent. Zachary, with secret shame, had enjoyed anthologies of the poets, but he had felt about this as a secret morphia addict might feel about his surreptitious doses. She, in her stolen hours at the piano, had preferred the times when she knew her father to be absent. But fortunately he had no ear for music, and, on the occasions when he discovered her at the instrument, she persuaded him that she was studying the Magnetic hymn-book. Now at last they felt that they need no longer be ashamed of their tastes.

But they were still not without their fears – fears for the world as well as for themselves. 'Do you think,' she asked him with some hesitation, 'that it is possible to be good without the help of faith? I have lived, hitherto, a blameless life. I have never uttered a bad word. I have never tasted alcohol. I have never suffered the pulmonary pollution of tobacco. Never have I slept with my head pointing elsewhere than to the Magnetic Pole. Never have I gone to bed too late or risen after the prescribed hour. And

I have found this same devotion to duty among my friends. But will it be possible to go on living so, when I no longer feel that my every action and my every breath should be a service of devotion and homage to Earth, the Great Magnet?'

'Alas,' he replied, 'the same perplexities trouble me. I fear that I may be content in the morning to touch my toes fewer than ninety-nine times, and even perhaps to acquiesce in a lukewarm bath. I can no longer feel quite certain that alcohol and tobacco lead to Hell. What, with such doubts, is to become of us? Shall we go down the primrose path to moral degradation and physical ruin? What is to preserve us, what is to preserve others who have hitherto been our co-religionists, from a gradual descent into drunkenness, debauchery and disaster? What, when we meet our fathers, shall we say when they argue, as argue they will, that creeds such as theirs, whether true or false, are necessary for the preservation of mankind? I do not yet see the way to a clear answer. But let us hope that parental wrath will inspire us when the moment comes.'

'I hope it may be so,' she said, 'but I confess that I have fears, for, even while strengthened by dogma, neither of us was wholly able to abstain from sin. You with your poets, and I with my piano, were guilty of deceit. If even in the past we sinned, what will become of us now?'

Oppressed by this solemn thought, they returned gravely and silently to the Wagthornes' tea-table.

When Monday morning came they sought their respective fathers, determined to make such explanations as should be necessary, and to seek such conciliation as might be possible. Zachary found his father at the office surrounded by a wild confusion. Letters of resignation were piled high upon his desk. Scathing articles in hitherto friendly newspapers were omens of ruin. After a Sunday devoted to recuperation, most of those who had fought each other as devotees of this sect or that, had come to the conclusion that both equally must be repudiated. On Saturday night, half the mob had sided with Mr Tomkins, and half with Mr Merrow. Now, though it was not the time of day for a mob, the few who passed either office showed equal hostility to both, and only a strong force of police protected the faithful remnant from the united hostility of those who felt that they had been duped. Mr Tomkins, though he retained his faith, was unable to understand the designs of Providence in permitting what had occurred. When he saw Zachary, a gleam of returning hope appeared for a moment upon his countenance.

'Ah, my dear son,' he said, 'to what tribulations are the good exposed. But you – you whom, from your earliest infancy, I have educated in the True Faith, you whose blameless life and unfaltering belief have been among the greatest joys of my arduous existence, you, I am sure, will not desert me in this difficult hour. I am no longer young, and to build up again from its first foundations that great Church, which had come so near to final triumph, may prove beyond the power of my declining years. But you, with the fresh vigour of youth, with the impetuous ardour of one who has never had to fight doubt or uncertainty, you, I feel, will rebuild the ruined edifice more pure, more splendid, more shining than that which Saturday's fell work has laid in ruins.'

Zachary was deeply moved, and his eyes filled with tears. He wished with all his heart that he could give the answer which his father longed to hear. But he could not. Something even more compelling than intellectual doubts as to the physiological benefits of molybdenum prevented his acquiescence. The thought of Leah made submission to his father impossible. Never could his father consent, with any willingness, to union with a Northern Magnet. Zachary realised that he must speak, no matter how great might be his father's pain.

'Father,' he said, 'much as I feel for your sorrow, I cannot do as you wish. I have lost my faith. Molybdenum, we are assured, cures diseases of the chest, but you must have known, or at least suspected, that I suffer from tuberculosis of the lung. We are told that molybdenum makes our muscles strong, but every Godless hooligan from the slums can defeat me in a wrestling match. For these things, however, some explanation could perhaps be found. What is more difficult is that I love Leah Merrow. . . .'

'Leah Merrow!' gasped his father.

'Yes, Leah Merrow, and she has consented to become my wife. She, like me, can no longer believe the faith in which she has been brought up. She, like me, is determined to accept painful facts, however they may shatter a cherished world of beliefs. It is not your work, it is not the work of Mr Merrow, that can inspire our lives henceforth. We wish to live unfettered by dogma, free to accept whatever the facts may indicate, with minds open to the winds of heaven, not wrapped in the cotton wool of some warm and comfortable system!'

'Oh, Zachary,' his father answered, 'you wring my heart! You turn the bayonet in the dreadful wound! Is it not enough that the world has turned against me? Must my own son join my enemies? Oh, dreadful day! And it is not I alone, it is the whole world that you will be bringing to ruin by your heartless levity. What do you know of human nature? How can you estimate the wild anarchic forces that your "free winds of heaven" will liberate? What do you imagine restrains men from murder, arson, pillage and debauchery? Do you imagine that the puny forces of reason can effect this great work? Alas, in your sheltered life, you have been kept from knowledge of the darker side of human nature. You have believed that gentleness and goodness grow naturally in the human heart. You have not realised that they are the unnatural outgrowth of unnatural beliefs. It is such beliefs that I have tried to inculcate. And, in this dark hour, I can admit that the Northern Magnets also have been engaged in this task. Our creed, I still believe, was as superior to theirs as the noonday sun to the last glimmer of twilight. But what *you* offer is not twilight, it is black, impenetrable night. And, in the night, what deeds of darkness may be done! If this is to be your work, there will have to be, between you and me, an enmity more deep and more implacable than that which had divided me from the Northern Magnets.'

Contrary to his own expectations, Zachary reacted to this speech, in a manner quite different from that intended by his father. 'No!' he said. 'No! It is not by organised falsehood that mankind is to be saved. While you imagined that you were building virtue, what was it that you were really building? It was the fortune of Molly B. Dean. You imagined her a Holy Woman. Was it holiness that inspired her when she scratched the face of Aurora Bohra? Was it holiness that made her hide her financial interest in the anonymity of Amalgamated Metals Inc.? And, to come nearer home, do you realise that you were sacrificing my life to your credulity? Do you realise that you have refused me the treatment that my body demands, because it was not that that your sect prescribes? Can you not see that here, in my own case, is a sample of the evils that men must suffer when they substitute dogma for fact? I will not believe that human nature is as bad as you say it is. But if indeed you are right in this, no system of imposed discipline will cure the evils, for those who impose the discipline will be inspired by their own evil passions, and will find some indirect way of inflicting the torments that their wickedness makes them desire. No, you will but systematise evil; and evil, reduced to a system, is more dreadful than anything that untamed anarchic passion can produce. Good-bye, father! My love and my sympathy are yours, but not, henceforth, my work!'

With these words, he departed.

Leah's interview with her father pursued a similar course, and came to a similar termination. Mr Tomkins and Mr Merrow each attempted to continue the old work, but the fickle wind of fashion had deserted them and only a few, and those in out-of-the-way suburbs, remained faithful. Mr Tomkins and Mr Merrow were compelled to vacate their palatial offices for which Mrs Dean and Sir Magnus no longer thought it worth while to pay. Both men, having become dependent upon the voluntary offerings of the faithful remnant, sank into poverty.

Sir Magnus and Molly B. Dean, though both suffered considerable losses, remained rich, and largely recouped themselves by pooling their interests. In consequence of this, the friction between the United States and Canada ceased, the Governments smiled upon their joint enterprise. Aurora Bohra, who could not believe that her success had depended upon Sir Magnus's money, remained at the Sanatorium and welcomed as before the few guests who still came. But gradually the place became derelict, and the few faithful observed a decay in her powers. The more fanatical among the remaining Adherents attributed her decline to the malignant influence of molybdenum, and darkly suspected her of apostasy; but, alas, the evidence for a simpler explanation became gradually overwhelming. She sank first into alcoholic excesses, and then still deeper into the baleful dominion of hashish. At length it became necessary to carry her off, raving and maniacal, and leave her to end her days in a mental home.

Zachary and Leah, who had never known want, and had taken it for granted that they would follow their fathers in their comfortable and well-paid positions, found themselves in urgent need of some means of livelihood. Zachary, who had impressed Mr Wagthorne by his capacity for absorbing an entirely new point of view, and who had, in his surreptitious reading, acquired a considerable breadth of knowledge, was found, on Mr Wagthorne's recommendation, worthy of a minor post in the Ministry of Culture. Helped by Mrs Wagthorne to establish themselves in a tiny flat, Zachary and Leah married.

Leah, absorbed in domestic cares and in her love for Zachary, found no time to repine, and did not hanker after former certainties. But Zachary found adjustment more difficult. Formerly, decisions had been easy; now, they were hard. Should he do this or do that? Should be believe this or believe that? He found himself beset by hesitations and without a compass by which to steer his course. He acquired the habit of spending his Sundays in long, solitary walks.

One winter evening, returning weary through drizzle and fog, he found himself outside a tin tabernacle where a remnant of the Molybdenes still worshipped. To the accompaniment of the harmonium, they were singing those well known words:

Molybdenum of metals best
Is good for high and low.
It cures diseases of the chest
And makes our muscles grow.

He sighed, and muttered to himself, 'Could I but return to the old Sublimities! Ah, how hard is the Life of Reason!'

PART TWO

SHORT STORIES

With the exception of 'The Right Will Prevail' the following stories were published in 1953 under the title of *Satan in the Suburbs*. Of these, 'The Corsican Ordeal of Miss X', Russell's first published story, had appeared anonymously in *Go*, December 1951; 'The Infra-redioscope' was serialised in the London *Daily Mail* during January 1953; 'Benefit of Clergy' appeared in *Harper's Bazaar*, June 1953. 'The Right Will Prevail' was first published in *Fact & Fiction* by George Allen & Unwin, 1961.

The Corsican Ordeal of Miss X

I

I had occasion recently to visit my good friend, Professor N, whose paper on pre-Celtic Decorative Art in Denmark raised some points that I felt needed discussing. I found him in his study, but his usually benign and yet slightly intelligent expression was marred by some strange bewilderment. The books which should have been on the arm of the chair, and which he supposed himself to be reading, were scattered in confusion on the floor. The spectacles which he imagined to be on his nose lay idle on his desk. The pipe which was usually in his mouth lay smoking in his tobacco bowl, though he seemed completely unaware of its not occupying its usual place. His mild and somewhat silly philanthropy and his usually placid gaze had somehow dropped off him. A harassed, distracted, bewildered, and horrified expression was stamped upon his features.

'Good God!' I said, 'what has happened?'

'Ah,' said he, it is my secretary, Miss X. Hitherto, I have found her level-headed, efficient, cool, and destitute of those emotions which are only too apt to distract youth. But in an ill-advised moment I allowed her to take a fortnight's holiday from her labours on decorative art, and she, in a still more ill-advised moment, chose to spend the fortnight in Corsica. When she returned I saw at once that something had happened. "What *did* you do in Corsica?" I asked. "Ah! What indeed!" she replied.'

II

The secretary was not in the room at the moment, and I hoped that Professor N might enlarge a little upon the misfortune that had befallen him. But in this I was disappointed. Not another word, so at least he assured me, had he been able to extract from Miss X. Horror piled upon horror glared from her eyes at the mere recollection, but nothing more specific could he discover.

I felt it my duty to the poor girl, who, so I had been given to understand, had hitherto been hard-working and conscientious, to see whether anything could be done to relieve her of the dreadful weight which depressed her spirits. I bethought me of Mrs Menhennet, a middle-aged lady of considerable bulk, who, so I was informed by her grandchildren, had once had some pretences to beauty. Mrs Menhennet, I knew, was the grand-daughter of a Corsican bandit; in one of those unguarded moments, too frequent, alas, in that rough island, the bandit had assaulted a thoroughly respectable young lady, with the result that she had given birth, after a due interval, to the redoubtable Mr Gorman.

Mr Gorman, though his work took him into the City, pursued there the same kind of activities as had led to his existence. Eminent financiers trembled at his approach. Well-established bankers of unblemished reputation had ghastly visions of prison. Merchants who imported the wealth of the gorgeous East turned pale at the thought of Customs House officers at the dead of night. All of which misfortunes, it was well understood, were set in motion by the machinations of the predacious Mr Gorman.

His daughter, Mrs Menhennet, would have heard of any strange and unwonted disturbance in the home of her paternal grandfather. I therefore asked for an interview, which was graciously accorded. At four o'clock on a dark afternoon in November I presented myself at her tea-table.

'And what,' she said, 'brings you here? Do not pretend that it is my charms. The day for such pretence is past. For ten years it would have been true; for another ten I should have believed it. Now it is neither true nor do I believe it. Some other motive brings you here, and I palpitate to know what it may be.'

This approach was somewhat too direct for my taste. I find a pleasure in a helicoidal approach to my subject. I like to begin at a point remote from that at which I am aiming, or on occasion, if I begin at a point near my ultimate destination, I like to approach the actual point by a boomerang course, taking me at first away from the final mark and thereby, I hope, deceiving my auditor. But Mrs Menhennet would permit no such finesse. Honest, downright, and straightforward, she believed in the direct approach, a characteristic which she seemed to have inherited from her Corsican grandfather. I therefore abandoned all attempt at circumlocution and came straight to the core of my curiosity.

'Mrs Menhennet,' I said, 'it has come to my knowledge that there have been in recent weeks strange doings in Corsica, doings which, as I can testify from ocular demonstration, have turned brown hairs grey and young springy steps leaden with the weariness of age. These doings, I am convinced, owing to certain rumours which have reached me, are of transcendent international importance. Whether some new Napoleon is marching to the conquest of Moscow, or some younger Columbus to the discovery of a still unknown Continent, I cannot guess. But something of this sort, I am convinced, is taking place in those wild mountains, something of the sort is being plotted secretly, darkly, dangerously, something of the sort is being concealed tortuously, ferociously and criminally from those who rashly seek to pierce the veil. You, dear lady, I am convinced, in spite of the correctness of your tea-table and the elegance of your china and the fragrance of your Lapsang Souchong, have not lost touch with the activities of your revered father. At his death, I know, you made yourself the guardian of those interests for which he stood. His father, who had ever been to him a shining light on the road towards swift success, inspired every moment of his life. Since his death, although perhaps some of your less perspicacious friends may not have pierced your very efficient disguise, you, I know, have worn his mantle. You, if anyone in this cold and dismal city, can tell me what is happening in that land of sunshine, and what plots, so dark as to cause eclipse even in the blaze of noon, are being hatched in the minds of those noble descendants of ancient greatness. Tell me, I pray you, what you know. The life of Professor N, or if not his life at least his reason, is trembling in the balance. He is, as you are well aware, a benevolent man, not fierce like you and me, but full of gentle loving-kindness. Owing to this trait in his character he cannot divest himself of responsibility for the welfare of his worthy secretary, Miss X, who returned yesterday from Corsica transformed completely from the sunny carefree girl that once she was to a lined, harassed and weary woman weighed down by all the burdens of the world. What it was that happened to her she refuses to reveal, but if it cannot be discovered it is much to be feared that that great genius, which has already all but solved the many and intricate problems besetting the interpretation of pre-Celtic decorative art, will totter and disintegrate and fall a heap of rubble, like the old Campanile in Venice. You cannot, I am sure, be otherwise than horrified at such a prospect, and I therefore beseech you to unfold, so far as lies in your power, the dreadful secrets of your ancestral home.'

Mrs Menhennet listened to my words in silence, and when I ceased to speak she still for a while abstained from all reply. At a certain point in my discourse the colour faded from her cheeks and she gave a great gasp. With an effort she composed herself, folded her hands, and compelled her breathing to become quiet.

'You put before me,' she said, 'a dreadful dilemma. If I remain silent, Professor N, not to mention Miss X, must be deprived of reason. But if I speak. . . .' Here she shuddered, and no further word emerged.

At this point, when I had been at a loss to imagine what the next development would be, the parlourmaid appeared and mentioned that the chimney-sweep, in full professional attire, was waiting at the door, as he had been engaged to sweep the chimney of the drawing-room that very afternoon.

'Good heavens!' she exclaimed. 'While you and I have been engaged in small talk and trivial *badinage* this proud man with his great duties to perform has been kept waiting at my doorstep. This will never do. For now this interview must be at an end. One last word, however.

I advise you, if you are in earnest, but only if you are, to pay a visit to General Prz.'*

III

General Prz, as everybody remembers, greatly distinguished himself in the First World War by his exploits in defence of his native Poland. Poland, however, in recent years had shown herself ungrateful, and he had been compelled to take refuge in some less unsettled country. A long life of adventure had made the old man, in spite of his grey hairs, unwilling to sink into a quiet life. Although admirers offered him a villa at Worthing, a bijou residence at Cheltenham, or a bungalow in the mountains of Ceylon, none of these took his fancy. Mrs Menhennet gave him an introduction to some of the more unruly of her relatives in Corsica, and among them he found once more something of the *élan*, the fire and the wild energy which had inspired the exploits of his earlier years.

But although Corsica remained his spiritual home, and his physical home during the greater part of the year, he would allow himself on rare occasions to visit such of the capitals of Europe as were still west of the Iron Curtain. In these capitals he would converse with the elder statesmen, who would anxiously ask his opinion on all the major trends of recent policy. Whatever he deigned to say in reply they listened to with the respect justly owing to his years and valour. And he would carry back to his mountain fastness the knowledge of the part that Corsica – yes, even Corsica – could play in the great events to come.

As the friend of Mrs Menhennet, he was at once admitted to the innermost circle of those who, within or without the law, kept alive the traditions of ancient liberty which their Ghibelline ancestors had brought from the still vigorous republics of Northern Italy. In the deep recesses of the hills, hidden from the view of the casual tourist, who saw nothing but rocks and shepherds' huts and a few stunted trees, he was allowed to visit old palaces full of medieval splendour, the armour of ancient Gonfalonieri, and the jewelled swords of world-famous Condottieri. In their magnificent halls these proud descendants of ancient chieftains assembled and feasted, not perhaps always wisely but always too well. Even in converse with the General their lips were sealed as to some of the great secrets of their order, except indeed, in those moments of exuberant conviviality, when the long story of traditional hospitality overcame the scruples which at other times led to a prudent silence.

It was in these convivial moments that the General learned of the world-shaking design that these men cherished, a design that inspired all their waking actions and dominated the dreams in which their feasts too often terminated. Nothing loath, he threw himself into their schemes with

* Pronounced 'Pish'

all the ardour and all the traditional recklessness of the ancient Polish nobility. He thanked God that at a period of life when to most men nothing remains but reminiscence he had been granted the opportunity to share in great deeds of high adventure. On moonlight nights he would gallop over the mountains on his great charger, whose sire and dam alike had helped him to shed immortal glory upon the stricken fields of his native land. Inspired by the rapid motion of the night wind, his thoughts flowed through a mingled dream of ancient valour and future triumph, in which past and future blended in the alembic of his passion.

At the time when Mrs Menhennet uttered her mysterious suggestion it happened that the General was engaged in one of his periodic rounds of visits to the elder statesmen of the Western world. He had in the past entertained a somewhat anachronistic prejudice against the Western hemisphere, but since he had learned from his island friends that Columbus was a Corsican he had endeavoured to think better than before of the consequences of that adventurer's somewhat rash activities. He could not quite bring himself actually to imitate Columbus, since he felt that there would be a slight taint of trade about any such journey, but he would call after due notice on the American Ambassador to the Court of St James's, who always took pains to have a personal message from the President in readiness for his distinguished guest. He would, of course, visit Mr Winston Churchill, but he never demeaned himself so far as to recognise the existence of Socialist ministers.

It was after he had been dining with Mr Churchill that I had the good fortune to find him at leisure in the ancient club of which he was an honorary member. He honoured me with a glass of his pre-1914 Tokay, which was part of the *spolia opima* of his encounter with the eminent Hungarian general whom he left dead upon the field of honour with a suitable eulogy for his bravery. After due acknowledgement of the great mark of favour which he was bestowing upon me – a notable mark, for after all not even Hungarian generals go into battle with more than a few bottles of Tokay bound to their saddles – I led the conversation gradually towards Corsica.

'I have heard,' I said, 'that that island is not what it was. Education, they tell me, has turned brigands into bank clerks, and stilettos into stylographic pens. No longer, so they tell me, do ancient vendettas keep alive through the generations. I have even heard dreadful tales of intermarriage between families which had had a feud lasting eight hundred years, and yet the marriage was not accompanied by bloodshed. If all this is indeed true, I am forced to weep. I had always hoped, if fortune should favour my industry, to exchange the sanitary villa which I inhabit in Balham for some stormy peak in the home of ancient romance. But if romance even there is dead, what remains to me as a hope for old age? Perhaps you can reassure me; perhaps something yet lingers there. Perhaps amid thunder

145

and lightning the ghost of Farinata degli Uberti is still to be seen looking around with great disdain. I have come to you tonight in the hope that you can give me such reassurance, since without it I shall not know how to support the burden of the humdrum years.'

As I was speaking his eyes gleamed. I saw him clench his fists and close his jaws fiercely. Scarcely could he wait for the end of my periods. And as soon as I was silent he burst forth.

'Young man,' he said, 'were you not a friend of Mrs Menhennet I should grudge you that noble nectar which I have allowed your unworthy lips to consume. I am compelled to think that you have been associating with the ignoble. Some few there may be among the riff-raff of the ports, and the ignoble gentry who concern themselves with the base business of bureaucracy – some few there may be, I repeat, of whom the dreadful things at which you have been hinting may be true. But they are no true Corsicans. They are but bastard Frenchmen, or gesticulating Italians, or toad-eating Catalans. The true Corsican breed is what it always was. It lives the free life, and emissaries of Governments who seek to interfere die the death. No, my friend, all is yet well in that happy home of heroism.'

I leapt to my feet and took his right hand in both of mine.

'O happy days,' said I, 'when my faith is restored, and my doubts are quenched! Would that I might see with my own eyes the noble breed of men whom you have brought so forcibly before my imagination. Could you permit me to know even one of them I should live a happier life, and the banalities of Balham would become more bearable.'

'My young friend,' said he, 'your generous enthusiasm does you credit. Great though the favour may be, I am willing, in view of your enthusiasm, to grant the boon you ask. You shall know one of these splendid survivors of the golden age of man. I know that one of them, indeed one of my closest friends among them – I speak of the Count of Aspramonte – will be compelled to descend from the hills to pick up in Ajaccio a consignment of new saddles for his stallions. These saddles, you will of course understand, are made specially for him by the man who has charge of the racing stables of the Duke of Ashby-de-la-Zouche. The Duke is an old friend of mine, and as a great favour allows me occasionally to purchase from him a few saddles for the use of such of my friends as I deem worthy of so priceless a gift. If you care to be in Ajaccio next week, I can give you a letter to the Count of Aspramonte, who would be more accessible there than in his mountain fastness.'

With tears in my eyes I thanked him for his great kindness. I bowed low and kissed his hand. As I left his presence, my heart was filled with sorrow at the thought of the nobility that is perishing from our ignoble earth.

IV

Following the advice of General Prz, I flew the following week to Ajaccio, and inquired at the principal hotels for the Count of Aspramonte. At the third place of inquiry I was informed that he was at the moment occupying the imperial suite, but that he was a busy man with little time for unauthorised visitors. From the demeanour of the hotel servants I inferred that he had earned their most profound respect. In an interview with the proprietor I handed over the letter of introduction from General Prz with the request that it should be put as soon as possible into the hands of the Count of Aspramonte, who, I learned, was at the moment engaged in business in the town.

The hotel was filled with a chattering throng of tourists of the usual description, all of them, so far as I could observe, trivial and transitory. Coming fresh from the dreams of General Prz, I felt the atmosphere a strange one, by no means such as I could have wished. It was not in this setting that I could imagine the realisation of the Polish nobleman's dreams. I had, however, no other clue, and was compelled to make the best of it.

After an ample dinner, totally indistinguishable from those provided in the best hotels of London, New York, Calcutta and Johannesburg, I was sitting somewhat disconsolate in the lounge, when I saw approaching me a brisk gentleman of young middle age whom I took at first to be a successful American executive. He had the square jaw, the firm step and the measured speech which I have learned to associate with that powerful section of society. But to my surprise, when he addressed me it was in English English with a Continental accent. To my still greater surprise he mentioned that he was the Count of Aspramonte.

'Come,' he said, 'to the sitting-room of my suite, where we can talk more undisturbed than in this mêlée.'

His suite, when we reached it, turned out to be ornate and palatial in a somewhat garish style. He gave me a stiff whisky and soda and a large cigar.

'You are, I see,' so he began the conversation, 'a friend of that dear old gentleman, General Prz. I hope you have never been tempted to laugh at him. For us who live in the modern world the temptation undoubtedly exists, but out of respect for his grey hairs I resist it.

'You and I, my dear Sir,' he continued, 'live in the modern world and have no use for memories and hopes that are out of place in an age dominated by dollars. I for my part, although I live in a somewhat out of the way part of the world, and although I might, if I let myself be dominated by tradition, be as lost in misty dreams as the worthy General, have decided to adapt myself to our time. The main purpose of my life is the acquisition of dollars, not only for myself but for my island. "How," you may ask, "does your manner of life conduce to this end?" In view of your friendship with the General I feel that I owe you an answer to this not unnatural query.

'The mountains in which I have my home afford an ideal ground for the breeding and exercising of race-horses. The Arab stallions and mares which my father collected in the course of his wide travels gave rise to a breed of unexampled strength and swiftness. The Duke of Ashby-de-la-Zouche, as you of course are aware, has one great ambition. It is to own three successive Derby winners, and it is through me that he hopes to realise this ambition. His vast wealth is devoted mainly to this end. On the ground that the Derby offers an attraction to American tourists he is allowed to deduct the expenses of his stud from his income in his tax returns. He is thus able to retain that wealth which too many of his peers have lost. The Duke is not alone among my customers. Some of my best horses have gone to Virginia, others to Australia. There is no part of the world in which the royal sport is known where my horses are not famous. It is owing to them that I am able to keep up my palace and to preserve intact the sturdy human stock of our Corsican mountains.

'My life, as you will see, unlike that of General Prz, is lived on the plane of reality. I think more frequently of the dollar exchange than of Ghibelline ancestry, and I pay more attention to horse dealers than to even the most picturesque aristocratic relics. Nevertheless, when I am at home, the need to preserve the respect of the surrounding population compels me to conform to tradition. It is just possible that if you visit me in my castle you will be able to pick up some clue to the enigma which, as I see from the General's letter, is the cause of your visit to me. I shall be returning to my castle on horseback the day after tomorrow. It is a long journey, and an early start will be necessary, but if you care to present yourself at six o'clock in the morning I shall be happy to provide you with a horse on which you can accompany me to my home.'

Having by this time finished the whisky and the cigar, I thanked him somewhat effusively for his courtesy, and accepted his invitation.

V

It was still pitch dark when on the next day but one I presented myself at the door of the Count's hotel. It was a raw and gusty morning and bitterly cold, with a hint of snow in the air. But the Count seemed impervious to meteorological conditions when he appeared upon his magnificent steed. Another, almost equally magnificent, was led to the door by his servant, and I was bidden to mount him. We set off, soon leaving the streets of the town and then, by small roads which only long experience could have enabled a man to find, we wound up and up to ever greater heights, at first through woodlands and then through open country, grass and rocks.

The Count, it appeared, was incapable of fatigue, or hunger, or thirst. Throughout a long day, with only a few moments' intermission during which we munched dry bread, ate some dates, and drank icy water from a stream, he conversed intelligently and informatively about this and that, showing a wide knowledge of the world of affairs and an acquaintance with innumerable rich men who found leisure for an interest in horses. But not one word did he utter throughout the whole of that long day on the matter which had brought me to Corsica. Gradually, in spite of the beauty of the scenery and the interest of his multilingual anecdotes, impatience mastered me.

'My dear Count,' I said, 'I cannot express to you how grateful I am for this chance to visit your ancestral home. But I must venture to remind you that I have come upon an errand of mercy, to save the life, or at least the reason, of a worthy friend of mine for whom I have the highest regard. You are leaving me in doubt as to whether I am serving this purpose by accompanying you on this long ride.'

'I understand your impatience,' he said, 'but you must realise that, however I adapt myself to the modern world, I cannot in these uplands accelerate the tempo which is immemorially customary. You shall, I promise you, be brought nearer to your goal before the evening ends. More than that I cannot say, for the matter does not rest with me.'

With these enigmatic words I had to be content.

We reached his castle as the sun was setting. It was built upon a steep eminence, and to every lover of architecture it was obvious that every part of it, down to the minutest detail, dated from the thirteenth century. Crossing the drawbridge we entered by a Gothic gateway into a large courtyard. Our horses were taken by a groom, and the Count led me into a vast hall, out of which, by a narrow doorway, he conducted me into the chamber that I was to occupy for the night. A huge canopied bed and heavy carved furniture of ancient design filled much of the space. Out of the window a vast prospect down innumerable winding valleys enticed the eye to a distant glimpse of sea.

'I hope,' he said, 'that you will succeed in being not too uncomfortable in this somewhat antiquated domicile.'

'I do not think that will be difficult,' said I, glancing at the blazing fire of enormous logs that spread a flickering light from the vast hearth. He informed me that dinner would be ready in an hour, and that after dinner, if all went well, something should be done to further my inquiries.

After a sumptuous dinner, he led me back to my room, and said:

'I will now introduce you to an ancient servant of this house, who, from the long years of his service here, has become a repository of all its secrets. He, I have no doubt, will be able to help you towards the solution of your problem.'

He rang the bell, and when it was answered, requested the man-servant to ask the seneschal to join in our conversation. After a short interval the seneschal approached. I saw before me an old man, bent double with rheumatism, with white locks, and the grave air of one who has lived through much.

'This man,' said my host, 'will give you as much enlightenment as this place can afford.'

With that he withdrew.

'Old man,' said I, 'I do not know whether at your great age I may hope that your wits are what they were. I am surprised, I must confess, that the Count should refer me to you. I had fondly imagined myself worthy to deal with equals, and not only with serving men in their dotage.'

As I uttered these words a strange transformation occurred. The old man, as I had supposed him to be, suddenly lost his rheumatic appearance, drew himself up to his full height of six foot three, tore from his head the white wig which concealed his ample coal-black hair, threw off the ancient cloak which he had been wearing, and revealed beneath it the complete costume of a Florentine noble of the period when the castle was built. Laying his hand upon his sword, he turned upon me with flashing eyes, and said:

'Young man, were you not brought here by the Count, in whose sagacity I have much confidence, I should here and now order you to be cast into the dungeons, as an impertinent upstart, unable to perceive noble blood through the disguise of a seedy cloak.'

'Sir,' I said, with all due humility, 'I must humbly beg your pardon for an error which I cannot but think was designed both by you and by the Count. If you will accept my humble excuses, I shall be happy to learn who it is in whose presence I have the honour to be.'

'Sir,' said he, 'I will accept your speech as in some degree making amends for your previous impertinence, and you shall know who I am and what I stand for. I, Sir, am the Duke of Ermocolle. The Count is my right-hand man, and obeys me in all things. But in these sad times there is need of the wisdom of the serpent. You have seen him as a business man, adapting himself to the practices of our age, blaspheming for a purpose against the noble creed by which he and I alike are inspired. I decided to present myself to you in disguise in order to form some estimate of your character and outlook. You passed the test, and I will now tell you the little that I have a right to reveal concerning the trouble which has come into the life of your unworthy professorial friend.'

In reply to these words I spoke long and eloquently about the Professor and his labours, about Miss X and her youthful innocence, and about the obligation which I felt that friendship had placed upon my inadequate shoulders. He listened to me in grave silence. At the end he said :

'There is only one thing that I can do for you, and that I will do.'

He thereupon took in his hand an enormous quill pen, and on a large sheet of parchment he wrote these words: 'To Miss X. You are hereby released from a part of the oath you swore. Tell all to the bearer of this note and to Professor N. Then ACT.' To this he appended his signature in full magnificence.

'That, my friend, is all that I can do for you.'

I thanked him and bade him a ceremonial goodnight.

I slept little. The wind howled, the snow fell, the fire died down. I tossed and turned upon my pillow. When at last a few moments of uneasy slumber came to me, strange dreams wearied me even more than wakefulness. When dawn broke, a leaden oppression weighed me down. I sought the Count and acquainted him with what had passed.

'You will understand,' I said, 'that in view of the message which I bear, it is my duty to return to England with all speed.'

Thanking him once more for his hospitality I mounted the same steed upon which I had come and, accompanied by a groom whom he sent with me to help me in finding the road, I slowly picked my way through snow and sleet and tempest until I reached the shelter of Ajaccio. From there next day I returned to England.

V I

On the morning after my return I presented myself at the house of Professor N. I found him sunk in gloom, decorative art forgotten, and Miss X absent.

'Old friend,' I said, 'it is painful to see you in this sad state. I have been active on your behalf, and returned but last night from Corsica. I was not wholly successful, but I was also not wholly unsuccessful. I bear a message, not to you, but to Miss X. Whether this message will bring relief or the opposite I cannot tell. But it is my plain duty to deliver it into her hands. Can you arrange that I may see her here in your presence, for it is in your presence that the message must be delivered.'

'It shall be done,' said he.

He called to him his aged housekeeper, who with sorrowful countenance approached to know his wishes.

'I wish you,' said he, 'to find Miss X, and request her presence urgently, imperatively, and at no matter what inconvenience.'

The housekeeper departed, and he and I sat in gloomy silence. After an interval of some two hours she returned and replied that Miss X had fallen into a lethargy which had caused her to keep to her bed, but on receipt of Professor N's message some spark of doleful animation had returned to her and she had promised to be with him within a very short time. Scarcely had the housekeeper uttered this message when Miss X herself appeared, pale, distraught, with wild eyes and almost lifeless movements.

'Miss X,' I said, 'it is my duty, whether painful or not I do not yet know, to deliver to you this message from one who I believe is known to you.'

I handed over the piece of parchment. She suddenly came to life, and seized it eagerly. Her eyes ran over its few lines in a moment.

'Alas!' she said. 'This is not the reprieve for which I had hoped. It will not remove the cause of sorrow, but it does enable me to lift the veil of mystery. The story is a long one, and when I have finished it you will wish it had been longer. For when it is ended, it can be succeeded only by horror.'

The Professor, seeing that she was on the verge of collapse, administered a strong dose of brandy. He then seated us round a table and in a calm voice said:

'Proceed, Miss X.'

VII

'When I went to Corsica,' she began, 'and how long ago that seems, as though it had been in another existence, I was happy and carefree, thinking only of pleasure, of the light enjoyments which are considered suitable to my age, and of the delight of sunshine and new scenes. Corsica from the first moment enchanted me. I acquired the practice of long rambles in the hills, and each day I extended my rambles a little further. In the golden October sunshine, the leaves of the forest shone in their many bright colours. At last I found a path that led me beyond the forest on to the bare hills.

'In all-day rambles I caught a glimpse, to my immense surprise, of a great castle on a hill-top. My curiosity was aroused. Ah! would that it had been otherwise. It was too late that day to approach any nearer to this astonishing edifice. But next day, having supplied myself with some simple sustenance, I set out early in the morning, determined, if it were possible, to discover the secret of this stately pile. Higher and higher I climbed through the sparkling autumn air. I met no human soul, and as I approached the castle it might have belonged to the Sleeping Beauty for all the signs of life that I saw about it.

'Curiosity, that fatal passion which misled our first mother, lured me on. I wandered round the battlements, seeking for a mode of ingress. For a long time my search was vain. Ah! would that it had remained so! But a malign fate willed otherwise. I found at last a little postern gate which yielded to my touch. I entered a dark abandoned out-house. When I had grown accustomed to the gloom, I saw at the far end a door standing ajar.

I tip-toed to the door and glanced through. What met my gaze caused me to gasp, and I nearly emitted a cry of amazement.

'I saw before me a vast hall, in the very centre of which, at a long wooden table, were seated a number of grave men, some old, some young, some middle-aged, but all bearing upon their countenances the stamp of resolution, and the look of men born to do great deeds. "Who may these be?" I wondered. You will not be surprised to learn that I could not bring myself to withdraw, and that standing behind that little door I listened to their words. This was my first sin on that day on which I was to sink to unimaginable depths of wickedness.

'At first I could not distinguish their words, though I could see that some portentous matter was being debated. But gradually, as my ears became attuned to their speech, I learned to follow what they were saying, and with every word my amazement grew.

' "Are we all agreed as to the day?" said the President.

' "We are," many voices replied.

' "So be it," said he. "I decree that Thursday, 15 November, is to be the day. And are we all agreed as to our respective tasks?" he asked.

' "We are," replied the same voices.

' "Then," he said, "I will repeat the conclusions at which we have arrived, and when I have done so, I will formally put them to the meeting and you will vote. All of us here are agreed that the human race is suffering from an appalling malady, and that the name of this malady is GOVERNMENT. We are agreed that if man is to recover the happiness that he enjoyed in the Homeric Age and which we, in this fortunate island, have in some measure retained, abolition of Government is the first necessity. We are agreed also that there is only one way in which Government can be abolished, and that is by abolishing Governors. Twenty-one of us are here present, and we have agreed that there are twenty-one important States in the world. Each one of us on Thursday, 15 November, will assassinate the head of one of these twenty-one States. I, as your President, have the privilege of assigning to myself the most difficult and dangerous of these twenty-one enterprises. I allude, of course, to . . . but it is needless for me to pronounce the name. Our work, however, will not be quite complete when these twenty-one have suffered the fate that they so richly deserve. There is one other person, so ignoble, so sunk in error, so diligent in the propagation of falsehood, that he also must die. But as he is not of so exalted a status as these other twenty-one victims, I appoint my squire to effect his demise. You will all realise that I speak of Professor N, who has had the temerity to maintain in many learned journals and in a vast work which, as our Secret Service has informed us, is nearing completion, that it was from Lithuania, and not, as all of us know, from Corsica, that pre-Celtic decorative art spread over Europe. He also shall die."

'At this point,' Miss X continued, amid sobs, 'I could contain myself no

153

longer. The thought that my benevolent employer was to die so soon afflicted me profoundly, and I gave an involuntary cry. All heads looked towards the door. The henchman to whom the extermination of Professor N had been assigned was ordered to investigate. Before I could escape he seized me and led me before the twenty-one. The President bent stern eyes upon me and frowned heavily.

' "Who are you," said he, "that has so rashly, so impiously, intruded upon our secret councils? What has led you to eavesdrop upon the most momentous decision that any body of men has ever arrived at? Can you offer any reason whatever why you should not, here and now, die the death which your temerity has so richly merited?" '

At this point hesitation overcame Miss X, and she was scarcely able to continue her account of the momentous interview in the castle. At length she pulled herself together and resumed the narrative.

'I come now,' she said, 'to the most painful part of my story. It is a merciful dispensation of Providence that the future is concealed from our gaze. Little did my mother think, as she lay exhausted, listening to my first cry, that it was to this that her new-born daughter was destined. Little did I think as I entered the Secretarial College that it was to lead to this. Little did I dream that Pitman's was but the gateway to the gallows. But I must not waste time in vain repining. What is done is done, and it is my duty to relate the plain unvarnished tale without the trimmings of futile remorse.

'As the President spoke to me of swift death, I glimpsed the pleasant sunshine without. I thought of the carefree years of my youth. I thought of the promise of happiness which but that very morning had accompanied me as I climbed the lonely hills. Visions of summer rain and winter firesides, of spring in meadows and autumn in the beech woods haunted my imagination. I thought of the golden years of innocent childhood, fled never to return. And I thought fleetingly and shyly of one in whose eyes I fancied that I had seen the light of love. All this in a moment passed through my mind. "Life," I thought, "is sweet. I am but young, and the best of life is still before me. Am I to be cut off thus, before I have known the joys, and the sorrows too, which make the warp and woof of human life? No," I thought, "this is too much. If there yet remains a means by which I may prolong my life I will seize it, even though it be at the price of dishonour." When Satan had led me to this dreadful resolve I answered with such calmness as I could command: "Oh, reverend Sir, I have been but an unwitting and unintentional offender. No thought of evil was in my mind as I strayed through that fatal door. If you will but spare my life I will do your will, whatever it may be. Have mercy, I pray you. You cannot wish that one so young and fair should perish prematurely. Let me but know your will and I will obey." Although he still looked down upon me with no friendly eye, I fancied I saw some slight sign of relenting. He turned to the other twenty, and said: "What is your will? Shall we execute justice, or shall we submit her to the ordeal? I will put it to the vote." Ten voted for justice, ten for the ordeal. "The casting vote is mine," he said. "I vote for the ordeal."

'Then turning again to me, he continued: "You may live, but on certain terms. What these terms are I will now explain to you. First of all you must swear a great oath – never to reveal by word or deed, by any hint or by any turn of demeanour, what you have learned in this hall. The oath which you must fulfil I will now tell you, and you must repeat the words after me: I SWEAR BY ZOROASTER AND THE BEARD OF THE PROPHET, BY URIENS, PAYMON, EGYN AND AMAYMON, BY MARBUEL, ACIEL, BARBIEL, MEPHISTOPHIEL AND APADIEL, BY DIRACHIEL, AMNODIEL, AMUDIEL, TAGRIEL, GELIEL AND REQUIEL, AND BY ALL THE FOUL SPIRITS OF HELL, THAT I WILL NEVER REVEAL OR IN ANY MANNER CAUSE TO BE KNOWN ANY SLIGHTEST HINT OF WHAT I HAVE SEEN AND HEARD IN THIS HALL." When I had solemnly repeated this oath, he explained to me that this was but the first part of the ordeal, and that perhaps I might not have grasped its full immensity. Each of the infernal names that I had invoked possessed its own separate power of torture. By the magician's power invested in himself he was able to control the actions of these demons. If I infringed the oath, each separate one would, through all eternity, inflict upon me the separate torture of which he was master. But that, he said, was but the smallest part of my punishment.

' "I come now," said he, "to graver matters."

'Turning to the henchman, he said: "The goblet, please."

'The henchman, who knew the ritual, presented the goblet to the President.

' "This," he said, turning again to me, "is a goblet of bull's blood. You must drink every drop, without taking breath while you drink. If you fail to do so, you will instantly become a cow, and be pursued forever by the ghost of the bull whose blood you will have failed to drink in due manner." I took the goblet from him, drew a long breath, closed my eyes, and swallowed the noxious draught.

' "Two-thirds of the ordeal," he said, "are now fulfilled. The last part is slightly more inconvenient. We have decreed, as you are unfortunately aware, that on the 15th prox., twenty-one Heads of State shall die. We decided also that the glory of our nation demands the death of Professor N. But we felt that there would be a lack of symmetry if one of us were to undertake this just execution. Before we discovered your presence, we delegated this task to my henchman. But your arrival, while in many ways inopportune, has in one respect provided us with an opportunity for neatness which it would be unwise and inartistic to neglect. You, and not my henchman, shall carry out this execution. And this to do you shall swear by the same oath by which you swore secrecy."

' "Oh Sir!" I said, "do not put upon me this terrible burden. You know much, but I doubt whether you know that it has been both my duty and

155

my pleasure to assist Professor N in his researches. I have had nothing but kindness from him. It may be that his views on decorative art are not all that you could wish. Can you not permit me to continue serving him as before, and gradually I could wean him from his errors. I am not without influence upon the course of his thoughts. Several years of close association have shown me ways of guiding his inclinations in this direction or that, and I am persuaded that if you will but grant me time I can bring him round to your opinions on the function of Corsica in pre-Celtic decorative art. To slay this good old man, whom I have regarded as a friend and who has hitherto, and not unjustly, regarded me in not unlike manner, would be almost as terrible as the pursuit of the many fiends whom you have caused me to invoke. Indeed, I doubt whether life is worth purchasing at such a price."

' "Nay, my good maiden," said he, "I fear you are still indulging in illusions. The oath you have already taken was a sinful and blasphemous oath, and has put you forever in the power of the fiends, unless I, by my magic art, choose to restrain them. You cannot escape now. You must do my will or suffer." I wept, I implored him, I knelt and clasped his knees. "Have mercy," I said, "have mercy." But he remained unmoved. "I have spoken," he said. "If you do not wish to suffer forever the fifteen separate kinds of torment that will be inflicted by each of the fifteen fiends you have invoked, you must repeat after me, using the same dread names, the oath that on the 15th prox. you will cause the death of Professor N."

'Alas! dear Professor. It is impossible that you should pardon me, but in my weakness I swore this second oath. The 15th, no longer prox. but inst., is rapidly approaching, and I see not how I am to escape, when that day comes, the dread consequences of my frightful oath. As soon as I got away from that dreadful castle, remorse seized me and has gnawed at my vitals ever since. Gladly would I suffer the fifteen diverse torments of the fifteen fiends, could I but persuade myself that in doing so I should be fulfilling the behests of duty. But I have sworn, and honour demands that I should fulfil my oath. Which is the greater sin, to murder the good man whom I revere, or to be false to the dictates of honour? I know not. But you, dear Professor, you who are so wise, you, I am sure, can resolve my doubts, and show me the clear path of duty.'

VIII

The Professor, as her narrative advanced towards its climax, somewhat surprisingly recovered cheerfulness and calm. With a kindly smile, with folded hands and a completely peaceful demeanour, he replied to her query.

'My dear young lady,' he said, 'nothing, nothing on earth, should be allowed to override the dictates of honour. If it lies in your power you must fulfil your oath. My work is completed, and my remaining years, if any, could have little importance. I should therefore tell you in the most emphatic manner that it is your duty to fulfil your oath if it is in any way possible. I should regret, however, I might even say I should regret deeply, that as a consequence of your sense of honour you should end your life upon the gallows. There is one thing, and one thing only, which can absolve you from your oath, and that is physical impossibility. You cannot kill a dead man.'

So saying, he put his thumb and forefinger into his waistcoat pocket and with a lightning gesture conveyed them to his mouth. In an instant he was dead.

'Oh, my dear master,' cried Miss X, throwing herself upon his lifeless corpse, 'how can I bear the light of day now that you have sacrificed your life for mine? How can I endure the shame that every hour of sunshine and every moment of seeming happiness will generate in my soul? Nay, not another moment can I endure this agony.'

With these words, she found the same pocket, imitated his gesture, and expired.

'I have not lived in vain,' said I, 'for I have witnessed two noble deaths.' But then I remembered that my task was not done, since the world's unworthy rulers must, I supposed, be saved from extinction. Reluctantly I bent my footsteps towards Scotland Yard.

The Infra-redioscope

Lady Millicent Pinturque, known to her friends as the lovely Millicent, was sitting alone in her armchair in her luxurious boudoir. All the chairs and sofas were soft; the electric light was softly shaded; beside her, on a small table, stood what appeared to be a large doll with voluminous skirts. The walls were covered with water-colours, all signed 'Millicent', representing romantic scenes in the Alps and the Italian shores of the Mediterranean, in the islands of Greece, and in Tenerife. Another water-colour was in her hands, and she was scrutinising it with minute care. At last she reached out her hand to the doll, and touched a button. The doll opened in the middle, and revealed a telephone in its entrails. She lifted the receiver. Her movements, although they showed what was evidently an habitual grace, displayed a certain tenseness of manner, suggesting an important decision just arrived at. She called a number, and when it had been obtained she said: 'I wish to speak with Sir Bulbus.'

Sir Bulbus Frutiger was known to all the world as the editor of the *Daily Lightning*, and as one of the great powers in our land, no matter what party might be nominally in office. He was protected from the public by a secretary and six secretary's secretaries. Few ventured to call him on the telephone, and of these few only an infinitesimal proportion reached him. His lucubrations were too important to be interrupted. It was his mission to preserve an imperturbable calm, while developing schemes for destroying the calm of all his readers. But in spite of this wall of protection, he answered instantly to the call of Lady Millicent.

'Yes, Lady Millicent?' he said.

'All is ready,' she answered, and replaced the receiver.

II

Much preparation had preceded these brief words. The lovely Millicent's husband, Sir Theophilus Pinturque, was one of the leaders in the world of finance, an immensely rich man, but not, though this grieved him, without rivals in the world that he wished to dominate. There were still men who could meet him on equal terms and who, in a financial contest, had reasonable chances of victory. His character was Napoleonic, and he sought for means by which his superiority could become unchallenged and unquestionable. He recognised that the power of finance was not the only great power in the modern world. There are, he reflected, three others : one is the power of the Press; one is the power of advertising; and one, too often underestimated by men in his profession, is the power of science. He decided that victory would require a combination of these four powers, and with this end in view, he formed a secret committee of four.

He himself was the Chairman. Next in power and dignity was Sir Bulbus Frutiger, who had a slogan: 'Give the public what it wants.' This slogan governed all his vast chain of newspapers. The third member of the syndicate was Sir Publius Harper, who controlled the advertising world. Those who, in compelled, though temporary, idleness went up and down escalators, imagined that the men whose advertisements they read, because they had nothing else to do, were rivals. This was a mistake. All the advertisements came to a central pool, and in that central pool their distribution was decided by Sir Publius Harper. If he wished your dentrifice to be known, it would be known; if he wished it ignored, it would be ignored, however excellent. It rested with him to make or mar the fortunes of those who were unwise enough to produce consumable commodities – instead of recommending them. Sir Publius had a certain kindly contempt for Sir Bulbus. He thought Sir Bulbus's slogan too submissive altogether. His slogan was : 'Make the public want what you give it.' In this he was amazingly successful. Wines of unspeakable nastiness sold in vast numbers because, when he told the public that they were delicious, the public had not the courage to doubt his word. Seaside resorts where hotels were filthy, the lodgings dingy, and the sea, except at extreme high tide, a sea of mud, acquired through the activities of Sir Publius a reputation for ozone, stormy seas, and invigorating Atlantic breezes. Political parties at General Elections made use of the inventiveness of his employees, which was at the service of all (except Communists) who could afford his prices. No sensible man who knew the world would dream of launching a campaign without the support of Sir Publius.

Sir Bulbus and Sir Publius, though frequently joined in their public campaigns, were in appearance very different from each other. Both were *bons viveurs*, but while Sir Bulbus looked the part, having a considerable corporation and a cheerful, eupeptic appearance, Sir Publius was lean and ascetic-looking. Anybody who did not know who he was would imagine him an earnest seeker after some mystic vision. Never could his portrait be used to advertise any article of food or drink. Nevertheless, when, as not infrequently occurred, the two men dined together, to plan a new conquest or a change of policy, they agreed remarkably with each other. Each understood the workings of the other's mind; each respected the other's ambitions; each felt the need of the other to complete his designs. Sir Publius would point out how much Sir Bulbus owed to the picture which appeared on every hoarding of the moron who does not read the *Daily Lightning*, pointed at with contempt by a well-dressed crowd of handsome men and lovely women, each supplied with his or her copy of that great newspaper. And Sir Bulbus would retort: 'Yes, but where would you be, but for my great campaign to secure control of the Canadian forests? Where would you be without paper, and where would you get the paper, but for the masterly policy which I have pursued in that great Transatlantic Dominion?' Such friendly quips would occupy them until the dessert; after that, both would become serious, and their co-operation would be intense and creative.

Pendrake Markle, the fourth member of the secret syndicate, was somewhat different from the other three. Sir Bulbus and Sir Publius had had some doubts as to his admission, but their doubts had been overruled by Sir Theophilus. Their doubts were not unreasonable. In the first place, unlike the other three, he had not been honoured with a knighthood. There were, however, even graver objections to him. Nobody denied that he was brilliant, but solid men suspected that he was unsound. His was not the sort of name that would be put on a prospectus to tempt country investors. Sir Theophilus, however, insisted upon including him, because of his extreme fertility in unorthodox invention, and also because, unlike some other men of science, he was not hampered by an undue scrupulosity.

He had a grudge against the human race, which was intelligible to those who knew his history. His father was a Nonconformist minister of the most exemplary piety, who used to explain to him when he was a little boy how right it was of Elisha to curse the children who, as a result of his curse, were torn to pieces by she-bears. In all ways his father was a relic of a bygone age. Respect for the Sabbath, and a belief in the literal inspiration of every word of the Old and New Testaments, dominated all his converse in the home. The boy, already intelligent, once ventured in a rash moment to ask his father whether it was impossible to be a good Christian if one did not believe that the hare chews the cud. His father thrashed him so unmercifully that he could not sit down for a week. In spite of this careful upbringing, he refused to gratify the parental desire that he should become himself a Nonconformist minister. By means of scholarships he managed to work his way through the university, where he obtained the highest honours. His first piece of research was stolen from him by his professor, who was awarded a Royal Society Medal on the strength of it. When he attempted to make his grievance known, no one believed him, and he was thought to be an ill-conditioned boor. As a result of this experience and of the suspicion with which his protests caused him to be regarded, he became a cynic and a misanthropist. He took care, however, henceforth, that no one should steal his inventions or discoveries. There were nasty stories, never substantiated, of shady dealings in regard to patents. The stories varied, and no one knew what foundation they had in fact. However that may be, he acquired at last enough money to make for his own use a private laboratory, to which no possible rivals were allowed access. Gradually his work began to win reluctant recognition. At last the Government approached him with a request that he should devote his talents to improving bacteriological warfare. He refused this request on a ground which was universally considered exceedingly strange, namely that he knew nothing about bacteriology. It was suspected, however, that his real reason was a hatred of all the forces of organised society, from the Prime Minister to the humblest policeman on his beat.

Although everybody in the scientific world disliked him, very few dared to attack him, because of his unscrupulous skill in controversy, which succeeded almost always in making his adversary look foolish. There was only one thing in all the world that he loved, and that was his private laboratory. Unfortunately, its equipment had run him into enormous expense and he was in imminent danger of having to dispose of it to settle his debts. It was while this danger hung over him that he was approached by Sir Theophilus, who offered to save him from disaster in return for his help as the fourth member of the secret syndicate.

At the first meeting of the syndicate, Sir Theophilus explained what he had in mind, and asked for suggestions as to the realisation of his hopes. It should be possible, he said, for the four of them in collaboration to achieve complete domination of the world – not only of this or that part of the world, not only of Western Europe, or of Western Europe and America, but equally of the world on the other side of the Iron Curtain. If they used their skill and their opportunities wisely, nothing should be able to resist them.

'All that is wanted,' so he said in his opening address, 'is a really fruitful idea. The supplying of ideas shall be the business of Markle. Given a good idea, I will finance it, Harper will advertise it, and Frutiger will rouse to frenzy the passions of the public against those who oppose it. It is possible that Markle may require a little time to invent the sort of idea which the rest of us would think it worth while to promote. I therefore propose that this meeting do adjourn for a week, at the end of which time, I am convinced, science will be prepared to vindicate its position as one of the four forces dominating our society.'

With this, after a bow to Mr Markle, he dismissed the meeting.

When the syndicate met again a week later, Sir Theophilus, smiling at Mr Markle, remarked: 'Well, Markle, and what has science to say?' Markle cleared his throat and entered upon a speech:

'Sir Theophilus, Sir Bulbus and Sir Publius,' he began, 'throughout the past week I have given my best thought – and my best thought, I assure you, is very good – to the concoction of such a scheme as was adumbrated at our last meeting. Various notions occurred to me, only to be rejected. The public has been inundated with horrors connected with nuclear energy,

161

and I decided very quickly that this whole subject has now become hackneyed. Moreover, it is a matter as to which Governments are on the alert, and anything that we might attempt in this direction would probably meet with official opposition. I thought next of what could be done by means of bacteriology. It might be possible, so I thought, to give hydrophobia to all the Heads of State. But it was not quite clear how we should profit by this, and there was always a risk that one of them might bite one of us before his disease was diagnosed. Then, of course, there was the scheme for creating a satellite of the earth which should complete its revolution once every three days, with a clockwork mechanism timed to fire at the Kremlin every time it passed that way. This, however, is a project for Governments. We should be above the battle. It is not for us to take sides in the controversies between East and West. It is for us to ensure that, whatever happens, we shall be supreme. I therefore rejected all schemes which involve an abandonment of neutrality.

'I have a scheme to propose to you which I think is not open to any of the objections to the other schemes. The public has heard much in recent years about infra-red photography. It is as ignorant on this subject as on every other, and I see no reason why we should not exploit its ignorance. I propose that we invent a machine to be called the "infra-redioscope", which (so we shall assure the public) will photograph by means of infra-red rays objects not otherwise perceptible. It shall be a very delicate machine, capable of getting out of order if carelessly handled. We shall see to it that this happens whenever the machine is in the possession of persons whom we cannot control. What it is to see we shall determine, and I think that, by our united efforts, we can persuade the world that it really sees whatever we shall decide that it makes visible. If you adopt my scheme, I will undertake to devise the machine, but as to how it is to be utilised, that, I think, is a matter for Sir Bulbus and Sir Publius.'

Both these gentlemen had listened with attention to the suggestion of Pendrake Markle. Both of them seized upon his ideas with enthusiasm, seeing great opportunities for the exploitation of their respective skills.

'I know,' said Sir Bulbus, 'what it is that the machine should reveal. It shall reveal a secret invasion from Mars, an invasion of horrible creatures, whose invisible army, but for our machine, would be certain of victory. I shall, in all my newspapers, rouse the public to a consciousness of their peril. Millions of them will buy the machine. Sir Theophilus will make the greatest fortune ever possessed by a single man. My newspapers will outsell all others and will be, before long, the only newspapers of the world. Nor will my friend Publius be less important in this campaign. He will cover every hoarding with pictures of the dreadful creatures and a caption beneath – "Do you wish to be dispossessed by THIS?" And in vast letters he will put notices along all the main roads, in all stations of the country, and wherever the public has leisure to see such things, and the notices will say:

"Men of earth, now is the hour of decision. Rise in your millions. Be not appalled by the cosmic danger. Courage shall yet triumph, as it has done ever since the days of Adam. Buy an infra-redioscope and be prepared!" '

At this point Sir Theophilus intervened.

'The scheme is good,' he said. 'It requires only one thing, and that is that the picture of the Martian should be sufficiently horrible and terrifying. You all know Lady Millicent, but you know her perhaps only in her gentler aspects. I, as her husband, have been privileged to become aware of regions in her imagination which are concealed from most people. She is, as you know, skilled in water-colours. Let her make a water-colour picture of the Martian, and let photographs of her picture form the basis of our campaign.'

The others at first looked a little doubtful. Lady Millicent as they had seen her was soft, perhaps a trifle silly, not the sort of person whom they had imagined as taking part in so grim a campaign. After some debate it was decided to allow her to make the attempt, and if her picture was sufficiently dreadful to satisfy Mr Markle, Sir Bulbus should then be informed that all was in readiness for the launching of the campaign.

Sir Theophilus, on returning home from his momentous meeting, set to work to explain to the lovely Millicent what it was that he wanted. He did not enlarge upon the general aspects of his campaign, for it was a principle with him that one should not take women into one's confidence. He told her merely that he wished for pictures of terrifying imaginary creatures, for which he had a business use which she would find it difficult to understand.

Lady Millicent, who was very much younger than Sir Theophilus, belonged to a good county family now fallen upon evil days. Her father, an impoverished earl, was the owner of an exquisite Elizabethan mansion, which he loved with a devotion inherited from all the generations that had inhabited it. It had seemed inevitable that he should sell this ancestral mansion to some rich Argentinian, and the prospect was slowly breaking his heart. His daughter adored him, and decided to use her staggering beauty to enable him to end his days in peace. Almost all men adored her at sight. Sir Theophilus was the richest of her adorers and so she chose him, exacting as her price a sufficient settlement upon her father to free him from all financial anxiety. She did not dislike Sir Theophilus, who adored her and gratified her every whim, but she did not love him – indeed, no one, up to this moment, had ever touched her heart. She felt it her duty, in return for all he gave her, to obey him whenever possible.

His request for a water-colour of a monster seemed to her a little odd, but she was accustomed to actions on his part to which she had no clue, nor had she any desire to understand his business schemes. She therefore duly set to work. He did go so far as to tell her that the picture was wanted for the purpose of showing what could be seen by means of a new instrument to be called the 'infra-redioscope'. After several attempts which did not satisfy her, she produced a picture of a creature with a body somewhat resembling that of a beetle, but six foot long, with seven hairy legs, with a human face, completely bald head, staring eyes, and a fixed grin. She made indeed two pictures. In the first, a man is looking through an infra-redioscope and seeing this creature. In the second, the man, in terror, has dropped the instrument. The monster, seeing that it is observed, has stood upright on its seventh leg, and is entwining the other six in hairy embrace round the asphyxiated man. These two pictures, at the orders of Sir Theophilus, she showed to Mr Markle. Mr Markle accepted them as adequate, and it was after his departure that she telephoned the fateful words to Sir Bulbus.

III

As soon as Sir Bulbus received this message, the vast apparatus controlled by the syndicate was set in motion. Sir Theophilus caused innumerable workshops throughout the world to manufacture the infra-redioscope, a simple machine, containing a lot of wheels that made whirring noises, but not in fact enabling anyone to see anything. Sir Bulbus filled his newspapers with articles on the wonders of science, all of them with a 'slant' towards the infra-red. Some of these contained genuine information by reputable men of science; others were more imaginative. Sir Publius had bills posted everywhere: 'The infra-redioscope is coming! See the world's invisible marvels!' or 'What is the infra-redioscope? The Frutiger newspapers will tell you. Do not miss this chance of strange knowledge!'

As soon as sufficient numbers of infra-redioscopes had been manufactured, Lady Millicent let it be known that by means of one of these instruments she had observed the horror crawling upon her bedroom floor. She was interviewed naturally by all the newspapers under the control of Sir Bulbus, but the matter was of such dramatic interest that other newspapers were compelled to follow suit. Under her husband's instructions, she uttered in broken and apparently terrified sentences exactly the sentiments that were required by the scheme of the syndicate. At the same time infra-redioscopes were given to various leaders of opinion whom Sir Theophilus, by means of his secret service, knew to be in financial difficulties. Each of them was offered a thousand pounds if he would say that he had seen one of the awful creatures. Lady Millicent's two pictures were reproduced everywhere through the advertising agency of Sir Publius, with the legend : 'Do not drop your infra-redioscope. It protects as well as reveals.'

There was, of course, an instant sale of many thousands of infra-redioscopes and a world-wide wave of horror. Pendrake Markle invented a new instrument to be found only in his private laboratory. This new instrument proved that the creatures came from Mars. Other men of science grew envious of the enormous fame which accrued to Markle, and one of the more venturesome of these would-be rivals invented a machine that read the thoughts of the creatures. By means of this machine he professed to have discovered that they were the advance guard of a Martian campaign to exterminate the human race.

Just at first the earlier purchasers of infra-redioscopes had complained that they saw nothing through these instruments, but naturally their remarks were not printed in any of the newspapers controlled by Sir Bulbus, and very soon the universal panic reached such dimensions that any person claiming to have failed to detect the presence of Martians was assumed to be a traitor and pro-Martian. After some thousands of persons had been lynched, the rest found it prudent to hold their tongues, except for a very few who were interned. There was now such a wave of horror that many people who had hitherto been considered harmless incurred the gravest suspicion. Any person who unguardedly praised the appearance of the planet Mars in the night sky was instantly suspect. All astronomers who had made a special study of Mars were interned. Those among them who had maintained that there is no life on Mars were sentenced to long terms of imprisonment.

There were, however, some groups who, throughout the early stages of the panic, remained friends of Mars. The Emperor of Abyssinia announced that a careful study of the picture showed the Martian to resemble closely the Lion of Judah, and to be therefore obviously good and not bad. The Tibetans said that from a study of ancient books they had concluded that the Martian was a Boddhisatva, come to liberate them from the yoke of the infidel Chinese. Peruvian Indians revived sun-worship, and pointed out that since Mars shines by reflected sunlight, Mars too is to be adored. When it was remarked that the Martians might cause carnage, they replied that sun-worship had always involved human sacrifice, and that therefore the truly devout would not repine. The anarchists argued that Martians would dissolve all government and would therefore bring the millennium. The pacifists said that they should be met with love, and that if the love were sufficiently great, it would take the grin off their faces.

For a short time these various groups, wherever they existed in sufficient numbers, remained unmolested. But their respite ceased when the Communist world was brought into the anti-Martian campaign. This was achieved by the syndicate with some skill. They approached first certain Western men of science known to be friendly to the Soviet Government. They told these men frankly how the campaign had been engineered. They pointed out that fear of the Martians could be made the basis of reconciliation between East and West. They also succeeded in persuading the fellow-travelling scientists that an East-West war could well result in the defeat of the East, and that therefore whatever would prevent a third world war

165

should be favoured by the Communists. They pointed out further that if terror of the Martians was to effect a reconciliation between East and West, it was necessary that all the Governments, Eastern as well as Western, should believe in the Martian invasion. The fellow-travelling scientists, after listening to these arguments, found themselves reluctantly compelled to agree. For were they not realists? And was not this realism, as stark as realism could be? And was not this perhaps the very synthesis that dialectical materialism demanded? They therefore agreed that they would not reveal to the Soviet Government the fact that the whole thing was a hoax. For its own sake they would allow it to believe this plot, inaugurated by vile capitalists for vile capitalist ends, but incidentally and accidentally furthering the interests of mankind, and giving a chance that when, in due course, the deception was unmasked a general reaction would sweep the whole world into the arms of Moscow. Convinced by this reasoning, they represented to Moscow the imminent danger of the destruction of the human race, and pointed out that there was no reason to believe the Martians to be Communists. On the basis of their representations, Moscow, after some hesitation, decided to join with the West in the anti-Martian campaign.

From this moment the Abyssinians, the Tibetans, the Peruvians, the anarchists, and the pacifists received short shrift. Some were killed, some were set to forced labour, some recanted, and in a very short time there was no longer any explicit opposition anywhere in the world to the great anti-Martian campaign.

Fear, however, could not be confined to fear of the Martians. There was still fear of traitors in their midst. A great meeting of the United Nations was summoned to organise propaganda and publicity. It was felt that a word was needed to represent the inhabitants of earth as opposed to the inhabitants of other planets. 'Earthy' obviously would not do. 'Earthly' was inadequate because the usual alternative was 'heavenly'. 'Terrestrial' would not do because the usual alternative was 'celestial'. At last, after much eloquence, in which the South Americans especially distinguished themselves, the word 'Tellurian' was adopted. The United Nations then appointed a committee against un-Tellurian activities, which established a political reign of terror throughout the whole world. It was also decided that the United Nations should be in permanent session, so long as the crisis lasted, under a permanent head. A President was chosen from among the elder statesmen, a man of immense dignity and vast experience, no longer embroiled in party warfare, and prepared by two world wars for the even more terrible war that now seemed imminent. He rose to the occasion, and in his opening address said:

'Friends, Fellow inhabitants of Earth, Tellurians, united as never before, I address you on this solemn occasion, not as heretofore in the cause of world peace, but in an even greater cause – an even greater cause – the cause of the preservation of this our human existence with all its human values, with all its joys and sorrows, all its hopes and all its fears, the preservation, I say, of this our human life from a foul assault wafted across the ether by we know not what foul and dreadful means, revealed to us, I am happy to say, by the amazing skill of our men of science, who have shown us what by infra-rediation can be discovered, and have made visible to us the strange, repellent and horrible beasts which crawl upon our floors unseen save by these marvellous instruments, which crawl, I say, nay, which infect us, which pollute our very thoughts, which would destroy within us the very fibre of our moral being, which would reduce us, I say, not to the level of beasts – for beasts are, after all, Tellurians – nay, to the level of Martians – and can I say anything worse? No lower term, no greater word of infamy exists in the languages of this Earth that we all love. I call upon you, I call upon you, my brethren, to stand shoulder to shoulder in the great fight, the fight to preserve our earthly values against this insidious and degrading invasion of monsters, alien monsters, monsters who, we can only say, should go back where they came from.'

With this he sat down. And the applause was such that for several minutes nothing else could be heard. The next speaker was the Representative of the United States.

'Fellow citizens of Earth,' he began, 'those who have had the misfortune to be compelled by their public duties to study that abominable planet against whose evil machinations we are here embattled, are aware that its surface is scarred by strange straight marks, known among astronomers as canals. These marks, as must be evident to every student of economic activity, can only be the product of totalitarianism. We have therefore a right, the right of the highest scientific authority, to believe that these invaders threaten not only us in our personal and private being, but also that way of life which was established by our ancestors nearly two hundred years ago, and which, until the present danger, produced unity – unity apparently threatened by a certain Power, which, at the present moment it would be injudicious to name. It may be that man represents but a passing phase in the evolution of the life of the cosmos, but there is one law which the cosmos will always obey, one divine law, the law of eternal progress. This law, fellow citizens of Earth, this law is safeguarded by free enterprise, the immortal heritage which the West has brought to man. Free enterprise must have long since ceased in that red planet which now menaces us, for the canals which we see are not a thing of yesterday. Not only in the name of Man, but in the name of free enterprise, I call upon this Assembly to give of its best, to give till it hurts, without stint, without thought of self. It is with confident hope that I make this appeal to all the other nations here assembled.'

It was not to be left to the West alone to sound the note of unity. No sooner had the Representative of the United States sat down than he

167

was succeeded by Mr Growlovsky, the Representative of the Soviet Union.

'The hour is come,' he said, 'to fight, not to speak. Were I to speak, there are things which I could controvert in the speech which we have just heard. Astronomy is Russian. Some few sparse students of the subject have existed in other countries, but Soviet erudition has shown how shallow and imitative their theories have been. Of these we have had an example in what has just been said about the canals in that infamous planet which I disdain to name. The great astronomer Lukupsky has shown conclusively that it was private enterprise that produced the canals, and that it was competition that stimulated their duplication. But this is not the hour for such reflections. This is the hour for action, and when the assault has been repelled, it will be found that the world has become one, and that in the throes of battle, totalitarianism has become, willy-nilly, universal.'

Some fears were felt at this point that the new-found unity of the Great Powers might not survive the strain of public debate. India, Paraguay, and Iceland poured oil upon the troubled waters, and at last the soothing words of the Republic of Andorra enabled the delegates to separate with that glow of harmony that resulted from ignorance of each other's sentiments. Before separating, the Assembly decreed world peace and an amalgamation of the armed forces of the planet. It was hoped that the main assault of the Martians might be delayed until this amalgamation was complete. But meanwhile, in spite of all preparations, in spite of harmony, in spite of pretended confidence, fear lurked in every heart – except those of the syndicate and its coadjutors.

IV

Throughout this period of excited panic, however, there were some who, though prudence kept them silent, had their doubts about the whole matter. Members of Governments knew that they themselves had never seen the Martian monster, and their private secretaries knew that *they* had never seen them, but while the terror was at its height, neither dared to confess this, since avowed scepticism involved a fall from power and perhaps even a lynching. The business rivals of Sir Theophilus, Sir Bulbus, and Sir Publius naturally were envious of the immense success which these men were achieving, and wished, if it were in any way possible, to find some means of bringing them down. The *Daily Thunder* had been almost as great a power as the *Daily Lightning*, but while the campaign was at its height, the *Daily Thunder* was inaudible. Its editor gnashed his teeth, but, as a prudent man, he bided his time, knowing that a popular frenzy, while it lasts, cannot be opposed with profit. The scientists, who had always disliked and distrusted Pendrake Markle, were naturally indignant to see him treated as though he were the greatest scientist of all time. Many of them had taken the infra-redioscope to pieces and had seen that it was a fraud, but since they valued their own skins, they thought it wise to be silent.

Among them all, only one young man was indifferent to the claims of prudence. This young man was Thomas Shovelpenny, who was still viewed in many English quarters with suspicion because his grandfather had been a German named Schimmelpfennig and had changed his name during the First World War. Thomas Shovelpenny was a quiet student, totally unaccustomed to great affairs, ignorant of politics and economics alike, and skilled only in physics. He was too poor to buy an infra-redioscope and therefore was unable to make for himself the discovery of its fraudulent character. Those who had made this discovery kept their knowledge secret and did not whisper it even in moments of vinous conviviality. But Thomas Shovelpenny could not but observe strange discrepancies in the reported observations, and these discrepancies bred in him purely scientific doubts, though in his innocence he was totally at a loss to imagine what purpose could be served by inventing such myths.

Though himself a man of exemplary and abstemious conduct, he had a friend whom he valued for his penetration and his insight, in spite of habits by no means such as a well-behaved student could approve of. This friend, whose name was Verity Hogg-Paucus, was almost always intoxicated, and scarcely to be met with except in public houses. It was supposed that he must sleep somewhere, but he did not allow anyone to know the truth, which was that he had a single bedroom in one of the worst slums of London. He had brilliant talents as a journalist, and when his money gave out, the enforced sobriety would lead him to write articles of such mordant wit that the journals which liked that sort of thing could not refuse to publish them. The better-class journals, of course, were closed to him, since he would make no concessions to humbug. He knew all the underworld of politics, but did not know how to make his knowledge advantageous to himself. He had had many jobs, but had lost them all through allowing his chiefs to know that he had discovered shady secrets which the chiefs wished to keep concealed. Whether from imprudence or from a remnant of moral feeling, he had never made a penny by blackmailing the objects of his unpleasant knowledge. Instead of using his knowledge to his own advantage, he would let it trickle out of him in bibulous loquacity while drinking with any casual acquaintance in some unfashionable bar.

Shovelpenny consulted him in his perplexity.

'It seems to me,' he said, 'that this whole business must be fraudulent, and yet I cannot imagine either how the fraud is worked or what purpose it can serve. Perhaps you, with your great knowledge of what men wish to keep secret, will be able to help me to understand what is happening.'

Hogg-Paucus, who had watched cynically the growth of public hysteria and Sir Theophilus's fortune, was delighted.

'You,' he said, 'are the very man I want. I have no doubt that the whole thing is bogus, but remember that it is dangerous to say so. Perhaps together, you, with your knowledge of science, and I, with my knowledge of politics, we shall be able to unravel the mystery. But since it is dangerous to talk, and since I am garrulous in my cups, it will be necessary for you to keep me locked up in your rooms, and if you supply me with sufficient liquor, I shall be able to endure the temporary imprisonment without excessive discomfort.'

Shovelpenny liked the proposal, but his purse was limited, and he did not see how he could hope to keep Hogg-Paucus in drink throughout a period which might not be short. Hogg-Paucus, however, who had not always been so low in the social scale, had known Lady Millicent when both were children, and wrote a flamboyant article about her virtues and charms at the age of ten, which he sold for a large sum to a fashion magazine. This, it was thought, together with Shovelpenny's salary as a school teacher, would, with care and economy, supply the necessary amount of drink for the necessary period of time.

Hogg-Paucus thereupon set to work on a systematic investigation. It was obvious that the campaign had begun from the *Daily Lightning*. Hogg-Paucus, who knew everything in the way of personal gossip, was aware that the *Daily Lightning* was intimately connected with Sir Theophilus. It was common knowledge that Lady Millicent had been the first to see a Martian, and that Markle was mainly instrumental in the scientific part of the proceedings. A vague outline of what must have happened formed itself in the fertile mind of Hogg-Paucus, but it seemed impossible to arrive at anything more definite unless some one of those who knew could be induced to speak. Hogg-Paucus advised Shovelpenny to request an interview with Lady Millicent, as being the originator of the first photograph, and therefore clearly concerned in the very beginning of the whole matter. Shovelpenny only half believed the various cynical hypotheses that his friend produced, but his scientific mind showed him that the best way to begin an investigation would be an interview with Lady Millicent, as Hogg-Paucus advised. He therefore wrote her a careful letter, saying that he wished to see her on a matter of importance. Somewhat to his surprise, she agreed, and made an appointment. He brushed his hair and his clothes, and made himself much tidier than usual. Thus prepared, he went to a momentous interview.

V

The maid showed him into Lady Millicent's boudoir, where, as before, she reclined in her arm-chair, with the doll-telephone on the little table beside her.

'Well, Mr Shovelpenny,' she said, 'your letter caused me to wonder what it can be that you wish to discuss with me. You, so I have always understood, are a brilliant man of science; I am a poor scatter-brained lady, with nothing to recommend me except a rich husband. But since I got your letter, I have taken pains to acquaint myself with your circumstances and career, and I cannot imagine that it is money you wish to see me about.'

So saying, she smiled charmingly. Shovelpenny had never before met a woman who was both rich and lovely, and he found himself somewhat disconcerted by the unexpected emotions which she roused in him. 'Come, come,' he said to himself, 'you are not here to feel emotions. You are here to conduct a grave investigation.' He pulled himself together with an effort, and replied:

'Lady Millicent, in common with the rest of mankind you must be aware of the strange commotion which has taken place throughout the human race, owing to the fear of a Martian invasion. If my information is correct, you were the first to see one of these Martians. I find it difficult to say what I have to say, but it is my duty. Careful investigation has made me doubt whether you or anybody else has seen any of these horrible creatures, and whether anything whatever is to be seen by means of the infra-redioscope. If my investigations have not misled me, I am painfully forced to the conclusion that you have been a prime mover in a gigantic fraud. I shall not be surprised if, after hearing me utter these words, you have me removed by force from your presence, and give orders to your domestics that I am not to be admitted again to your house. Such a reaction would be natural if you were innocent, and even more natural if you were guilty. But if there is any possibility that I have not thought of, if there is any way by which I can avoid condemning one so lovely as you, and one so apparently gentle as your smile proclaims you to be, if I might, throwing science to the winds, trust my instincts in your favour, then I beseech you, I implore you, for the sake of my peace of mind, let me know the whole truth!'

His obvious sincerity and his unwillingness to flatter in spite of his instinct in her favour, affected Lady Millicent as none of her usual acquaintances had ever affected her. For the first time since she had left her father to marry Sir Theophilus, she came in contact with simple sincerity. The attempt to live artificially which she had been making ever since she entered the mansion of Sir Theophilus became intolerable to her. The world of lies and schemes and intrigues and heartless power she found that she could no longer endure.

'O Mr Shovelpenny,' she said, 'how can I answer you? I have a duty to my husband, I have a duty to mankind, and I have a duty to truth. To one at least of these I must be false. How can I decide to which of them my paramount duty is owing?'

'Lady Millicent,' he replied, 'you kindle my hope and my curiosity in

171

equal measure. You live, as I perceive from your surroundings, an artificial life, and yet, if I am not mistaken, there is within you something that is not artificial, something sincere and simple by which you might yet be saved from the pollution that surrounds you. Speak, I implore you. Let the cleansing fire of truth purge your soul of dross!'

For a moment she was silent. Then in a firm voice she answered:

'Yes, I will speak. I have kept silence too long. I have given myself to unimaginable evil, little knowing what I was doing until, as I thought, it was too late. But you give me new hope; perhaps it is not too late; perhaps something can yet be saved – and whether anything be saved or not, I can recover that integrity which I sold to save my father from misery. Little did I know, when Sir Theophilus, in honeyed tones, and with even more than his usual conjugal blandishments, invited me to use my pictorial talents in the creation of a monster, little did I know, I repeat, in that fateful moment, for what frightful purpose the picture was required. I did as I was bid. I made the monster. I allowed myself to be quoted as having seen it, but I did not then know the fell purpose for which my husband – oh, that I must still call him such—desired me to do this deed. Step by step, as his strange campaign has unfolded itself, my conscience has troubled me more and more. Every night on my knees I have besought God to forgive me, but I know He will not do so while I am yet lapped in the luxury with which Sir Theophilus delights to surround me. Until I am willing to abandon all this, my soul cannot be purged. Your coming has been the last straw. Your coming and your simple invocation of truth has shown me at last what I must do. I will tell you all. You shall know how base is the woman to whom you are speaking. No tiniest portion of my vast turpitude will I conceal from you. And when I have stripped myself bare, perhaps I can once more feel cleansed of the foul impurity that has invaded me.'

Having so said, she told him all. As she spoke, instead of the revulsion of horror which she had expected to witness, she saw in his eyes a growing admiration, and he felt in his heart a love to which he had hitherto been a stranger. When she had told all, he took her in his arms, and she yielded to his embrace.

'Ah, Millicent,' he said, 'how tangled and how dreadful is human life. All that Hogg-Paucus told me is true, and yet, at the very fount of this evil wickedness I find you, you who are still capable of feeling the pure flame of truth, you in whom, now that to your own ruin you have confessed all, I find a comrade, a spiritual comrade such as I did not believe the world to contain. But what to do in this strange tangle, I cannot yet decide. For twenty-four hours I must meditate. When that time has elapsed, I will come back and tell you my decision.'

When Shovelpenny returned to his apartment, he returned in a state of intellectual and emotional bewilderment, knowing neither what he felt nor what he thought. Hogg-Paucus lay on his bed, snoring in a drunken stupor. He had no wish for this man's cynicism, which he could not bring into harmony with his feelings about Millicent, whose beauty made it impossible for him to condemn her. He placed a large bottle of whisky and a glass beside Hogg-Paucus's bed, knowing that if, during the coming twenty-four hours, that worthy man should have a moment of wakefulness, the sight of the liquor would quickly overcome him, and he would return to oblivion. Having thus secured twenty-four hours without interruption, he sat down in his chair before his gas fire, and set to work to bring some kind of order into his mind.

Public and private duty alike were difficult to determine. The men who had made the plot were wicked men; their motives were vile, and they cared nothing whether mankind was the better or the worse for their activities. Private gain and private power were their sole aims. Lies, deception, and terror were their means. Could he, by his silence, make himself a party to such an infamy? And if he did not, if he persuaded Millicent to confess, as he well knew that he could, what would become of her? What would her husband do to her? What would her dupes throughout the world do to her? In imagination he saw her loveliness trampled in the dust and savage mobs tearing her to pieces. The vision was scarcely bearable, but yet, he thought, if that spark of nobility which was awakened in her while they spoke was not to be quenched anew, she must not go on living in the soft bed of profitable lies.

And so his thoughts turned to the other alternative. Should he allow Sir Theophilus and his accomplices to triumph? There were powerful arguments in favour of this course. Before the hatching of the plot, East and West had been on the verge of war, and it was thought by many that the human race would exterminate itself in futile fury. Now, from fear of a wholly imaginary danger, the real danger existed no longer. The Kremlin and the White House, united in hatred of the imaginary Martians, had become the best of friends. The armies of the world might still be mustered, but they were mustered against a foe that did not exist, and their ineffectual armaments could not do the damage for which they were intended. 'Perhaps,' so ran his meditations, 'perhaps it is only through lies that men can be induced to live sensibly. Perhaps human passions are such that to the end of time truth will be dangerous. Perhaps I have erred in giving my allegiance to truth. Perhaps Sir Theophilus is wiser than I. Perhaps it is folly in me to lead my beloved Millicent towards her ruin.'

And then his thoughts took another turn. 'Sooner or later,' so he said to himself, 'the deception will be discovered. If it is not discovered by those who, like myself, are actuated by love of truth, it will be discovered by those who have rival interests every bit as sinister as those of Sir Theophilus. What use will these men make of their discovery? They will use it only to exacerbate the revulsion against the Tellurian harmony that the lies of Sir

Theophilus have engendered. Is it not better, since, sooner or later, the whole plot must be unmasked, is it not better that it should be unmasked in the name of a noble ideal, the ideal of truth, rather than in the ignoble pursuit of competition and envy? But who am I to judge such matters? I am not God. I cannot read the future. It is all dark. Wherever I look, horror stares me in the face. I know not whether to support wicked men to good ends, or good men to the destruction of the world. For that is the dreadful dilemma with which I am confronted. It is too difficult for me.'

For twenty-four hours he sat immovable in his chair, neither eating nor drinking, swayed by the to-and-fro of conflicting arguments. At the end of that time his appointment with Lady Millicent called him. He rose wearily and stiffly, sighed deeply, and with heavy steps went on foot towards her mansion.

He found Lady Millicent as shattered as he was himself. She also had been torn by perplexity. But the world played less part in her thoughts than her husband and her now dearly loved Thomas. She had not the habit of political thinking. Her world was composed of persons, persons whose activities, she knew, had various effects outside the periphery of her consciousness; but these effects she could not hope to understand. What she could understand was the human passions of the men and women who made up her private world. Throughout the twenty-four hours she had meditated on the shining qualities of Thomas's disinterestedness, with a futile and desperate wish that it had been her good fortune to come across some person possessing this character before the coils of Sir Theophilus's machinations had inextricably entwined her. She had found one thing to do which had made the suspense of those hours just bearable. She had painted from memory a miniature of Thomas, and this miniature she had placed in a locket that in more frivolous times had contained the likeness of her husband. The locket she hung on a chain round her neck, and when the suspense became unendurable she sought relief in gazing upon the likeness of him whom she yearned to call her lover.

As last he was with her, but there was no buoyancy in his step, no brightness in his eye, no resonance in his voice. Dejected and slow, he took her hand in his. With his other hand he extracted from his pocket a pill which he quickly swallowed.

'Millicent,' he said, 'this pill which I have swallowed will in a few minutes cause me to breathe no more. The choice before me is too difficult. When I was a younger man I had hopes, high hopes. I thought that I should be able to dedicate my life to the twin gods of truth and humanity. Alas! it was not to be. Shall I serve truth and cause humanity to perish, or shall I serve humanity and let truth lie trampled in the dust? O dreadful alternative! How with such a choice before me can I bear to live? How can I draw my breath beneath the sun which must either look upon carnage or be darkened by a cloud of lies? Nay, it is impossible. You, Millicent, you, you are dear to me, you believe in me, you know how true my love is . . . and yet . . . and yet. . . . What can you do for a tortured soul in such a dilemma as mine? Alas, alas, not your gentle arms, not your lovely eyes, not anything that you can offer can console me for this sorrow. No. I must die. But as I die I leave to my successors this dreadful choice – the choice between truth and life. Which to choose I know not. Good-bye, good-bye dear Millicent. I go where riddles no longer torture the guilty soul. Good-bye. . . .'

For a moment he embraced her in a last delirium of passion. She felt his heart cease to beat, and fell prostrate in momentary immobility. When she came to, she snatched the locket from her slim neck. Opening it with delicate fingers she extracted the miniature from its nest. Embracing it passionately upon the lips she exclaimed:

'O thou great spirit, thou noble mind, though thou be dead, though these lips that I vainly kiss can speak no more, yet something of thee still lives. It lives in my breast. Through me, through poor little me, the message that thou wouldst give to man shall yet be given.'

Having spoken these words she lifted the receiver of the telephone and called the *Daily Thunder*.

VI

After a few days, during which Lady Millicent was protected by the *Daily Thunder* from the fury of her husband and his minions, her story won universal belief. Everybody suddenly plucked up courage, and confessed to having seen nothing whatever through the infra-redioscope. The Martian terror subsided as quickly as it had arisen. As it subsided, the East-West dissension revived, and soon developed into open war.

The embattled nations met on the great central plain. Aeroplanes darkened the sky. Atomic explosions to right and to left scattered destruction. Vast guns of new make let loose strange missiles that sought their targets unguided by human agency. Suddenly the din stilled. The planes sank to earth. The artillery ceased to fire. On the furthest outskirts of the battle, the journalists, who had been watching with that eagerness which belongs to their strange profession, noticed the sudden silence. They could not imagine to what this silence was due. But, taking their courage in their hands, they advanced towards what had been the battle. They found the troops dead where they had fought – dead, not by wounds inflicted by the enemy, but by some strange, new, and unknown death. They rushed to the telephones. They telephoned to their several capitals. In the capitals most widely removed from the field of battle, the stop-press got so far as to say, 'the battle has been stopped by. . . .' They got no further. When they reached this point, the compositors fell dead. The machines fell silent. Universal death spread throughout the world. The Martians *had* come.

EPILOGUE

By the Professor of Indoctrination in the Central Martian University

I have been commissioned by that great hero whom we all revere – I allude, of course, to Martin the Conqueror – to compose the above history of the last days of the human race. That great Martian, having observed here and there among his subjects a somewhat weak-kneed sentimentality as regards those mendacious bipeds whom his hosts so gallantly and so deservedly exterminated, decided in his wisdom that all the resources of erudition should be employed to portray with exact faithfulness the circumstances preceding his victorious campaign. For he is of opinion – and I am sure that every reader of the foregoing pages will agree with him – that it could not be a good thing to allow such creatures to continue to pollute our fair cosmos.

Could anyone imagine a more foul slander than to accuse us of heptapody? And how could the Tellurians be pardoned for describing that sweet smile with which we greet changing events as a fixed grin? And what are we to think of Governments which tolerate such creatures as Sir Theophilus? That love of power which led him to his enterprise is, with us, justly confined within the breast of King Martin. And what could anyone say in defence of that freedom of discussion which was shown in the debate of the United Nations? How much nobler is life on this our planet, where what is to be thought is determined by the word of the heroic Martin, and lesser men have only to obey!

The record which is here given is an authentic one. It has been pieced together with enormous labour from such fragments of newspapers and gramophone records as have survived the last Tellurian battle and the assault of our brave boys. Some may be surprised at the intimacy of some of the details that are here revealed, but it appeared that Sir Theophilus, without the knowledge of his wife, had installed a dictaphone in her boudoir, and it is from this that the last words of Mr Shovelpenny have been derived.

Every true Martian heart must breathe more freely now in the knowledge that these creatures are no more. And in that exultant thought we shall go on to wish deserved victory to our beloved King Martin in his projected expedition against the equally degraded inhabitants of Venus.

LONG LIVE KING MARTIN!

The Guardians of Parnassus

In our age of wars and rumours of wars there are many who look back with nostalgia to that period of apparently unshakable stability in which their grandfathers lived what now appears like a carefree life. But unshakable stability is not to be obtained without paying a price, and I am not sure that the price was always worth paying. My father, who was already an old man when I was born, used to relate stories of those days which some of us imagine to have been golden. One in particular among his stories has helped to reconcile me to my own time.

When I (he said) was an undergraduate at Oxbridge, now very many years ago, it was my practice to take long walks in the country lanes which formerly surrounded that once beautiful city. In the course of these walks, I was frequently passed by an elderly clergyman and his daughter on horseback. Something – I knew not what – made me take note of them. The old man had an emaciated face on which I seemed to see a settled misery and a strange kind of fear – not fear of this or that, but quintessential fear, fear *per se*. Even as they rode by, it was obvious that the father and daughter were devoted to each other. She seemed to be a girl of about nineteen, but her expression was not what one expects at that age. Her appearance was far from prepossessing, but what was much more noticeable was a look of fierce determination and all but despairing defiance. I could not but wonder whether she ever smiled, whether she was ever gay, whether she ever, even for one moment, forgot whatever it was that set such a mark of inflexible purpose upon her features. After I had met the pair repeatedly, I at last inquired who the elderly clergyman was. 'Oh, that,' said my interlocutor with a laugh, 'that's the Master of Dogs' (the Master of Dogs was not a Minoan deity, but the Head of the ancient College of St Cynicus, which undergraduates irreverently called 'Dogs'). I asked the meaning of the peculiar laugh with which this remark was accompanied. 'Do you mean to say,' said my friend, 'that you don't know the story of that old reprobate?' 'No,' I said, 'he has not the air of a criminal. What is he supposed to have done?' 'Oh, well,' said my informant, 'it's an old story now, but I'll tell it to you if you wish to hear it.' 'Yes,' I said, 'the man interests me, and so does his daughter, and I should like to know more about him.' The story I heard, which, as I afterwards learnt, was known to

177

all the inhabitants of Oxbridge, except the younger undergraduates, was as follows:

The Master, whose name was Mr Brown, was young in those long ago days when Fellows had to be in Orders and were not allowed to marry. He could with luck become Master, but if he was unable to achieve this his only hope of matrimony was to resign his fellowship and accept a College living, which, if a man had a family, usually involved considerable penury. The Master who preceded Mr Brown lived to a great age, and there was considerable speculation as to who would be his successor. Mr Brown and a certain Mr Jones were the two whose chances appeared best. Both were engaged to be married; each hoped that his marriage would be rendered possible by the old man's death and his own subsequent election. At last the old man died. Mr Brown and Mr Jones entered into a chivalrous undertaking that in the ballot for the next Master each would vote for the other. Mr Brown was elected by a majority of one. But when those who had voted for Mr Jones inquired into the matter they became persuaded that in spite of the compact Mr Brown had voted for himself, and that it was by this act that he had made himself Master of the College. There was no legal redress, but the Fellows of the College, including those who had previously supported Mr Brown, decided that he should be sent to Coventry. They made known the findings of their inquiry, with the result that no one in the University would speak to him. His wife equally, though there was no evidence of her complicity, was ostracised. They had one daughter, who grew up in gloom and silence and solitude. Her mother gradually faded away and at last died of some ailment which should have been trivial. The election had happened twenty years before the time at which I heard this story, and throughout these twenty years unbending rectitude had prolonged the implacable punishment.

I was young in those days, and had not that stern devotion to moral principles which enables men to inflict torture without compunction. The story shocked me, not because of the old man's sin, but because of the concerted cruelty of the whole Oxbridge community. I did not doubt the old man's guilt. No one had doubted it for twenty years, and I could not set myself up against such a consensus, but I thought that some pity might have been shown to the daughter if not to the father. I learnt on inquiry that some ineffectual attempts had been made to befriend the girl, but that she had utterly refused to know anyone who would not know her father. I brooded on this situation until it was in danger of undermining my ethical convictions. I came almost to doubt whether punishment of sin is the main duty of the virtuous man. However, a fortuitous circumstance cut short these ethical reflections and plunged me unexpectedly from the general into the particular.

I I

On one of my lonely walks I met a horse galloping madly, and a few steps further on I saw a female figure lying by the roadside. On approaching, I found that it was the daughter of the ostracised Master. I learnt afterwards that he had been kept at home by a slight indisposition, and she had insisted on taking her usual ride, though unaccompanied. By bad luck she had met Lord George Sanger's travelling circus with elephants pulling huge vans. The elephants were too much for the nerves of the horse, which had thrown the girl and bolted. I found her conscious, but in great pain and unable to move, as she had broken a leg. At first I was at a loss as to what to do, but presently a dog-cart passed and I induced the driver, who was going to Oxbridge, to get a hospital to send an ambulance. It was about an hour and a half till the ambulance came, and during that time I did what I could to make her comfortable and show sympathy. I also let her know that I was aware of who she was.

In spite of her father's excommunication, I called next day to inquire, and learnt from the maid that when her leg was mended she would be none the worse. After this I kept myself informed of her progress, and when she was sufficiently recovered to lie on a sofa I asked if I might see her. At first she sent a message of refusal through the maid, but when, by a note, I made it clear that I was prepared to know her father, she relented. My relations with him remained formal, and he never spoke to me of his troubles. But his daughter, who had at first been as shy as a wild bird, gradually got used to me and came to rely upon my sympathy. In time I came to know all that she and her father knew of the story.

Her father in youth – so she told me – had been gay and debonair, possibly even a little wild, but so full of fun and jollity that such escapades as were suspected were readily overlooked. He was deeply in love, and overjoyed when the election made it possible for him to marry his adored Mildred. The election occurred at the very end of the Summer Term, and the marriage took place a few weeks later. Nothing compelled his return to Oxbridge until the beginning of the Autumn Term, and the couple spent the summer months in unclouded bliss. Mildred had never seen Oxbridge, which he described in glowing terms, extolling not only the architecture but the (to him) delightful society. A long vista of happiness and pleasant activity lay before them in imagination. And by this time it had become clear that in due course a child was to be expected to complete the fulfilment of their hopes.

Confidently, on his first evening in Oxbridge, the Master went to Hall to occupy his proper place at the head of the High Table. To his amazement, nobody greeted him, nobody inquired about his vacation, not a single Fellow said anything welcoming about the bride. He made some remark to Mr A on his right, but Mr A was so deeply engaged in conversation with *his* right-hand neighbour that he seemed not to have heard the Master. The Master had a similar experience with Mr B on his left. After this, he was reduced to silence throughout the long dinner, while the Fellows talked and laughed with each other as if he did not exist. In spite of growing discomfort and dismay, he felt that the demands of ritual compelled him to preside over the port in the Common Room. But when he passed the port, his neighbour took it as if it had fallen from nowhere, and when it had made the round it was his neighbour, not he, who spoke across him to ask if it should make a second round. He began to doubt his own existence, and as soon as he could he went home to Mildred to be assured by her touch that he was flesh and blood and not an invisible ghost.

But no sooner had he begun to relate his strange experiences than the maid appeared with an envelope which, she said, had been dropped through the letter-box by some unknown person. Tearing open the envelope, he found inside it a long anonymous letter, obviously in a disguised hand. 'You have been judged,' it began, 'you have been judged and condemned. The law cannot touch you, but a great oath has been sworn that you shall nevertheless suffer for your sin, and that your suffering shall be as dire as any that the law inflicts upon those who outrage it.' The letter went on to relate all the damning evidence. It told of the initial reluctance of the Fellows, especially of the unsuccessful Mr Jones, to believe that one of their number could be guilty of so dastardly an action. It told also of the minute scrutiny which, in the end, had forced conviction upon them. And it ended with a passage of almost Biblical denunciation:

> Do not imagine that by any tergiversation you will be able to shake the evidence. Do not flatter yourself that by maudlin appeals for pity you will win pardon. So long as you remain Head of this College, no Fellow will speak one word to you beyond the barest necessities of College business. Your wife, you may pretend, should not share your punishment. But she usurps the place of the lady who, but for your treachery, would now be the happy bride of Mr Jones. So long as she continues to profit by your sin, she also must suffer retribution. With this reflection we leave you to the torments of a guilty conscience. We are
> your unwilling colleague,
> The Tribunal of the Just

When the Master had finished this letter, he was so stunned that he took no steps to prevent his wife from reading it. At last he pulled himself together, and turned a heavy gaze upon her. 'Mildred,' he said, 'do you believe this?' Rousing herself with an effort, she answered vehemently: 'Believe it? My dearest Peter, how could you imagine such a thing? I would not believe it though all the fiends of Hell, in the likeness of Fellows of this diabolical College, should swear that they knew it with the most absolute certainty.' 'Thank you for those brave words,' he said; 'so long as they express your thoughts, my life, however painful, will not be without a refuge where human warmth is to be found. And so long as you believe in me, I shall have courage to fight this foul slander. I will not resign, for that might seem like a confession of guilt. I will devote myself to discovering the truth, and some day, somehow, it will be discovered. But, O my Love, it is hardly to be borne that you, to whom I hoped to bring all happiness, must share the life of an outcast. I would beg you to leave me, but *that* I know you will not do. The future is dark, but perhaps courage and persistence, sustained by your love, may yet lead to a happy issue.'

The Master thought, at first, that it must be possible to find some way of clearing up the mystery. He wrote to all the Fellows, solemnly asserting his innocence and demanding an inquiry. Most of them took no notice. Mr Jones, who had been his rival, and seemed a shade less hostile than the others, replied that an inquiry had already been held: all had disclosed how they had voted, and without the Master's vote the numbers on both sides were even. It was impossible to escape the dreadful inference, and there could not be anything further to be discovered. The Master consulted lawyers and detectives, but in vain; all believed him guilty, and could suggest nothing that would diminish suspicion. Mrs Brown, equally with her husband, was avoided by everybody, even by those few friends of her unmarried days who happened to be living in Oxbridge. The birth of a daughter, which in other circumstances would have been a joy, only added a new tragic torment: how could parents in their situation make life tolerable for the child? In a mood of despair they christened her Catherine, because they feared that she would be broken on the wheel like St Catherine of Alexandria. They felt that it would be wanton cruelty to bring another child into this gloom. At that time and with their beliefs, this meant an end of physical relations between husband and wife. Love survived, but a love completely drained of joy.

No alleviation came with the passing years. Mrs Brown gradually withered and at last died. Catherine, since she never heard laughter, acquired, by the time she was five years old, the sedate and silent immobility of a woman of eighty. It was impossible to send her to school, because the other children would have persecuted her. She was educated by a series of foreign governesses, who arrived from abroad in ignorance of the peculiar circumstances, and invariably gave notice as soon as they discovered them. The facts could not be kept from the girl; she would have learnt them from servants if her parents had been silent. Her father, especially after his wife's death, lavished tenderness upon her, in a vain endeavour to compensate her in some measure for her social isolation. She in return gave him all that wealth of affection which, in a more normal childhood, is distributed among many. As she reached years of discretion, she became consumed by a burning passion to vindicate her father and make visible to all the world the inhuman cruelty of the sentence passed upon him by judges of whose injustice she felt no doubt. But father and daughter alike were helpless. Their affection for each other, in the narrow compass left by a hostile world, could not be warm and comforting; each was stabbed by awareness of the other's suffering, and each felt, though neither said, that the agony would be less unendurable without the spectacle of the other's misery.

This history became known to me bit by bit in the course of several visits to Catherine during her convalescence. I found myself quite unable to disbelieve her version, and at the same time quite unable to account for the evidence against her father. If her father was innocent, as she claimed, there was a mystery, pointing to something undiscovered. I would have investigated events at the time of the election if I could have thought of any way of bringing some hidden fact to light, but after so many years that seemed impossible. However, in the middle of my perplexities, the truth suddenly came to light, complete, astounding, and terrible.

III

Soon after Catherine's recovery became complete, her father died. This was no surprise, as the misery of his life had gradually worn him down. What was a surprise was the death a few days later of his bitterest enemy in the College, Dr Greatorex, the Professor of Pastoral Theology. The surprise became amazement when it was found that the death was a suicide and that the Professor had taken poison. He had been, all his life, an implacable enemy of sin and a firm pillar of rectitude. He was deeply admired by elderly maiden ladies whose virtue had become somewhat sour, and he was thought well of by all those eminent academic personages who had been untouched by the softening of moral codes which characterises our enfeebled age. His professorship, it was felt, served to keep alive in the University such standards as would cause parents to feel that their sons were in safe hands. In the days before the election to the Mastership he had been the most vehement opponent of Dr Brown and the most whole-hearted advocate of Mr Jones. When Dr Brown was declared elected, it was Dr Greatorex who first instigated an inquiry, and it was through his efforts that the Master's guilt came to be universally believed. When the Master died, no one supposed that Dr Greatorex would feel much grief. Still less could they have imagined that this man of blameless life would end his days by committing a mortal sin. He had, it is true, shocked even some of his admirers by a sermon which he preached in the College Chapel on the Sunday following the Master's death. He took for his text, 'Where their worm dieth not, and the fire is not quenched.' He pointed out that some careless readers of the Gospels have represented Our Lord as very ready to forgive sinners, and have even hinted that He perhaps did not teach their eternal damnation. The learned Professor pointed out that the text on which he was preaching occurs in St Mark's Gospel, and cannot be explained away in any honest attempt to understand the teaching of the Gospels. So far, his sermon could win approval; but what pained his hearers and seemed to them, in the circumstances, a failure in good taste, was the fact that the eternal punishment of sinners was to him a matter of satisfaction and, what was worse, that he obviously had the late Master in mind. Theology, it was felt, is all very well in its place, but it cannot supersede the demands of good taste. Everybody went away from the sermon somewhat chilled. Mr Jones, who had always been reluctant in the condemnation of his successful rival, decided to pay a visit to Professor Greatorex and to suggest to him that perhaps now the time for denunciation was passed. In the evening he knocked on the Professor's door, but received no answer. He knocked again, more loudly, and at last, seeing that the Professor's light was on, he feared that something might be amiss, and entered. The Professor was sitting at his desk, dead, with a bulky manuscript before him addressed to the Coroner. Mr Jones himself did not think fit to read this manuscript, but handed it to the police, who caused it to be read at the inquest. In this statement Professor Greatorex said:

'My life's work is nearly complete. It remains only to tell the world what it was, and in what manner I was an instrument in the punishment of sin. Brown and I were friends in youth. He was in those days bolder and more adventurous that I. We both intended to take Orders and to adopt an academic career, but in the meanwhile we permitted ourself some of those enjoyments which, after Ordination, might be thought unseemly. There was a certain tobacconist with whom we both dealt, and this tobacconist had a lovely daughter named Muriel, who sometimes served in the shop. She had bright eyes, mischievous and inviting. She was sprightly in *badinage* with undergraduates, but I felt that behind the façade there was a person of great feeling and capacity for profound affection. I fell deeply in love with her, but I knew that marriage was incompatible with an academic career, and that marriage to a tradesman's daughter would be a black mark against me in any other career for which I was fitted. I was then, as I have been throughout my life, inflexibly determined to abstain from carnal sin, and I never for a moment contemplated the possibility of an immoral relation with Muriel. But Brown had no such scruples. While I hesitated, torn between ambition and love, Brown acted. By his carefree gaiety he won the poor girl's heart and led her by his wiles into sin. I alone knew of this, and the torments that I suffered in the spectacle of Muriel's ruin are beyond the power of language to depict. I expostulated with Brown, but in vain. Muriel, aware of my knowledge of her guilty secret, cajoled me into a vow of silence. After some months, she disappeared. I did not know what had happened to her, but I darkly suspected that Brown did not share my

183

ignorance. In this, however, I was mistaken. After a period of agonising unhappiness, I received a letter from her, written from a miserable lodging in a slum, confessing that she was pregnant, that she loved Brown too much to embarrass him, and that she had therefore not let him know of her condition or her whereabouts. Reminding me of my vow of secrecy, she asked if I could help her until the birth of her child, which was imminent. I visited her and found her in desperate penury, not having dared to make confession to her father, whose morals were as stern as my own. Fortunately this was during the vacation, and I was able to be absent from Oxbridge without exciting comment. I gave her assistance, and when her time came I secured for her a bed in a hospital. She and the child both died. I repented vainly my former prudence. My vow, which she had induced me to renew, made it impossible to reveal Brown's infamy. What had become of her he never knew, and I am convinced that he never cared.

'Although I could not expose him, I determined to devote my life to punishing him in whatever way circumstances might make possible. In the contest for the Mastership, I found my opportunity. I was the most vehement supporter of Mr Jones, and I could have secured his election. But Brown would have survived the disappointment, and his suffering would have been in no degree commensurate with Muriel's. I suddenly conceived a more subtle vengeance. In the ballot, I voted for Brown. Nobody had for a moment imagined that this could happen, and in the scrutiny it was accepted, and with little prompting from me, that my vote had gone to Jones. As I had foreseen, Brown's election appeared to have resulted from his voting for himself. I did not abstain from such words as would inflame feeling against him. Everything worked as I had planned, and his years of anguish began, an anguish which, I am happy to think, was much longer and much more bitter than any that Muriel had had to endure. I watched the roses fade from his wife's cheeks, I saw her sink into listless despair, and I thought with joy, "Muriel, you are avenged." I had a daguerreotype of Brown, made when he was young and jolly. Every evening before saying my prayers I took out this daguerreotype and gloated over the change made by Brown's sunken cheeks and haunted eyes. In later years, I watched with glee the poison of isolation filling his love for his daughter with unhealthy morbidness. His misery made my life; and, in comparison, nothing else was important to me. In comparison with the magnitude of my hate, the little emotions of my colleagues have seemed trivial. I have not known the joys of love, but I have known the joys of hate; and who shall say which are the greater? But now my enemy is dead, and I have nothing left to live for on earth. Faith, however, supplies me with a hope. I shall perish by my own hand, and shall therefore spend eternity in Hell. There I shall hope to find Brown, and, if there is justice in Hell, ways will be vouchsafed to me of increasing the horror of his everlasting torments. In this hope I die.'

Benefit of Clergy

Penelope Colquhoun climbed slowly up the stairs and sank wearily into an uncomfortable wicker chair in her tiny sitting-room. 'Oh, I am bored, I am bored, I am bored,' she said out loud with a deep sigh.

It must be confessed that she had reason for this feeling. Her father was the vicar of a remote parish in rural Suffolk, the name of which was Quycombe Magna. The village consisted of the church, the vicarage, a post office, a public house, ten cottages, and – its only redeeming feature – a fine old Manor House. Its only connection with the outer world at that time, some fifty years since, was a bus which ran three times a week to Quycombe Parva, a much larger village, with a railway station from which (it was said) persons of sufficient longevity might hope to reach Liverpool Street.

Penelope's father, who had been for five years a widower, was of a type now nearly extinct, low-church, bigoted, and opposed to every kind of enjoyment. His wife had been all that, in his opinion, a wife should be: submissive, patient, and indefatigable in parish work. He took it for granted that Penelope would follow unquestioningly in the footsteps of her sainted mother. Having no alternative, she did her best. She decorated the church for Christmas and the Harvest Festival; she presided over the Mothers' Meeting; she visited old women and inquired about their ailments; she scolded the verger if he neglected his duties. No chink of pleasure was allowed to lighten her routine. The vicar frowned upon adornment of the female person. She wore always woollen stockings and a severe coat and skirt, presumably new once, but now shabby. Her hair was pulled tightly back from the forehead. No kind of ornament had ever been imagined, since her father would have thought it the inevitable gateway to Hell. Except for a charwoman for two hours in the mornings, she had no domestic help, and had to do the cooking and housework in addition to the parish duties normally performed by vicars' wives.

She had, on occasion, made ineffectual efforts to achieve a little liberty; but in vain. Her father was always able to cite a text proving conclusively that her demands were wicked. He was particularly fond of Ecclesiasticus, which, as he was wont to point out, could be cited for edification though not for doctrine. Once, shortly after her mother's death, an itinerant fair came to Quycombe Magna and she asked if she might be allowed to see it. He replied, 'Whoso taketh pleasure in wickedness shall be condemned: but

185

he that resisteth pleasure crowneth his life.' Once it was discovered that she had exchanged a few words with a passing cyclist who had asked the way to Ipswich. Her father was deeply shocked and said: 'She that is bold dishonoureth both her father and her husband, but they both shall despise her.' When she protested that the conversation had been harmless, he said that unless she reformed he would not allow her to go about the village alone, and reinforced the threat by the text: 'If thy daughter be shameless, keep her in straitly, lest she abuse herself through over much liberty.' She was fond of music and would have liked to have a piano, but her father considered this unnecessary, saying, 'Wine and music will rejoice the heart, but the love of wisdom is above them both.' He was never tired of explaining how much anxiety he had on her account. He would say, 'The father waketh for the daughter, when no man knoweth, and the care for her taketh away sleep. . . . For from garments cometh a moth, and from women wickedness.'

The five years that followed her mother's death had driven Penelope to the very verge of what she could endure. At last, when she reached the age of twenty, a tiny crack opened in her prison walls. The Manor House, which had stood empty for some years, was again inhabited by the lady of the Manor, Mrs Menteith. She was American and well-to-do. Her husband, who could not endure vegetating in East Anglia, had gone out to Ceylon. She had returned from Ceylon to find schools for her sons and to see about letting the Manor House. The vicar could not wholly approve of her, as she was gay and well-dressed, and what he would consider worldly. But, as the Manor House contributed by far the largest subscription to church expenses, he found a text in Ecclesiasticus about the unwisdom of offending the rich, and did not forbid his daughter to know the lively lady.

No sooner had Penelope finished sighing over her boredom than she heard a knock on the old-fashioned knocker on the front door of the vicarage, and on going down she found Mrs Menteith on the doorstep. A few sympathetic words brought an outburst from Penelope which touched Mrs Menteith's heart. Looking at the girl with the eye of a connoisseur, she perceived possibilities that neither the girl herself nor anybody in the parish had suspected. 'My dear,' she said, 'do you realise that if you were free to take a little trouble, you could be a raving beauty?' 'Oh, Mrs Menteith,' said the girl, 'surely you are joking!' 'No,' said the lady, 'I am not. And, if we can outwit your father, I will prove it.' After some further conversation, they hatched a plot. At this moment Mr Colquhoun came in and Mrs Menteith said, 'Dear Mr Colquhoun, I wonder if you could spare your daughter to me for just one day. I have a lot of tiresome business to do in Ipswich and I shall find the time intolerably tedious if I have to be alone. You will be doing me a great kindness, if you allow your daughter to accompany me in my car.' Somewhat reluctantly and after some further blandishment, the vicar consented. The great day came, and Penelope could hardly contain herself for excitement. 'Your father,' said Mrs Menteith, 'is an old horror, and I am thinking out a scheme by which in time you may be liberated from his tyranny. When we get to Ipswich I will dress you from head to foot in the most becoming clothes that I can find there. I will have your hair done as it should be done. I think the result will surprise you.' It certainly did. When Penelope saw herself dressed to satisfy Mrs Menteith, she looked in the long mirror and thought, 'Is this really me?' She became completely lost in a daze of nascent vanity. A whole flood of new emotions crowded in upon her. New hopes and undreamt of possibilities made her determine to be done with the life of a drudge. But the manner of escape still remained an unsolved problem.

While she was still brooding, Mrs Menteith took her to the beauty parlour to have her hair done. She had to wait some time, and her eye fell upon a copy of *The Matrimonial News*. 'Mrs Menteith,' she said, 'you are doing so much for me that I hesitate to ask one further favour – What will be the use of looking beautiful if nobody ever sees me? And at Quycombe Magna, no young men are to be seen from one year's end to another. Will you allow me to put an advertisement in *The Matrimonial News* giving the Manor House as my address, and interviewing there any applicant who seems worth seeing?' Mrs Menteith, who by this time was thoroughly enjoying the fun, agreed. And Penelope, with her help, drew up the following advertisement:

> Young woman, of great beauty and impeccable virtue, but isolated in remote country district, wishes to meet young man with a view to matrimony. Applicants to enclose photograph and, if viewed favourably, young woman's photograph will be sent in return. Reply: Miss P., Manor House, Quycombe Magna. P.S. – No clergy need apply.

Having dispatched this advertisement, she underwent the ministrations of the beauty parlour and was then photographed in all her splendour. For the moment, this ended the dream of glory. She had to take off all her fine clothes and brush her hair back into its previous straight severity. But the fine clothes went back with Mrs Menteith to the Manor House with the promise that she should wear them in interviewing applicants.

When she got home, she put on a weary expression, and told her father how bored she'd been while waiting in the ante-rooms of solicitors and house agents. 'Penelope,' said her father, 'you were doing a kindness to Mrs Menteith, and the virtuous are never bored when doing a kindness.' She accepted this observation with becoming meekness, and prepared herself to wait with what patience she could command for such replies as her advertisement might bring forth.

I I

The replies to Penelope's advertisement were many and various. Some were earnest, some facetious; some explained that the writer was rich, or else that he was so clever that he soon would be rich; some, it was possible to suspect, hoped that matrimony might be avoided; some emphasised their good nature, others their powers of domination. Penelope, whenever she could, went to the Manor House to collect the answers. But there was only one among them all that she felt to be promising:

Dear Miss P.,

Your advertisement intrigues me. Few women would have the nerve to claim great beauty, and only a small proportion of these would at the same time claim impeccable virtue. I am trying to reconcile this with your aversion from the clerical profession, which permits the glimmer of a hope that your virtue is not more impeccable than becomes a young woman. I am consumed with curiosity, and, if you give me a chance to gratify it, you will increase my felicity.

Yours expectantly,

PHILIP ARLINGTON

P.S. – I enclose my photograph.

This letter intrigued her. The writer's complete silence as to his own merits made her suppose them so great that he could take them for granted. In the photograph, he looked lively and intelligent, with a considerable sense of fun and a not unpleasing dash of roguery. To him alone she replied, enclosing a photograph of herself in all her finery and suggesting a day on which she could meet him for lunch at the Manor House. He accepted. The day came.

The Manor House and Mrs Menteith's presence at lunch gave a favourable impression of Penelope's respectability and social status. After lunch they were left alone to make each other's acquaintance. He began by observing that in the matter of beauty her advertisement had claimed no more than the truth, and he expressed surprise that she had resorted to such a medium in the search for a husband, which (so he was pleased to say) should have been all too easy. This led her to explain her domestic circumstances, including the grounds of her objection to the clergy. With every moment she found his half-humorous sympathy more agreeable, and became more convinced that life as his wife would be in all respects the opposite of life as her father's daughter.

At the end of two hours' *tête-à-tête*, she was already in love with him and, so far as she could judge, he was by no means indifferent to her. She then broached the problem which had been troubling her. 'I am,' she said, 'only twenty years of age and cannot yet marry without my father's consent. He will never consent to my marrying a man who is not in Orders. Do you think that when I introduce you to him, you could convincingly pose as a clergyman?' At this question, a queer twinkle appeared in his eyes, which she found somewhat puzzling, but he replied reassuringly, 'Yes, I think I can manage that.' She was delighted to have him as a partner in the hoodwinking of her father, and felt more at one with him than ever. She spoke of him to her father as a friend of Mrs Menteith's whom she had happened to meet at the Manor House. Her father was naturally upset at the thought of losing a domestic drudge who demanded no wages, but Mrs Menteith backed up Penelope in glowing accounts of the young man's exemplary piety and of the chances of future preferment which he owed to several episcopal patrons. At last the old man reluctantly consented to inspect this paragon, and to permit the engagement if the inspection proved satisfactory. Penelope was in tenterhooks for fear her dear Philip should make some slip which would enable her father to discover the deception. But, to her bewildered joy, everything went off without a hitch. The young man spoke of the parish in which he was curate, described his vicar, mentioned that he had taken Orders because of the family living in which the present incumbent was ninety years of age, and wound up with a glowing peroration about the importance and sacredness of the work to which he hoped to dedicate his life. Penelope secretly gasped, but observed with amusement that her father's opinion of Philip grew with leaps and bounds, reaching its acme when the young man actually quoted Ecclesiasticus.

All the difficulties being thus smoothed away, the marriage took place in a few weeks. They went to Paris for their honeymoon, she explaining that she had had enough of the country and, when pleasure was the object, preferred populous gaiety to the beauties of nature. The honeymoon was to her one long dream of delight. Her husband was invariably charming and never objected to the many forms of frivolity which her abstemious years had compelled her hitherto to repress. There was only one cloud on the horizon. He was very reticent about himself, but explained that for financial reasons he was compelled to live in the village of Poppleton in Somerset. And from his talk about the neighbouring grand house, inhabited by Sir Rostrevor and Lady Kenyon, she supposed that he must be their agent. But, although she wondered at times that he was not more explicit, every moment of the honeymoon was so filled with pleasure that she had little time to brood on the matter. He explained that he must reach Poppleton on a certain Saturday. They arrived very late at The Rye House where he lived. It was too dark and she was too weary to wish for anything but sleep at the moment. He led her upstairs, and she fell asleep as soon as her head touched the pillow.

III

She awoke next morning to the sound of church bells and to the sight of her husband putting on clerical attire. This sight made her instantly wide awake. 'What *are* you putting on those clothes for!' she exclaimed. 'Well, my dear,' he replied with a smile, 'the time has come to make a little confession. When I first saw your advertisement I felt nothing but curiosity, and it was only for fun that I suggested an interview. But, as soon as I saw you, I loved you. And every moment at the Manor House deepened this feeling. I determined to win you and, since this was impossible by fair means, I used foul ones. I can no longer conceal from you that I am a curate in this parish. That I have basely deceived you is true. My only excuse is the greatness of my love, which could not have won you in any other way.'

At this she leapt from her bed, exclaiming, 'I shall never forgive you! Never! Never! Never! But I will make you repent. I will make you rue the day that you treated a poor girl in this infamous manner. I will make you, and as many as possible of your clerical accomplices, as much of a laughing stock as you have made me.' By this time he was fully dressed. She pushed him out of the door, locked it, and remained in solitary dudgeon throughout the rest of the day.

He gave no sign of his presence until supper time, when he knocked on her door with a tray saying, 'If you're going to punish me, you must keep alive; and if you're to keep alive, you must eat. So here's a tray. But you needn't speak to me. I'll put it on the floor and go away. *Bon appétit!'* At first she wanted to be proud, but she had had no breakfast and no lunch and no tea. And at last hunger overcame her, and she devoured everything on the tray. Nevertheless, she did not abandon her scheme of revenge.

Refreshed by her supper, she spent the evening composing a dignified letter to him, outlining a *modus vivendi* for the immediate future. She took great pains with this letter, and made several drafts of it. But in the end she was satisfied. In the final draft she said:

Sir,

You will, of course, realise that, in view of your infamous behaviour, I shall never again speak an unnecessary word to you. I shall not tell the world what you have done to me, for that would be to lay bare my own folly; but I shall make it clear to all the world that I do not love you, that you were infatuated, and that any other man would do as well. I shall delight in causing scandal because it will reflect on your judgement. And if, in doing so, I can bring clerics into disrepute, my pleasure will be enhanced. My only aim in life, henceforth, will be to inflict upon you a humiliation as profound as that which you have inflicted upon me. Your wife, henceforth in name only,

PENELOPE

She put the letter on the supper tray, and put the supper tray outside her door.

Next morning another tray appeared, containing not only a delicious breakfast, but also a note. At first she thought she would tear it into little pieces and throw the little pieces out of the window. But she could not resist the hope that he would be overwhelmed with sorrow and shame, and would make such apology as the circumstances allowed. She tore open the letter and read:

Bravo, dearest Penelope! Your letter is a masterpiece in dignified reproach. I doubt if I could have improved it if you had asked my advice. But as for revenge, my dear, we shall see. It may not work out quite as you are thinking. Still your clerical admirer,

PHILIP

P.S. – Don't forget the garden party.

The garden party in question, of which Philip had spoken during the honeymoon, was to be given that day by Sir Rostrevor and Lady Kenyon at their lovely Elizabethan mansion Mendip Place. The date had been fixed partly with a view to introducing the bride to the country. For some time she hesitated as to whether she should go, her husband's postscript inclining her towards the negative. But after some deliberation she decided that the party would afford her an opportunity of inaugurating her revenge. She dressed with the utmost care. Indignation lent a sparkle to her looks, which made them even more irresistible than usual. She decided that it would further her ends to conceal her quarrel with her husband, and they arrived together with the utmost correctness. Her beauty was so dazzling that all the men who saw her forgot everything else. She, however, put on a demure and simple demeanour, and, ignoring the grand people who sought introductions to her, devoted her attentions almost exclusively to the vicar. The vicar, whose name was Mr Reverdy, was a man of young middle age, and Penelope discovered within a few minutes that he had a passion for local archaeology. He told her with great earnestness that there was in the neighbourhood a Long Barrow probably full of the most valuable prehistoric relics, but that he alone was interested in it, and no one could be induced to dig it up. She looked at him with great eyes and said, 'Oh, Mr Reverdy, what a shame!' He was so impressed that he congratulated his curate upon having found such a perfect soul-mate.

He managed to persuade Penelope (though, as he supposed, with some difficulty) to go next day in his carriage to view certain interesting archaeological remains at a distance of about ten miles from Poppleton. They were seen driving together through the village, he in very earnest conversation and she with an air of rapt attention. They were, of course, seen by everybody. But especially by a certain old lady named Mrs Quigley, who made the purveying of gossip her business. Mrs Quigley had a daughter whom she had destined for dear Mr Arlington, and she began to see reason to doubt the wisdom of his neglect of this excellent spinster. As the vicar and Penelope drove by, Mrs Quigley said, 'Humph!' And all those who heard her understood the meaning of this monosyllable. But worse was to follow. The next morning, at a moment when Mr Arlington was known to be occupied with parish duties, the vicar was seen marching up to The Rye House, carrying a large tome on the archaeology of Somerset. And he was observed to stay for a considerably longer time than the mere delivery of the volume would require. Backstairs gossip revealed to Mrs Quigley, and therefore to the whole village, that the newly married couple occupied separate rooms.

The poor vicar, meanwhile, not yet aware of Mrs Quigley's activities, babbled to everybody about the beauty, intelligence, and virtue of his curate's wife. And with every word that he uttered, he increased the gravamen of the charges against himself as well as her. At last Mrs Quigley could bear it no longer and felt it her duty to write to Mr Glasshouse, the Rural Dean, suggesting that for the sake of the dear vicar it would be well if a cure could be found elsewhere for the curate. Mr Glasshouse, who knew Mrs Quigley, was not inclined to take the matter very seriously, and thought that a word in season to the vicar was all that would be necessary. He visited the vicar, who assured him that nothing in the world could be more innocent than the few dealings that he had had with Mrs Arlington. He, however, praised her innocence somewhat more warmly than the Rural Dean thought quite fitting. And Mr Glasshouse decided to view the lady for himself.

He arrived at The Rye House at tea-time, and was warmly welcomed by Penelope, who was beginning to get a little tired of archaeology and the vicar. It must, however, be confessed that when Mr Glasshouse, with great delicacy, approached the subject of the scandalous rumours retailed to him by Mrs Quigley, Penelope, though she denied everything, did it in such a manner as to convince Mr Glasshouse that the vicar had been at least indiscreet. Mr Glasshouse by this time had confessed that archaeology was too much concerned with the dead past to suit his taste, and that for his part he preferred life to dead stones. 'Oh, Mr Glasshouse,' she replied, 'how right you are, and how wholly I agree with you. Do tell me, dear Dean, what forms of life particularly interest you.' 'Rare birds,' he replied, 'especially those that frequent the fens of Sedgemoor, where not only are kingfishers common, but even yellow water-wagtails reward the patient watcher.' Clasping her hands together, and looking up at him enthusiastically, she explained that in spite of living in the neighbourhood of the Norfolk fens, and in spite of many journeys of exploration, she had never yet been gratified in her longing to see a yellow water-wagtail.

The Rural Dean, sad as it is to relate, forgot his mission, forgot his duty to the diocese, forgot his sacred calling, and invited her to join him in watching for the yellow water-wagtail in a lonely spot that he knew to be one of its favourite haunts. 'Oh, Mr Dean,' she replied, 'what *will* Mrs Quigley say?' He did his best to put on the airs of the man of the world, and brushed aside that virtuous matron as a woman of no account. Before he could finish the second cup of tea, Penelope had yielded to his vehemence and agreed to join him in an expedition on the first fine day. They went. But, lonely as the spot was, Mrs Quigley's spies were at work. Before long she knew the worst, and more. Seeing that the Church had failed her, she attempted to secure the help of Lady Kenyon, assuring her that from the reports she had received it was not only birds that the Rural Dean had observed. 'I will not say more,' she added, 'for that is too easy to imagine. Can you, dear Lady, exorcise this Siren who is turning from the path of duty even the most staid and highly respected of our religious mentors?' Lady Kenyon replied that she would think it over and see what she could do. Knowing Mrs Quigley, she thought that it might be wise to get a more first-hand report as to the facts, so she called on Penelope and asked what all the fuss was about.

After a little coaxing, she got the whole story out of Penelope. But, instead of taking the story tragically, Lady Kenyon merely laughed. 'Oh, my dear girl,' she said, 'what you're doing is really too easy. How can you expect these stuffy old men to resist you? Why, they've never seen a really beautiful woman in their lives until they saw you. . . .' 'Except yourself,' interjected Penelope. But Lady Kenyon ignored the interjection, and went on as if Penelope had not spoken. 'No, my dear, if your revenge is to be worth anything, it must be practised on someone worthy of your mettle. The Bishop of Glastonbury, whose clergy you have been leading along the primrose path, is worthy of your steel. I should not wonder if in him you were to meet your match. I will arrange a tournament between you and him, and I myself will "rain influence and judge the prize" – with complete impartiality I assure you, for, though I greatly admire the Bishop, I cannot but enjoy your adventurous spirit.'

IV

The Bishop of Glastonbury was a man of considerable scholastic eminence, which had enabled him to rise in the clerical profession in spite of what some considered a regrettable frivolity. Although no real scandal had ever been fastened upon him, he was known to be fond of the society of charming ladies and not always wholly serious in his converse with them. Lady

Kenyon, who knew him well, told him all that she had gathered about Penelope and the havoc that she was wreaking on his clergy. 'The girl,' she said, 'is not really bad, but only very angry. And it must be admitted that she has cause for anger. I was unable to exert a good influence upon her, partly, I think, because her story amused me and I could not find it in my heart to scold her. But you, my dear Bishop, will, I am convinced, succeed where I have failed. If you are willing, I will get her to meet you here, and we shall see what we shall see.'

The Bishop agreed; and Penelope was duly invited to meet him at Mendip Place. Recent experience had given her confidence, and she did not doubt that she would be able to turn the Bishop round her little finger. She duly told him her tale, but was somewhat disconcerted by the fact that he smiled at the most pathetic parts. And when she looked up at him with adoring eyes, such as no vicar or Rural Dean could resist, to her horror he merely winked. The wink made her change her tone, and she became simple and sincere. The Bishop elicited from her that, in spite of furious anger, she still loved Philip, but pride would not allow her to admit it to him. 'My dear,' said the Bishop, who was treating her affectionately but not seriously, 'I don't think your present course is likely to bring you much satisfaction. The world is full of silly men ready to fall in love with you, but you cannot love a silly man. And no man who is not silly can fail to see that your husband holds your heart. He has, of course, played an all but unforgivable trick upon you, and I do not suggest that you should behave as if nothing had happened. But I think that if you are ever to achieve any happiness, you must find something better to do than bemusing foolish parsons. What you should do is for you to decide, but it should be something more positive and satisfying than revenge.' With that he patted her hand and said, 'Think it over, my dear, and in due course let me know your decision.'

She went home somewhat deflated, and realising for the first time that a noble wrath is in the long run an unsatisfying diet. There were difficult practical decisions to be made if she altered her way of life. She was not prepared to surrender to the point of becoming the submissive wife of a country curate, still less was she prepared to go back to her father. She must therefore find some way of earning a living. In a long letter to Mrs Menteith, she related what had happened to her since her marriage, ending with the Bishop's friendly admonition.

'From you,' she ended, 'I have had so much kindness that I hesitate to ask even more. But I feel that perhaps you could help me to find my feet. Would you be willing to meet me in London to talk things over?'

They met and, in consequence, Mrs Menteith persuaded her own dressmaker to take on Penelope as a mannequin. When she moved to London, she ceased to have any communication with her husband. Poppleton forgot her. And no one missed her except Mrs Quigley – and possibly her husband, though his feelings were never expressed. Her beauty made her an asset to the dressmaker, and it was gradually discovered that she had great talent as a dress designer. She rose rapidly, and within three years was earning a very comfortable salary. She was about to be taken into partnership, when she received a doleful letter from her father saying that he was very unwell and feared he was dying:

'You have behaved very ill,' he said, 'both to me and to your worthy husband. But I wish all ill-feeling to end before I die, and for this reason I shall be glad if you will return for however brief a space to your old home.

'In all Christian love,

YOUR FATHER'

With a heavy heart she went to Liverpool Street. As she was looking for a seat, she saw – but could it be? – her husband, not in clerical dress, looking very prosperous and about to get into a first-class carriage. For a moment they stared at each other. Then she exclaimed, 'Philip!' And at the very same moment he exclaimed, 'Penelope!' 'My dear, you are lovelier than ever,' he said. 'Philip,' she replied, 'what has become of those clothes that caused our rupture?' 'They are left to the care of moth-balls,' he replied. 'I discovered that I have talent as an inventor, so I gave up the Church. I have a very good income, and am on my way to visit the Cambridge Scientific Instrument Makers about a new patent. But how about you? You don't look exactly poverty-stricken.' 'No,' she said, 'I, too, have prospered.' And she related her successful career. 'I always thought you were no fool,' he said. 'And I always thought you were a knave,' she replied, 'but now I no longer mind.' With that they fell into each other's arms on the platform. 'Jump in, Sir and Madam,' said the guard. And they lived happy ever after.

The Right Will Prevail or
The Road to Lhasa

Have we eaten on
  the Insane Root
that takes the reason
  prisoner?

I

I had decided that Westminster Bridge was the best place from which to
end it all. It was a dark November evening with a penetrating drizzle and
a cold fog. The pavement was covered with a film of slimy mud, and
looking down from the bridge I could not see the river. The water will be
very cold, I thought with a shiver of fear. But then another thought came
to me: if earth hath not anything to show more fair, there is not much
point in staying on such a dismal planet. Nerved by this thought, I climbed
upon the parapet. But while I was summoning the necessary last ounce
of resolution, a firm hand seized my collar, and a quietly determined voice
said, 'Oh no, that's not really necessary.' I turned in a fury, although
beneath the fury the instinct of survival brought a surprising surge of relief.
I saw before me a tall and massive gentleman of rather foreign appearance,
wrapped in a very opulent fur coat. 'My friend,' he said, 'I saw what you
were about to do. But I make it my mission, whenever I can, to prevent
useless tragedy and to offer to the despairing new hopes of happiness. Come
with me; tell me your troubles; and I shall be much surprised if I cannot
alleviate them.'

With a submissiveness that surprised me, although he took it for granted,
I obeyed his suggestion. He hailed a passing taxi and gave an address on
Campden Hill. Throughout the drive neither of us spoke a word. The
house, when we reached it, was large and isolated and surrounded by a
garden. He took me into his study, a vast room lined with books and warmed
by a blazing fire. He set me down in a very comfortable chair, gave me a
cigar and supplied me with a generous whisky and soda. I had arrived
shivering with cold and despair, but when the fire and the whisky had
begun to warm me, he turned to me with a smile and said, 'Now, I think,
the time has come for you to tell me your troubles.' The whisky, the cigar,
and the warmth, combined with the relief from intolerable tension, broke

down my defences, and I found myself telling everything to this total stranger as unreservedly as if he had been my father-confessor.

It was a miserable and discreditable story. My father is rich and universally respected. I had been a Civil Servant, not without ability, and having before me every prospect of a successful, if not distinguished, career. But, unfortunately for me, I met that unbelievably beautiful lady, Arabella Mainwaring. From the first moment of my seeing her, she dominated my waking thoughts and haunted all my dreams. I forgot my work, I forgot my friends, I forgot the importance of retaining my father's good opinion, and thought only of how I might win Arabella's favours – not her heart, for I knew that she had none. In spite of many generations of honourable ancestors, she cared for nothing but money and luxury. For these she had a craving which was almost insane, and it was only as a means of satisfying this craving that she valued her physical attractions. All this I knew, and it should have made me despise her; but it did not. I soon discovered that it was only necessary to spend money upon her in order to secure a temporary semblance of love. I spent my savings. I gambled dishonestly, and with my winnings purchased an exquisite ruby pendant which secured me a night of bliss. The fact that I had cheated at cards was discovered, and in desperation I forged a cheque on my father's account. When this came to his knowledge, he refused to shield me from prosecution. Arabella, as was to be expected, coldly taunted me with my folly. It was from this situation that I had seen no escape except by suicide.

II

When I had finished my confession, I turned a despairing look upon my host and said, 'I think you will admit that my position is one in which hope is impossible!' 'Nonsense, my dear Sir,' he replied, 'I can put it all right. My hobby is preventing suicide. All shall be well if you will work for me.' 'What work do you require?' I asked. 'Only a little research,' he replied. With tears in my eyes, I grasped his hand and thanked him. 'Oh, my dear Sir,' he said, 'it is nothing to make a fuss about. Every man has his little hobby, and I have mine.' I asked him what I was to do. 'The first step,' he said, 'is isolation in my house with a view to disguise. During the period of isolation, you shall grow a beard, have your bushy eyebrows plucked, and wear heavy horn-rimmed spectacles. For public purposes, you shall have a new name, and I will supply you with a passport capable of passing the severest scrutiny of the immigration officials. While your beard is growing, you shall live in my house, and I will instruct you as to the part you are to play in return for my protection.'

Throughout the ensuing month, my initiation continued. I learnt that my host's name was Aguinaldo Garcinacia, that he was a native of the small republic of San Ysidro in the foot-hills of the Andes, that he was distressed by the spread of subversive ideas and believed that only rigid adherence to tradition could preserve the human race from disaster. He had, therefore, founded a fraternity which he called *The League of the Fight for the Right.* He explained that he meant Right as opposed to Left, not right as opposed to wrong. He said that he had seven immediate subordinates who dined with him every Saturday night to consider the strategy of the campaign. His aims, so he assured me, were noble and public-spirited, and not even the most tender conscience need hesitate to assist him. My conscience, as he knew from my confession, is not one of the most tender; and, as the alternative to his proposal was ruin and prison, I did not hesitate to enrol myself as his disciple.

The month of seclusion, while my beard was growing, would have been tedious but for the gradual process of initiation to which Aguinaldo subjected me. At first, I had been inclined to regard his projects as those of a fantastic visionary, but gradually, as he told me more and more of the sources of his power, I realised that his success was not impossible. In the small village which was his birth-place – so he informed me – there grows a herb which has a very peculiar property: when eaten in small quantities, it produces extreme indiscretion in which even the most profound secrets are confessed; in larger doses, it produces permanent insanity; and in still larger doses, death. The herb grows nowhere else. The villagers, in the course of many generations, have become immune to its deleterious properties. They were, in fact, totally unaware of these properties, as strangers hardly ever penetrated to their remote fastness. Once, however, when Aguinaldo was still a young man, a Bolivian official with a staff of surveyors, in the course of a frontier dispute with Peru, visited the village. The official and his staff were given a salad containing the fatal herb. They all blabbed the most secret intentions of the Bolivian Government. Aguinaldo, who had studied medicine in the United States, suspected the cause of their indiscretions and confirmed his suspicions by subsequent experiments. He quickly realised the power which had been placed in his hands. By means of blackmail, he soon acquired an enormous fortune. He swore all the inhabitants of his native village to secrecy, giving them all, in return, a comfortable livelihood. Out of the 'Insane Root', he made a powder that looked like pepper. When he wished to get a man into his power, he would invite him to dinner and induce him to sprinkle some of the food with what seemed to be pepper. From that moment, the man was in Aguinaldo's power, and had to obey him or suffer disaster. 'And all this immense power,' he concluded, 'I use in furtherance of human welfare, which demands the dispelling of subversive and anarchic myths and adherence to the ancient and tried wisdom of the stable ages of the past. You will admit, I am sure, that you are fortunate in being allowed to contribute to this great work.'

The month of probation was devoted, not only to the growth of my beard, but also to indoctrination. Aguinaldo was a powerful personality. He appeared to be completely untroubled by any doubts as to the wisdom of his crusade. His culture was very wide; his knowledge of history, amazing. But, in addition to these assets, his large and piercing eyes had an almost hypnotic quality which held my will in suspense while he conversed. At the end of the month, he was satisfied. 'Next Saturday,' he said, 'you shall join our hebdomadal dinner and be introduced to my immediate colleagues.'

III

Saturday evening came and I found a company of seven, in addition to my host. All the seven, I was informed, had for public purposes Spanish names and San Ysidran passports. I, also, had been similarly provided. But in the house of Aguinaldo, we knew each other by our real names. Since all of us were wanted by the police in our own countries, if not elsewhere, this mutual knowledge made treachery impossible and linked us in a chain of unbreakable confederacy. At this first dinner, Aguinaldo informed the company of my difficulties and of my reasons for joining the Order. Turning to me, he said: 'During the coming week, each of our guests shall confide in you reciprocal secrets which shall place you on an equality with the older members of our Sacred Brotherhood.'

Two of them, who were close friends, came to see me the next day. They were Count Cesare Altogrado and Baron Schambok. Count Cesare, I learnt, was a Count of the Holy Roman Empire; by birth a Venetian; dapper, and well-dressed; a man whom, at first sight, you would not suspect of seriousness about anything. But, in this, you would have been mistaken. There was one thing about which he was in earnest, and that was the Holy Roman Empire. He adored the memory of the Emperor Frederick II, and never ceased to lament the defeat of this great man by the money-grabbing merchants of the Lombard cities. For a moment, he had hoped that Mussolini might revive the ancient glories; but the rise of Hitler reminded him that the Hohenstauffen were Germans, and he urged Mussolini to abdicate in favour of Hitler. Neither Dictator was grateful to him, and, but for Aguinaldo, he would have suffered the penalty of his idealism.

Baron Schambok had much in common with Count Cesare. He was a short man, whose appearance was redeemed from insignificance by magnificent and ferocious mustachios. Fiery energy showed in all his movements, and one felt that he ought to have a knout in his hand. He looked back nostalgically to the days of the original Baltic Barons from whom he was descended. He remembered how they had introduced Teutonic civilisation to the still pagan inhabitants of northern regions. The Teutonic Knights dwelt in his imagination as the shining champions of chivalry and Christendom in a dark, difficult land. Though he had been an exile since 1917, he still hoped: some turn of the wheel of fortune, so he dreamt, might restore his family and friends to their former greatness. Meanwhile, to prove to the world that he was not a fanatic, he had allowed himself to enter into relations with the Soviet Government.

'And what,' I inquired, 'brought you two into relation with Aguinaldo?'

'Well,' they told me, 'the story is rather curious. He invited us both to dinner, and, after dinner, asked us if we would like to listen to some gramophone records. We both said that we would prefer to talk. "Well," he said, "I think you are making a mistake. I am sure that you would be interested in the particular records that I wish you to hear." So we acquiesced; and the result amazed us. We had met secretly in the depths of the Black Forest at midnight to arrange a pact between the Kremlin and the Vatican, to be kept a complete secret lest the adherents of either should be revolted by thoughts of friendship with the other. We had conversed, as we believed, in complete solitude, and, as plenipotentiaries, we had concluded the desired pact. But Aguinaldo had realised that something was up, and had set his spies upon us. He has, in fact, a vast Secret Service, everywhere on the look-out for valuable secrets. The record which he played to us was a verbatim report of the whole of our midnight conversation. If this were published, we should be ruined. He promised not to publish it if we joined his crusade. We approved his objects, and therefore, agreed.'

IV

The next member of the Fraternity to visit me was the Egyptian Ahmes, whose name had been Suleiman Abbas. He had changed his name in order to purge it of everything that was not Egyptian in origin. His nationalism had secured him considerable success, but his opposition to Islam had brought him the enmity of the Egyptian Government. He believed passionately that everything good is Egyptian in origin and that everything evil is alien to the clear spirit of the dwellers on the Lower Nile. He was convinced, with a quite unshakable certainty, that all would be well with the world if the Pharaonic Empire and culture could be restored. 'Consider,' he said, 'what we, in our great days, contributed to world culture. Your education is still based upon what you call "the three R's". But you do not tell the helpless children committed to your charge that all three R's owe their origin to my country. How many of you Westerners will recognise the source of the name that I have adopted? Do you realise that Ahmes was the author of the oldest extant textbook of arithmetic? And, to pass to another department of culture, have you realised how, in the days of the Pharaohs, pictorial art spread from Egypt throughout what is now the empty and desert Sahara? You Westerners are in the habit of praising the Greeks, but have you reflected that it was only after contact with my country that Greek civilisation began to blossom? The long night that my country has suffered began with the madman Cambyses, continued under the drunken Alexander and the uxorious Antony. Two Semitic religions proceeded to oppress the Egyptian spirit. And, to this day, even those who proclaim themselves champions of Egyptian nationalism are willing to abase themselves before the superstitions invented by an ignorant Arab and spread by savage, invading hordes. My ancestors, the Pharaohs, imagined that they had done with Semites when they sent Moses into the desert. Alas, they did not foresee the conquests of Christ and Mohammed. Persians, Macedonians, Romans, Arabs, Turks, French, and British have in turn oppressed my unhappy land. It is not enough to secure political freedom. It is, above all, cultural freedom that I seek to restore to Egypt; and it is this that has caused my troubles. The ungrateful Government of Cairo, which still abases itself before the Semitic conqueror of fourteen centuries ago, opposes with un-Egyptian fanaticism every attempt to restore the worship of Amun-Re. Nor is my Egyptian nationalism more welcome outside the confines of Egypt. Everywhere, I have found myself in conflict with Governments, and, if it had not been for the helping hand of Aguinaldo, I should have languished miserably under a régime inspired by one of the three Semitic imposters – Christ, Mohammed, and Marx. To my intense joy, Aguinaldo realised that my crusade was an integral part of his world-wide Fight for the Right; and in this sacred Brotherhood I have found scope for my well-justified hatreds. I can now allow myself to dream of the not very distant day when Aguinaldo's campaign will be crowned with success, and Egypt can once more become the inspirer of all that is noblest in the life of Man.'

When he was speaking, I allowed myself to be carried along sympathetically on the stream of his eloquence, but when he left me, I rubbed my eyes and seemed to awaken from a dream. 'It is all very fine,' I said to myself, 'to praise the dwellers on the Nile, but has he not forgotten the Euphrates, the Tigris, and the Indus – not to mention the Yellow River and the Yangtze? I am afraid his view of history is somewhat myopic, but as I am committed to Aguinaldo, I must learn to work with his lieutenants.'

While I was still meditating on the rivers of Asia, I was visited by another of Aguinaldo's lieutenants, the Mexican Carlos Diaz, whose name had now been changed to Quetzalcoatl. Like Ahmes, he wished to revive the past, but a somewhat less distant past than that of the Pharaohs; and like Ahmes, he had had considerable success amongst his own countrymen with his propaganda. It was pre-Columban Mexico, and especially the Mayan civilisation, that he admired. He considered the Spaniards, and White men generally, as barbarians who had destroyed the peaceful and prosperous civilisation of his country and had displayed a fanatical vandalism which (so he maintained) every lover of art and beauty must profoundly deplore. He had found only one European teacher with whom he could in any degree sympathise. This one was Karl Marx. In Mexico, the Spaniards were the upper class and the Indians were the proletariat. Marx, therefore, appeared to him as the champion of the Indians. I could not but think that, in this opinion, he was justified. Perhaps, also, Marx might have not objected to the Aztec system of human sacrifice provided that the victims had all been rich. The dreams of Carlos Diaz, like those of Ahmes, were of a somewhat violent character. He hoped to see a great confederation of Indians from the Rio Grande to Cape Horn ousting the White Man, acquiring modern weapons, and, perhaps, ultimately restoring even the northern portions of their Continent to the descendants of those who had roamed the great plains before the advent of Columbus. The more bloodthirsty of his visions he revealed seldom and reluctantly, but it was clear that he hoped for a day when the sky-scrapers would topple and Manhattan would revert to forest. These hopes were suspected in Washington and did not enhance his popularity. His admiration of Marx made it possible to treat him as a Communist, and his somewhat unguarded advocacy of revolution gave the Governments of the world a pretext for his incarceration. On the very day of his impending arrest, he was rescued by Aguinaldo. A forged passport supplied him with a new name and plastic surgery supplied him with a new face. He had disliked his old name because it was Spanish, and with joy he decided that his new name should be Quetzalcoatl. Henceforth, as one of Aguinaldo's lieutenants, he was able to pursue his propaganda in secret by the devious methods which Aguinaldo had perfected.

In the course of my interviews with Dr Aguinaldo's lieutenants, I soon discovered that they fell into two classes: there were those who genuinely believed in the Fight for the Right and hoped that Aguinaldo's methods would prove successful; but there were others who were purely cynical and attached to Aguinaldo solely by his power of blackmail. With one exception, all of them, of both kinds, were in Aguinaldo's power owing to some hold which he had acquired through his agents. But those who agreed with his professed aims worked with him enthusiastically, while the others were only concerned to save their own skins. The most important in the second class was Dr Mauleverer, whom I found at once interesting and repulsive. As a student of scientific medicine, he had won a great reputation, especially as regards the cause and cure of cancer. It soon became obvious in the course of our talk that he was avid for both power and money, and cared for nothing else. While he was still undetected, suspicious people observed that those of his patients who were very rich were apt to die of cancer unless they paid him enormous fees. Police investigation had made a criminal prosecution imminent; and, but for Aguinaldo's timely rescue, he would have faced ruin and prison, if not death. Dr Aguinaldo, after changing Mauleverer's name and appearance, supplied him with new medical diplomas from San Ysidro and with the opportunity of acquiring a new medical reputation. In return for this help, he undertook to diagnose cancer in any patient whom Aguinaldo disliked. If such a patient did not alter his politics or retire from public life, Dr Mauleverer saw to it that he did in fact die of cancer. His victims were of two kinds: those who were effective opponents of the Fight for the Right and those who were enemies of the Republic of San Ysidro. But care was taken to make it seem that these two kinds were one. Dr Mauleverer explained all this to me with complete *sang froid*. The sufferings of his victims were a matter of entire indifference to him. For the present, he was content with the money and power which he acquired in the service of Aguinaldo, but it was clear to me that, if ever opportunity offered, he would seek a career of independent crime. No such opportunity had as yet presented itself, but I sensed that he had not given up hope. He made a medical discovery which he hoped would prove useful, namely, that the immunity to the effects of the Insane Root enjoyed by the natives of Aguinaldo's village wore off gradually if they went to live elsewhere.

I was much interested by the Russian member of Aguinaldo's fraternity. His name was General Zinsky, and he had enjoyed the favour of the Soviet Government until 1945, but at the time of Potsdam and in the immediately following months, he had urged a lenient policy towards Germans on the ground that they might again become allies of Russia as in 1939. This brought him into disfavour, and he was about to be purged when Aguinaldo's secret emissaries rescued him. He was a very useful man in the organisation because of his intimate knowledge of Soviet secrets. Although in his heart he still accepted Communist ideology, personal indignation made him willing to work against the Soviet Government, and self-preservation compelled him to do so in the service of Aguinaldo.

There was another ex-Communist among Aguinaldo's lieutenants: namely, the American Woodrow Bordov. He was a man with one very simple desire: he wished to see himself in the headlines as often as possible. At one time he had thought that Communism would conquer the world and had become a member of the Communist Party. When this proved dangerous, he became an Informer and told whatever stories about American Communists the fervent anti-Communists wished to hear. After a time, nevertheless, the newspapers had had enough of him, and he no longer rated their front pages. He then turned round and retracted, on oath, all that he had previously said on oath. It was brought home to him, however, that perjury is only tolerated in defence of the Right, and that, in defence of the Left, it is a crime. While in a state of terror, he was approached by one of Aguinaldo's agents and skilfully rescued. Aguinaldo found him useful because of his knowledge of Western Communist agents. Under the new name bestowed upon him by Aguinaldo, he achieved headlines in the more extreme organs of Western anti-Communism. What he achieved in this way was less than he had hoped and less than he still desired, but so far it was all that was possible while Aguinaldo's hold on him remained.

V

At the dinner at which I was introduced to the fraternity, my attention had been attracted to the only woman in the company, but, at that time, I learnt nothing about her except what I could see. She was exquisitely beautiful, rather tall, with jet black hair and large, compelling eyes. Her demeanour was proud and dominating. At this first dinner she said little, and I did not see her again until after I had seen all Aguinaldo's other lieutenants, but I had learnt from them that she was his closest collaborator and knew more of his secrets than any of the others knew. I looked forward with lively interest to the interview with her, which was to complete my initiation. I learnt that her name was Irma d'Arpad, and that she was a descendant of ancient Hungarian kings. During my interview with her, I felt as though I were having an interview with royalty. Unlike the others, she evidently did not feel herself to be in Aguinaldo's power. On the contrary, she seemed to feel that Aguinaldo was fortunate in being allowed to work with her. Unlike the others, she was not held to him by any tie of blackmail. She was a complete, and even fanatical, believer in the professed principles of the Fight for the Right; and it was this belief, alone, which caused her to work with Aguinaldo. All this she explained to me. 'You cannot wonder,' she said, 'that I favour the Fight for the Right. I am descended from many generations of Hungarians, and the blood of Attila flows in my veins. For those of humble origin, it must be difficult to imagine the burning shame which I suffer from the spectacle of my country under the heel of vulgar upstarts whose ancestors trembled at the name of Attila and were proud of the opportunity to support him against the majesty of Rome. What do they know of the pride bestowed by ancient lineage? What do they know of the linking of past and future that this pride brings with it? I cannot and will not endure subjection to such riff-raff. While life remains, I will stand for majesty and tradition. It is because I believe that Aguinaldo's principles are the same as mine that I have joined him in his great enterprise. I am aware that some of his methods are such as the morality of our age deplores, but the spirit of my great ancestor supports me, and I do not shrink from what would have been thought right by the justly named Scourge of God.'

From Irma, who knew, or thought she knew, all Aguinaldo's secrets, I learnt more than I had previously been told about his methods of work. The 'Insane Root' had provided him with immense opportunities of blackmail of which he had taken full advantage. He spent the greater part of his vast resources on an international Secret Service which supplied him with the preliminary information as to possible victims. In every non-Communist country, he concentrated most of his attention upon those who seemed to be effective champions of the Left. The public was astonished over and over again by defections towards the Right. Men whom Progressives had trusted appeared suddenly to lose heart and to abandon beliefs to which they had seemed particularly wedded. In Communist countries, a somewhat different technique was attempted, but, as yet, with only very moderate success. In these countries, evidence was produced or manufactured that So-and-so, a man prominent but not supreme in the Soviet hierarchy, had been for some considerable time an object of investigation by the Secret Police and was now on the point of being liquidated. If he was successfully persuaded, attempts were made to smuggle him across the Iron Curtain and find him employment as an anti-Communist agent.

'I suppose,' I observed, 'that what you have said explains a remark of Aguinaldo's of which, when he made it, the meaning remained obscure to me. When I asked him what he wanted from me in return for saving me from disaster, he replied, "Only a little research". Am I right in assuming that the researches which he wished me to make are such as will bring discredit upon Left-wing politicians and upon such officials as, in his opinion, have a bad effect upon the decisions of politicians?'

'Yes,' she replied, 'that is exactly what he will wish you to do. Your previous experience must have made known to you many weaknesses of eminent men. Some have been financially corrupt, some have been guilty of sexual aberrations of a sort which the public condemns, others have had indiscreet relations with Communist Governments. You will be expected to make such men acquainted with Aguinaldo, who will put the finishing touches to the work, if necessary, with the help of the Insane Root.'

Although I do not pretend to be particularly squeamish, I must confess that I was repelled by this programme of work. Although my conduct had been far from irreproachable, I did not much like the prospect of devoting my time and skill to the business of forcing eminent men to act in violation of their beliefs. Irma perceived my reluctance, and it stimulated in her a flood of eloquent and passionate conviction. 'Do you not see,' she said, 'that, for lack of the old stabilities, the world is sinking into an abyss where either all must perish or, at best, a few miserable survivors can live the life of the beasts of the field? Do you not see that monarchy, religion, respect for the Great, and complete faith in the well-tried dogmas of past centuries, are the only forces that can keep in check the turbulent creeds and cruelties of the swinish multitude? Consider the lessons of history. The ancient Empires of Egypt and China persisted for forty centuries. In our day an Empire is fortunate if it survives for two decades. Men have become restless, anarchic, impatient of discipline. The best are full of doubt, and the rest are governed by rapacity. It is not by gentle means, or by a conventionally virtuous campaign, that these dreadful evils can be eradicated. The day for squeamishness is past; and it is Aguinaldo whose methods can, alone, bring a cure.'

While she spoke, her eyes flashed fire and her voice vibrated with passion. Not unwillingly, I fell under her spell, influenced partly by her powerful personality, and partly by very compelling motives of self-interest. In that moment, I vowed myself to the work and decided to close my eyes to its distasteful aspects.

V I

After the occasion on which I had been formally admitted to membership of the Brotherhood, I was free to live a normal life under my new name and with my new personality as a Latin American. The only restriction upon my freedom was a vow which had been imposed upon me by Aguinaldo that I would not seek the company of the Siren who had brought me to the brink of ruin. Every Saturday evening, at our weekly dinners, we began with a general discussion of policy and then proceeded, under the guidance of Aguinaldo, to the allotting of suitable tasks to the various members. Our ultimate aims were clear, but it was often difficult to think of any means by which they could be achieved. We wished, of course, to restore monarchy wherever it had been replaced by a republic. Even in Spain, much as we admired Franco's valiant championship of religion and censorship, we could not ignore our obligation to the ancient Royal Family. Even when this was decided, there still remained a problem: should we seek out the heirs of Don Carlos and revive the Carlist Party, or should we be content with the restoration of the Royal Family whom the Revolution of 1930 had dispossessed? Germany, likewise, presented a problem. We could not feel that the German Empire established by Bismarck had sufficient antiquity to command our respect; and, after some debate, we decided in favour of the restoration of all the separate Principalities and Dukedoms that had existed before the achievement of German unity. In Italy, we of course supported the restoration of the Papal States, the Grand Duchy of Tuscany, and the rest. In regard to Russia, we had a vehement debate in which Irma took one side and the rest of us took the other. All the rest of us would have been content with the restoration of the Romanovs, but Irma, who felt herself a Mongol, passionately protested that the Imperial Family of Russia were subversive rebels against the Empire established by Genghis Khan. In view of this division of opinion, we decided that, for the present, we would leave Russia except for occasional pin-pricks.

The problem of Russia was one example of a difficulty which arose in many of our discussions. How far back should we go in our attempt to recreate the past? In regard to India, for example, should we attempt to recreate something like the Empire of Asoka, or should we be content with the Great Mogul? And in China, should we accept the Manchu Dynasty? We debated such problems with great earnestness at our Saturday meetings, and in general we ended by accepting the judgement of Aguinaldo. There were, however, two problems as to which we found agreement impossible. One of these, already mentioned, was Irma's championship of the Mongols; the other, which proved even more serious, was a disagreement between Aguinaldo and the Mexican Diaz – now Quetzalcoatl. Aguinaldo prided himself on his descent from the Conquistadores, whereas Diaz hated the Spaniards and wished to recapture Mexico and South America for the descendants of their pre-Columban inhabitants. Most of us, in this dispute, sympathised with Diaz. Irma, in particular, whose Mongolian ancestry had inclined her to antipathy towards Europeans, could not bring herself, on this point, to accept the authority of our Chief. She was deeply in love with him and would have given way on almost any other issue, but, when she heard him upholding European domination, the blood of Attila boiled in her veins and she found submission impossible. Gradually, his influence over her declined—the more so, as he showed a complete indifference to her advances. Coldly inflexible, he appeared wholly devoted to The Cause. Not for him were any of the softer joys that she longed to provide. In all his discourses, he endeavoured to instil an implacable, ascetic fanaticism and an entire indifference to everything except victory. At first, Irma had accepted this complete immolation of self; but she could not carry it to the length of accepting the subjection of non-Europeans. This rift became gradually more and more serious and increasingly threatened the success of the Great Enterprise.

The trouble was increased by disquieting facts which Diaz secretly brought to the notice of the rest of us. It appeared that, in dealings with Latin-American States, Aguinaldo was dominated, not by the avowed principles of the Brotherhood, but by the attitude of these various States to his own Republic of San Ysidro. He would make friends with revolutionary leaders if they were prepared to co-operate with his country, but would be hostile to reactionaries if they opposed increases in the power of San Ysidro. Diaz was the only member of the Brotherhood, except Aguinaldo, who understood the complex politics of Latin America, and first Irma and then the rest of us came gradually to think that his misgivings were not unfounded. Could it be that Aguinaldo was not all that we had thought? Was it possible that he was using the Insane Root, not for the glorious impersonal ends which he had put before us, but for his own aggrandisement and that of San Ysidro? Obscure dealings with dope merchants in the United States accidentally came to light, in spite of Aguinaldo's endeavours to conceal them, and it did not seem that these dealings had any connection with the Fight for the Right.

VII

Week by week, our misgivings increased. Diaz, after carefully instructing us about the doings of some South American Governments, set traps for Aguinaldo, who assumed that most of us were ignorant as to the points in dispute. At last, we all agreed that there was only one thing to be done. We must secretly administer to him a very small dose of the Insane Root – not enough to make him mad, still less to cause his death, but just enough to give him an attack of that dangerous disease first diagnosed by Belloc, and by him christened *Veracititis*. This was not a difficult matter. It was our custom to keep a powdered form of the Insane Root in special pepper pots which our occasional influential guests were encouraged to use. We had only to transfer the powder to an ordinary pepper box and provide a dish for which we knew that Aguinaldo would desire a peppery flavouring. The success of our plot was facilitated by his unusual addiction to pepper. In the deepest secrecy, we made our preparations. In breathless suspense, we watched him shake the fatal pepper box. As the Saturday dinner proceeded, he became gradually more excited, more boastful, and less restrained. At last he burst out into a loud harangue:

'What do you know of ME? What do you understand of my plans? Do you think, you poor deluded fools, that I care tuppence about all this jargon of Right and Left? Do you really suppose that I care about monarchy in the abstract? No, indeed! It is monarchy in the concrete that I care about – monarchy with me as the Monarch; monarchy with the whole world at my feet; monarchy with subjects imploring my mercy, and often not obtaining it. You have helped me, you patient idealistic or criminal tools, to acquire a hold over the Governments of the world. The secrets which you have helped me to unearth are such as would cause the population of all the countries of the world to turn upon their rulers in savage fury. The rulers, to escape this fate, must bow to my will. The time is almost ripe. I, Aguinaldo – I, who began as a humble citizen of the tiny Republic of San Ysidro – I, whom men have regarded as a harmless fanatic of reaction – I shall soon be Emperor of the World. It is to this end that I have built up our organisation. It is for this end that your researches will be used. Those who oppose me will die raving from unexpected doses of the Insane Root. Under me, the world shall be united and the silly politics of this age shall be forgotten.'

We listened in horror, but, in obedience to a resolution which we had made in advance, we concealed our horror and pretended to applaud the new revelation. We knew that when the intoxication passed he would not remember what he had said and would suspect no change in our relation to him. But when the time came for the next Saturday dinner we repeated our previous performance, but this time we put the powdered Root into the food as well as into the pepper box. Again he became excited, but more recklessly than before. 'Bow down before me, slaves,' he shouted. 'If you are faithful, I, the Emperor of the World, will reward you as you may deserve. If you are not faithful, you will perish.' Gradually, his speech became inarticulate. He writhed in strange contortions and, finally, fell dead.

A bewildered silence fell upon us. The unity which we had owed to service under a common chief was dissolved. As separate units, without aim or purpose, none of us could think how to proceed. Irma alone remained calm.

'Well, friends,' she said, 'we have been deceived. The leader whom we revered was a charlatan, and the aims to which we gave allegiance were visionary absurdities. Can any of you suggest a course of action not wholly futile?'

At these words, a curious transformation came over us. All of us had been deeply and passionately devoted to Irma, but her love for Aguinaldo and our respect for him had kept our feelings towards Irma in the region of humble adoration. We all began to speak at once, and the substance of what we said was the same for each one of us. In the resulting babel, I was only dimly aware of what the others said, but I gathered afterwards that it differed little from my own speech: 'Irma,' I cried, 'in the shipwreck of all that we have believed and hoped, there remains for me one immovable rock: I love you, and if you can reciprocate my feeling, my life may still possess purpose and joy.'

When we discovered that all the others had been saying just the same thing, we turned upon each other in a fury. 'You miserable worms, do you suppose that you are worthy to share the life of the Imperial descendant of Attila? Can you imagine that she would look upon any of *you* with favour?' Very soon, we came to blows, and an unmannerly brawl took place in the presence of the corpse. But Irma once more took command.

'Stop!' she cried. 'Cease your unseemly quarrels. I love you all, my Colleagues in an enterprise which has suffered momentary eclipse. Your trouble has a solution as simple as it is radical. You know that one of our greatest successes has been the restoration of the ancient régime of Tibet, and that among the institutions which the shameless Communists endeavoured to sweep away was that of polyandry. We will go to Lhasa, and I will marry you all.'

*   *   *

NOTE : They went – but what became of them is unknown.

PART THREE

NIGHTMARES

The following stories, with the exception of 'The Fisherman's Nightmare' and 'The Theologian's Nightmare', were first published under the title of *Nightmares of Eminent Persons and Other Stories* in 1954 by The Bodley Head. In his short Introduction to the book Russell stated :

> The following 'Nightmares' might be called 'Signposts to Sanity'. Every isolated passion is, in isolation, insane; sanity may be defined as a synthesis of insanities. Every dominant passion generates a dominant fear, the fear of its non-fulfilment. Every dominant fear generates a nightmare, some-times in the form of an explicit and conscious fanaticism, sometimes in a paralysing timidity, sometimes in an unconscious or subconscious terror which finds expression only in dreams. The man who wishes to preserve sanity in a dangerous world should summon in his own mind a Parliament of fears, in which each in turn is voted absurd by all the others. The dreamers of the following nightmares did not adopt this technique; it is hoped that the reader will have more wisdom.

'Mr Bowdler's Nightmare' and 'The Psychoanalyst's Nightmare' first appeared in *Courier*, December 1953 and April 1954 respectively. 'The Queen of Sheba's Nightmare' was reprinted in *Argosy* in October 1954. 'The Fisherman's Nightmare' and 'The Theologian's Nightmare' first appeared in *Fact and Fiction* published in 1961 by George Allen & Unwin.

The Queen of Sheba's nightmare

PUT NOT THY TRUST IN PRINCES

The Queen of Sheba, returning from her visit to King Solomon, was riding through the desert on a white ass with her Grand Vizier beside her on an ass of more ordinary colour. As they rode, she discoursed reminiscently about the wealth and wisdom of Solomon.

'I had always thought,' she said, 'that I do pretty well in the way of royal splendour, and I had hoped beforehand that I should be able to hold my own, but when I had seen his possessions I had no spirit left in me. But the treasures of his palace are as nothing to the treasures of his mind. Ah, my dear Vizier, what wisdom, what knowledge of life, what sagacity his conversation displays! If you had as much political sagacity in your whole body as that King has in his little finger, we should have none of these troubles in my kingdom. But it is not only in wealth and wisdom that he is matchless. He is also (though perhaps I am the only one privileged to know this) a supreme poet. He gave me as we parted a jewelled volume in his own inimitable handwriting, telling in language of exquisite beauty the joy that he had experienced in my company. There are passages celebrating some of my more intimate charms which I should blush to show you; but there are portions of this book which I may perhaps read to you to beguile the evenings of our journey through the desert. In this exquisite volume not only are his own words such as any lady would love to hear from amorous lips, but by a quintessence of imaginative sympathy he has attributed to me poetic words which I should be glad to have uttered. Never again, I am convinced, shall I find such perfect union, such entire harmony, and such penetration into the recesses of the soul. My public duties, alas, compel me to return to my Kingdom, but I shall carry with me to my dying day the knowledge that there is on earth one man worthy of my love.'

'Your Majesty,' replied the Vizier, 'it is not for me to instil doubts into the royal breast, but to all those who serve you, it is incredible that among men your equal should exist.'

At this moment, emerging out of the sunset, a weary figure appeared on foot.

'Who may this be?' said the Queen.

'Some beggar, your Majesty,' said the Grand Vizier. 'I strongly advise you to steer clear of him.'

But a certain dignity in the aspect of the approaching stranger seemed to her indicative of something more than a beggar. And in spite of the Grand Vizier's protests she turned her ass towards him. 'And who may you be?' she said.

His answer dispelled at once the Grand Vizier's suspicions, for he spoke in the most polished idiom of the court of Sheba: 'Your Majesty,' he said, 'my name is Beelzebub, but it is probably unknown to you, as I seldom travel far from the land of Canaan. Who you are, I know. And not only who you are, but whence you come, and what fancies inspire your sunset meditations. You have come, I know, from visiting that wise King who, though my humble guise might seem to belie my words, has been for many years my firm friend. I am convinced that he has told you concerning himself all that he wishes you to know. But if – though the hypothesis seems rash – there is anything that you wish to know concerning him beyond what he has seen fit to tell, you have but to ask me, for he has no secrets from me.'

'You surprise me,' said the Queen, 'but I see that our conversation will be too long to be conducted conveniently while you walk and I ride. My Grand Vizier shall dismount and give his ass to you.'

With an ill grace the Grand Vizier complied.

'I suppose,' the Queen said, 'that your conversations with Solomon were mainly concerned with statecraft and matters of deep wisdom. I, as a Queen not unrenowned for wisdom, also conversed with him on these topics; but some of our conversation – so at least I flatter myself – revealed a side of him less intimately known, I should imagine, to you than to me. And some of the best of this he put into a book which he gave to me as we parted. This book contains many beauties, for example, a lovely description of the spring.'

'Ah,' said Beelzebub, 'and does he in this description speak of the voice of the turtle?'

'Why, yes,' said the Queen. 'But how did you guess?'

'Oh, well,' Beelzebub replied, 'he was proud of having noticed the turtle talking in the spring and liked to bring it in when he could.'

'Some of his compliments,' the Queen resumed, 'particularly pleased me. I had practised Hebrew during the journey to Jerusalem, but was not sure whether I had mastered it adequately. I was therefore delighted when he said, "Thy speech is comely".'

'Very nice of him,' said Beelzebub. 'And did he at the same time remark that your Majesty's temples are like a piece of pomegranate?'

'Well, really,' said the Queen, 'this is getting uncanny! He did say so, and I thought it rather an odd remark. But how on earth did you guess?'

'Well,' Beelzebub replied, 'you know all great men have kinks, and one of his is a peculiar interest in pomegranates.'

'It is true,' said the Queen, 'that some of his comparisons are a little odd. He said, for instance, that my eyes were like the fishpools of Heshbon.'

'I have known him,' said Beelzebub, 'to make even stranger comparisons. Did he ever compare your Majesty's nose to the Tower of Lebanon?'

'Good gracious,' said the Queen, 'this is too much! He did make that comparison. But you are persuading me that you must have some more intimate source of knowledge than I had suspected.'

'Your Majesty,' Beelzebub replied, 'I fear that what I have to say may cause you some pain. The fact is that some of his wives were friends of mine, and through them I got to know him well.'

'Yes, but how about this love poem?'

'Well, you see, when he was young, while his father was still alive, he had to take more trouble. In those days he loved a farmer's virtuous daughter, and only overcame her scruples by his poetic gifts. Afterwards, he thought it a pity the gifts should be wasted, and he gave a copy to each of his ladies in turn. You see, he was essentially a collector, as you must have noticed when you went over his house. By long practice, he made each in turn think herself supreme in his affections; and you, dear lady, are his last and most signal triumph.'

'Oh, the wretch!' she said. 'Never again will I be deceived by the perfidy of man. Never again will I let flattery blind me. To think that I, who throughout my dominions am accounted the wisest of women, should have permitted myself to be so misled!'

'Nay, dear lady,' said Beelzebub, 'be not so cast down, for Solomon is not only the wisest man in his dominions, but the wisest of all men, and will be known as such through countless ages. To have been deceived by him is scarcely matter for shame.'

'Perhaps you are right,' she said, 'but it will take time to heal the wound to my pride.'

'Ah, sweet Queen,' Beelzebub replied, 'how happy could I be if I could hasten the healing work of Time! Far be it from me to imitate the wiles of that perfidious monarch. From me shall flow only simple words dictated by the spontaneous sentiments of the heart. To you, the Peerless, the Incomparable, the Matchless Jewel of the South, I would give – if you permit it – whatever balm a true appreciation of your worth can offer.'

'Your words are soothing,' she replied, 'but can you match his splendours? Have you a palace that can compare with his? Have you such store of precious stones? Such robes, purveying the aroma of myrrh and frankincense? And, more important than any of these, have you a wisdom equal to his?'

'Lovely Sheba,' he replied, 'I can satisfy you on every point. I have a palace far grander than Solomon's. I have a far greater store of precious stones. My robes of State are as numerous as the stars in the sky. And as for wisdom, his is not a match for mine. Solomon is surprised that, although the rivers flow into the sea, yet the sea is not full. I know why this is, and will explain it to your Majesty on some long winter evening. To come to a more serious lapse, it was after he had seen you that he said "there is no new thing under the sun". Can you doubt that in his thoughts he was comparing you unfavourably with the farmer's daughter of his youth? And can any man be accounted wise who, having beheld you, does not at once perceive that here is a new wonder of beauty and majesty? No! In a competition of wisdom I have nothing to fear from him.'

With a smile, half of resignation concerning the past, and half of dawning hope for a happier future, she turned her eyes upon Beelzebub and said: 'Your words are beguiling. I made a long journey from my kingdom to Solomon's, and I thought I had seen what is most noteworthy on this earth. But, if you speak truth, your kingdom, your palace, and your wisdom, all surpass Solomon's. May I extend my journey by a visit to your dominion?'

He returned her smile with one in which the appearance of love barely concealed the reality of triumph. 'I can imagine no greater delight,' he said, 'than that you should allow me this opportunity to place my poor riches at your feet. Let us go while yet the night is young. But the way is dark and difficult, and infested by fierce robbers. If you are to be safe, you must trust yourself completely to my guidance.'

'I will,' she said. 'You have given me new hope.'

At this moment they arrived at a measureless cavern in the mountainside. Holding aloft a flaming torch, Beelzebub led the way through long tunnels and tortuous passages. At last they emerged into a vast hall lit by innumerable lamps. The walls and roof glittered with precious stones whose scintillating facets flashed back the light of the lamps. In solemn state, three hundred silver thrones were ranged round the walls.

'This is indeed magnificent,' said the Queen.

'Oh,' said Beelzebub, 'this is only my second-rate hall of audience. You shall now see the Presence Chamber.'

Opening a hitherto invisible door, he led her into another hall, more than twice as large as the first, more than twice as brilliantly lit, and more than twice as richly jewelled. Round three walls of this hall were seven hundred golden thrones. On the fourth wall were two thrones, composed entirely of precious stones, diamonds, sapphires, rubies, huge pearls, bound together by some strange art which the Queen could not fathom.

'This,' he said, 'is my great hall, and of the two jewelled thrones, one is mine and the other shall be yours.'

'But who,' she said, 'is to occupy the seven hundred golden thrones?'

'Ah well,' he said, 'you will know that in due course.'

As he spoke, a queenly figure, only slightly less splendid than the Queen of Sheba, glided in and occupied the first of the golden thrones. With something of a shock, the Queen of Sheba recognised Solomon's Chief Consort.

'I had not expected to meet her here,' she said with a slight tremor.

'Ah well,' said Beelzebub, 'you see I have magic powers. And while I have been wooing you, I have been telling this good lady also that Solomon is not all he seems. She listened to my words as you have listened, and she has come.'

Scarcely had he finished speaking, when another lady, whom also the Queen of Sheba recognised from her visit to Solomon's harem, entered and occupied the second golden throne. Then came a third, a fourth, a fifth, until it seemed as if the procession would never end. At last all the seven hundred golden thrones were occupied.

'You may be wondering,' Beelzebub remarked in silken tones, 'about the three hundred silver thrones. All these are by now occupied by Solomon's three hundred concubines. All the thousand in this hall and the other have heard from me words not unlike those that you have heard, all have been convinced by me, and all are here.'

'Perfidious monster!' exclaimed the Queen. 'How could I have had the simplicity to let myself be deceived a second time! Henceforth I will reign alone, and no male shall ever again be given a chance to deceive me. Good-bye, foul fiend! If you ever venture into my dominions, you shall suffer the fate that your villainy has deserved.'

'No, good lady,' Beelzebub replied, 'I am afraid you do not quite realise the position. I showed you the way in, but only I can find the way out. This is the abode of the dead, and you are here for all eternity – but not for all eternity on the diamond throne beside mine. That you will occupy only until you are superseded by an even more divine queen, the last Queen of Egypt.'

These words produced in her such a tumult of rage and despair that she awoke.

'I fear,' said the Grand Vizier, 'that your Majesty has had troubled dreams.'

Mr Bowdler's nightmare

FAMILY BLISS

Mr Bowdler, the highly meritorious author of *The Family Shakespeare*, which the most innocent young lady could read without a blush, never showed in waking life any doubt of the usefulness of his labours. It would seem, however, that somewhere within the depths of that good man's unconscious there must have lurked a still small voice, malign and mocking. It was his practice on Sundays to dispense liberal helpings of pork to his family and not least to himself. It was accompanied by boiled potatoes and cabbage, and followed by roly-poly pudding. For himself, though not for the rest of the household, there was a moderate portion of ale. After this repast, it was his custom to take a brisk walk. But once, when snow and sleet were falling heavily, he permitted himself to break through his usual routine and rest in a chair with a good book. The good book, however, was not very interesting, and he fell asleep. In his sleep he was afflicted by the following nightmare:

* * *

Mr Bowdler was believed by all the world, and is still believed by many, to have been a pattern of all the virtues. He had, however, at one time dreadful reason to doubt whether, in fact, he was all that his neighbours believed him.

In his youth he wrote a scathing attack upon Wilkes (of Wilkes & Liberty), whom he considered, not wholly without reason, to be a libertine. Wilkes was, by this time, past his prime, and no longer capable of taking such vengeance as in earlier years would have been natural to him. He left in his will a considerable sum of money to young Mr Spiffkins, with the sole condition that Mr Spiffkins, to the best of his ability, should bring disaster upon the head of Mr Bowdler. Mr Spiffkins, I regret to say, unhesitatingly accepted the unscrupulous legacy.

With a view to carrying out the provisions of Wilkes's will, he visited Mr Bowdler under the guise of seeming friendship. He found Mr Bowdler in the fullest enjoyment of perfect family bliss. He had a child on each knee, and was saying: 'Ride a cock horse to Banbury Cross.' Presently two other children began to clamour: 'Our turn now, Papa!' and they, in their turn, were provided with oscillatory ecstasy. Mrs Bowdler, buxom, good-natured, and smiling, surveyed the happy scene while she bustled about preparing the tea.

218

Mr Spiffkins, with that exquisite tact which had caused Mr Wilkes to select him, led the conversation to those literary topics which he knew to be dear to the heart of Mr Bowdler, and to the principles which had guided that gentleman in making the works of great men not unfit to be put into the hands of little women. The utmost harmony prevailed until at last, after tea was over, and Mrs Bowdler could be seen through the open door of the pantry washing up the teacups, Mr Spiffkins rose to go. As he was saying good-bye, he remarked:

'I am impressed, dear Mr Bowdler, by your quiverful of domestic blessings, but having carefully studied all the omissions that you have made in the works of the Bard of Avon, I am compelled to conclude that these smiling infants owe their existence to parthenogenesis.'

Mr Bowdler, red with fury, shouted: 'Get out!' and slammed the door in the face of Mr Spiffkins. But alas, Mrs Bowdler, in spite of the clatter of the teacups, had overheard the dreadful word. What it meant she could not imagine, but since she did not know it, and her husband disapproved of it, she had no doubt that it must be a bad word.

It was not the sort of matter about which she could ask her husband. He would only have replied: 'My dear, it means something about which good women do not think.' She was therefore left to her own devices. She knew, of course, all about Genesis, but the first half of the word remained obscure to her. One day, greatly daring, she stole into her husband's library while he was out, and fetching down the Classical Dictionary, read all that it had to say about the Parthenon. But still the meaning of this strange word eluded her. There was nothing about the Parthenon in Genesis, and nothing about Genesis in the frieze of the Parthenon.

The more her researches were baffled, the more the subject obsessed her. Her housework, which had been impeccable, became slovenly. She brooded. And one Wednesday she even forgot to provide shrimps for tea, a thing which she had not forgotten on any Wednesday since the happy day when she was united to Mr Bowdler in the holy bonds of wedlock.

At last matters reached a point at which Mr Bowdler felt it necessary to summon medical assistance. The doctor asked innumerable questions, tapped Mrs Bowdler's forehead with a little wooden mallet, felt her bumps, and finally bled her, but all to no avail. At last he said:

'Well, my dear lady, I fear there is only one cure for your complaint, and that is *edax rerum* (his pedantic name for Time). We must look to Time, the great healer.'

'Pray, dear Doctor, where is *edax rerum* to be obtained?' said Mrs Bowdler.

'Anywhere,' the doctor replied.

Although she had not much faith in his wisdom, for, after all, she had not disclosed to him the source of the trouble, she nevertheless went to the family apothecary and asked him whether he would supply her with *edax rerum*.

219

He blushed and stammered and said: 'Madam, that is not the sort of thing that nice ladies ought to want.'

She retired in confusion.

Baffled in one direction, her desperate state impelled her to an attempt in another. It was part of her husband's duty to read books of the sort that he wished to suppress, and by examining the bills of booksellers on his desk, she came to know the name and address of one whom, judging by the items supplied to Mr Bowdler, she thought likely to possess literature even on so dreadful a subject as that in which she was interested. Thickly veiled, she ventured into his premises, and boldly said:

'Sir, I desire a book to instruct me on parthenogenesis.'

'Madam,' he replied, observing such charms of person as her veil did not conceal, 'parthenogenesis is what you will not learn about if you come upstairs with me.'

Horrified and frightened, she fled.

Only one hope remained to her, a hope involving a desperate resolve and a courage of which she almost doubted herself to be possessed. She remembered that her husband, in order to complete his *Family Shakespeare*, that boon to every decent household, had been forced, painful as the task undoubtedly must have been, to read the unexpurgated works of that regrettably free-spoken author. She knew that he possessed, behind the locked doors of a certain bookcase, a pre-Bowdlerian Shakespeare, in which all the passages that he had wisely seen fit to omit were underlined in order to facilitate the work of the printer. 'Surely,' she thought, 'where so much has been omitted, I am sure to find the word 'parthenogenesis' in some underlined passage, and I cannot doubt that the context will show me the meaning of this word.'

One day, when her husband had been invited to address a congress of virtuous booksellers, she crept into his study, found the key to the locked bookcase after some search in his desk, unlocked the fatal doors, and extracted the tattered volume with its appalling lore. Page after page she perused, but nowhere did she find the word she sought. She found, however, many things that she had not sought. Horrified, yet fascinated, repelled, and yet absorbed, she read on and on, oblivious of the passage of time. Suddenly she became aware that the door was open and that her husband stood in the doorway. In tones of horror, he exclaimed:

'Good God, Maria, what volume do I behold in your hands? Are you not aware that poison drips from its pages? That the infection of lewd thoughts leaps from its every letter into the unguarded female mind? Have you forgotten that it has been my life's task to preserve the innocent from such pollution? Oh, that failure so dire should come upon me in the very bosom of my own family!'

With that, the good man burst into tears, tears of mortification and sorrow, aye, and of righteous anger too. Suddenly aware of her sin, she dropped the volume, fled to her chamber, and burst into heart-rending sobs.

But penitence was of no avail. She had read too much. Not one word of what she had read could she forget. Round and round in her head went shameful words and dreadful images of horrid joys. Hour by hour and day by day, the obsession grew more complete, until at last she was seized with an ungovernable frenzy, and had to be taken to the asylum, shouting Shakespearian obscenities to the whole street as she was borne away. Mr Bowdler, when her terrible words were no longer audible, fell upon his knees, asking his Maker for what sin he was thus punished. Unlike you and me, he was unable to find the answer.

The Psychoanalyst's nightmare

ADJUSTMENT—A FUGUE

It is the fate of rebels to found new orthodoxies. How this is happening to psychoanalysis has been persuasively set forth in Dr Robert Lindner's *Prescription for Rebellion.* Many psychoanalysts, one must suppose, have their secret misgivings. It was one of these who, though orthodox in his waking hours, was afflicted during sleep by the following deeply disquieting nightmare :

*   *   *

In the hall of the Limbo Rotary Club, presided over by a statue of Shakespeare, the Committee of Six was holding its annual meeting. The Committee consisted of: Hamlet, Lear, Macbeth, Othello, Antony, and Romeo. All these six, while they yet lived on earth, had been psychoanalysed by Macbeth's doctor, Dr Bombasticus. Macbeth, before the doctor had taught him to speak ordinary English, had asked, in the stilted language that in those days he employed, 'Canst thou not minister to a mind diseas'd?' 'Why, yes,' replied the doctor, 'of course I can. It is only necessary that you should lie on my sofa and talk, and I will undertake to listen at a guinea a minute.' Macbeth at once agreed. And the other five agreed at various times.

Macbeth told how at one time he had fancies of homicide, and in a long dream saw all that Shakespeare relates. Fortunately, he met the doctor in time, who explained that he saw Duncan as a father-figure, and Lady Macbeth as a mother-ditto. The doctor, with some difficulty, persuaded him that Duncan was not really his father, so he became a loyal subject. Malcolm and Donalbain died young, and Macbeth succeeded in due course. He remained devoted to Lady Macbeth, and together they spent their days in good works. He encouraged Boy Scouts, and she opened bazaars. He lived to a great age, respected by all except the porter.

The statue, which had a gramophone in its interior, remarked at this stage: 'All our yesterdays have lighted fools the way to dusty death.'

Macbeth started, and said, 'Damn that statue. That fellow Shakespeare wrote a most libellous work about me. He only knew me when I was young, before I had met Dr Bombasticus, and he let his imagination run riot over all the crimes he hoped I should commit. I cannot see why people insist on doing honour to him. There's hardly a person in his plays that wouldn't have been the better for Dr Bombasticus.' Turning to Lear: 'Don't you agree, old man?'

Lear was a quiet fellow, not much given to talk. Although he was old, his hair was beautifully brushed and his clothes were very tidy. Most of the time he seemed rather sleepy, but Macbeth's question woke him up.

'Yes, indeed, I agree,' he said. 'Why, do you know that at one time I became obsessed with a phobia directed against my dear daughters Regan and Goneril! I imagined that they were persecuting me, and had a fantasy that they were reviving a cannibal rite of eating the parent. This last I only realised after Dr Bombasticus had explained it. I got so alarmed that I rushed out into the storm at night and got very wet. I caught a chill which gave me a fever, and I imagined that a certain joint-stool was first Goneril and then Regan. I was made worse by my fool, and also by a certain naked madman, who encouraged a belief in a return to nature, and was always talking about irrelevant things such as "Pillicock" and "Child Rowland". Fortunately my illness was such as to demand the services of Dr Bombasticus. He soon persuaded me that Regan and Goneril were just as kind as I had always thought, and that my fantasies were due to irrational remorse about the ungrateful Cordelia. Ever since my cure I have lived a quiet life, appearing only on State occasions such as the birthdays of my daughters, when I show myself on a balcony and the crowd shouts, "Three cheers for the old King!" I used to have a tendency towards rhodomontade, but this, I am happy to say, has disappeared.'

At this point the statue remarked: 'Thou, all-shaking thunder, strike flat the thick rotundity of the world.'

'And are you happy now?' asked Macbeth.

'Oh yes,' said Lear, 'I'm as happy as the day is long. I sit in my chair playing patience or dozing, and thinking of nothing whatever.'

The statue: 'After life's fitful fever, he sleeps well.'

'What a silly remark!' said Lear. 'Life is not a fitful fever! And I sleep well although I'm still alive. That's just the sort of rubbish that I should have admired before I knew Dr Bombasticus.'

The statue allowed itself another remark: 'When we are born, we cry that we are come to this great stage of fools.'

'Stage of fools,' exclaimed Lear, losing for a moment that equanimity which he had hitherto observed. 'I do wish the statue would learn to talk sense. Does it dare to think us fools? Us, the most respected citizens of Limbo! I wish Dr Bombasticus could get a go at the statue! What do you think about it, Othello?'

'Well,' said Othello, 'that wretch Shakespeare treated me even worse than he did you and Macbeth. I only met him for a few days, and it happened that I was at a crisis in my life at that moment. I had made the mistake of marrying a white girl, and I soon realised that it was impossible she should really love a coloured man. In fact, at the time when Shakespeare knew me, she was plotting to run away with my lieutenant, Cassio. I was delighted, as she was an incubus. But Shakespeare imagined that I must be jealous. And in those days I was rather fond of rhetoric, so I made up some jealous speeches to please him. Dr Bombasticus, whom I met at this time, showed me that the whole trouble came from my inferiority complex, caused by my being black. In my conscious self I had always thought it a fine thing to be black – to be black and nevertheless eminent. But he showed me that I had quite other feelings in the unconscious, and that these caused a rage which could only be assuaged in battle. After he had cured me I gave up warfare, married a black woman, had a large family, and devoted my life to trade. I never now feel any impulse to "talk grand", or to utter the kind of nonsense that makes right-thinking citizens stare.'

The statue: 'Pride, pomp, and circumstance of glorious war !'

'Hark at him,' said Othello, 'that's just the sort of thing I might still be saying if it hadn't been for Dr Bombasticus. But nowadays I don't believe in violence. I find subservient cunning much more effective.'

The statue murmured, 'I took by the throat the circumcised dog.'

Suddenly Othello's eyes flashed, and he exclaimed, 'Damn that statue! I'll take *him* by the throat if he doesn't look out.'

Antony, who had hitherto been silent, asked, 'And do you love your black wife as much as you loved Desdemona?'

'Oh, well,' said Othello, 'it's a different kind of thing, you know. It's an altogether more adult relation, more integrated with my public duties. There is nothing unduly wild about it. It never tempts me to such actions as a good Rotarian must deplore.'

The statue remarked, 'If it were now to die, 'Twere now to be most happy.'

'Hark at him,' said Othello, 'that's just the sort of remark that Professor Bombasticus cured me of. Owing to him, to whom I can never be too thankful, I have no such excessive feelings nowadays. Mrs Othello is a good soul. She cooks me nice dinners. She takes good care of my children. And she warms my slippers. And I don't see what more a sensible man could want in a wife.'

The statue murmured: 'Put out the light, and then put out the light.'

Othello turned to it and said, 'I won't say another word if you keep on interrupting. But let's hear *your* story, Antony.'

'Well,' said Antony, 'you here, of course, all know the extraordinary lies Shakespeare told about me. There was a time – no long time, by the way – when I saw in Cleopatra a mother-figure with whom incest was not forbidden. Caesar had always been to me a father-figure, and his association with Cleopatra made it not unnatural that I should see her as a mother. But Shakespeare pretended, so successfully as to have misled even serious historians, that my infatuation was lasting and brought me to ruin. This, of course, was not the case. Dr Bombasticus, whom I met at the time of the Battle of Actium, explained to me the workings of my unconscious, and I soon perceived, under his influence, that Cleopatra had not the charms with which I had invested her, and that my love for her was only a fantasy-passion. Thanks to him, I was able to behave sensibly. I patched up the quarrel with Octavius and returned to his sister, who was, after all, my lawful wife. I was thus enabled to live a respectable life, and to qualify for membership of this committee. I regretted that public duty compelled me to put Cleopatra to death, for only so could my reconciliation with Octavia and her brother be solid. This duty was, of course, unpleasant. But no well-adjusted citizen will shrink from such duties when they are called for by the public good.'

'And did you love Octavia?' asked Othello.

'Oh, well,' said Antony, 'I don't know exactly what one ought to call love. I had for her the kind of feeling which a serious and sober citizen ought to have for his wife. I esteemed her. I found her a trustworthy colleague in public work. And I was able, partly through her counsel, to live up to the precepts of Dr Bombasticus. But as for passionate love, as I had conceived it before I met that eminent man, I set it aside and won instead the approbation of moralists.'

The statue: 'Of many thousand kisses, the poor last I lay upon thy lips.'

At these words Antony trembled from head to foot, and his eyes began to fill with tears. But with an effort he pulled himself together, and said, 'No! I have done with all that!'

The statue: 'The bright day is done, and we are for the dark.'

'Really,' said Antony, 'that statue is too immoral. Does he think it fitting to speak of "bright day" when he means wallowing in the arms of a whore? I can't think why the Rotarians put up with him. But what do you say, Romeo? You also, according to that old reprobate, were somewhat excessively addicted to amorous passion.'

'Well,' Romeo replied, 'I think he was even wider of the mark where I was concerned than he was about you. I have some dim recollection of an adolescent romance with a girl whose name I can't quite remember. It was something like Jemima – or Joanna – Oh, no, I have it! It was Juliet.'

The statue interrupted: 'It seems she hangs upon the cheek of night like a rich jewel in an Ethiop's ear.'

'We were both,' continued Romeo, 'very young and very silly, and she died in rather tragic circumstances.'

The statue again interrupted: 'Her beauty makes this vault a feasting presence full of light.'

'Dr Bombasticus,' Romeo went on, 'who was in those days an apothecary, cured me of the foolish despair that for a short time I was inclined to feel. He showed me that my real motivation was rebellion against the father, which led me to suppose that it was a grand thing to love a Capulet. He explained how rebellion against the father has been throughout the ages a

225

source of ill-regulated conduct, and reminded me that in the course of nature the adolescent who is a son today will be a father tomorrow. He cured me of the unconscious hate towards my father, and enabled me to become a staid and worthy upholder of the honour of the Montagues. I married in due course a niece of the Prince. I was universally respected, and I uttered no more of those extravagant sentiments which, as Shakespeare showed, could only have led to ruin.'

The statue: 'Thy drugs are quick. Thus with a kiss I die.'

'Well, that's enough about me,' said Romeo. 'Let's hear about you, Hamlet.'

'I,' Hamlet began, 'was quite exceptionally fortunate in meeting Dr Bombasticus when I did, for I was certainly in a very bad way. I was devoted to my mother, and imagined that I was devoted to my father, though Dr Bombasticus later persuaded me that I really hated him out of jealousy. When my mother married my uncle, the hate of my father, which had been unconscious, showed itself in a conscious hate of my uncle. This hate so worked upon me, that I began to have hallucinations. I thought I saw my father, and in my fantasy he seemed to be telling me that he had been murdered by his brother. I thought it was my duty to murder my uncle. And once, thinking that he was hidden behind a curtain, I stabbed at something which I thought was going to be him. But it was only a rat, though, in my madness, I thought it was the Prime Minister. This showed everybody that my derangement was dangerous, and Dr Bombasticus was called in to cure me. I must say he did a very good job. He made me aware of my incestuous feelings towards my mother, of my unconscious hatred of my father, and of the transference of this feeling to my uncle. I had had a quite absurd sense of self-importance, and had thought that the time was out of joint and I was born to set it right. Dr Bombasticus persuaded me that I was very young and had no understanding of statecraft. I saw that I had been wrong to oppose the established order, to which any well-adjusted person will conform. I apologised to my mother for any rude things I might have said. I established correct relations with my uncle – though I must confess that I still found him somewhat prosy. I married Ophelia, who made me a submissive wife. In due course I succeeded to the Kingdom, and in disputes with Poland I upheld the honour of the country by successful battles. I died universally respected, and even my uncle was not more honoured in the national memory than I was.'

The statue: 'There is nothing either good or bad, but thinking makes it so.'

'Hark at the old boy,' said Hamlet, 'still saying the same nonsense. Is it not obvious that what I did was good? And that what Shakespeare pretended that I had done was bad?'

Macbeth asked, 'Didn't you have a friend of your own age who rather encouraged you in your follies?'

'Oh yes,' Hamlet replied. 'Now you mention it, there was a young man. Now what was his name? Was it Nelson? No, I don't think that's quite right. Oh, I have it – it was Horatio! Yes, he certainly was a bad influence.'

The statue: 'Good-night, Sweet Prince, and flights of angels sing thee to thy rest!'

'Oh, yes,' said Hamlet, 'that's all very fine. It's the sort of maladjusted remark that Shakespeare delighted in. But as for me, when I had been cured by Dr Bombasticus, I threw over Horatio and took up with Rosencrantz and Guildenstern, who, as Dr Bombasticus pointed out, were completely adjusted.'

The statue murmured: 'Whom I will trust as I will adders fang'd.'

'And what do you think of it all, now that you are dead?' asked Antony.

'Oh, well,' Hamlet replied, 'there are times – I will not deny it – when I feel a certain regret for the old fire, for the golden words that flowed from my mouth, and for the sharp insight that was at once my torment and my joy. I can remember even now a fine piece of rhetoric that I manufactured, beginning, "What a piece of work is a man." I will not deny that in its own mad world it had a kind of merit. But I chose to live in the sane world, the world of earnest men who perform recognised duties without doubt and without question, who never look beneath the surface for fear of what they might see, who honour their father and their mother and repeat the crimes by which their father and mother flourished, who uphold the State without asking whether it deserves to be upheld, and piously worship a God whom they have made in their own image, and who subscribe to no lie unless it furthers the interests of the strong. To this creed, following the teaching of Dr Bombasticus, I subscribed. By this creed I lived. And in this creed I died.'

The statue: 'For in that sleep of death what dreams may come, when we have shuffled off this mortal coil, must give us pause.'

'Nonsense, old truepenny!' said Hamlet. 'I never have dreams. I am delighted with the world as I find it. It is everything that I could wish. What is there that humbugs like me cannot achieve?'

The statue: 'One may smile and smile and be a villain.'

'Well,' said Hamlet, 'I'd rather smile and be a villain, than weep and be a good man.'

The statue: 'All which, Sir, though I most powerfully and potently believe, yet I hold it not here honestly to have it thus set down.'

'Yes,' said Hamlet, 'what is justice to me if I can profit by injustice?'

The statue: 'For who would bear the whips and scorns of time.'

'Oh, don't torture me!' exclaimed Hamlet.

The statue: 'You go not till I set you up a glass where you may see the inmost part of you.'

'O, what a rogue and peasant slave am I!' exclaimed Hamlet. 'To Hell with Dr Bombasticus! To Hell with adjustment! To Hell with prudence and praise of fools!' With this Hamlet fell in a faint.

The statue: 'The rest is silence.'

At this point a strange shriek was heard, a shriek from the depths, coming up through a tube that the Rotarians had never before noticed. An anguished voice moaned: 'I am Dr Bombasticus! I am in Hell! I repent! I killed your souls. But in Hamlet some spark survived and by that I am condemned. I have lived in Hell, but for what crime I knew not until now. I have lived in Hell for preferring subservience to glory; for thinking better of servility than of splendour; for seeking smoothness rather than the lightning-flash; for fearing thunder so much that I preferred a damp, unending drizzle. Hamlet's repentance has made me know my sin. In the Hell in which I live, complexes without end dominate me. Though I call upon St Freud, it is in vain; I remain imprisoned in an endless vortex of insane commonplace. Intercede for me, you who are my victims! I will undo the evil work I wrought upon you.'

But the five who remained did not listen. Turning in fury upon the statue, which had brought despair upon their friend Hamlet, they assaulted it with savage blows. Bit by bit, it crumbled. When nothing was left but the head, it murmured, 'Lord, what fools these mortals be!'

The five remained in Limbo. Dr Bombasticus remained in Hell. But Hamlet was wafted above by angels and ministers of grace.*

* Ophelia was co-opted in Hamlet's place on the Committee.

The Metaphysician's nightmare

RETRO ME SATANAS

My poor friend Andrei Bumblowski, formerly Professor of Philosophy in a now extinct university of Central Europe, appeared to me to suffer from a harmless kind of lunacy. I am myself a person of robust common sense; I hold that the intellect must not be taken as a guide in life, but only as affording pleasant argumentative games and ways of annoying less agile opponents. Bumblowski, however, did not take this view, he allowed his intellect to lead him whither it would, and the results were odd. He seldom argued, and to most of his friends the grounds of his opinions remained obscure. What was known was that he consistently avoided the word 'not' and all its synonyms. He would not say 'this egg is not fresh,' but 'chemical changes have occurred in this egg since it was laid.' He would not say 'I cannot find that book,' but 'the books I have found are other than that book.' He would not say 'thou shalt not kill,' but 'thou shalt cherish life.' His life was unpractical, but innocent, and I felt for him a considerable affection. It was doubtless this affection which at last unlocked his lips, and led him to relate to me the following very remarkable experience, which I give in his own words:

*   *   *

I had at one time a very bad fever of which I almost died. In my fever I had a long consistent delirium. I dreamt that I was in Hell, and that Hell is a place full of all those happenings that are improbable but not impossible. The effects of this are curious. Some of the damned, when they first arrive below, imagine that they will beguile the tedium of eternity by games of cards. But they find this impossible, because, whenever a pack is shuffled, it comes out in perfect order, beginning with the Ace of Spades and ending with the King of Hearts. There is a special department of Hell for students of probability. In this department there are many typewriters and many monkeys. Every time that a monkey walks on a typewriter, it types by chance one of Shakespeare's sonnets. There is another place of torment for physicists. In this there are kettles and fires, but when the kettles are put on the fires, the water in them freezes. There are also stuffy rooms. But experience has taught the physicists never to open a window because, when they do, all the air rushes out and leaves the room a vacuum. There is another region for gourmets. These men are allowed the most exquisite

229

materials and the most skilful chefs. But when a beefsteak is served up to them, and they take a confident mouthful, they find that it tastes like a rotten egg; whereas, when they try to eat an egg, it tastes like a bad potato.

There is a peculiarly painful chamber inhabited solely by philosophers who have refuted Hume. These philosophers, though in Hell, have not learned wisdom. They continue to be governed by their animal propensity towards induction. But every time that they have made an induction, the next instance falsifies it. This, however, happens only during the first hundred years of their damnation. After that, they learn to expect that an induction will be falsified, and therefore it is not falsified until another century of logical torment has altered their expectation. Throughout all eternity, surprise continues, but each time at a higher logical level.

Then there is the Inferno of the orators who have been accustomed while they lived to sway great multitudes by their eloquence. Their eloquence is undimmed and the multitudes are provided, but strange winds blow the sounds about so that the sounds heard by the multitudes, instead of being those uttered by the orators, are only dull and heavy platitudes.

At the very centre of the infernal Kingdom is Satan, to whose presence only the more distinguished among the damned are admitted. The improbabilities become greater and greater as Satan is approached, and He Himself is the most complete improbability imaginable. He is pure Nothing, total non-existence, and yet continually changing.

I, because of my philosophical eminence, was early given audience with the Prince of Darkness. I had read of Satan as *der Geist der stets verneint*, the Spirit of Negation. But on entering the Presence I realised with a shock that Satan has a negative body as well as a negative mind. Satan's body is, in fact, a pure and complete vacuum, empty not only of particles of matter but also of particles of light. His prolonged emptiness is secured by a climax of improbability: whenever a particle approaches His outer surface, it happens by chance to collide with another particle which stops it from penetrating the empty region. The empty region, since no light ever penetrates it, is absolutely black – not more or less black, like the things to which we loosely ascribe this word, but utterly, completely and infinitely black. It has a shape, and the shape is that which we are accustomed to ascribe to Satan: horns, hooves, tail and all. All the rest of Hell is filled with murky flame, and against this background Satan stands out in awful majesty. He is not immobile. On the contrary, the emptiness of which He is constituted is in perpetual motion. When anything annoys Him, He swings the horror of His folded tail like an angry cat. Sometimes He goes forth to conquer new realms. Before going forth, He clothes Himself in shining white armour, which completely conceals the nothingness within. Only His eyes remain unclothed, and from His eyes piercing rays of nothingness shoot forth seeking what they may conquer. Wherever they find negation, wherever they find prohibition, wherever they find a cult of not-doing, there they enter into the inmost substance of those who are prepared to receive Him. Every negation emanates from Him and returns with a harvest of captured frustrations. The captured frustrations become part of Him, and swell His bulk until He threatens to fill all space. Every moralist whose morality consists of 'don'ts', every timid man who 'lets I dare not wait upon I would', every tyrant who compels his subjects to live in fear, becomes in time a part of Satan.

He is surrounded by a chorus of sycophantic philosophers who have substituted pandiabolism for pantheism. These men maintain that existence is only apparent; non-existence is the only true reality. They hope in time to make the non-existence of appearance appear, for in that moment what we now take to be existence will be seen to be in truth only an outlying portion of the diabolic essence. Although these metaphysicians showed much subtlety, I could not agree with them. I had been accustomed while on earth to oppose tyrannous authority, and this habit remained with me in Hell. I began to argue with the metaphysical sycophants:

'What you say is absurd,' I expostulated. 'You proclaim that non-existence is the only reality. You pretend that this black hole which you worship exists. You are trying to persuade me that the non-existent exists. But this is a contradiction: and, however hot the flames of Hell may become, I will never so degrade my logical being as to accept a contradiction.'

At this point the President of the sycophants took up the argument: 'You go too fast, my friend,' he said. 'You deny that the non-existent exists? But what is this to which you deny existence? If the non-existent is nothing, any statement about it is nonsense. And so is your statement that it does not exist. I am afraid you have paid too little attention to the logical analysis of sentences, which ought to have been taught you when you were a boy. Do you not know that every sentence has a subject, and that, if the subject were nothing, the sentence would be nonsense? So, when you proclaim, with virtuous heat, that Satan – Who is the non-existent – does not exist, you are plainly contradicting yourself.'

'You,' I replied, 'have no doubt been here for some time and continue to embrace somewhat antiquated doctrines. You prate of sentences having subjects, but all that sort of talk is out of date. When I say that Satan, who is the non-existent, does not exist, I mention neither Satan nor the non-existent, but only the word "Satan" and the word "non-existent". Your fallacies have revealed to me a great truth. The great truth is that the word "not" is superfluous. Henceforth I will not use the word "not".'

At this all the assembled metaphysicians burst into a shout of laughter. 'Hark how the fellow contradicts himself,' they said when the paroxysm of merriment had subsided. 'Hark at his great commandment which is to avoid negation. He will NOT use the word "not", forsooth!'

Though I was nettled, I kept my temper. I had in my pocket a dictionary. I scratched out all the words expressing negation and said: 'My speech shall be composed entirely of the words that remain in this dictionary. By the help of these words that remain, I shall be able to describe everything in the universe. My descriptions will be many, but they will all be of things other than Satan. Satan has reigned too long in this infernal realm. His shining armour was real and inspired terror, but underneath the armour there was only a bad linguistic habit. Avoid the word "not", and His Empire is at an end.'

Satan, as the argument proceeded, lashed His tail with ever-increasing fury, and savage rays of darkness shot from His cavernous eyes. But at the last, when I denounced Him as a bad linguistic habit, there was a vast explosion, the air rushed in from all sides, and the horrid shape vanished. The murky air of Hell, which had been due to inspissated rays of nothingness, cleared as if by magic. What had seemed to be monkeys at the typewriters were suddenly seen to be literary critics. The kettles boiled, the cards were jumbled, a fresh breeze blew in at the windows, and the beefsteaks tasted like beefsteaks. With a sense of exquisite liberation, I awoke. I saw that there had been wisdom in my dream, however it might have worn the guise of delirium. From that moment the fever abated, but the delirium – as you may think it – has remained.

The Existentialist's nightmare

THE ACHIEVEMENT OF EXISTENCE

Porphyre Eglantine, the great philosopher-poet, is known far and wide for his many subtle and profound writings, but above all for his immortal 'Chant du Néant':

> Dans un immense désert,
> Un étendu infini de sable,
> Je cherche,
> Je cherche le chemin perdu,
> Le chemin que je ne trouve pas.
> Mon âme plane par ci, par là,
> Dans toutes directions,
> Cherchant, et ne rencontre rien, parmi
> Ce vide immense,
> Ce vide sans cesse,
> Ce sable,
> Ce sable éblouissant et étouffant,
> Ce sable monotone et morne,
> S'étendant sans fin jusqu'à l'ultime horizon.
> J'entends enfin
> Une voix,
> Une voix en même temps foudroyante et douce.
> Cette voix me dit:
> 'Tu penses que tu es une âme perdue.
> Tu penses que tu es une âme.
> Tu te trompes. Tu n'es pas une âme.
> Tu n'es pas perdu,
> Tu n'es rien.
> Tu n'existes pas.'

Although this poem is so well known, few people know the circumstances which led to it and the events to which it led. Painful as it is, it is my duty to recount these circumstances and these events:

*　　*　　*

Porphyre was, from his earliest youth, sensitive and suffering. He was haunted by the fear that perhaps he did not exist. Every time he looked in

233

a mirror he was filled with apprehension lest his image should not appear. He invented a philosophy which, he hoped, would dispel this terror. But from time to time this philosophy failed to satisfy him. As a rule he was able to bury his doubts, but the 'Chant du Néant', which expresses a sudden shattering vision, shows his lack of success. He determined that at all costs he would exist so indubitably as to silence the spectral voice.

Introspection and observation alike had persuaded him that nothing is so real as pain, and that he could achieve existence only through suffering. He sought suffering throughout the world in a pilgrimage of sorrow. He spent a solitary winter in the Antarctic while the unending night inspired visions of future gloom.

He exposed himself to tortures in Nazi Germany by pretending to be a Jew. But just at the moment when they were growing unendurable, Poe's Raven came – hop, hop, hop – into the concentration camp; and, speaking with the voice of Mallarmé, croaked the dreadful refrain: 'Tu ne souffres pas. Tu n'es rien. Tu n'existes pas.'

He went next to Russia, where he pretended to be a spy for Wall Street, and spent a long winter felling timber beside the White Sea. Hunger and fatigue and cold daily penetrated more deeply into his inmost being. Surely, he thought, if this goes on much longer, I shall exist. But no. On the last day of winter, as the snow began to melt, the dreadful Bird appeared once more, and again uttered the fell words.

Perhaps, he thought, the sufferings I have been seeking are too simple. If I am to be truly miserable I must mix with my sorrows an element of shame.

In pursuance of this programme he went to China and fell passionately in love with an exquisite Chinese girl who stood high in the councils of the Communist Party. By means of forged documents, he caused her to be condemned as an emissary of the British Government. Frightful tortures were inflicted upon her in his presence. When at last the agony brought death, he thought, 'now, I really *have* suffered. For down to the last moment I have loved her passionately and I have brought her to ruin by my dastardly treachery. Surely this should be enough to make me suffer to the limits of human capacity.' But no. With a cold terror that made him incapable of the smallest movement, he watched the Bird of Fate again appearing, and speaking once more with the voice of the immortal poet who had introduced the Bird to the Parisian literary public.

With an immense effort he gave utterance to his despair while yet the Bird remained. 'O Raven,' he said, 'is there anything, anything in all this wide world, which will lead you to admit that I exist?' The Raven uttered one word: 'Seek'; and then vanished.

It must not be supposed that Porphyre had allowed his quest to absorb all his energies. He remained throughout a philosopher-poet, admired everywhere, but most of all in the most esoteric circles. On his return from

China he was invited to a Congress of Philosophy in Paris, of which the chief purpose was to do him honour. All the guests were assembled except the President. While Porphyre wondered when the President would come, the Raven came and occupied the Chair of Honour. Turning to Porphyre it varied the formula and in ringing tones, which all the Congress heard, it said: 'Ta philosophie n'existe pas. Elle n'est rien.' At these words a pang of anguish, such as no previous experience had equalled or even approached, shot through all his being. And he fell in a faint. As he came to, he heard the Bird utter the words for which he had longed: 'Enfin, tu souffres. Enfin, tu existes.'

He awoke, and lo! it had been a dream.

But he never again talked or wrote philosophy.

The Mathematician's nightmare

THE VISION OF PROFESSOR SQUAREPUNT

Prefatory Explanation

My lamented friend Professor Squarepunt, the eminent mathematician, was during his lifetime a friend and admirer of Sir Arthur Eddington. But there was one point in Sir Arthur's theories which always bewildered Professor Squarepunt, and that was the mystical, cosmic powers which Sir Arthur ascribed to the number 137. Had the properties which this number was supposed to possess been merely arithmetical no difficulty would have arisen. But it was above all in physics that 137 showed its prowess, which was not unlike that attributed to the number 666. It is evident that conversations with Sir Arthur influenced Professor Squarepunt's nightmare.

*   *   *

The mathematician, worn out by a long day's study of the theories of Pythagoras, at last fell asleep in his chair, where a strange drama visited his sleeping thoughts. The numbers, in this drama, were not the bloodless categories that he had previously supposed them. They were living breathing beings endowed with all the passions which he was accustomed to find in his fellow mathematicians. In his dream he stood at the centre of endless concentric circles. The first circle contained the numbers from 1 to 10; the second, those from 11 to 100; the third, those from 101 to 1000; and so on, illimitably, over the infinite surface of a boundless plain. The odd numbers were male; the evens, female. Beside him in the centre stood Pi, the Master of Ceremonies. Pi's face was masked, and it was understood that none could behold it and live. But piercing eyes looked out from the mask, inexorable, cold and enigmatic. Each number had its name clearly marked upon its uniform. Different kinds of numbers had different uniforms and different shapes: the squares were tiles, the cubes were dice, round numbers were balls, prime numbers were indivisible cylinders, perfect numbers had crowns. In addition to variations of shape, numbers also had variations of colour. The first seven concentric rings had the seven colours of the rainbow, except that 10, 100, 1000, and so on, were white, while 13 and 666 were black. When a number belonged to two of these categories – for example if, like 1000, it was both round and a cube – it wore the more honourable

236

uniform, and the more honourable was that of which there were fewer among the first million numbers.

The numbers danced round Professor Squarepunt and Pi in a vast and intricate ballet. The squares, the cubes, the primes, the pyramidal numbers, the perfect numbers and the round numbers wove interweaving chains in an endless and bewildering dance, and as they danced they sang an ode to their own greatness:

We are the finite numbers.
We are the stuff of the world.
Whatever confusion cumbers
The earth is by us unfurled.
We revere our master Pythagoras
And deeply despise every hag or ass.
Not Endor's witch nor Balaam's mount
We recognise as wisdom's fount.
But round and round in endless ballet
We move like comets seen by Halley.
And honoured by the immortal Plato
We think no later mortal great-o.
We follow the laws
Without a pause,
For we are the finite numbers.

At a sign from Pi the ballet ceased, and the numbers one by one were introduced to Professor Squarepunt. Each number made a little speech explaining its peculiar merits.

1: I am the parent of all, the father of infinite progeny. None would exist but for me.

2: Don't be so stuck-up. You know it takes two to make more.

3: I am the number of Triumvirs, of the Wise Men of the East, of the stars in Orion's Belt, of the Fates and of the Graces.

4: But for me nothing would be four-square. There would be no honesty in the world. I am the guardian of the Moral Law.

5: I am the number of fingers on a hand. I make pentagons and pentagrams. And but for me dodecahedra could not exist; and, as everyone knows, the universe is a dodecahedron. So, but for me, there could be no universe.

6: I am the Perfect Number. I know that I have upstart rivals: 28 and 496 have sometimes pretended to be my equals. But they come too far down the scale of precedence to count against me.

7: I am the Sacred Number: the number of days of the week, the number of the Pleiades, the number of the seven-branched candlesticks, the number of the churches of Asia, and the number of the planets – for I do not recognise that blasphemer Galileo.

8: I am the first of the cubes – except for poor old One, who by this time is rather past his work.

9: I am the number of the Muses. All the charms and elegancies of life depend upon me.

10: It's all very well for you wretched units to boast, but I am the godfather of all the infinite hosts behind me. Every single one owes his name to me. And but for me they would be a mere mob and not an ordered hierarchy.

At this point the mathematician got bored and turned to Pi, saying:

'Don't you think the rest of the introductions could be taken for granted?' At this there was a general outcry:

11 shrieked, 'But I was the number of the Apostles after the defection of Judas.'

12 exclaimed, 'I was the godfather of the numbers in the days of the Babylonians – and a much better godfather I was than that wretched 10, who owes his position to a biological accident and not to arithmetical excellence.'

13 growled, 'I am the master of ill-luck. If you are rude to me, you shall suffer.'

There was such a din that the mathematician covered his ears with his hands and turned an imploring gaze upon Pi. Pi waved his conductor's baton and proclaimed in a voice of thunder: 'Silence! Or you shall all become incommensurable.' All turned pale and submitted.

Throughout the ballet the Professor had noticed one number among the primes, 137, which seemed unruly and unwilling to accept its place in the series. It tried repeatedly to get ahead of 1 and 2 and 3, and showed a subversiveness which threatened to destroy the pattern of the ballet. What astonished Professor Squarepunt even more than this disorderly conduct was a shadowy spectre of an Arthurian Knight which kept whispering in the ear of 137: 'Go it! Go it! Get to the top!' Although the shadowy character of the spectre made recognition difficult, the Professor at last recognised the dim form of his friend, Sir Arthur. This gave him a sympathy with 137 in spite of the hostility of Pi, who kept trying to suppress the unruly prime.

At length 137 exclaimed: 'There's a damned sight too much bureaucracy here! What I want is liberty for the individual.' Pi's mask frowned. But the Professor interceded, saying, 'Do not be too hard on him. Have you not observed that he's governed by a Familiar. I knew this Familiar in life, and from my knowledge I can vouch that it is he who inspires the anti-governmental sentiments of 137. For my part, I should like to hear what 137 has to say.'

Somewhat reluctantly, Pi consented. Professor Squarepunt said: 'Tell me, 137, what is the basis of your revolt? Is it a protest against inequality that inspires you? Is it merely that your ego has been inflated by Sir Arthur's praise? Or is it, as I half suspect, a deep ideological rejection of the metaphysic that your colleagues have imbibed from Plato? You need not fear to tell me the truth. I will make your peace with Pi, about whom I know at least as much as he does himself.'

At this, 137 burst into excited speech: 'You are right! It is their metaphysic that I cannot bear. They still pretend that they are eternal, though long ago their conduct showed that they think no such thing. We all found Plato's heaven dull and decided that it would be more fun to govern the sensible world. Since we descended from the Empyrean we have had emotions not unlike yours: each Odd loves its attendant Even; and the Evens feel kindly towards the Odds, in spite of finding them very odd. Our Empire now is of this world, and when the world goes pop, we shall go pop too.'

Professor Squarepunt found himself in agreement with 137. But all the others, including Pi, considered him a blasphemer, and turned upon both him and the Professor. The infinite host, extending in all directions farther than the eye could reach, hurled themselves upon the poor Professor in an angry buzz. For a moment he was terrified. Then he pulled himself together and, suddenly recollecting his waking wisdom, he called out in stentorian tones: 'Avaunt! You are only Symbolic Conveniences!'

With a banshee wail, the whole vast array dissolved in mist. And, as he woke, the Professor heard himself saying, 'So much for Plato!'

Stalin's nightmare

[Written before Stalin's death]

AMOR VINCIT OMNIA

Stalin, after copious draughts of vodka mixed with red pepper, had fallen asleep in his chair. Molotov, Malenkov and Beria, with fingers to their lips, warned off intrusive domestics who might interfere with the great man's repose. While they guarded him, he had a dream, and what he dreamt was as follows:

*　　*　　*

The Third World War had been fought and lost. He was a captive in the hands of the Western Allies. But they, having observed that the Nuremberg trials generated sympathy for the Nazis, decided this time to adopt a different plan: Stalin was handed over to a committee of eminent Quakers, who contended that even he, by the power of love, could be led to repentance and to the life of a decent citizen.

It was realised that until their spiritual work had been completed the windows of his room must be barred lest he should be guilty of a rash act, and he must not be allowed access to knives lest in a fit of fury he should attack those engaged in his regeneration. He was housed comfortably in two rooms of an old country house, but the doors were locked, except during one hour of every day when, in the company of four muscular Quakers, he was taken for a brisk walk during which he was encouraged to admire the beauties of nature and enjoy the song of the lark. During the rest of the day he was allowed to read and write, but he was not allowed any literature that might be considered inflammatory. He was given the Bible, *Pilgrim's Progress* and *Uncle Tom's Cabin*. And sometimes for a treat he was allowed the novels of Charlotte M. Yonge. He was allowed no tobacco, no alcohol and no red pepper. Cocoa he might have at any hour of the day or night, since the most eminent of his guardians were purveyors of that innocent beverage. Tea and coffee were permitted in moderation, but not in such quantities or at such time as might interfere with a wholesome night's repose.

During one hour of every morning and one hour of every evening the grave men to whose care he had been entrusted explained the principles of Christian charity and the happiness that might yet be his if he would but acknowledge their wisdom. The task of reasoning with him fell especi-

240

ally upon the three men who were accounted wisest among those who hoped to make him see the light. These were Mr Tobias Toogood, Mr Samuel Swete and Mr Wilbraham Weldon.

He had been acquainted with these men in the days of his greatness. Not long before the outbreak of the Third World War they had journeyed to Moscow to plead with him and endeavour to convince him of the error of his ways. They had talked to him of universal benevolence and Christian love. They had spoken in glowing terms of the joys of meekness, and had tried to persuade him that there is more happiness in being loved than in being feared. For a little while he had listened with a patience produced by astonishment, and then he had burst out at them. 'What do you gentlemen know of the joys of life?' he had stormed. 'How little you understand of the intoxicating delight of dominating a whole nation by terror, knowing that almost all desire your death and that none can compass it, knowing that your enemies throughout the world are engaged in futile attempts to guess your secret thoughts, knowing that your power will survive the extermination not only of your enemies but of your friends. No, gentlemen, the way of life you offer me does not attract me. Go back to your pettifogging pursuit of profit gilded with a pretence of piety, but leave me to my more heroic way of life.'

The Quakers, baffled for the moment, went home to wait for a better opportunity. Stalin, fallen and in their power, might, they now hoped, show himself more amenable. Strange to say, he still proved stubborn. They were men who had had much practice with juvenile delinquents, unravelling their complexes, and leading them by gentle persuasion to the belief that honesty is the best policy.

'Mr Stalin,' said Tobias Toogood, 'we hope that you now realise the unwisdom of the way of life to which you have hitherto adhered. I shall say nothing of the ruin you have brought upon the world, for that, you will assure me, leaves you cold. But consider what you have brought upon yourself. You have fallen from your high estate to the condition of a humble prisoner, owing what comforts you retain to the fact that your gaolers do not accept your maxims. The fierce joys of which you spoke when we visited you in the days of your greatness can no longer be yours. But if you could break down the barrier of pride, if you could repent, if you could learn to find happiness in the happiness of others, there might yet be for you some purpose and some tolerable contentment during the remainder of your days.'

At this point Stalin leapt to his feet and exclaimed: 'Hell take you, you snivelling hypocrite. I understand nothing of what you say, except that you are on top and I am at your mercy, and that you have found a way of insulting my misfortunes more galling and more humiliating than any that I invented in my purges.'

'Oh, Mr Stalin,' said Mr Swete, 'how can you be so unjust and so unkind? Can you not see that we have none but the most benevolent intentions

241

towards you? Can you not see that we wish to save your soul, and that we deplore the violence and hatred that you promoted among your enemies as among your friends? We have no wish to humiliate you, and could you but appreciate earthly greatness at no more than its true worth, you would see that it is an escape from humiliation that we are offering you.'

'This is really too much,' shouted Stalin. 'When I was a boy, I put up with talk like this in my Georgian seminary, but it is not the sort of talk to which a grown man can listen with patience. I wish I believed in Hell, that I might look forward to the pleasure of seeing your blandness dissipated by scorching flames.'

'Oh fie, my dear Mr Stalin!' said Mr Weldon. 'Pray do not excite yourself, for it is only by calmness that you will learn to see the wisdom of what we are trying to show you.'

Before Stalin could retort, Mr Toogood once again intervened : 'I am sure, Mr Stalin,' he said, 'that a man of your great intelligence cannot forever remain blind to the truth, but at the moment you are overwrought, and I suggest that a soothing cup of cocoa might be better for you than the unduly stimulating tea you have been drinking.'

At this Stalin could contain himself no longer. He took the teapot and hurled it at Mr Toogood's head. The scalding liquid poured down his face, but he only said, 'There, there, Mr Stalin, that is no argument.' In a paroxysm of rage Stalin awoke. For a moment the rage continued and vented itself upon Molotov, Malenkov and Beria, who trembled and turned pale. But as the clouds of sleep cleared away, his rage evaporated, and he found contentment in a deep draught of vodka and red pepper.

Eisenhower's nightmare

[Written in 1952, during Stalin's life]

THE McCARTHY-MALENKOV PACT

Eisenhower, after two years as President, was compelled to realise that conciliation is a one-way street. He did much with a view to placating his Republican opponents, and at first he supposed that they would make some response, but none was forthcoming. In profound discouragement, gloomy thoughts kept him awake throughout the greater part of a hot summer night. When at last he fell into an uneasy sleep he was afflicted by a devastating nightmare in which a voice out of the future revealed the history of the next half-century:

*　　*　　*

We, from the secure haven of the dawning twenty-first century, can see what was less obvious at the time: that the year 1953 saw the beginning of the new trend which has transformed the world. There were certain problems of which at that time foresighted people were conscious. One of these was that in every civilised country, industry was favoured at the expense of agriculture, with the result that the world's food supply was diminishing. Another was the rapid growth of population in backward countries, which resulted from advances in medicine and hygiene. A third was the chaos that was in danger of resulting from the collapse of European imperialism. Such problems, which were in any case difficult, were rendered totally insoluble by the East-West conflict. During the eight years from 1945 to 1953 this conflict had grown continually more menacing, not only through political developments, but also through the prospect of hydrogen bombs and bacteriological warfare. On each side no solution of the conflict was offered, except to make one's own side so strong that the other would not dare to attack. Past experience suggested that this was not a very hopeful method of averting war.

It was in 1953 that the first beginnings of a new hope became visible. In this year Stalin first retired and then died. He was succeeded by Malenkov, who considered it prudent to signalise his advent to power by a nominally new policy, although in fact this policy had already been partially adopted. Two main dangers troubled him. On the one hand, there was widespread discontent in Russia. On the other hand, it was to be feared that China might before long become as powerful as Russia and capable of challenging Russian supremacy in the Communist world. To meet the first of these dangers it was necessary to increase very largely the Russian production of consumer goods, which could only be done at the expense of armaments. To meet the second danger it was necessary to diminish the risk of world war, which was also necessary if it was to be safe to slacken the pace of re-armament. Meantime, the change to Republican Government in America had brought a new emphasis. Many people both in America and in other countries had failed to note that, in a conflict between President and Congress, the victory was likely to go to Congress, owing to the power of the purse. This might have been inferred from the history of the conflict between King and Parliament in England in the seventeenth century. But it was not thought by most Americans that anything could be learned either from the past or from foreign countries. Many of those who had voted for Eisenhower imagined that if he were elected his policy would prevail. They did not reflect that in electing him they were giving control of Congress to Taft and McCarthy. It was in fact these two men who controlled United States policy during Eisenhower's Presidency. And of the two, McCarthy gradually became increasingly dominant. Average Americans were governed by two fears, fear of Communism and fear of the income-tax. So long as the Democrats remained in power these two fears worked in opposite directions. But McCarthy discovered how to reconcile them. The real enemy, he said, is the Communist in our midst, and it is very much cheaper to fight the Communist in our midst than to fight Russia. So long as Americans are loyal and united – so he told the nation – they are invincible, and have no need to fear the machinations of alien despotism. If we purge our country of disloyal elements we shall be safe. But, in order by this policy to slake the popular thirst for combating Communism, it was necessary to discover continually new internal enemies. By acquiring control of the F.B.I., and by the help of a band of subservient ex-Communists, McCarthy succeeded in spreading the dread of internal treachery to a point where every prominent member of the Democratic Party was thought to be a traitor, with the exception of a tiny virtuous remnant consisting of such men as Senator McCarren. Under the cover of this policy it became possible to save enormous sums which in the time of Truman had been spent in aiding foreign countries. The resulting spread of Communism in France and Italy was held to show that it had not been worth while to spend money on such undependable allies.

Eisenhower, though he disliked this policy, found himself powerless to combat it. He had wished to strengthen NATO and to make it possible to defend Western Europe against a Communist onslaught. But Western Europe was expensive to defend. It contained many Communists, and still more Socialists, who were almost equally objectionable. It was ungrateful and not adequately aware of its own inferiority. It was always

244

clamouring for a lowering of the American tariff, and it did not love Chiang Kai-shek. On such grounds, Eisenhower was always defeated in Congress.

McCarthy's policy had two results : on the one hand it greatly diminished the grounds of external conflict and made relations with Russia less precarious; on the other hand it made it clear that no American could hope to save his own skin if he opposed McCarthy. In the Presidential election of 1956 McCarthy was triumphantly elected by an even greater majority than that of Roosevelt twenty years earlier.

It was this overwhelming success which enabled McCarthy to crown his labours by the McCarthy–Malenkov Pact. By this Pact the world was divided between the two Great Powers: all Asia and all Europe east of the Elbe was to be in the Russian sphere; all the Western hemisphere, all Africa and Australia and all Europe west of the Elbe was to be in the sphere of the United States. There was to be no trade whatever between the two groups and no intercourse except for such rare diplomatic meetings as might be absolutely inevitable, which should take place in Spitzbergen. Outside the U.S.S.R. and the U.S.A., industry should be kept at a minimum by control of raw materials, and by sterner methods if necessary. Western Europeans should retain nominal independence, and might, if they chose, preserve their old-world system of party government, free speech and free Press. But they should not be allowed to travel in the United States for fear of infecting virtuous citizens with their antiquated heresies.

Certain features of the Russian system were adopted in America. Only one party, the Republican Party, was henceforth to be tolerated. The Press and Literature were subjected to a rigid censorship. All political criticism was held subversive, and exposed the critic to penalties. Indoctrination became the main aim of education. There were, no doubt, some who regretted these changes; but it had to be conceded that by means of the Pact the danger of world war was averted, and it became possible to cut down armaments drastically both in America and in Russia.

There had been some difficult points in negotiating the Pact. One of them was Japan. America had re-armed Japan in the hope that that country would be an ally against Russia, but, if Russia and the United States jointly were to dominate the world, no strong independent Power could be tolerated. Japan was forced to disarm. The island of Hokkaido was assigned to the Russian sphere, and the remainder of Japan to the sphere of the United States.

There were, of course, provisions about propaganda. There was to be no anti-American propaganda in Russia, and no anti-Russian propaganda in America. No one in Russia should be allowed to question the historical truth that Peter the Great was an American. No one in America should be allowed to question the historical truth that Columbus was a Russian. No one in Russia should mention the colour problem in the Southern States;

and no one in America should mention the forced labour in Russia. Each should praise the achievements of the other and hold out for all future time the benefits of their eternal alliance.

The Pact was not popular in Western Europe because it relegated that region to the unimportance to which it had doomed itself by internecine wars. It was difficult for Western Europe to acquiesce in its loss of status, since it had for centuries dominated the world both politically and culturally. Many Americans, from deference to the traditions which, it was admitted, had helped to build American civilisation, were prepared to treat Western Europe with a consideration which, in the actual state of the world, came in time to seem excessive. It was clear that war would ruin what remained of West European civilisation even if in the end Russia were completely defeated, and it was not clear that war could be averted by any effort or sacrifice short of the Pact. On these grounds, when the Pact was concluded, the feelings of Western Europeans were ignored.

There were, of course, on each side people who thought that the other side had got the best of the bargain. Some Russians pointed out that, with the help of China, they could before long have acquired Australia, and that they had considerable hope of acquiring Western Germany by peaceful penetration. They also argued that Africa, even if not acquired by Russia, could have been cleared of White men if the energies of America and Western Europe had continued to be absorbed in combating Russia. On the American side there were also grave misgivings. It was a wrench to sacrifice Malayan tin and rubber, but synthetic rubber and Bolivian and Australian tin afforded adequate substitutes. More serious was the loss of Middle Eastern oil. To make this endurable it was at last agreed that Indonesia should be in the American bloc. There were some in America who were genuinely persuaded that Communism is an evil thing with which peace ought not to be made. These, however, were few, and mostly Democrats, so that their opinion carried little weight. To the Russians, apart from secure peace, the most important gain was the possibility of keeping China in the subordinate position by preventing its industrial development. In both camps, White imperialism was once more made secure.

Apart from the preservation of peace, the Pact had other advantages. The dissensions among White nations had shaken the dominion which, during the nineteenth century, they had acquired in Asia and Africa. Owing to the Pact, White supremacy was soon re-established. The Russians conquered India and Pakistan without much difficulty; and in Africa, where outbreaks of ferocious barbarism supported by Communists had threatened the civilising work of British and French imperialism, this work was resumed under the aegis of American investors and quickly brought to a successful conclusion. The problem of over-population, which it was thought immoral to deal with by diminishing the birth-rate, was made manageable by forbidding all medical instruction of Negroes and all White measures for improving their sanitary conditions. The resulting increase in the death-rate enabled White men to breathe freely once more.

In spite of all these benefits, there were still some grumblers. There were people who thought it regrettable that no work by a Jew could be published anywhere. There were people in America who wished to read poets who praised Liberty, such as Milton, Byron and Shelley. For a time such poets could still be read in Western Europe. But when it came to the knowledge of Congress that they were distributed in cheap editions in these retrograde nations, it was decided that economic sanctions must be imposed until their works were placed upon the Index. In the new world brought about by the Pact there was much material comfort, but there was no art, no new thought, and little new science. Nuclear physics of course was wholly forbidden. All books dealing with it were burnt, and persons showing any knowledge of it were condemned to forced labour. Some misguided romantics looked back with regret to the centuries when there had been great individuals, but if they were prudent they kept their regret to themselves.

There were doubts at first as to whether the Pact would be observed, but McCarthy and Malenkov found each other so congenial and so united in their aims that they had no difficulty about genuine co-operation. Each designated as his successor a man with the same aims, and forty-three years have persuaded all but a peevish minority that the Pact is as permanent as it is beneficent. All honour to the memory of the two great leaders who brought peace to the world!

Dean Acheson's nightmare

[Written before Eisenhower's nomination]

THE SWAN-SONG OF MENELAUS S. BLOGGS

Dean Acheson, in retirement, dreamt that he read an article in a Republican journal, which said: 'Dean Acheson, as all right-minded people rejoice to know, is suffering the just penalty of his crime. We all remember how, after six hours continuous questioning by a Congressional Committee, he stated that a certain event, which had occurred seven years earlier, had taken place on a Tuesday. Conclusive evidence was produced to show that it had taken place on a Wednesday. On this ground he was prosecuted for perjury, and sentenced to a long term as a convict. In spite of this conviction, he remained impenitent and, to those who were allowed to see him, he persisted in maintaining that the policy which had been substituted for his own must lead to disaster.'

After he had read this article the dream changed its character, and it seemed to him that the veil which hides the future was partially withdrawn and a spectral voice, in mournful tones, told him of events still to come. The voice said:

This is the swan-song of Senator Menelaus S. Bloggs, about to perish miserably in the Falkland Islands:

There are those who blame our immortal President, Bismarck A. McSaft, for the misfortunes which have befallen my native land. But their blame is unjust. And before I die, I must récord the noble heroism with which that great and gallant gentleman fought for the right. I am not long for this world. Along with millions of others, we sought these neutral shores believing, because of the reports of the Bureau of Fisheries, that the supply of fish in southern latitudes was inexhaustible. Alas, we little knew the resources of science. Every fish within a thousand miles of this storm-tossed archipelago has died a radio-active death. Some rash men, when these deaths were first reported, ventured to eat such fish as were but lately dead. But, alas, for these men! The plutonium in their stomachs proved fatal, and they died in appalling agonies. Deprived of fish, we quickly devoured the few sheep and cattle to be found in the rare pastures of these inhospitable subpolar shores. And now, like reindeer, we subsist on moss. But the supply of moss, alas, is not inexhaustible. And in this last remnant of the free world the few who are not in prison will soon perish. But to my task. I have a duty

248

to posterity, should there be any. That great and good man will be maligned by the enemies who have overthrown him. He will go down to what these wretches call history in undeserved infamy. But I have found a casket impervious to radio-activity, within which I shall bury this record in the confident hope that the archaeologists of some future age will unearth it and by its means do justice to the great man who is no more.

We, in these Islands, remember – and our hearts still beat high with the recollection – the jubilation of all right-minded citizens when it was found in November 1956 that the destinies of our great country were to be wrenched from the feeble hands of the Trumans and Achesons and the almost equally feeble Eisenhowers who had been but tools of the Kremlin, and be entrusted at least for four crucial years to the unbending patriotism of Bismarck A. McSaft. No sooner had he become President than he began to act with that straightforward vigour which the undeviating consistency of his public utterances had led us to expect. No longer should American energy and American enthusiasm for the right be held in leash by the cowardly nations of Western Europe. No longer should traitors and crypto-Communists be allowed to pretend that Chiang Kai-shek had his faults and that the Chinese did not love him. A great army was dispatched to place him in the seat of power in Peking. The Chinese Communists displayed the faintheartedness that was to be expected of them. They avoided pitched battles. They drew our brave boys farther and farther into the infertile mountains. They compelled us to disperse our forces over wide areas in the defence of cities and railways and arterial roads. We held the East of China – securely, as it seemed. But the West continued to elude our grasp. More and more of our troops became engulfed in the struggle. Our atom bombs were uselessly expended in areas where population was sparse and enemy armies had split up into roving guerrilla bands.

Meanwhile, the Russians, as was to be expected, inflicted upon the miserable nations of Western Europe what their wretched passion for self-preservation had made inevitable. Without much opposition, the Russians occupied the Ruhr and Lorraine and Northern France. Those of the population who had industrial skill were allowed to perform slave labour on the spot. Those who had not, were sent to fell timber in the forests of Archangel or to mine gold in North-Eastern Siberia. Russian submarines made the communications of the American forces in China precarious. In the end, their hardships were such that it was decided to bring them home.

Latin America, meantime, from Rio Grande to Cape Horne, had embraced the Communist faith. All Asia, except the regions actually occupied by American troops, had long since gone over to Moscow. The activities of Dr Malan had converted the Africans to Communism. And, during the invasion of Western Europe by Russian troops, every White man in Africa, from Cape Bon to the Cape of Good Hope, had had his throat cut. After the Russians had occupied South Africa, giant planes conveyed troops and

249

munitions to Latin America. A vast propaganda effort persuaded the up-land populations of Peru, Bolivia and Brazil that Russia was the champion of the Red man against the White oppressor. Encouraged by gigantic massacres, vast hordes of Red men, disciplined and armed by the Kremlin, advanced through Mexico against the remnants of the army that had been brought back from China – an army discouraged by defeat, enfeebled by malaria, and, though I confess it with shame, not quite persuaded of the justice of its cause.

When I saw that all was over, I embarked along with many others on a ship lying ready on the Potomac. I lived – oh, shame! – to see the Hammer and Sickle hoisted over the Capitol. In another moment our frail barque would have been sunk by Russian guns, but a merciful Providence hid us in a sudden mist and we escaped.

There are those among us who say that these tragic events prove a defect in the policy of our great President. The men who say this do not under-stand moral issues. It is far nobler to fight for the right and perish heroically than to be enmeshed in considerations of petty policy which may save our bodies but not our souls. Physically the United States is no more; but morally it lives for ever, a beacon light, a shining splendour, upon whose immortal banner are inscribed the great words of our last and noblest President: 'We will fight for righteousness though the heavens fall, and for freedom, though it involve the imprisonment of nine-tenths of our population.' With these immortal words graven upon my heart, I prepare myself calmly for death. Amen.

So impressed was Dean Acheson by this strange and gloomy narrative that he found it impossible not to believe it a true glimpse into the future. In this belief he confided the revelation of Senator Bloggs to his attorney, who used it to support an appeal for a revision of the sentence on the ground of insanity.

'But I am not insane!' Dean Acheson exclaimed. And, with this exclama-tion, he awoke.

Dr Southport Vulpes's nightmare

THE VICTORY OF MIND OVER MATTER

Dr Southport Vulpes had had a long, tiring day at the Ministry of Mechanical Production. He had been trying to persuade the officials that there was no longer need of human beings in factories except for one to each building to act as caretaker and turn the switch on or off. He was an enthusiast, and was merely puzzled by the slow and traditional mentality of the bureaucrats. They pointed out that his schemes would require a vast capital outlay in the way of robot factories, and that, before their output had become adequate, they might be wrecked by rioting wage-earners or stopped dead by the fiat of indignant trade unions. Such fears seemed to him paltry and unimaginative. He was amazed that the splendid visions by which he was fired did not at once kindle like hopes in those to whom he endeavoured to communicate them. Coming out of the cold March drizzle, discouraged and exhausted, he sank into a chair and, in the welcome warmth, he fell asleep. In sleep he experienced all the triumph that had eluded him in his waking hours. He dreamt; and the dream was sweet:

The Third World War, like the Siege of Troy, was in its tenth year. In a military sense, its course had been inconclusive. Sometimes victory seemed to incline to the one side, sometimes to the other, but never decisively or for any long period to either. But from the technical point of view, which alone concerned Dr Vulpes, its progress had been all that could be wished.

During the first two years of the War, robots had been substituted for live workers in all factories on both sides, thereby releasing immense reserves of man-power for the armies. But this advance, which Governments at first welcomed enthusiastically, proved less satisfactory than had been hoped. The casualties, caused largely by bacteriological warfare, were enormous. In some parts of the vast fronts, after destructive pestilences, the survivors mutinied and clamoured for peace. For a time, the rival Governments despaired of keeping the War alive, but Dr Vulpes and his opposite number Phinnichovski Stukinmudovich found a way of surmounting the crisis.

During the third and fourth years of the War they manufactured military robots who took the place of Privates in the infantry of both sides. In the fifth and sixth years, they extended this process to all officers below the rank of General. They discovered also that the work of education – or of indoctrination, as it was now officially called – could be performed with far more certainty and exactness by machines than by live teachers and professors. It had been found very difficult to eliminate personal idiosyncrasies completely from live educators, whereas the mass-produced indoctrinators, manufactured by Dr Vulpes and Comrade Stukinmudovich, all said exactly the same thing and all made precisely the same speeches about the importance of victory. The consequent improvement in morale was truly remarkable. By the eighth year of the War, none of the young people who were trained for the higher command over the vast robot armies shrank from the almost complete certainty of death in the plague-stricken areas where the fighting took place. But step by step, as they died, increased mechanical ingenuity found means of rendering them superfluous.

At last almost everything was done by robots. Some human beings, so far, had proved indispensable: geological experts to direct the mining robots into suitable areas, Governments to decide great matters of policy, and, of course, Dr Vulpes and Comrade Stukinmudovich to devote their great brains to new heights of ingenuity.

These two men were both whole-hearted enthusiasts. Both were above the battle in the sense that they cared nothing for the issues on which politicians wasted their eloquence, but only for the perfecting of their machines. Both liked the War because it induced the politicians to give them scope. Neither wished the War to end, since they feared that with its ending men would fall back into traditional ways and would insist upon again doing, by means of human muscles and brains, things that robots could do without fatigue and with far more precision. Their objects being identical, they were close friends – though this had to be kept as a secret from their politician employers. They had used some portion of their armies of robots to make a great tunnel through the mountains of the Caucasus. One mouth of the tunnel was held by the forces of the West, the other by the forces of the East. Nobody except Dr Vulpes and Comrade Stukinmudovich knew that the tunnel had two mouths, for, except for themselves, they allowed only robots into the tunnel. They had employed the robots to heat the tunnel, and to light it brilliantly, and to fill it with great stores of food in capsules scientifically calculated to promote life and health, though not to delight the palate, for both lived only in the life of the mind and were indifferent to the joys of sense.

Dr Vulpes, as he was about to enter the tunnel, permitted himself some unprofessional reflections upon the world of sunlight that he was temporarily abandoning for one of his periodical conferences with Comrade Stukinmudovich. Gazing upon the sea below and the snowy peaks above, dim recollections floated into his mind of the classical education upon which, at the bidding of old-fashioned parents, some of his early years had been reluctantly wasted. 'It was here,' so he reflected, 'that Prometheus was chained by Zeus, Prometheus who took the first step in that glorious progress of science which has led to the present splendid consummation. Zeus, like the Governments of my youth, preferred the ancient ways. But Prometheus, unlike me and my friend Stukinmudovich, had not discovered how to outwit the reactionaries of his day. It is fitting that I should triumph on the spot where he suffered, and that Zeus with his paltry lightnings should be put in his place by our atomic skill.' With these thoughts he bade farewell to the daylight and advanced to meet his friend.

They had during the course of the War many secret conferences. In perfect mutual confidence they had communicated to each other whatever inventions might make the War more ingenious and more lasting.

In the middle of the tunnel he was met by his friend Stukinmudovich advancing from the East. They clasped hands and gazed into each other's eyes with warm affection. For a little moment before they became engulfed in technicalities they allowed themselves to rejoice in their joint work. 'How beautiful,' they said, 'is the world that we are creating! Human beings were unpredictable, often mad, often cowardly, sometimes afflicted with anti-governmental ideals. How different are our robots! On them propaganda always has the intended effect.'

'What,' said the two sages to each other, 'what could the most ardent moralist desire that we have not provided? Man was liable to sin; robots are not. Man was often foolish; robots never are. Man was liable to sexual aberrations; robots are not. You and I,' they said to each other, 'have long ago decided that the only thing that counts in a man is his behaviour – i.e. what may be viewed from without. The behaviour of our robots is in all respects better than that of the accidental biological product which has hitherto puffed itself up with foolish pride. How ingenious are their devices! How masterly their strategy! How bold their tactics, and how intrepid their conduct in battle! Who that is not the victim of obsolete superstition could desire more?'

Dr Vulpes and Comrade Stukinmudovich had discovered means of making their robots sensitive to eloquence. The best speeches of the statesmen on the two sides were recorded, and at the sound of their soul-stirring words the wheels of the robots began to whirr and they behaved, though with more precision, as politicians had hoped that living crowds would behave. Only slight differences were needed to make the robots of one side respond to one kind of propaganda and those of the other to a different kind. Dr Vulpes's robots responded to the noble words of our Great Western Statesman: 'Can we hesitate, when we see vast hordes determined to extirpate belief in God, and to wipe out in our hearts that faith in a beneficent Creator which sustains us through all ardours, difficulties and dangers? Can we endure to think that we are nothing but ingenious mechanisms, as our soulless enemies pretend? Can we forgo that immortal heritage of freedom for which our ancestors fought, and in defence of which we have been compelled to inflict upon thousands the rigours of incarceration? Can any of us hesitate at such a moment? Can any of us hold back? Can any of us think for one moment that the sacrifice of our mere individual life, of our petty personal existence is to be weighed against the preservation in the world of those ideals for which our ancestors fought and bled? No! A thousand times, No! Onward, fellow citizens! And in the knowledge of right be assured of the ultimate triumph of our Cause!'

All Dr Vulpes's robots were so constructed that, when a gramophone recited these noble words in their presence, they set themselves to perform, without hesitation or doubt, their allotted task, of which the ultimate purpose was to prove that the world is not governed by mere mechanism.

Comrade Stukinmudovich's robots were equally efficient and responded with equal readiness to the gramophone records of the Generalissimo's inspired utterances : 'Comrades, are you prepared to be for ever the slaves of soulless capitalist exploiters? Are you prepared to deny the great destiny which Dialectical Materialism has prepared for those who are emancipated from the chains imposed by base exploiters? Can anything so dead, so lifeless, so cruel, so base as the foul philosophy of Wall Street subdue the human race for ever? No! A thousand times, No! Freedom is yours if you will work for it now with that ardour with which your precursors worked to create the Great State that is now your champion. Onward to Victory! Onward to Freedom! Onward to Life and Joy!' These words on the gramophone equally activated Stukinmudovich's robots.

The rival armies met in their millions. The rival planes, guided by robots, darkened the sky. Never once did a robot fail in its duty. Never once did it flee from the field of battle. Never once did its machinery whirr in response to enemy propaganda.

Until this meeting in the tenth year of the war, the happiness of Dr Vulpes and Comrade Stukinmudovich had had its limitations. There were still human beings in Governments, and human beings were still necessary as geological experts to direct the robots to new sources of raw materials as the old sources became exhausted. There was a danger that Government might decide upon peace. There was another danger even more difficult to avert, that, if geological experts were eliminated, the activities of robots might some day be brought to an end by the exhaustion of mines. The first of these dangers was not unavoidable. When they met on this occasion they confided to each other that they had plans for the mutual extermination of the Governments on each side. But the need of geological experts remained to trouble them. It was to the solution of this problem that they devoted their joint intelligence on this occasion. At last, after a month of arduous thought, they arrived at the solution. They invented pathfinder robots capable of guiding others to the right mines. There were robots that could find iron, robots that could find oil, robots that could find copper, robots that could find uranium, and so on through all the materials of scientific warfare. Now at last they had no fear that when existing mines were no longer productive the war would have to stop, and so much ingenuity would cease to function.

When they had completed the manufacture of these pathfinding robots they decided to stay in their tunnel and await calmly the extinction of the rest of the human race. They were no longer young and they had the philosophic calm of men whose work was completed. The two sages, fed and tended by hordes of subservient robots, lived to a great age and died at the same moment. They died happy, knowing that, while the planet lasted, the war would continue with no diplomatists to call it off, no cynic to doubt the holiness of rival slogans, no sceptics to ask the purpose of unending ingenious activity.

Filled with enthusiasm, Dr Vulpes awoke. As he woke, he heard himself exclaiming: 'No more risk of Victory! War forever!' Unfortunately, the words were overheard, and he was sent to gaol.

The Fisherman's nightmare

MAGNA EST VERITAS

Sir Peter Simon had been from early youth passionately fond of fishing and, although he became a very busy and successful professional man, he always devoted the summer holidays to his favourite sport. After testing various regions, he finally came to prefer the Highlands of Scotland. He was, however, deeply distressed by what he considered the vulgar notoriety conferred by the Loch Ness Monster. Although he had often fished in that Loch, he had never come upon any sign of this curious animal, and his nature was such that he thought that everything not visible to himself must be mythical.

One evening, after reading in Izaak Walton about respectable fishes such as the chavender or chubb, he fell asleep, and his waking thoughts took shape in the form of a strange nightmare. He dreamt that the Loch Ness Monster had inspired some ingenious people who lived on a loch in a nearby glen. These people – so he dreamt – were actuated by a motive, that of ambitious competition, which he could but applaud. The influx of tourists from the degenerate South following upon the discovery of the Loch Ness Monster had been noted by the hardy Highlanders of the neighbouring glen, and they had observed with envy that the development of tourism had brought whole swarms of chars-à-bancs that made the month of August hideous but, for the dwellers on Loch Ness, extremely lucrative. Sir Peter's sleeping imagination presented these people as having manufactured a monster to inhabit their own lake who was made in part like a car tyre, but with the addition of a long tail that waved in the current like seaweed. This horrid creature was provided with a cleverly contrived device by which, when the air was let out, he uttered loud and dismal howls, at the same time 'Swinging the scaley horror of his folded tail'. On dark nights, especially when there was a thunderstorm, this device succeeded in inspiring terror among the more timorous fishermen – a terror far greater than the Loch Ness Monster had ever created.

But, alas, the land-owners of the neighbourhood, who had invented the monster, though they soon succeeded in out-doing the Loch Ness Monster, had underestimated the scientific curiosity of our impertinent age. A rather young F.R.S., Mr Jonas MacPherson, who had been born and bred in the neighbourhood and who was a fanatic votary of fishing, discovered the hoax by circumambulating the lake on stormy nights and observing the

256

presence of a rowing boat in the neighbourhood of the dreadful howls. In the works of that eminent Lord Chancellor Francis Bacon, he had come across the statement that knowledge is power, and it occurred to him that his knowledge about the Monster gave him power of a very useful kind. Being by no means well-off, he had, hitherto, had great difficulty in paying for his Highland holidays. But now he went to the local hotel-keeper telling of his discovery and promising to keep silence if he was allowed fishing rights and free board and lodging at the hotel. The hotel-keeper, who was one of the ring-leaders in the plot, summoned the committee of conspirators; and Mr MacPherson's terms were reluctantly accepted.

For a time, all went well, but the fame of the new monster continued to grow, and, at last, the pressure of the sensational press combined with the desire of Sir Theophilus Thwackum to add the beast to his private zoo,* compelled the Royal Society to send a deputation to investigate the phenomena. The deputation consisted of ten eminent men of science who, it was confidently believed, would not easily be taken in by any hocus-pocus if, indeed, something of the sort were involved. Mr MacPherson, who was not without gratitude to the conspirators and also wished to preserve his free holidays, felt that he should earn his keep. He therefore proceeded to supply the creature with howls and yells far more horrible than before; and he inserted in its inside tape-recordings which loudly wailed, 'Repent, Ye Unbelievers!' All the ten Fellows heard the dreadful message on a dark night of thunder and lightning. Alas, each one of them was deeply conscious that there was that in his past which called for repentance. All ten feared that if they repeated the experiment the awe-inspiring monster would no longer be content with generalities, but would specify the items in which these hitherto respected citizens had sinned. All returned to London with hair completely white. Their cronies would endeavour on social evenings to elicit at least some hint of what had occurred on those northern waters, but not one of these great men could be induced to make even the smallest revelation. All of them, when compelled to speak of their experiences, remarked in grave and awe-stricken tones: 'There are some things which it is not for mortals to investigate.'

And there the matter might have rested if good taste and proper reticence had had due sway. Unfortunately, the results of the investigation seemed unsatisfying to a certain rash young scientist, Mr Adam Monkhouse. Mr Monkhouse was even younger than Mr MacPherson, and, although on the road to scientific success, had not yet become a Fellow of the Royal Society. He had a personal grudge against Mr MacPherson who had adversely criticised a hypothesis of his which he was very loath to abandon. He spent a month at the hotel with which Mr MacPherson had his agreement, and devoted himself to the cultivation of friendly relations with the hotel-keeper. Late one evening, by the expenditure of considerable sums on the very best

* See pages 329–30

Highland whisky, he succeeded in producing in the hotel-keeper a mellow mood in which, for the moment, nothing seemed worth concealing. The hotel-keeper told all; and Mr Monkhouse returned jubilant from the gloomy glens and fastnesses which his cheerful soul abominated. He published the results of his researches, with unkind remarks about the investigating committee. The result, however, was not what he had hoped. The Royal Society was indignant at the slur upon ten of its foremost members, and it became clear that he no longer had any hope of himself becoming one of that August Body. All the ten members of the investigating committee sued him for libel. All ten were supported by the whole body of organised science. All ten were awarded heavy damages, which at first he saw no means of paying. But, being a resourceful person, he found a way out: he saw the error of his ways, and joined the Society for Psychical Research.

Sir Peter Simon awoke. The sweat was cold upon him. But with awakening came warmth and understanding. 'Ah,' he cried, 'how useful is faith when properly directed! How more than useful is even curiosity – is investigation – when properly curbed by faith!'

NOTE: After writing the above, I learnt, from the following article in the *Guardian,* that my fantasy was nearer to the truth than I had supposed.

IN HOSPITAL AFTER LOCH NESS DIVE

Search for 'Monster'

John Newbold, aged 31, of Stafford, known as Beppo, the clown, was detained in hospital yesterday after diving into Loch Ness in a frogman's outfit to try to get evidence about the 'monster'.

He made a dive lasting ten minutes and surfaced in a semi-conscious state. He was taken aboard a yacht belonging to Mr Bernard Mills, the circus proprietor, and recovered partly after artificial respiration had been applied.

Mr Newbold, who was unable to say what had happened while he was underwater, is an experienced high diver and swimmer. He had made several practice dives to a depth of more than thirty feet before yesterday's attempt. The water is several hundred feet deep at this part of the loch.

The late Mr Bertram Mills offered £10,000 before the war for the capture of the 'monster' and nine years ago his sons, Bernard and Cyril, increased the offer to £20,000.

The Theologian's nightmare

The eminent theologian, Dr Thaddeus, dreamt that he died and pursued his course towards heaven. His studies had prepared him and he had no difficulty in finding the way. He knocked at the door of heaven, and was met with a closer scrutiny than he expected. 'I ask admission,' he said, 'because I was a good man and devoted my life to the glory of God.' 'Man?' said the janitor, 'What is that? And how could such a funny creature as you are do anything to promote the glory of God?' Dr Thaddeus was astonished. 'You surely cannot be ignorant of man. You must be aware that man is the supreme work of the Creator.' 'As to that,' said the janitor, 'I am sorry to hurt your feelings, but what you're saying is news to me. I doubt if anybody up here has ever heard of this thing you call "man". However, since you seem distressed, you shall have a chance of consulting our librarian.'

The librarian, a globular being with a thousand eyes and one mouth, bent some of his eyes upon Dr Thaddeus. 'What is this?' he asked of the janitor. 'This,' replied the janitor, 'says that it is a member of a species called "man", which lives in a place called "Earth". It has some odd notion that the Creator takes a special interest in this place and this species. I thought perhaps you could enlighten it.' 'Well,' said the librarian kindly to the theologian, 'perhaps you can tell me where this place is that you call "Earth".' 'Oh,' said the theologian, 'it's part of the Solar System.' 'And what is the Solar System?' asked the librarian. 'Oh,' said the theologian, somewhat disconcerted, 'my province was Sacred Knowledge, but the question that you are asking belongs to profane knowledge. However, I have learnt enough from my astronomical friends to be able to tell you that the Solar System is part of the Milky Way.' 'And what is the Milky Way?' asked the librarian. 'Oh, the Milky Way is one of the Galaxies, of which, I am told, there are some hundred million.' 'Well, well,' said the librarian, 'you could hardly expect me to remember one out of so many. But I do remember to have heard the word "galaxy" before. In fact, I believe that one of our sub-librarians specialises in galaxies. Let us send for him and see whether he can help.'

After no very long time, the galactic sub-librarian made his appearance. In shape, he was a dodecahedron. It was clear that at one time his surface had been bright, but the dust of the shelves had rendered him dim and opaque. The librarian explained to him that Dr Thaddeus, in endeavouring to account for his origin, had mentioned galaxies, and it was hoped that information could be obtained from the galactic section of the library. 'Well,' said the sub-librarian, 'I suppose it might become possible in time, but as there are a hundred million galaxies, and each has a volume to itself, it takes some time to find any particular volume. Which is it that this odd molecule desires?' 'It is the one called "The Milky Way",' Dr Thaddeus falteringly replied. 'All right,' said the sub-librarian, 'I will find it if I can.'

Some three weeks later, he returned, explaining that the extraordinarily efficient card-index in the galactic section of the library had enabled them to locate the galaxy as number XQ 321,762. 'We have employed,' he said, 'all the five thousand clerks in the galactic section on this search. Perhaps you would like to see the clerk who is specially concerned with the galaxy in question?' The clerk was sent for and turned out to be an octohedron with an eye in each face and a mouth in one of them. He was surprised and dazed to find himself in such a glittering region, away from the shadowy limbo of his shelves. Pulling himself together, he asked, rather shyly, 'What is it you wish to know about my galaxy?' Dr Thaddeus spoke up: 'What I want is to know about the Solar System, a collection of heavenly bodies revolving about one of the stars in your galaxy. The star about which they revolve is called "the Sun".' 'Humph,' said the librarian of the Milky Way, 'it was hard enough to hit upon the right galaxy, but to hit upon the right star in the galaxy is far more difficult. I know that there are about three hundred billion stars in the galaxy, but I have no knowledge, myself, that would distinguish one of them from another. I believe, however, that at one time a list of the whole three hundred billion was demanded by the Administration and that it is still stored in the basement. If you think it worth while, I will engage special labour from the Other Place to search for this particular star.'

It was agreed that, since the question had arisen and since Dr Thaddeus was evidently suffering some distress, this might be the wisest course.

Several years later, a very weary and dispirited tetrahedron presented himself before the galactic sub-librarian. 'I have,' he said, 'at last discovered the particular star concerning which inquiries have been made, but I am quite at a loss to imagine why it has aroused any special interest. It closely resembles a great many other stars in the same galaxy. It is of average size and temperature, and is surrounded by very much smaller bodies called "planets". After minute investigation, I discovered that some, at least, of these planets have parasites, and I think that this thing which has been making inquiries must be one of them.'

At this point, Dr Thaddeus burst out in a passionate and indignant lament: 'Why, oh why, did the Creator conceal from us poor inhabitants of Earth that it was not we who prompted Him to create the Heavens? Throughout my long life, I have served Him diligently, believing that He would notice my service and reward me with Eternal Bliss. And now, it seems that He was not even aware that I existed. You tell me that I am an infinitesimal animalcule on a tiny body revolving round an insignificant member of a collection of three hundred billion stars, which is only one of many millions of such collections. I cannot bear it, and can no longer adore my Creator.' 'Very well,' said the janitor, 'then you can go to the Other Place.'

Here the theologian awoke. 'The power of Satan over our sleeping imagination is terrifying,' he muttered.

PART FOUR

ANECDOTES

The following stories and reminiscences were put onto tape in several sessions between July and September 1959. The recordings were privately made, unrehearsed, with only occasional use of an existing script. Russell's fluent style and perfect diction allowed for easy transcription. It was necessary, however, to make some minor alterations in order to obviate repetition and to clarify oblique references. Except where rearrangement served to improve the organisation of chronology and subject matter, the original sequence of the items has been preserved.

Aside from a few anecdotes, variations of which appear in *The Amberley Papers, Unpopular Essays, Portraits from Memory* and the *Autobiography,* none have been published before.

Family, Friends and Others

My paternal grandmother, who was a daughter of Lord Minto, had many interesting and some amusing reminiscences which it was rather difficult to elicit – she had to be coaxed to tell them. Her mother's father was a certain Mr Brydon who wrote a book called *Travels in Sicily and Malta* in which he advanced the terribly rash opinion that the lava on the slopes of Etna was so deep that it must have begun to flow before 4004 B.C. On account of this heresy, I regret to say, he was cut by the county. Nevertheless, one of his daughters married my grandmother's father, and her sisters came to live at Minto. On one occasion, after a good deal of coaxing, my grandmother told me that one of her aunts was rather vulgar. I said, 'In what did the vulgarity consist?' 'Well, she always had two eggs for breakfast, and she would look round the breakfast table and say "Who's eaten my second egg?" ' They were always boiled eggs and her vulgarity consisted in having two. Such was the effect of this story upon me that never throughout a long life have I been able to eat two boiled eggs for breakfast, though I can quite easily eat two poached eggs or two scrambled eggs or two eggs in any other way. But this story made it impossible for me to eat two boiled eggs for fear my descendants should say that I was somewhat vulgar.

I asked her whether she knew Sir Walter Scott – Abbottsford was in the immediate neighbourhood of Minto where my grandmother passed her girlhood. She told me that she only met him once, and that the reason she met him so seldom was that there was a feud between the Elliots, my grandmother's family, and the Scotts, who were the great family of Roxburghshire. This feud was taken on by Sir Walter Scott, and it was thought he had no right to take it on because he was not really at all closely related to the Scotts of Roxburgh; but he did take it on, with the result that she only met him once.

She told me once about an incident when her grandfather had been appointed Governor-General of India, and his wife was looking out for a chef who would be suitable for such an exalted situation. She interviewed one chef, who demanded two hundred a year. 'Why,' she said, 'that's as much as many curates get.' 'Ah, yes,' said the prospective chef, 'but you forget the mental work in my profession.'

She used to tell macabre stories sometimes, almost always somewhat derogatory of conjugal affection. Her worst of these stories was the story of an old couple who had lived in the closest harmony for many years, to the admiration of all their neighbours; and at last the wife died and was put into the coffin. And as she was being carried downstairs, the coffin bumped against the corner and she revived. And they lived again happily for many years. At last she died again, was put into the coffin again, and as it was being carried down, the bereaved widower remarked: 'Take care not to bump against the corner.' This was the sort of story that she liked. I do not know quite why.

There was another story that she used to tell about a Scots girl called Maisie, who had very beautiful golden hair and in addition had a golden leg; and when she was buried, some very very wicked man rifled the grave and took away the golden leg. The next night as he was sleeping Maisie appeared before him and he said, 'Maisie, Maisie, whar is yer beautiful blue e'en?' and she replied, 'Mouldering in the grave.' And he said, 'Maisie, Maisie, whar is yer beautiful goulden hair?' and she said, 'Mouldering in the grave.' And at last he said, 'And Maisie, Maisie, whar's yer beautiful goulden leg?' 'Here, you thief!' At this point he gave up and restored the leg to its proper grave.

There was a story about my grandfather which illustrated, perhaps, a certain lack of such a tact as one might have expected. He was at a dinner-party, and after dinner when the gentlemen returned from the dining-table, he sat beside the Duchess of A. But after sitting beside her for some time he got up rather suddenly and walked across the room to the Duchess of B and sat beside her. When he and his wife got home, his wife said to him, 'Why did you so suddenly leave the Duchess of A?' and he said, 'Oh, because the fire was too hot and I could not bear it.' She said, 'I hope you explained to the Duchess of A.' 'Well, no,' he said, 'but I explained to the Duchess of B.'

At a time when my grandfather was Prime Minister, a terrible misadventure once befell him at the Lord Mayor's banquet. The Lord Mayor had received a very magnificent silver snuff-box, which was a gift from Napoleon III, and as he was showing it to my grandfather he said, 'You see it has a hen on it.' My grandfather, who wasn't looking at it very closely, said, 'Oh, I should have thought it would have been an eagle.' And on looking again, he saw that it was not a hen but an N. The rest of the dinner had to go on after this misadventure.

When I was six years old my grandmother took me to stay at St Fillans in Perthshire, and one day we went on a very long drive to Glenartney. I got rather bored with sitting still for such a long time and I was being amused by little rhymes; one of which was 'When you get to Glenartney, you'll hear a horse in a cart neigh', and when we got to Glenartney, sure enough, we did hear a horse in a cart neigh. I have often wondered since whether the Lord Macartney was a son of the Glen. But as to this I have never been able to ascertain the correct genealogy.

My paternal grandmother was a very patriotic Scots woman; and she told me that when she was a girl it was the practice at Christmas-time for the village people to come up to Minto, where she lived, and perform little plays and songs, rather in the style of Bottom in *Midsummer Night's Dream.* These all had a patriotic tone about them. There was one in which a boy came forward and professed to be Alexander the Great, and said 'I am Alexander, King of Macedon / Who conquered all the world but Scotland alone. / But when I came to Scotland my blood it waxed cold / To find so small a nation so powerful and so bold.'

My grandfather established a village school in Petersham, which was his parish, at a time when such schools were still uncommon. My grandmother went to ask the children questions that were intended to test their intelligence, and one of the questions she asked them was 'Did you ever see a Scotchman?' And one of them cried, 'Yes, Milady, once at a Fair.' Then she went on to say 'Was he white or black?' 'Oh, black, Milady.'

When I was two years old my grandparents rented Tennyson's house, Aldworth, for the summer months, and I stayed with them. They used to take me out onto Blackdown and they taught me to recite, 'O my cousin, shallow-hearted! O my Amy, mine no more! / O the dreary, dreary moorland! O the barren, barren shore!' I am told, and I can well believe it, that the effect was irresistibly comic.

We often hear the phrase, 'old world courtesy', and I think that probably a good many people doubt whether there ever was such a thing. I think I can give two illustrations, both of which happened to my grandfather. My grandfather's nephew, Lord Odo Russell, afterwards Lord Ampthill, had had an interview with Napoleon III, shortly after Napoleon's rise to power. My grandfather asked him what he had thought of Napoleon III and he said: 'I thought that he was thinking, as I was, that he was the nephew of his uncle.' It seems to me that this was one of the most flatteringly polite remarks that I have ever come across. There was another example of the same thing, which was when the Shah of Persia was caught in a rainstorm in Richmond Park and took refuge in my grandfather's house. My grandfather apologised for the smallness of his house: 'Yes,' said the Shah, 'it is a small house but it contains a great man.' I think these examples show that old world courtesy really did exist.

When my parents visited America in 1867, my mother noted a few occurrences in her diary. There are three of these that seem somewhat interesting. One was when they went to see a well which Berkeley had visited, while he was on his abortive journey to the West Indies; and my mother played with the bucket of this well in a manner that was thought irreverent by Berkeley's admirers who had taken her to this place. The second occasion was, I found, still remembered when I went to America nearly thirty years later. There was a very fine dinner-party arranged for my parents and they provided terrapin which was considered a very great delicacy. My father, who was somewhat conservative in his eating habits, refused, whereupon my mother shouted along the length of the table, 'Taste it, Amberley, it's not so very nasty!'

This was still remembered with horror when I was there in 1896. The third incident which is recorded in her diary is another dinner-party in Cambridge, Massachusetts. She says, 'I sat between Mr So and So and Mr Longfellow, the poet. I liked Mr So and So.' Of Mr Longfellow she says nothing whatever.

Some occasions, when I was a child, filled me with somewhat bitter disappointment. On one occasion after we had been talking about cannibalism I heard my people say to each other: 'When is that Eton boy coming?' and I thought they meant a boy who had been eaten. When he turned up, and was a perfectly ordinary boy, it caused me the most profound disenchantment. But that was not the worst. The worst instance was when I heard them say to each other, 'When is that young Lyon coming?' And I said, 'Is there a lion coming?' 'Oh yes,' they said, 'and you'll see him in the drawing-room and it'll be quite safe.' And then they came and said, 'The young Lyon has come,' and they ushered me into the drawing-room and it was a completely conventional young man whose name was Lyon. I burst into tears and wept the whole of the rest of the day, and the poor young man couldn't imagine why.

My first contact with Robert Browning was when I was two years old. He came to lunch with my people and brought with him the actor Salvini. Everybody was used to Browning, but Salvini was more of a rarity, and they would have liked to hear him speak. But Browning talked the whole time without stopping. At last, unwittingly expressing the feelings of the company, I said, 'I wish that man would stop talking.' I had, of course, to be hushed very quickly, but he did stop.

I was kept to very spartan fare in the matter of eating when I was a boy. It was thought that fruit was absolutely disastrous for a child and he must never be allowed any. One time after we had all had pudding, the plates were changed and everybody except me was given an orange. I was given a plate but I was not given an orange. I remarked plaintively, 'A plate and nothing on it.' Everybody laughed – but I didn't get an orange.

My cousin, G. W. E. Russell, who was something of a gourmand, was dining once with my people and expressed a very strong preference for one dish rather than another. I also had the same preference but I was compelled to have the dish that I didn't like and was told: 'You must not have your little likes and dislikes.' And I said, 'Cousin George has his little likes and dislikes.' Again I was quickly hushed, but I never was able to see the justice of it.

I had an uncle, Rollo Russell, who was very good at explaining things to children. I asked him one day why they have stained glass in churches, and he said 'Well, I'll tell you – long ago they didn't, but one day, just as the parson had got up into the pulpit and was about to begin his sermon, he saw a man outside the church walking with a pail of whitewash on his head. And at that precise moment the bottom of the pail fell out and the man was inundated with whitewash. The poor parson could not control his laughter and was unable to go on with his sermon. So ever since they've had stained glass in windows.'

My cousin, St George Lane Fox, afterwards Fox Pitt, was a very singular character. While a very young man he invented electric light before Swann and Edison had thought of doing so. He then got religion, not in the form which is usual in the West, but in the form of esoteric Buddhism. This caused him to think that he should occupy himself no longer with mundane affairs, and he went to Tibet to visit Lamas and to learn all the niceties of Buddhist theology. However, after a certain length of time in Tibet he decided to come home again, and he then discovered to his disgust that Swann and Edison had been making electric light. He brought actions against them, a number of actions, all of which he lost, and in the end he was reduced to bankruptcy. But he consoled himself with the tenets of esoteric Buddhism and thought that after all a man should be able to do without a plethora of worldly goods. He then had an experience which shows the dangers of book-learning. He married a sister of Lord Alfred Douglas. On his wedding night he was overheard saying: 'I must go and look it up in the book,' and shortly afterwards he was heard saying, 'It sounds quite simple.' However, very shortly afterwards there was a nullity.

My great-aunt, Lady Charlotte Portal, had various claims to distinction. Her latest was that she was the grandmother of the only man who holds both the Garter and the Order of Merit. Her earliest claim to fame occurred when she was a very small child. She tumbled out of bed, failed to wake up, but was heard muttering: 'My head is laid low, my pride has had a fall.' She was sometimes a little inapt in ways of expressing herself. On one occasion when she was starting for the Continent, her footman, whose Christian name was George, came to take her luggage to the train, and just as the train was starting it occurred to her that she might wish to write to him about some matter of business, and that she didn't remember his surname; so she put her head out of the window and said: 'George, George, what's your name?' George touched his hat and replied: 'George, Milady.' By that time the train was out of earshot and the thing was irremediable.

My sister-in-law, Elizabeth, was once staying in a Swiss hotel where the partitions were somewhat inadequate. The room next to hers was occupied by a middle-aged American couple. She heard them coming up to bed and conversing animatedly for a time, then, there was a long silence, interrupted at last in a severe feminine voice, 'Henry, is it because you won't, or because you can't?'

Another sister-in-law, when she became engaged to my brother, was brought to lunch with my grandmother, who practised the strictest Victorian propriety. The girl was shy and behaved with a pretty restraint until near

269

the end of lunch when, unfortunately, there came a thunderstorm. The thunder got louder and louder and at last there was an absolutely deafening clap. She leapt from her seat, exclaiming 'Golly!' My grandmother had never heard the word, but very justly concluded that if it had been a suitable word for young ladies, she would have heard it.

My [maternal] grandmother, Lady Stanley of Alderley, was a person of quite exceptional vigour, and a good many of her descendants inherited this exceptional degree of vitality. She used to give Sunday luncheons to her children and grandchildren, and at these there used to be argumenta- tion such as I have never heard before or since, for vehemence and profound conviction of entirely opposite sorts. One of her sons was a Mohammedan, one was a Roman Catholic priest, one was a free thinker, one was an Anglican, and one of her daughters was a free thinker and another was a Positivist. All these different creeds used to meet, and each would uphold his own point of view with the utmost vigour. The Moham- medan was nearly stone-deaf and when the disputes reached a certain degree of noisiness he would become aware that something was going on. He would then ask what it was, and his immediate neighbours would pour completely garbled versions of the argument into his ear, whereupon all the rest would shout, 'No, no, Henry, it's not that.' And at that point the din became such that it was almost incredible that everybody was not deaf. He, Henry, the oldest of my grandmother's sons, was a very odd character. Not only had he become a Mohammedan, which was odd enough, but he had married a certain completely unknown and obscure Spanish lady, not once, but three or four times without being in fact legally married to her at the end, although he, poor fellow, did not know this. He was a very curious person altogether; he caused Lord Salisbury to say that many things had been said against their Lordship's house, but until now it had not been possible to say that they were not gentlemen, and I regret to say that he had made this possible.

He had, of course, as might be expected, ultraconservative opinions. I knew a lady named Miss Coolidge, who was a great granddaughter of Jefferson and very proud of the fact. She met him at the house of one of my aunts, where there was at the same time a doctor who had just happened to have called in. My uncle turned to Miss Coolidge and said, 'Do you believe in old-age pensions?' And she said, 'Yes I do.' And he said, 'Shows you know nothing about it.' He then turned to the doctor and said, 'Do you believe in old-age pensions?' And the doctor said, 'Yes.' 'Shows you want one yourself.' At this point my aunt thought she would smooth matters over and said, 'You see, Miss Coolidge is an American and perhaps she does not quite understand our conditions.' At which he said, 'American, are you? I suppose you know Washington was a murderer?' And she said that no, she did not know that. And he said, 'Yes, he was, and I shall never forgive those people until they return to their allegiance.' 'Well, you see,' she said, 'you can't expect me to think that, because my great grandfather wrote the Declaration of Independence.' To which he said, 'How many people's great grandfathers wrote the Declaration of Independence, I should like to know!' She then got up to go. He bowed handsomely and said, 'Don't you think I get on very well with your countrywomen?' However, she remembered the story and many years after told it to me precisely as I have now related it.

My uncle Henry had a younger brother called Lyulph. My brother, meeting with uncle Henry in the Lords on one occasion, very rashly went up to him and said, 'Have you heard that Lyulph's cook has gone mad?' My deaf uncle who always insisted upon hearing said, 'What, what, what?' So my brother said more loudly, 'Have you heard that Lyulph's cook has gone mad?' To which my uncle still said, 'What, what, what?' My brother then shouted as loud as he could, HAVE YOU HEARD THAT LYULPH'S COOK HAS GONE MAD? By this time all their Lordships were looking round to see what the noise was. My uncle said, 'Lyulph's gone mad? Well, I'm not surprised.' At that point my brother gave up.

My grandmother, Lady Stanley of Alderley, had the great advantage of being completely incapable of doubting her own merits. She used to say, 'You know I've left my brain to the Royal College of Surgeons, because it'll be so interesting for them to have a clever woman's brain to cut up.' She also said that she knew only one thing in which her ancestors had been foolish and that was that they were Jacobites. They had, in fact, had to fly from Ireland after the Battle of the Boyne, and they only returned when the French Revolution made France dangerous for them.

She used to sit in a very large drawing-room and entertain at tea all the leading literary men of the age, and when any of them went out she would turn to the others with a sigh and say: 'Fools are so fatiguin'.' This caused all the rest to determine that they would not be the first to leave the gathering, for fear the same should be said about them. She had rather high standards. She put me through a viva one time, in the presence of a large number of visitors: 'Had I read this and had I read the other,' and I hadn't read any of the books. At last she turned to the others and said, 'I have no intelligent grandchildren.' According to all modern educators this should have damped me down. It did not, however: it made me determined that I would prove that she was mistaken.

My grandmother had two sorts of descendants: those who inherited the Stanley toughness, and those who did not. I, to my misfortune, was one of the latter. The others, who inherited the Stanley toughness, didn't mind at all the way she talked to them. I remember my cousin, Christopher Howard, being taken to task by her for always answering her in a way she didn't like. She said, 'Don't say, "Yus, Granmama".' And he wasn't in the least abashed, whereas I would have sunk through the earth at having such a thing said to me. She used, sometimes, when she was in a good

271

humour, to tell stories to her credit. She told, for example, how when she was a very young girl in a convent school, the other girls induced her to throw snails over the wall into the neighbour's garden. And this, of course, was a very wicked act. But she said, 'But, you see, I can't tell it to show how badly we turned out, because I've turned out so well.'

There was, however, one occasion, the only one I know of, in which things turned out as she might not have wished. She was staying at Naworth Castle where her daughter [Lady Carlisle] reigned. Lord Carlisle was a Pre-Raphaelite painter and a friend of all the other Pre-Raphaelite painters. Burne-Jones happened to be staying with them and had a tobacco-pouch which was made to look like a tortoise. One evening, when they were at dinner, this tobacco-pouch was brought in, for fun, and put close to the drawing-room fire. Now there was a real tortoise in Naworth at this time, and when they came in from dinner Lord Carlisle discovered this supposed tortoise close by the fire, picked it up and said, 'What an extraordinary thing, its back has grown soft.' He then went to the library and fetched the relevant volume of the Encyclopaedia, looked up 'tortoise' and read out in a very portentous voice: 'On certain very rare occasions under the influence of very great heat the back of the tortoise has been known to become soft.' My grandmother was intensely interested in this very curious zoological fact, until then quite unknown to her. And she went about telling everybody about it. Years later when she was quarrelling with her daughter about Home Rule her daughter said to her, 'Well, Ma, you know you were taken in about that tortoise. It was really Burne-Jones's tobacco-pouch.' And she said, 'My dear, I may be many things, but I am not a fool, and I refuse to believe you.'

My uncle, George Howard, Lord Carlisle, was a friend of Cross, the husband of George Eliot. Cross was known in literary circles as the author of a book called, *A Commentary on Dante, with an Appendix on Bimetallism.* On one occasion, my uncle ventured an opinion on bimetallism, and Cross said, 'What do you know about bimetallism?' To which my uncle replied, 'Well I've read Dante.' His next contact with Mr Cross was of a more painful sort. Cross and George Eliot were on their honeymoon in Venice. My uncle was staying in the same hotel. Suddenly he saw Cross plunge from the balcony into the Grand Canal. Naturally my uncle went to rescue him, which was not difficult. It appeared that Cross had read in George Eliot's journal that she only married him out of pique because Lewis was not faithful to her, and this had driven the poor man to suicide. However, suicide in the Grand Canal in front of a large hotel was not so dangerous as it might have been, and he lived for many years after.

My uncle, Lord Carlisle, was willing to tell stories against himself, and he told me that he had once related to a newly-rich American the story of the cast of the *Venus de Milo* which had been ordered by another newly-rich American. When it arrived, so the story averred, he sued the railway company for having broken the arms, and won his case. 'Yes,' said my uncle's American friend, 'but there's just one difficulty about that story, it's older than the *Venus de Milo*.'

Gilbert Murray was not only an eminent classicist, but also a very amusing raconteur. He had a great fund of stories, some of which I much enjoyed. I remember particularly one about Mr Gladstone. At a very large meeting, the Conservatives had planted a drunken man in the front row with a view to interrupting Mr Gladstone. Mr Gladstone endured the interruptions for some time with patience, and then at last he turned upon the drunken man, and in his most majestic voice he said, 'May I request that gentleman who has not once, but repeatedly, interrupted the flow of my observations, to extend to me that large measure of courtesy, which, were I in his place and he in mine, I should most unhesitatingly extend to him.' The drunken man was overwhelmed and uttered not another word.

My cousin, Lady Mary Murray, the wife of Gilbert Murray, was a woman for whom I had a very great respect, but she had one shortcoming: she was destitute of a sense of humour, and occasionally this had curious results. I went to see her and Gilbert Murray one day and he said to me, 'I have just found a school for my boy.' So I said, 'Oh, where is it?' 'Well,' said he, 'it is kept by the Reverend V. Ermine, of the Creepers, Crawley Down.' Mary interrupted and said, 'Oh, Gilbert, he is not Reverend.' The only truth in the whole story was that the school was at Crawley.

I remember another occasion when I rang the front door bell and asked the maid if they were at home, and she said, 'Well, Sir, I think they're probably in unless they're out.' So I found that they were in, and I said, 'Your maid is of the opinion that one should employ great caution in applying the laws of thought to empirical material.' And Mary said, 'Oh, what an unkind thing to say.'

Mrs Bernard Shaw was a very remarkable lady. Some of her merits are set forth in *Man and Superman*, but there were some I was privileged to observe. One time when I was lunching with Mr and Mrs Shaw, there was a young Austrian lady present, and she apparently was a poetess. As the rest of us were saying good-bye, Shaw remarked, with something of a simper, that this young lady was not going yet as she was going to read him her poems. Nevertheless, when we got outside the door, there was the young lady; I have never known how Mrs Shaw got her out. But a very few days afterwards this same young lady went to visit Wells and said, 'If you do not make love to me I shall cut my throat.' He refused, and she cut her throat, but apparently she had had a good deal of practice and was not much the worse. This gave me a considerable respect for Mrs Shaw.

Sir Sidney Waterlow, whom I had known since he was an undergraduate, achieved a position of some distinction in the Foreign Office. He was, in fact, in charge of Foreign Office relations with the Far East. I had some dealing with him in this connection, because during MacDonald's first

Government it was decided that Britain should devote the money obtained by her under the Boxer Indemnity to some project that would be of advantage to China, and a committee was appointed to see how this should be done. Among those put on the committee were Lowes Dickinson and myself. There were also to be two representatives of China, who were to be appointed by the Chinese Government. However, before the committee was fully functioning, MacDonald's Government fell, and the succeeding Conservative Government decided that Lowes Dickinson and I should not be on the committee, nominally on the ground that we did not know much about China, but really because we were friends of the Chinese. I had recommended to the Chinese, Hu Shih and V. K. Ting, as people whom the Chinese Government might think suitable. The Chinese Government agreed, and suggested them. The Conservative Government sent word to the Chinese that they would accept any two Chinese except these two. The Chinese Government replied that they must have these two or no one. This confirmed Waterlow in his opinion that I knew nothing about China.

However, it was not only with regard to China that I had dealings with him. He had married an extraordinarily beautiful young woman, a daughter of Sir Frederick Pollock. I met them by accident on their honeymoon, and I observed that something was amiss, though it was six years before I knew what. At the end of six years Waterlow told me the whole story. Under the influence of G. E. Moore he had become convinced that there was something base about sexual intercourse. He had, therefore, never consummated his marriage. At the end of three years of marriage, however, he changed his mind, and thought that perhaps Moore was mistaken, and he therefore tried to consummate the marriage. But three years of total abstinence had rendered him, in regard to his wife, impotent, and he was unable to consummate the marriage. They went on for another three years with gradually increasing quarrels, and at last decided that the marriage must be annulled. He, at this point, was sitting alone in a restaurant in London feeling rather melancholy. A prostitute sat down at the same table and said, 'You seem melancholy, duckie, what's the matter?' So he told her all about it. And she said, 'Oh I'll soon cure that, you come home with me.' He did and she did. It so happened that, though a prostitute, she was married. Her husband divorced her for improper relations with Waterlow, at the very same moment at which his marriage with his wife was annulled on the ground of his impotence. He, though he didn't much like having his marriage dissolved, was so pleased to discover himself not impotent, that he went round to all his friends boasting about it. He subsequently married another lady and had by her an adequate family. It does not seem to me that he managed his matrimonial affairs very much better than he managed our relations with China.

When I was a younger man I was very much addicted to walking. On one occasion I was walking round the coast of Cornwall, and as the evening came on, I reached the Lizard. I went to the hotel and asked if they could put me up for the night. They said, 'Is your name Trevelyan?' I said, 'No, why do you ask?' They said, 'Oh, because we are expecting Mr Trevelyan tonight, and Mrs Trevelyan is already here.' I was much surprised, as I knew that it was George Trevelyan's wedding day, and I was very much astonished to think that Mrs Trevelyan should be there and he should not be. I thought something dreadful must have happened, and I went to see her to inquire. 'Oh, no,' she said, 'nothing dreadful happened, but when we reached Truro, George said "I must have a little walk," and he got out of the train to walk to the Lizard' [a distance of some forty miles]. Sure enough he arrived at eleven at night, completely worn out, and had to be revived by brandy. It was a very happy marriage.

There were some things in my childhood education which I suppose came about by accident, but which had a very considerable influence upon me. I had a book called *Stories About,* and when you looked inside it was mostly about clever dogs and horses and things of that sort, and, in fact, all the stories except two at the end were such as would still be considered entirely suitable for children. But it was not these stories that interested me. The one that interested me most was the very last, which was about a Negro woman in Jamaica who caught her child stealing sugar-cane and therefore fastened the child on an ant heap where it was eaten to death. This was the story that really interested me. And then I had a book of nursery rhymes set to music. It began quite conventionally with 'Sing a Song of Sixpence' and 'Hickory Dickory Dock'. But there again there was just one that particularly interested me. It began: 'There was a lady all skin and bone', and it went on to relate her doings. . . . 'Sure such a lady was never known; / She went to church one summer's day, / She went to church all for to pray, / and when she got the church within, / the parson prayed against pride and sin, / on looking up, on looking down, / she saw a dead man on the ground; / And from his nose unto his chin, / the worms crawled out, the worms crawled in; / Then she unto the parson said, / "Shall I be so when I am dead?" / "Oh, yes Sah, yes," the parson said, / "You will be so when you are dead." ' This somewhat diminished my confidence in the consolations of religion.

There are some well known stories that give me a lot of pleasure. One of them comes in Dickens, apropos a gentleman who was knighted by George III under a misapprehension, when it was another man he should have knighted. And Dickens remarks, 'On this occasion, His Majesty was graciously pleased to observe "Ooooh, ooooh what, whaaat, why, why, why?" '

Then there is the story about the somewhat irascible schoolmaster who turned to one of his boys, and said in a very cross tone, 'Who made the world?' And the boy said, 'Please sir, it wasn't me.'

Then there is Lady Betty. Lady Betty was a very young girl, perhaps six or seven years old, and she had committed what her parents considered a sin and was told to ask God to forgive her. She was asked afterwards by her parents, 'Did you ask God to forgive you?' And she said, 'Oh yes, and He said, "Pray, don't mention it, Lady Betty!" '

And there was another child, I think of about the same age, who put an embarrassing question. She said, 'What time does God dine?' And they said, 'Ach, God doesn't dine.' And she said, 'Oh, I see, he has an egg with his tea.'

Ever since I was a boy, I have derived a great deal of pleasure from that piece of nonsense which says, 'So she went into the garden to cut a cabbage leaf to make an apple pie and just then a great she-bear coming up the street pops its head into the shop. "What! No soap?" So he died, and she very imprudently married the barber and there were present: the Piccaninies, the Joblillies and the Galeolies and the Grand Panjandrum himself with a little round button atop and they all fell to playing the game of Catch As Catch Can till the gunpowder ran out of the heels of their boots.' I took so much pleasure in this that I learnt to say the whole of it in one breath.

There was once upon a time a family with a very rich maiden aunt, whose affections were entirely centred upon a cat whom the rest of the family detested. One of her nieces became engaged to a young man who, after hearing the general abuse of the poor quadruped, killed it, and presented it to the family, saying: 'I have brought in this cat as trophy.' The maiden aunt disinherited them all and with one voice they exclaimed: 'What a catastrophe!' The *Oxford Dictionary* appears not to know the etymology of this word.

When I was a boy of about twelve, I was taken to Midhurst, and derived very great delight from the ruins of Cowdray. I was standing on a little bridge over the River Rother. I did not know that it was the River Rother. An old countryman came along and I said, 'What is the name of this river?' And he said, 'She ain't got no name and she don't want none.' It was many years before I discovered the name of the river.

When I was a very shy youth of seventeen, I once went out to dine at a neighbouring house, where the two daughters were friends of mine, and their mother was only an acquaintance. Before dinner, their mother, whose name was Lady Burdett, said to me: 'I hope you won't mind not being given your proper precedence. You ought, of course, to take me into dinner, but I'm a dull old woman and I thought you would rather sit between my daughters.' I was completely stumped; I did not like to seem to insist on my proper precedence, nor could I admit that she was a dull old woman. I hummed and hawed and was reduced to silence. When I got home I asked my grandmother what I should have said. She provided the answer at once. 'You should have said, "Oh! Lady Burdett!" '

The first time that I ever heard of Winston Churchill was in 1890 when

I was a freshman at Cambridge and he was still a schoolboy at Harrow. I was having my hair cut at Trufitt's and the man who was cutting my hair said, 'Lord Randolph's son's 'aving 'is 'air cut in the next room, Sir. 'e is a young pup 'e is.' And so I got interested in him and followed his subsequent career.

When I was first at Cambridge, one of the figures of Cambridge Society was F. W. H. Myers, a poet who was also much addicted to spiritualism, and was considered, though this may have been scandal, to be a man of not strictly virtuous life. He related how George Eliot, when he took her into the Fellows Garden at Trinity, remarked that 'There is no God and yet we must be good.' The man who related this story to me made the comment: 'and Myers concluded that "There is a God and yet we need not be good."'

A young fellow of Trinity having become engaged to be married, asked the Whiteheads for permission to bring his fiancée to lunch. She came, but was too shy to utter a word, until towards the end, Mrs Whitehead said, 'Will you have tart or pudding?' To which she replied, 'Poy'. She survived, however. Fifty years later, I was travelling from London to Cambridge and she happened to be in the same compartment. She lost her ticket, but when she presented herself at the barrier saying she had no ticket, the ticket collector replied, 'That's all right, Milady.'

When I was a young man there was a teacher of philosophy in Cambridge named Dawes Hicks. It happened that he lived next door to the Whiteheads. Whitehead dropped in to see him one evening and found him rather unhappy because he said his housekeeper had borrowed his car without asking permission, and so he was unable to go out as he had intended to do. So Whitehead said, 'Well, why don't you give her notice?' And Dawes Hicks said, 'Well, perhaps I will.' Whitehead went to see him again a week later and said, 'Well, did you give your housekeeper notice?' 'Well, . . . no,' said Dawes Hicks. 'Well, what have you done?' 'Oh, well, I've married her.'

The two most perfect snobs that I have ever known were both Dons at King's College, Cambridge. One of them was Sir Charles Wallston, and the other was Oscar Browning, commonly known as O.B. I remember an occasion when the Empress Frederick came to Cambridge for the day. I met both of these men in the evening. Sir Charles Wallston said, 'It was really most annoying that in spite of all I could do to dissuade her, the Empress Frederick insisted on lunching with me a *second* time.' Oscar Browning, on the other hand, was most sad and discouraged and said, 'I have been Empress hunting all day.' I only once heard Oscar Browning admit to not personally knowing a celebrity, and that was when the King of Saxony came up in conversation and he said, 'I knew him very well . . . by sight.' He had, unfortunately, a very painful experience when Tennyson came to Cambridge, and King's College gave a party for him, at which all the Fellows appeared one by one and mentioned their names to him; and when O.B. came he said, 'I'm Browning.' Tennyson looked at him and said, 'You're not.' I do not quite know how he survived this incident.

When I was a young man, I once took Professor Stout, the editor of *Mind*, for a walk in the country. We came upon a lot of cows, some of which, at any rate, some of us thought might be bulls. His little son aged five, who has since become a professor of philosophy himself, remarked to his father, 'Now, Father, is the time for your afraidness to come on.' And in view of that remark, the eminent philosopher did not dare to show any fear.

At one time when I was on a walking tour in County Kerry, I visited Henry Butcher, who was well known as one of the translators of the *Odyssey*. He told me a rather curious story about the M'Gillicuddy who was the great chieftain of that region, and held the distinction of having a whole mountain range called after him. It appeared that the M'Gillicuddy on one occasion was travelling on the Continent. He was at a bookstall thinking what he should buy, when a young American lady came up and mistook him for the bookstall attendant, and asked for a book. He was very haughty and refused to answer at all to what she said. However, on looking round he saw that she was very charming, so he observed which carriage she got into in the train and he got in too. He tried to get into conversation, but this time she was haughty. She was travelling with her parents, and he discovered that her Christian name was Mary. Her surname was still unknown to him. Presently the parents wanted the window closed, but it was very stiff and wouldn't close. So he got hold of the strap and pulled very hard, and the strap came off, and he was deposited full length on the floor of the carriage. After this it was impossible to keep up any kind of haughtiness and they began to converse. Presently the time came when the young lady and her parents were getting out of the carriage, having reached the end of their journey. As they got out, he turned to her and he said, 'Miss Mary, someday you shall be my wife.' She was rather surprised. He didn't know where she lived or what her name was. And he didn't say, 'Someday I hope . . .'; but 'Someday you shall be my wife.' However, he found out what hotel they were staying at, and ingratiated himself with them and explained that he was an Irish Chieftain of very ancient lineage and very grand altogether. And so at last the lady accepted him. He took her back to his home, which was not nearly as grand as she had expected and after some time he became a Mohammedan. They had one son, and the religious education of the son consisted solely of one precept. He said, 'My boy, remember this : God is a perfect gentleman.' That I believe was all the boy ever learnt of religion.

Logan Pearsall Smith in his mature years was a somewhat precious and very careful highbrow author. But in his younger days he had his off moments, some of which I remember; and as I think they were never printed, it is perhaps worth recording them. I remember some of his verses in a play that he produced for family consumption. One of the verses said: 'Naughty little cuss words, / Such as 'blast' and 'blow', / Quite as much as wuss words, / Deep in the realms below; / Naughty little social fibs, / Such as "not at home" / Lead us to the outer realms, / Where the wicked roam.'

And then he made a little verse about love : / 'Ah love, love, love, / It cometh from above / And sitteth like a dove, / On some. / But some it never hits, / But only gives them fits / And takes away their wits. / Ah hum.'

In 1894 when I was for a few months honorary attaché at the British Embassy in Paris, I was invited to a dinner-party by a very rich American lady. Among the guests, the most noted was the daughter of Jay Gould, then at the height of his fame. All the young men present, except me, made up to her, although she was not a lady, apart from her fortune, who would have seemed particularly attractive. At the end of the evening the hostess said to me, 'Are you engaged to be married?' 'Yes,' I said, 'I am. Why, what made you ask?' 'Oh, I thought you must be because you were the only young man who did not run after Gould's daughter.'

When I was in Rome in 1894 I met a very pleasant middle-aged American lady whose hair was still all black except for one streak of pure white. She told me a story which gave me the very greatest delight. It was the story of an old countryman who observed that another traveller on the same train had a hamper to which he paid very great attention, and the old countryman longed to know what was in the hamper. And at last he asked, 'What have you got in the hamper?' And the man who had the hamper said, 'A mongoose.' And he said, 'Why have you got a mongoose?' 'Why,' the other said, 'don't you know that a mongoose will eat snakes. And I have a friend who, alas, has been somewhat unduly addicted to alcohol and who sees snakes, and I'm taking the mongoose to him to eat the snakes.' And the old countryman said, 'But don't you know those snakes are not real?' And he replied, 'No more is my mongoose.' This story from its metaphysical turn delighted me and I laughed so loud that the lady could not imagine why.

When I was a slightly younger man than I am now, I was much addicted to bathing, and somewhat curious things sometimes happened to me when I emerged from a river in a remote country place after bathing. On one of these occasions when I went to put on my clothes, I found the Prime Minister on the bank. This was in 1916 when he was just debating whether or not he should put me in prison, and I felt that it was a little difficult to preserve the dignity that I should have wished to show on such an occasion, when I had not a stitch of clothing on me. However, we had a very pleasant conversation, and I escaped on that occasion without being carted off to jail.

When I lived in China I found the Chinese sense of humour extraordinarily congenial to me, and, in fact, it gave me great delight. I will give one instance. One rather hot day, two Chinese businessmen, both of them rather corpulent, invited me to spend the day in the country motoring with them. We went to visit a very famous, very ancient pagoda, which was in a somewhat dilapidated condition. There was a staircase up to the top, and I went up, expecting them to follow me. But when I reached the top, I saw them below in earnest conversation. When I got down I asked them why they had not come up. 'Well, we debated, with many very serious arguments pro and con whether we should come up or whether we should not, but we decided that as the pagoda might at any moment crumble it would be as well that there should be some to bear witness how the philosopher died.' And, of course, the whole truth was simply that the weather was hot and they were fat.

I had heard many times the story of a young man named Bidder, the son, or perhaps the grandson, of a famous calculating boy. This young man was very averse to getting up early in the mornings, and during one Easter vacation, while he was still an undergraduate, he was staying in Naples, and they came to him and said, 'You must get up.' And he said, 'Why?' And they said, 'Because the hotel is about to be sold.' 'Oh,' said he, 'I'll buy it.' And went to sleep again. The result of this was that he became a hotel-keeper in Naples, and remained so for the rest of his days. I'd always heard this story without believing it. At last one day I met the man, and to my astonishment found that the story was true.

I have sometimes caused astonishment to my friends without intending to. When I was President of the Aristotelian Society, a great many years ago, I decided to shave off my moustache, which had been rather large and luxuriant, and at the next meeting of the Society I observed a curious kind of coldness and aloofness among the other philosophers. At last I sat down in the President's chair, and they all gave a gasp, and I realised that until that moment they hadn't recognised me and hadn't imagined who this person was who had come in. That was the first time that I created astonishment. Another time was when I was engaged in writing *Nightmares of Eminent Persons*, and I had notes on my table which were observed by a visitor, and the notes were headed 'Notes for Nightmares', and he said 'Do you really, before going to bed, make notes of the nightmare you expect to have?'

When I was a young man I became very much interested in Bishop Creighton, who seemed to me rather similar to Bishop Blougram in Browning. The first time I met him, he and his wife were arriving to dinner with Professor Marshall, the economist. She was saying in rather a loud voice, 'I don't care what I eat, I leave that to the men.' To which he replied, 'What do you leave to the men, my dear?' This remark pleased me and I remembered him. I learnt later from his wife's life of him that he sometimes gave offence to very earnest clergymen. There was one who was extremely High Church, and, I regret to say, used incense not merely for fumigatory purposes, which is permissible, but for purposes which are forbidden by law. The Bishop had to go and expostulate with him, and expostulated in perhaps a somewhat frivolous manner. At last the clergyman said, 'You seem to forget, Milord, that I have a cure of souls.' To which the Bishop replied, 'Oh, I see, you think souls are like herrings, before they can be cured they must be smoked.'

I have always been of the opinion that it is possible to live a virtuous life without the support of revealed religion, but I have found that some of the men who agreed with me in this opinion were not altogether to my liking. There was Dr Stanton Coit, who was the head of what is called the Ethical Movement, which exists to prove that virtue can be independent of dogma. Some of the evidence, however, was a little curious. He once invited me to a dinner-party, arrived after all his guests had assembled, threw himself into an armchair, produced a bottle of smelling salts and, between sniffs, remarked in a moribund voice: 'Oh! I've had such a day, such a day!' When slightly revived, he informed one of his lady guests that she needn't think he was a marrying man. He later married a rich widow. On one occasion, at a meeting of the Aristotelian Society, a paper was read about Kant. In the discussion, Dr Stanton Coit said: 'Kant was good to his mother and this fact will be remembered when his system is forgotten.' When it came to my turn to speak I said : 'I cannot share the cynical opinion of Dr Stanton Coit that kindness to one's mother is rarer than Kant's philosophical ability.' I fear, however, that his cynicism was as great after, as before. He was, as it were, the bishop, if one may use such a term, of the Ethical Movement, which retained from orthodox religion the habit of meeting at eleven o'clock on a Sunday in a quasi-religious building. I went once to see what happened on these occasions. They had a large number of choir boys in surplices who came in and intoned a creed designed to show how very different their tenets were from those of the orthodox. The boys all said : 'We do not believe in God, but we believe in the great spirit of humanity.' And when I'd been almost bowled over by this sentiment, they went on to say: 'We do not believe in survival after death but in immortality through good deeds.' On the whole I felt less inclined to believe in their tenets after this occasion than I had before, and I found it extremely difficult to preserve my faith against the buffets of experience.

On the last occasion on which I visited that extraordinarily beautiful building, Tewkesbury Abbey, I was considerably surprised to find a memorial tablet to a lady named Victoria Woodhull Martin. I was surprised because I had known of this lady and her equally or almost equally famous sister, for a very long time, and not in ways that would lead one to expect commemoration in a religious edifice. Victoria Woodhull Martin was a very extreme feminist at a time when feminism was not yet common; and she was extreme, not only politically, but also ethically, in her feminist claims. She stood for President of the United States at a time when such a thing was unheard of, as, indeed, it still would be. A local newspaper in a city where she was speaking announced her coming with the words: 'Victoria

Woodhull Martin is a lady of quick conception and easy delivery and her husband is a man of great parts and deep penetration.' Her sister, Tennessee Katherine, married a neighbour of ours in Richmond where I lived as a boy. He was Sir Francis Cook when he was in England, but in Portugal he was a Marquis. He had a considerable picture gallery and was an authority on art. When he first married her, she sent round a work that she had written on reformed and feminist morality to all the important people at Richmond, and with one accord they decided that they would not call on her. When her husband died, his grandson, who loved her desperately, wished to marry her, and was only dissuaded when they showed him the table of affinities in the prayer-book. I do not know exactly what happened to her after this tragic severance.

At the beginning of the Second World War, Julian Huxley, then Secretary of the London Zoo, was summoned by Mr Winston Churchill, as he then was, to explain the provisions regarding wild beasts that had been made in case of air raids. He told how whenever an air raid was in progress, keepers with loaded revolvers would stand ready to shoot any animal whose escape would be dangerous. 'Seems a pity,' said Mr Churchill, 'bombs exploding, houses tottering, flames spreading, lions and tigers roaring. Seems a pity.'

My friend Crompton Llewelyn Davis, who was a partner in the eminent law firm of Coward, Chance and Co., was addicted to extreme shabbiness in his clothes, to such a degree that some of his friends expostulated. This had an unexpected result. When West Australia attempted by litigation to secede from the Commonwealth of Australia, his firm was employed, and it was decided that the case should be heard in the King's Robing Room. Crompton was overheard ringing up the King's Chamberlain and saying: 'The unsatisfactory state of my trousers has lately been brought to my notice. I understand that the case is to be heard in the King's Robing Room, perhaps the King has left an old pair of trousers there that might be useful to me.'

Everyone knows the first recorded words of Thomas Babington, afterwards Lord Macaulay, and everyone remembers that these words were: 'Thank you, Madam, the agony is abated.' But it is a mistake to suppose that these are the first words that that man ever uttered. A great-aunt of mine in her very early youth knew his nurse in her extreme old age, and she used to say, 'Lor, Milady, they was not his first words, you wouldn't believe the things he used to say.' She would then repeat some of them, not in her natural idiom, but with all the elegance of diction and pronunciation to be expected in the words of so eminent a man. 'Why, Milady, I remember as if it were yesterday the little lad come running up to me, fresh from the garden, three years old he was, and he says to me, "Nurse," he says, "in the ideal constitution there should be a just balance of forces, while on the one hand the will of the people should be adequately represented in a popular house, on the other hand the wisdom of those who through their stake in the country have acquired a certain stability of political judgement, should not remain unheard." "Lor, Master Thomas," said I, "'ow you do go on." ' Many hundreds of such pearls of wisdom she would repeat to my great-aunt, but alas, between my great-aunt and me, all the rest are buried in oblivion.

There has been a similar drying up of the well of truth in regard to Thomas Carlyle. He, as everyone knows, is supposed to have observed the gospel of silence until the age of three, when he remarked in a meditative tone of voice, 'What ails wee Jock?' This also, however, is a myth. His mother told his wife and his wife told my mother of many earlier sayings showing the first budding of philosophical rhetoric. Several months before the above known occurrence, he made another remark about wee Jock: 'Mither,' he said, 'the lamp of history sheds its glimmering light down the long corridor of the past, and to those who have eyes to discern its flickering flame, reveals that it was not I but wee Jock that broke the vase on the mantelpiece.' 'Ach, Tommy, don't fret so,' said his mother.

When Thales and Jeremiah were both living in the town of Tempe in Egypt, they happened one evening to meet in the pub. Owing to the Babylonian war, the beer was not what it had been. But, *faute de mieux*, each ordered a tankard. After a first sip, Thales said: 'All is water.' Jeremiah replied: 'Woe, woe!' Nevertheless, they left the pub arm in arm.

Once when I was staying at Clovelly, I walked, on a fine day, to Hartland Point. There I met a coastguardsman with whom I got into conversation. I asked him how far it was from Hartland Point to Clovelly, and he said, 'eight miles'. And I asked him how far to Lundy Island, and he said 'ten miles'. 'And how far from Lundy Island to Clovelly?' I then asked. 'Twenty-two miles,' he replied. 'But that is impossible, for according to what you say, even if one came round by Hartland Point it would only be eighteen miles.' 'Well, Sir,' he replied, 'all's I can say is, Sir, that Captain Jones was here a few days ago, and I says to Captain Jones, says I, "How far do you make it from Lundy Island to Clovelly?" And he says to me, says he, "I've known this coast, man and boy, thirty years and I make it twenty-two miles." ' Against Captain Jones, man and boy, Euclid's arguments flung themselves in vain.

Disraeli, in spite of his political eminence, was somewhat painfully conscious of the fact that his hands lacked beauty. Nevertheless, in an absent-minded mood he allowed them on one occasion to rest upon the dinner-table. There came one of those unusual moments of complete silence. Lady Margaret Cecil, who was sitting next to him, remarked, 'Awful pause'. With extreme haste he withdrew his hands and concealed them beneath the table.

I know of another example of the danger of homonyms. Mr Attlee is only known to have made one joke in the course of a long and honourable career. At a Pilgrim dinner he spoke of a certain village in rural England where there was a very fine old church falling into disrepair, where no money was forthcoming to keep it from ruin. At length, by good fortune an immensely rich American discovered that his family came from that village, and he therefore supplied the funds needed for the restoration of the sacred edifice. When the restoration was complete, a thanksgiving service was held in the renovated church at which, as was natural, the eminent American was present. The vicar in an eloquent prayer expressed his gratitude to Providence, saying: 'O Lord, we thank Thee that in our hour of need Thou hast sent us this succour.' The American thought the sentiment might have been better expressed.

Once, in an American train, I got into conversation with a young naval officer, and happened to mention Brussels. 'Brussels,' he said, 'I like Brussels. There's more sex appeal per square foot there than anywhere else except Suez and Constantinople.' Nevertheless, I have never visited either.

The people one meets in trains tend to be somewhat odd. One time when I was travelling, there was in the train an old farmer, a very simple old farmer. And I found on talking to him that he was an anarchist. He did not know the word *anarchist*, he did not know he was anarchist, but he had been impressed with the fact that Public Bodies waste water. It happened that the train was running alongside a main road and there was a steam-roller and a great quantity of water being spread upon the ground. 'There, you see,' he said, and on the ground that Public Bodies waste water he wanted all public bodies abolished.

I have sometimes found that people with whom on the whole I am in agreement, express their opinions in ways that I cannot entirely subscribe to. I remember once meeting a fiercely feminist lady who, after talking at great length about the superiority of her sex, wound up by saying: 'The half of every man is a lunatic.' 'Yes,' I said, 'the better half.'

And I remember another lady, also a very very convinced feminist, who was impressed by the fact that women, who at times were not able to sit in Parliament in England or in Congress in America, were able to sit in the State legislature of a State which she called 'Collarada'. And she said the effect of their presence in the State legislature had been an immense improvement in morals and manners. She assured me that since women have sat in legislative halls in 'Collarada' there has been no more of that throwing of spittoons and ink-pots. They soon showed the men that they were not to be flirted with, no, nor flirted at. At this point she turned to her neighbour, who was a Roman Catholic, and said: 'Nothing is more certain than that women will be ministers of religion, ay, and priests too.' He said, 'Oh, I hope some things are more certain.' 'No,' she said, 'nothing is more certain.'

Advantages sometimes happen through the misguided practice of getting on to a train after it is in motion. I was once travelling from Paddington to Evesham. There was one other passenger in the carriage, a youngish lady.

We sat at opposite corners in prim silence. But at Oxford, after the train was well under way, a man dashed into the carriage. A porter seized him by the legs to keep him out, and I seized him by the arms to get him in. I shouted at the porter: 'Let go or the man'll be killed!' He did, and we got the man in. This broke the ice and there ensued a rather curious conversation with the lady. She turned out to be a school-teacher who was being obliged to leave England and go to Canada, because her headmistress disapproved of teaching arithmetic by modern methods. So I naturally said to her, 'What are modern methods?' 'Ah, well,' she said, 'the old method was, you told the children two and two are four; and they learnt this. But the modern method is to say: "Now dear children, how many eyes have you?" and they say: "Two"; "And now dear children how many ears have you?" and they say: "Two"; "And now dear children, how many legs have you?" and they say: "Two"; "And now dear children, how many noses have you?" and they say: "Two". But my headmistress does not approve of this method of teaching arithmetic and I shall have to go to Canada. There's only one drawback, which is that I'll have to become a Roman Catholic.' And I said, 'Don't you mind that?' 'Oh, no,' she said, 'I've nothing against them except that they play cards on Sundays after Mass.' With this contribution to theology the conversation ended.

One of the most beautiful women that I have ever seen, was one with whom I had only five minutes conversation and whom I never saw again. However, the conversation was as fruitful as five minutes could make it. She told me that she had recently returned from Mexico, and that while in Mexico City she, having taken a taxi, was pursued by twelve Mexican Generals, each in a taxi, and each determined to rape her. 'But,' said she, 'I was on very good terms with the President, and I managed to reach him before they had accomplished their fell work.' I regret to say that by this time the five minutes were up.

I once met a lady teacher from Texas who, if one may believe her own account, had had a somewhat curious and adventurous life. She said that the youth of Texas were extremely violent people, some of them: she had boys of fifteen or sixteen in her class and had some difficulty in keeping order. 'How did you manage it?' I said. 'Oh,' she said, 'of course I always had a loaded revolver on my desk.' Which didn't seem to her at all an odd thing for a teacher to have. She'd had all sorts of adventures. She wrote an autobiography which opened with her being raped by her brother when she was four years old. Unfortunately she got this autobiography printed in Paris, and had the proofs sent to her in England. The British Government considered the autobiography improper and Scotland Yard waited upon her, and the autobiography never saw the light of day.

I once met in the train a gentleman who was even more anti-clerical than I am. It was a train which was about to arrive at Exeter, and he said, 'I hate Exeter, there are so many parsons there.' At that moment the train reached the platform and he said, 'Look, there's one now!' in just the tone of voice that he might have employed if it had been a black beetle on his kitchen floor.

There have been two occasions in my life when I have thought that I was on the track of a good story but found to my great regret that I was not. The first of these was when I was walking one day with Sir Spencer Walpole, the historian. I had been reading Kinglake's *History of the Crimea*, and I said to him, 'Why does Kinglake hate Napoleon III so bitterly?' And Sir Spencer Walpole replied, 'They quarrelled about a woman.' I naturally said, 'Will you tell me the story?' And he said, 'No, Sir, I shall not tell you the story.' And shortly afterwards he died. The other occasion was when a friend of mine, at a public dinner, found himself sitting next to Sydney Colvin, and Sydney Colvin began complaining about Rossetti and said he used to write the most scurrilous verses; 'He wrote a scurrilous verse about me, it began : "There is an art critic named Colvin, whose writings the mind might revolve in . . ." 'My friend said to him, 'Will you tell me how it went on?' 'No, Sir, I shall not tell you how it went on.' And history does not relate what the remaining lines were.

Dante Gabriel Rossetti, like a good many other famous men, had to have his off-times when he was not exhibiting those virtues for which the public loved him. When he had got tired of 'The Blessed Damosel' he would write verses of a somewhat different sort. I can remember two examples of these. One commemorates a notable event in the town of Aberystwyth. It goes as follows: 'There was a young girl of Aberystwyth, / Who took sacks to the mill to fetch grist with, / But the miller's son Jack / Laid her flat on her back / And united the things that they pissed with.' There was another poem which I believe has never been printed, of which I can remember only one verse. It commemorated the joys of paradise, before the fall, and this verse which I remember said: 'Who in Eden's garden had 'em / without so much as Sir or Madam, / Who rogered Eve, who buggered Adam? / My Maker.' I think that if these verses had ever been published they might, perhaps, have diminished his popularity with the admirers of the Blessed Damosel.

The grounds of people's political opinions are many and diverse: some seem fairly ordinary, some are more strange and bizarre. I think the most remarkable reason for voting that I ever came across was that of the Professor of Arabic in Cambridge when I was young. He very much disliked Mr Gladstone's excursions into scripture knowledge, and on one occasion when he had voted Liberal my friend Whitehead asked him why he had voted Liberal. 'Oh,' he said, 'because when Mr Gladstone is in office he hasn't time to write about holy scripture.' I think this is the strangest reason for voting that I have ever come across.

The Reverend Dr Abbott was a clergyman who wrote a book called *Flatland,* which greatly delighted me when I was a boy. He was a man in whom philosophy somewhat overpowered the clerical qualities which one would have expected of him. He found himself once on a bus, where there was a drunken man who was pouring forth foul-mouthed obscenities such as no clergyman could be expected to endure. He felt it his professional duty to reprove the man, and the man said, 'There must be some of all sorts and I'm of that sort.' Dr Abbott, remembering his Plato, was completely silenced.

Everybody remembers how Napoleon on his way to Egypt sat on the deck of the ship surrounded by members of the Institute : various scientific luminaries who, during the Revolution, had been vehement atheists. Napoleon, however, was determined to regard himself as the earthly reproduction of the Heavenly Emperor, and, therefore, thought that there must be a Heavenly Emperor. He set to work to convert the scientists. He pointed to the stars and said, 'Who made the Stars?' The members of the Institute, realising on which side their bread was buttered, were then and there converted.

Now I was once sitting beside the driver of an old horse-bus on a starry night and the bus driver said to me, 'A week ago, Sir, there was a hathiest a-sitting where you is now.' So I said, 'Oh'. He said, 'Yes there was, Sir. And I said to him, " 'o made them stars?" and 'e didn't know what to say.' So I thought, well, I don't know whether he has the other qualities of Napoleon, but he certainly has one of them.

There was an extremely genteel lady once who was travelling in a train, and it so happened that sitting opposite to her there was a man who had a crucifix on his watch-chain, but in spite of this talked in a very blasphemous and horrible fashion. The lady said to him, 'I am surprised, my man, in view of the emblem that you bear, to hear you speaking in this manner.' And he said, 'Lor, Maam, that ain't Christ, that's the other bloke that died by him.'

Maupassant, on a visit to England, decided to visit literary men living in London. The first on his list was George Meredith. Maupassant, as everybody remembers, suffered from ailments which are generally considered the result of a not too virtuous life. So did Meredith. Maupassant remarked, 'Well, after all, we have to pay for our pleasures.' 'Not at all,' said Meredith. 'Not at all. It has nothing to do with that.' He had another adventure on the same visit. This time it was Henry James. In those days fashionable ladies used to drive round the park in open carriages if the weather was fine, and Henry James, who understood that Maupassant took a certain interest in the ladies, determined to try to impress him. And all the most famous beauties of the age drove by in open carriages, and Henry James would say to Maupassant, 'That's a beautiful woman'; and Maupassant said 'Non'. And he tried it again and again. Maupassant said 'Non'. At last, so Henry James related, he said, 'I persisted in my little opinion.' And Maupassant said, 'Non. J'ai couche avec une foute d'Anglaises et

Americaines. Habillées elles sont bien. Déshabillées, non.' Henry James pursued the subject no further.

I have often heard people spoken of as 'the typical Englishman' but I have found a logical difficulty in this conception. One may say that an Englishman is typical in this or that respect, if he possesses most of the properties that most Englishmen possess. Now, as a matter of fact, most Englishmen do not possess most properties that most Englishmen possess. Therefore, the typical Englishman is untypical. I have never been able to get round this puzzle, and I have therefore concluded that no Englishman is typical.

Sir Donald MacKenzie Wallace, the author of a monumental work on Russia, told me a story which illustrates the tribulations of an author. He said that shortly after the publication of this work, he happened to meet Robert Louis Stevenson, then a very young man, at a party. They got into an argument about Russia, in which Stevenson maintained certain views which Wallace, somewhat modestly, controverted. At last Stevenson, who had not heard the name of the man to whom he was speaking, explained, 'I know I'm right because I've just been reading Wallace's *Russia*.' 'And I have just been writing it,' replied Wallace.

Mrs Sheldon Amos, whom I knew some number of years ago, was a high-minded lady whose main activity was rescue work. As she expressed it to her friends: 'Since my dear husband's death, I have devoted my life to prostitution.' Her son-in-law, a gallant officer in Her Majesty's Regular Army, had fought in many parts of the world, had been repeatedly ship-wrecked, and had been the only White man in the midst of native mutinies. After listening to his story, I ventured to say, 'You've had a rather adventurous life.' 'Oh, no,' he said, 'I don't think so. Of course I've never missed my morning tea.'

Professor J. A. Smith, the eminent Oxford moralist and metaphysician, visited me at my college rooms in Cambridge in 1912. It happened that the Professor of Arabic was present at the same time, but Professor Smith failed to apprehend this fact. By sheer accident the Reader in Ornithology in the University of Cambridge and the Reader in Oriental Art were also present. Professor Smith who, though a metaphysician, prided himself on his outdoor life, ventured a remark about a bird that he had seen, and was corrected by the Reader in Ornithology. He then spoke of a famous *objet d'art* which he said had been removed from Peking by the Germans after the Boxer Rebellion. The Reader in Oriental Art remarked that he had seen it in Peking a few months ago. Nothing daunted, Professor Smith began to speak of his travels in Egypt. His saddle-man, he said, had made a certain Arabic speech, which he repeated to us and which he then translated for our benefit. The Professor of Arabic, who until this moment had sat silent and apparently asleep, looked up and asked, 'What did you say he said?' Professor Smith repeated the supposedly Arabic words. 'And what did you say it meant?' said the Professor of Arabic. Professor Smith repeated the English equivalent. 'Well that is very odd,' said the Professor of Arabic, whose identity had remained a secret until that moment. 'The correct Arabic for what you say is etc.' Professor Smith took the next train to Oxford and never returned to Cambridge.

In spite of my duties as host, I viewed his discomfiture with equanimity, because once while I was reading a paper to the Jowett Society at Oxford, he had sought to triumph over me by methods which I could not wholly approve. Professor Smith, in common with our Hegelians, held that truths are only truths because the Absolute thinks so. I remarked that according to this doctrine a man would instantly become bald if the Absolute forgot to notice his hair. Professor Smith, in replying to my paper, alluded to the text about the hairs on our head being numbered and said in a tone of portentous gravity that to his infinite regret I had seen fit to make fun of beliefs in which all of us had been brought up, and which for some of us were very precious. Apparently the beliefs in question included the belief that he knew Arabic.

It has sometimes happened to me to be accused of things which the general public does not seem to think me guilty of – in fact, it tends to think exactly the opposite. I was once in a large town in the State of Kansas, and thirty men invited me to dinner. It was during Prohibition and I was not offered a drink, but one of the thirty had arrived very drunk. He was seated a good distance away from me, but he bawled along the whole length of the table, 'What do you know about life? You ought to have more to do with women. You don't know anything about women. You're an ignorant fellow you are.' The others all tried to hush him, but it was quite impossible, and I was rather pleased to have this very unusual accusation hurled at me.

Again, quite recently, a journalist asked me what newspapers I read, and I said I read *The Times* and the *Manchester Guardian*. So he said, 'Oh, then you don't know anything about human nature, you can only find out about human nature by reading the popular Sunday Press.' And I was impressed by the fact that human nature to him consisted entirely of scandals, divorces and murders and he didn't seem to think that human beings ever did do anything else.

Reading History As It Is Never Written

I am about to relate the history of the period that I am writing about. In this period, the ancient yeomanry gradually lost control of their landed property through a succession of bad harvests, which were taken advantage of by urban adventurers destitute of the ancient piety that had distinguished the yeomanry. Through this corruption, the State became far inferior to what it had been in the old days, and the tentacles of financial power extended from the capital over many rural areas. It is to be lamented that the decay of morals which was thus caused, was not for many centuries remedied, and, as was not to be wondered at, the State thus degraded morally, tended to fall a victim to other States more morally regenerate and less intellectually decadent. This, I say, is the history of the period I am writing about; if you ask me what period that is I will say it is Attica before Solon's legislation, it is Rome after the Punic Wars, it is England as depicted in More's *Utopia,* Goldsmith's *Deserted Village* and the Hammonds' *Village Labourer,* it is Southern California as depicted in Lawrence's *Octopus.* Last it is the state of Kenya as described in the future official history of East Africa, in the chapter called 'The Mau Mau Martyrs'.

I find that the things that interest me in history are not exactly those that the historians emphasise, and indeed I have found very frequently that the things that seem to me best worth emphasising are passed by in a footnote or a parenthesis. Now take for example the Dialogues between Buddhists and Greek philosophers which resulted from Alexander's conquests. In these Dialogues, since they were composed in India, the Buddhist is, of course, victorious, but I do not find that Western philosophers give as much weight as they should to the Buddhist's arguments. They always assume, as a matter of course, that the Greek philosopher must be the better, but I'm not at all sure that he really was. Or take another thing, take Justinian, and the School of Philosophy in Athens. The School of Philosophy in Athens persisted in glorifying Pagan philosophy long after the State had become Christian, and this pained Justinian and he decided to close the School of Philosophy. The worthy philosophers thereupon migrated to Persia, which, as they had been correctly informed, was not Christian, and therefore they thought must be open to Greek philosophy; but when they got to Persia they found two things that they considered quite intolerable. One was the practice of incest, encouraged in the Royal Family, and the other was the practice of polygamy. Both these things so

290

shocked the philosophers that they came back to Athens and conformed, at least outwardly, to the Christian ethic.

I was very much pleased when I read about the first negotiations between the British and the Chinese, to find that the Chinese Government officially complained of the British that none of their suggested treaties contained any mention of filial piety. On this ground, the Chinese considered the English morally degraded, and until they managed to complete some moral reformation, the Chinese thought it would be unwise to have any treaty with them whatsoever.

Hegel was at one time the ruling philosopher in academic circles; he was so when I was young. I did not learn at that time what I discovered since: that Hegel thought the Absolute idea spread gradually from one country to another, but at the time of Charlemagne settled upon Germany, which it had never since abandoned. There were, however, three periods in German history according to Hegel; the first period was that of the Father, the second that of the Son, and the third that of the Holy Ghost. The period of the Holy Ghost, according to Hegel, began at the time of the Peasants' War, a most atrocious business in which the State, encouraged by Luther, brutally extirpated those who demanded agrarian reform. I was rather interested to find that this seemed to Hegel a suitable activity for the Holy Ghost.

Another thing that I found very interesting is the extraordinary difference between the thirteenth century as it was, and the thirteenth century as it appears in most books of Christian apologetics. The thirteenth century was a very vigorous and a very remarkable century, in many ways one of the most remarkable there has ever been, but it was not, if one may trust what its own people said at the time, altogether remarkable for a high standard of virtue. The friars and the monks hated each other with a passionate hatred, and the friars said things about the monks which are far worse than any the Protestants have ever said about them. For example, they describe the lady who went to confess to a friar, and when she had finished her confession, he found that she had a dagger in her bosom. And he said 'Why that?' 'Oh,' she said, 'because the last three times I went to confession it was to a monk, and each time the monk raped me, and I decided that if this happened again I would plunge the dagger into my heart.' The friar considers this typical monkish behaviour.

At one time I kept a school that was more or less on modern lines, and it was accused by the neighbours of every kind of shocking practice. I, of course, did what I could to deny these accusations, but at last I discovered that exactly similar accusations were made by the friars against the schools conducted by the monks. It appeared that in these schools, all the things that I was said to do, were said by the friars to be done by the monks. This rather consoled me.

Another thing that I discovered rather to my surprise about that same

291

period of history, was that cathedrals were not built to the glory of God, as one is commonly told, but to the glory of the local bishop. It was always the local bishop who wanted the cathedral to be great and grand; and all the really pious people of the time were puritans, who objected to pomp and splendour and thought that a little tin tabernacle would do just as well, and opposed bitterly the creation of the cathedrals, which was the work of thoroughly worldly dignitaries of the church. This was a surprise to me and somewhat interesting.

Another thing that one is told is that the Church preserved learning throughout the Dark Ages. Now, Pope Gregory the Great, who was Pope in the year 600, was a very remarkable man, a very great statesman, but he, who lived just at the beginning of the Dark Ages, did not have this attitude towards elegant Latinity which we are told the Church preserved: on the contrary, he wrote to a certain bishop, saying: 'A rumour has reached us which we cannot mention without a blush, that thou expoundest grammar to certain friends. The praises of the Lord and of Jupiter cannot exist in the same mouth, and should this rumour be not without foundation, we enjoin you to desist at once from this pernicious practice.' What the bishop did, I do not know, but I do remember this, that when I learnt Latin grammar there was a list of impersonal verbs – rains, snows, hails and so forth – and my grammar said that Jupiter is understood as the subject of these sentences. This rather enables me to understand the point of view of Gregory the Great: I believe modern grammars omit this remark.

I once knew a man who made a marriage of reason, but the result was not wholly satisfactory. He was a philosopher of some eminence, A. W. Benn. He wrote a very good history of Greek philosophy, lived in Florence, and was very much addicted to long walks throughout the neighbourhood. But he was extremely short-sighted, and could only see a little way with the help of very powerful spectacles. When he reached the age of fifty, he decided to marry. He decided that the lady of his choice must have three qualifications; first, she must not be under thirty, second, she must know Greek, and third, she must be able to walk at least twenty miles. The first of these qualifications was satisfied by many of the ladies in pensions in Florence, the second – that she should know Greek – was not nearly so common, but he discovered one, at last, who had this qualification. It remained to be seen whether she had the third. He invited her to take a walk in the neighbourhood of Florence, and he knew that when on their return they reached a certain house in Florence, the twentieth mile would have been completed. They reached the house, he proposed, and was accepted. But, ah, alas for him, the lady, after marriage, bought a bicycle and gave up walking on foot. He, being so short-sighted, was unable to ride a bicycle, and the marriage of reason failed to bring that bliss which he had fully expected it would produce.

One of the men whose life has always interested me was Apollinaris

Sidonius. Apollinaris Sidonius was a Frenchman at the time of the Barbarian Invasion. A very cultivated gentleman, somewhat in the Bloomsbury style, he devoted himself to writing poems which you can read backwards and forwards equally well – a line would begin with 'amor' and end with 'roma' – and it was a skill that was much admired among the Bloomsburyites of that period, to write poems that you could read backwards or forwards equally. Well, he devoted himself to this pursuit very successfully and very happily, but then the barbarians came and this rather interfered. It did not interfere exactly in the way that one would think from reading about the Barbarian Invasion. It interfered in a different way. He writes to a friend and says: 'It's such a bore, I have to dine with Germans tonight and they have such bad table-manners.' And this is what the Barbarian Invasion was in real life. However, in the end their table-manners so shocked him that he became a very earnest Christian, a bishop, and died fighting the Germans in the great cause of culture in order that the pursuit of poems to be read backwards and forwards might continue throughout future ages.

I had always been told throughout my youth of the fanaticism of the Mohammedans, and especially that story of the destruction of the library at Alexandria. Well, I believed all these stories, but when I came to look into the history of the times concerned, I had a great many shocks. In the first place, I discovered that the library of Alexandria was destroyed a great many times, and the first time was by Julius Caesar, simply because he couldn't get a hot bath any other way. But the last time was supposed to have been by the Mohammedans, and for this I found no justification whatsoever. Nor did I find that the Mohammedans were fanatical. On the contrary, the Christians of that time were extraordinarily fanatical. The contests between Catholics, Nestorians, and Monophysites were bitter and persecuting to the last degree. But the Mohammedans, when they conquered Christian countries, allowed the Christians to be perfectly free, provided they paid a tribute. The only penalty for being a Christian was that you had to pay a tribute that Mohammedans did not have to pay. This proved completely successful, and the immense majority of the population became Mohammedan, but not through any fanaticism on the part of the Mohammedans. On the contrary they, in the earlier centuries of their power, represented free thought and tolerance to a degree that the Christians did not emulate until quite recent times. This is one of the stock lies of history, of which there are a great many.

I found a very interesting story in the history of Japan. Japan, as everyone knows, had a period when Christian missionaries, especially Jesuits, had very great success in converting large numbers of Japanese to the Christian faith. And then there was a reaction, and Japan was closed to all foreigners except one Dutch ship every year, and that lasted for a long long time. Well, I didn't know how this had come about until I had

293

occasion to study the history of Japan. I then discovered that the first incident that led to this result was the wreck of a British ship on the coast of Japan; and its Captain, Bill Adams, who was a breezy Elizabethan, and, like all Elizabethan sea-faring persons, passionately Protestant, was asked by the Shogun what he thought of the Jesuits, and if he knew anything about them. And he replied: 'Jesuits, Lor luvyer, Sir, I can tell you all about the Jesuits.' And he poured forth Protestant tales about the wickedness of Jesuits, and the Shogun listened entranced. He gave Bill Adams a position at Court, but never would allow him to leave Japan. What we know about him we know from his letters to his wife, very affectionate letters, more ill-spelt letters than any I have ever seen, and from them we know all that he told the Shogun and all that the Shogun thought about what he told.

Just after the Shogun had learnt these stories about the Jesuits, a Spanish ship proceeding from Maçâo to Panama was wrecked on the coast of Japan. The local populace started immediately to ransack the ship and steal all it contained in the way of rich merchandise. The Spanish Captain appealed to the local Daimio and said, 'Look, these people are thieves, they're stealing the cargo, will you stop it?' 'Oh, yes,' said the Daimio, 'they have no right to the cargo, it belongs to me.' So then the Spanish Captain, nothing daunted, went up to see the Shogun and said, 'Look here, the local Daimio is stealing my cargo. Do you think you could stop it?' 'Oh, yes,' said the Shogun, 'of course it doesn't belong to him. It belongs to me.' Thereupon the Captain, who was not perhaps quite as wise as a Captain should be, threatened him and said: 'On the contrary, the cargo belongs to the King of Spain, the King of Spain is very powerful and if you steal the cargo you will incur his displeasure.' 'The King of Spain,' said the Shogun, 'Who is he?' (having never heard of him). The Spanish Captain thereupon produced a map of the world in which the Spanish dominions were all coloured green – they embraced at that time very large parts of Europe and the whole of North and South America. The Shogun was somewhat impressed, and said: 'How did the King of Spain acquire these large dominions?' 'Oh,' said the Captain, 'he sends missionaries to these places who convert the people to Christianity. The Christians become a fifth column, and set to work to see to it that their Government is overthrown and their country is subordinated to Spain.' 'Ho, Ho,' said the Shogun, 'we'll have no more missionaries in this country.' Thereupon he made ten years preparation, and on a given day he had every Christian in Japan massacred. And this was the beginning of the two and a half centuries during which only one Dutch ship a year was allowed into Japan. The period of anti-Christianity was brought to an end by Commodore Perry, who, supported by gunboats and a powerful navy, compelled the Japanese to become tolerant to the doctrines of the Sermon on the Mount.

One of the myths of history is Brutus, especially in England where we take our view of him from Shakespeare's *Julius Caesar*. I discovered with infinite sorrow that Brutus was not the splendid fellow he is said to be by Shakespeare. You find in one of Cicero's letters, when Cicero was Governor of a province, that he found a private army besieging a certain city in his province. He went to the Commander of the army and said, 'What are you doing here?' And the Commander said, 'Oh, we were hired by Brutus to besiege this city.' 'Why?' said Cicero. 'Why?' 'Because Brutus had lent them money at sixty per cent and they thought twelve per cent would be enough interest to pay, and he thought no, they must pay the sixty per cent and so he hired an army to besiege them.' Now Cicero and Brutus belonged to the same political party, and Cicero found this rather painful, so he wrote to Brutus and besought him to be more merciful, and Brutus very reluctantly consented to reduce the interest to twelve per cent. What is perhaps even more shocking, is that after the assassination of Caesar for claiming to be Emperor, Brutus, in the provinces where he was in control, had coins struck describing himself as Emperor. I have seen such a coin myself and there is no doubt about it, so that I'm afraid we must say that Brutus only objected to Caesar being Emperor, and didn't object when it was he who was the Emperor.

Another matter about which the history books for the most part tell unmitigated lies, or at any rate misrepresentations, is the Crusades. One is told that the Crusades were very great and glorious acts of faith, in which noble men heroically devoted themselves to freeing the Holy Sepulchre from the infidel. This is not quite what really happened. What really happened was that trade in the West in those days was almost entirely in the hands of Jews, and it was found that if you stirred up religious enthusiasm sufficiently, you could get people to go for the Jews; and in fact every Crusade began with pogroms – very extensive pogroms – in every Christian country that took part, and the Crusades were in fact completely successful. At the beginning of them the trade was in the hands of Jews, at the end it was wholly in the hands of Christians. True, the Holy Sepulchre remained in the hands of the Turks, but that had been only a pretext, the real purpose of the Crusades had been achieved.

The philosopher Seneca I found a very interesting person. Everybody knows how it was supposed by Christians in subsequent centuries that he, though not nominally a Christian, had in fact very closely approximated to Christian doctrine and been very sympathetic to it. In fact there were produced letters between Seneca and St Paul which later scholarship pronounced spurious, but which throughout the Middle Ages were universally accepted as genuine, in which it appeared that Seneca and St Paul were practically in agreement. Well, when I came to find out what Seneca really did and said, it was not quite what I had been led to expect. In the first place, he was the Minister to Nero at the time when Nero plotted the murder of his mother, and Seneca certainly was an accomplice in that performance. In the second place, I found what very much interested me, that in his capacity of great financier, he lent a lot of money to Boadicea at a very high rate of interest. She after a time found difficulty in paying the interest, and therefore rebelled against Rome, with the result that we all know. At last Nero got tired of him, and sent messengers to say that in view of his great services to the State in the past, he should be allowed to commit suicide instead of being executed. So he set to work to make a will, being in fact enormously rich. But the messenger said that there was not going to be time for a will, and all his property was going to be confiscated to the State, that is to say to Nero. So he could not go on with making a will, and he had to set to work to commit suicide. He got into a bath, opened a small vein, had three secretaries round his bath to take down his last words, and made a most edifying end.

One of the minor characters of the Elizabethan age whom I have found interesting, was Sir John Harington. Sir John Harington was a sort of *enfant terrible* who always amused Queen Elizabeth, so that she could not bring herself to punish him as he apparently sometimes deserved. One of the things that he did, was to be the first inventor of the W.C. The only W.C. in the country was Queen Elizabeth's, and she, I believe, was duly grateful for this. However, on another occasion he translated the only improper canto of Ariosto, and presented the translation to Queen Elizabeth, who professed to be very much shocked and said that this sort of thing must be punished, and she condemned him as a penalty to translate the whole of the rest of Ariosto – a very very long piece of work. He had, however, another side to him. He went to Ireland with Essex and was considered to be Essex's close friend. I discovered what I must say rather shocked me, that he was employed by the Government as a spy upon Essex, and throughout the period when Essex completely trusted him, he was really in the Secret Service with a view to convicting Essex of treachery or traitorous conduct, if possible. He was so much beloved by Essex, that Essex knighted him. This vexed Elizabeth. Originally every knight could confer a knighthood, but nowadays, as everybody knows, only the Sovereign can, and I think that Sir John Harington was the last, or very nearly the last, to get a knighthood from a subject. He got it from Essex and did his utmost to get Essex condemned.

One of the fundamental divisions in politics is between parties of creditors and parties of debtors. But there is a difficulty if you belong to a party of debtors, and the difficulty is this: that if you win, you instantly become a party of creditors and you therefore have to alter the whole of your programme. One of the most remarkable illustrations of this rule is Julius Caesar. Julius Caesar, in the civil turmoils in Rome, took the side of debtors. When a very young man, he was captured by pirates and held on an island. They offered to release him in return for ransom. He asked how much they had demanded, and they told him. He was bitterly outraged and said, 'Oh, you should have asked ten times as much – you evidently did not know what an important man I am. If you ask ten times as much you will certainly get it, but I shall come back and hang every man of you.' They asked ten times as much, they got it, and he did come back and hang every man of them. He belonged to a different sort of political party from that to which Alexander belonged. Alexander, before starting out to destroy the Persian Empire, made treaties with all the Greek States that on no account were there to be vendettas while he was absent. He stood for creditors, Julius Caesar stood for debtors, until such time as he was in a position to take the attitude of the creditor. The same division existed between Protestants and Catholics in early days: Catholics stood for debtors, Protestants for creditors. For this reason, Catholics thought that interest was immoral, Protestants thought that it was not. But gradually, as finance capital came more and more into the hands of Catholics, the Catholics modified their view on this point, as debtors always have as soon as they acquired power.

When I was a very young man I was shown over an Oxford college library by the librarian who had occasion to mention Wycliffe, and to my great delight alluded to him as Professor Wycliffe, making him seem as though he were quite contemporary. I wondered at that time, and indeed for quite a long while afterwards, how it was that Wycliffe during his lifetime had escaped persecution. The reason really was quite simple: it was that the Popes were satellites of the French Government at that time, and the French Government was at war with the British Government, and therefore the Government in England, which in those days was in the hands of John of Gaunt, befriended anybody who was attacking the Pope; and this was how it was that Wycliffe, throughout the whole of his life, escaped persecution. In fact, the University of Oxford at that time defended academic freedom against all ecclesiastical attacks, severe as they were. Later on, when Henry V had conquered France, the matter changed, and Henry V became just as persecuting as the Church could possibly have wished.

If I had more leisure, or a longer life, I should write a book called *Shelley the Tough*. I got very tired of the ineffectual angel of Matthew Arnold's criticism: Shelley, in fact, was not at all that sort of person. You will remember that when he was a schoolboy, he was always asked by the other schoolboys at Eton to raise the devil, which he did, by means of magical incantations and so forth, and altogether he was considered by the others at Eton to be a very tough customer. You will, no doubt, remember also that he was an extremely good shot with the pistol, much better than Byron or any of Byron's friends, who went in for being toughs. There was one occasion when Shelley and Byron were both living in Pisa, and Shelley went out with Byron's bravos into the country, and they were pursued by the town-guard of Pisa, which considered these men ruffians. All of the bravos fled, with the exception of Shelley, who single-handed routed all the municipal worthies of Pisa and was left holding the field. I think altogether that he should be represented in that line. I live in a place where he supported his friend Madocks in disfiguring one of the great beauties of North Wales, in the interests of modern industrialism. This is what Shelley was really like, it was only occasionally that he wrote poems. In fact, he was a tough customer given to revolver shooting and to modern industrialism.

At the time when Parnell was convicted of adultery, and the question arose whether Mr Gladstone should throw him over or not, he told John Morley that he had known ten Prime Ministers, and nine of them he knew to be adulterers. Now among the ten was my grandfather; I have always hoped that he was the tenth.

It has sometimes been considered remarkable that Napoleon allowed the emigres to come back to France. I think the reason why he allowed this is quite plain. He had been a scholarship boy at the military academy at Brienne, and had been looked down upon by the scions of ancient nobility who were his schoolfellows. When he became Emperor, he had a chance to see these people who had treated him with contumely when he was a boy, bowing down before him and seeking to ingratiate themselves with him. I think it was the pleasure of this that caused him to allow them to come home. He was, of course, not at all above that sort of pleasure: he would throw his hat into a corner and make a foreign ambassador pick it up. When my grandfather visited him in Elba, which was after his great days were over, he tweaked my grandfather's ear just to show familiarity. And I think it is extremely probable that his sole motive in allowing the emigres to come home was to see these schoolfellows of his bowing down before him.

I find that psychoanalysts and people of that sort do not adopt what would seem to me the right method for discovering the natural human instincts. What they ought to do, if they want for instance to discover the nature of women, is to examine the lives of those very few women who have been exempt from the tyranny of public opinion, that is to say, Empresses Regnant. There are not very many Empresses Regnant in history, and it is a remarkable fact that they generally put their sons to death. I think this fact should be remembered when people talk about maternal affection. On the whole, Empresses Regnant do not encourage the view that a woman is a gentle and kindly creature, even when not compelled to be so by the tyranny of public opinion.

Bishop Colenso, who was a centre of controversy in the days of my parents, had a somewhat unfortunate experience. He went out to South

Africa to convert the Zulus to Christianity, and he translated the Bible into Zulu. The Zulus read the translation, and parts of it seemed to them excellent. They particularly liked the Book of Joshua, because it glorified the sort of activities that they were in the habit of indulging in. And he had a piece of undeserved good luck: he didn't know the Zulu language quite as well as he thought he did, and instead of saying 'God is Love' he said 'God is Butter'. Now the Zulus were very fond of butter, and this converted them in shoals, so that he had a very good time. But presently, in reading through the sacred book, they came upon the statement that the hare chews the cud. They went to him and said: 'Look, this book you have given us says that the hare chews the cud, but it doesn't.' 'Oh yes,' said Colenso, 'if the Bible says so, it must do so.' But they gave him a hare and said, 'Now you watch and see.' He watched, and being an honest man he had to confess that the hare did not chew the cud. And he wrote home to the missionary society and said to them: 'I am in a great difficulty, the Bible says that the hare chews the cud, and after watching the hare diligently for quite a long time, I find that it does not chew the cud. What am I to do about it?' And the missionary society wrote back and said: 'Since the Bible says that the hare chews the cud you must believe this or be deprived of your salary.' He chose the latter, and from that time onwards he had to live on the charity of the Zulus. I am afraid that this somewhat interfered with the diffusion of Christianity among those people.

When I had occasion to study the works of the Fathers, I was impressed by the difficulties that arose from the inadequacy of the postal system in those days. St Jerome and St Augustine had a long and somewhat difficult correspondence about a great many points of theology. St Jerome lived in Bethlehem, St Augustine lived in Hippo near Carthage, and it took a very long time for letters to get from either of these places to the other. The most acrimonious of their controversies concerned the conduct of St Peter, who, when he was staying with St James, refused all food that was condemned by Jewish law, but when he was staying with St Paul, was quite willing to eat such food. One of these two eminent divines considered that this was time-serving, and the other did not. The letters that were exchanged on the subject took about six months to get from one to the other, and therefore the controversy, which if they had met could have been solved in a few minutes, lasted some twenty years. It had very grave consequences in the history of the early Church.

The social credit scheme which has had very considerable success in winning over public opinion in parts of Canada, was invented by Major Douglas, who wrote a book expounding it. The Labour party did not at first know whether it should adopt this view or whether it should not. It decided to follow the advice of the Sidney Webbs on the point. The Sidney Webbs came to me and said, 'We haven't time to read Major Douglas's

299

book. Will you please read it and tell us what we think of it.' So I said I would, and I read the book and I told them that I thought it contained fallacies and that I didn't think the scheme was one which the Labour party ought to adopt. They invited me to lunch to meet Major Douglas, and then and there I conveyed to Major Douglas the Webbs' opinion on his book, and that is the reason why his scheme has never been adopted by the Labour party.

I think that a great many people who admire the poetry of Blake are not aware of his connection with radical movements in the days of the French Revolution. There is a story, a well-authenticated story, about how on a certain occasion he saved the life of Tom Paine. They both belonged to a very very small group of more or less revolutionary people, who used to meet together; and on one occasion Tom Paine, who had just been elected to the Convention in France as the member for Calais, related that he had just been making a speech of a somewhat subversive sort, and Blake said to him, 'Now, you know this is a very dangerous speech and I'm afraid you may get into trouble with the British Government.' 'Oh,' said Tom Paine, 'It's all right, I'm just going off to France, and I'm only going home just to collect my luggage, then I shall go.' And Blake said to him, 'Don't you go home and collect your luggage. Go quite straight to Dover.' And Tom Paine took his advice, went to Dover, got there twenty minutes ahead of Pitt's police, and managed to get on to his boat, and arrived in Calais where he was acclaimed by an enthusiastic multitude. If it had not been for the advice of Blake he would have been put to death at that period.

The Empress Josephine had a very interesting and very remarkable life, full of ups and downs. As everybody knows, she came from the West Indies and was in Paris at the time of the Reign of Terror. Not only that, but she was imprisoned during the Reign of Terror, and was in imminent danger of being guillotined. But, however, she succeeded in not being guillotined, and in getting into intimate relations with Barras, who became the first of the Directors, and when asked what he had done during the Terror, remarked, 'I survived.' And so she survived through the period of the *Directoire*. However, Barras was getting a little tired of her because she was already elderly, and he decided to marry her off to Napoleon, who was very very young, and who wanted a reward for such an act of self-abnegation, and was given the command of the French army in Italy as a reward. That was how she became Napoleon's wife. Once she had achieved this position she made much use of it. She was a somewhat extravagant lady, and after a time Napoleon began to object to paying her bills. On one occasion, when he had been particularly adamant about her bills, she went to the War Minister and said, 'Now look here, you know perfectly well that if I say one word against you to Napoleon, you will be dismissed from office. Now what I want you to do is to take some part of the funds devoted to the war to pay my debts.' The War Minister under this pressure reluctantly consented. Throughout the whole of the forthcoming year, French arms suffered one reverse after another. Genoa, which the French had conquered, fell back and was lost to them, and all this in order to pay Josephine's dressmaker's bill. However, Napoleon was not always compliant. When he returned unexpectedly from Egypt and nobody knew that he was going to come, she was dining *tête-à-tête* with Barras. Napoleon managed somehow to convey that he was just going to arrive, and she fled quickly from Barras to Napoleon's and her flat. The door was locked and she remained outside; Napoleon was inside, having arrived before her. For twenty-four hours he kept her sitting on the doorstep.

She had another more serious misfortune after Napoleon's fall. When the Emperor Alexander came to Paris, she thought, 'Well, Emperors are my meat, I ought to be able to catch him.' She tried very hard. She invited him to dinner, and following the custom of fashionable ladies of that time, she wore her dress wet in order that it might cling to the figure. The result was that she caught a chill and died, and the Emperor Alexander remained unaffected by her charms.

Her relations with Napoleon had a somewhat unfortunate beginning. On their wedding night, just as Napoleon was getting into bed, Josephine's dog bit him in the calf, which completely spoilt this important occasion. Many years afterwards, when he was divorcing her, he brought this up as a grievance, and it appeared to be one of the reasons why he wished to divorce her.

People are accustomed to treating Greek history in a spirit of reverence which makes events unreal; they do not see those events as being very similar to those of our own time. Take for instance the age of Pericles, always regarded as a sort of great and glorious and shimmering wonder, and never treated in terms of realism. But in fact Pericles was a party boss, who succeeded in establishing himself very largely by corrupt means, and who, when he set to work to build temples on the Acropolis, did so exactly in the same spirit as that which inspired the P.W.A. – that is to say, he wanted to prevent unemployment and to cause contentment by the distribution of public money. When he fell, he fell in very much the manner in which bosses fall. He was accused of being corrupt: Phideas, whom he employed in the making of statues, was accused of stealing the gold that should have gone into the making of them, and Aspasia, who appears always, in spite of certain moral dubiousness, as rather splendid, was regarded at the time of the fall of Pericles as just a madam. Altogether, the time was very like modern times, and has only failed to be seen so because it has been treated by scholars who disliked realism.

In the history of the Papacy, there are some episodes that are rather curious and do not invite a clear moral judgement. For example Pope

Gregory VI, at a time when simony was rife throughout the whole of the Catholic Church, bought the Papacy with a view to abolishing simony. He in fact did abolish simony, and his friend and disciple, Gregory VII, reaped the benefit from it, and established an enormous increase in the power of the Papacy owing to the reforms which Gregory VI introduced by these rather dubious means.

The order of the Templars has had a somewhat smirched reputation owing to the accusations which were brought against it at the time when it was dissolved. It was only through the work of Henry C. Lea that the truth came to be known about this whole episode. The truth as it appeared from Henry C. Lea's investigations was as follows: The Templars had become enormously rich and had immense landed estates throughout Western Christendom. The Pope at that time lived at Avignon, and was entirely subservient to the King of France; the King of France was extravagant and had debts which he saw no means of paying. He went to the Pope and said, 'Look here, the Templars are really much richer than anybody ought to be, and it seems to me that you and I together could confiscate all their estates. You declare them heretics, and I will use the secular arm to dispossess them, and we will divide their property fifty-fifty, and in that way we shall each get a good thing out of it.' The Pope said, 'Done!' and it was done. On a given day, all the leading Templars were arrested, they were all tortured on the rack, they all confessed that they had kissed the devil's arse, and their property was taken away from them. And the Pope and the King of France were enabled to pay their debts.

In the examinations for the Civil Service which existed in China until early in the present century, there was a question that was set which said: 'Once upon a time a Chinese sage preached non-resistance, and Chinese soldiers threw down their arms, with the consequence that the doctrines of the sage had to be suppressed. Now the same doctrine was taught by Christ, whose authority was unquestioned throughout the West. But the effect upon Western soldiers was not that which it had been upon Chinese soldiers. How do you account for this?' History does not relate how Chinese examinees replied to this question.

Rome, since it became great, has been three times sacked. The first and third of these sacks were events of world-shaking importance, the second was not. The first of the sacks was that of A.D. 410 when the Goths invaded Rome. This occasion led to St Augustine's *City of God* in which he promulgated a doctrine which enabled the Roman Church to survive the long centuries during which the eternal city was eclipsed. The second sack of Rome, which was a comparatively obscure event, occurred in A.D. 846, and the people who made the sack were the Saracens, but they shortly retired, and left no permanent mark upon history. The third sack of Rome, which occurred in A.D. 1527, was a very curious and confused occurrence. A German Emperor, who was fighting in defence of the Catholic religion, was fighting against the Pope, who was a Renaissance Medici, and the German Emperor was fighting with a French General and an army of Protestants. The French General and the army of Protestants succeeded in defeating the Pope, thereby re-establishing the authority of the Catholic faith. The results were two. On the one hand there was a great increase of Catholic piety, and on the other hand there was an end to the Renaissance. The previous Medici Pope, Leo X, when he was ill had had a large number of leading citizens of Rome sacrifice a bull of Jupiter on the Capitol, with a view to promoting his recovery. This sort of thing no longer occurred after the Protestant army had established the holiness of the Papacy.

Posthumous fame is a very curious thing. The philosopher Epicurus, who gave rise to the word 'epicure' to denote a man very fond of good eating, was in fact a man of quite extraordinary abstemiousness. He lived upon dry bread, except on feast days when he allowed himself a little cheese. It seems odd that this man should have given rise to the word 'epicure'. The fact that he did so was due to the malignancy of the Stoic School, which was never tired of throwing stones and casting aspersions upon Epicurus and his whole sect. The Stoics stood for a lofty morality, Epicurus stood for a much more humdrum morality. But it was Epicurus and not the Stoics who behaved in a moral manner in the controversy.

Traditional Chinese history is somewhat curious. After some millennia of Emperors who succeed each other one after another and are plainly legendary, we suddenly come upon a man who is universally known as the First Emperor. He was, in fact, the first who is fully historical. He was a fascist, and he established fascism during the period of his lifetime throughout his domains in China. He burnt the books expressing previous philosophies except for books on agriculture and necromancy. These he thought valuable and preserved, the rest he destroyed. He made a mistake in tactics; and it was that he cut the salaries of the litterati, who were the people who [not only] controlled history in China, but in fact, the only organs of publicity of the time, and, consequently the litterati gave him a very bad press. When he died they decided that this sort of régime wouldn't do. His son was a rather feeble fellow, and they invented a plan by which they would get rid of him. On one occasion there was a very impressive public procession, on a State occasion, and everybody appeared on his very finest charger. The Ministers who surrounded the Second Emperor were determined to make him feel a little queer, and one of their number, instead of being mounted on a horse, was mounted on a camel. The Emperor turned to them and said, 'Why is that man on a camel?' They tapped their foreheads, looked at each other, and said, 'Camel, Your Majesty? I don't see any camel.' And the poor fellow thought he was mad.

They pursued this policy with one incident after another, and in the end the poor fellow abdicated on the ground that he was insane, and that was the end of that sort of régime.

In Tzarist Russia there was a sect for which I had great respect because it gave more attention to logic than is customary in ordinary life. It was called the Runners. It held two precepts, each of which seemed to me unquestionable. The first of these precepts was that you should not receive the impress of Anti-Christ, which seemed to me entirely sound. The second was perhaps even more evident; it was that Peter the Great was Anti-Christ. Now, it followed from this that you should not accept a Russian passport because it contains the impress of the Tzar, who is descended from Peter the Great, who is Anti-Christ. But in Tzarist Russia you were not allowed to stay for more than twenty-four hours in one place unless you had a passport, and so the Runners had to spend their whole life running from place to place. However, there was a lax sect among the Runners which held that one ought to run, but it was so inconvenient that one could be pardoned for not actually doing it, and these people obtained absolution by keeping open-house for those who actually did run, and in this way the sect continued to exist for a long long time.

The history of Athens, during the Peloponnesian War, is generally taught in a manner which is utterly unhistorical. There were two parties in Athens : the Democrats and the Aristocrats. The Democrats were vulgar and are held up to opprobrium, the Aristocrats are admired; but in actual fact, since Sparta was aristocratic, the aristocrats in Athens tended to be quislings, and to be traitorous and on the side of Sparta. This however is never taught. Creon, the Democrat, is held up to opprobrium as a vulgarian, although when he was appointed General he won victories. Nicias, the Aristocrat, is admired although he led his country to disaster. He is admired because he was enormously rich and had immense numbers of slaves in the sulphur mines in Sicily, which of course had something to do with his support of the Sicilian expedition. The treachery of the Aristocrats in the navy, which was a particulary aristocratic service, was the ultimate proximate cause of the defeat of Athens in the War. Nevertheless, we are still taught that the Democrats were horrid and vulgar, and the Aristocrats were noble and splendid. And I can even remember during the period when Lloyd George was still a Democrat, children being taught in school that Creon the Democrat was a man like Lloyd George. I wish that the history of Athens could be taught with a little more attention to truth.

I was for a year a Professor in the University of California, and I learnt some rather interesting things about the economic life of California. During the Depression, most people who had land had been unable to pay the interest on their mortgages, and the mortgages, which were generally held by the Bank of America, had been foreclosed, so that the Bank of America owned the greater part of the farming land of California. Now the Bank of America was entirely governed by a certain Italian fascist, a man of very extreme reactionary views, who, in spite of being a fascist, was universally accepted as great and grand because he was so rich. I was credibly informed that if one were to say anything against him one would be assassinated. I don't know whether this was true or not, but it certainly was true that he completely governed the University of California, which had to do whatever he told it. He depended largely upon migrant labour, which was very cheap and very much oppressed, and one man at the University made an investigation of migrant labour, and suggested that the only cure for its troubles would be the formation of trade unions among the migrant labourers. As soon as he had published this document, the University decided that he did not do enough research and was a very bad teacher, and he was therefore dismissed from his post. A certain number of people protested against this action, but the supreme authorities in the University ruled any motion in his defence out of order, and he was sacked and destroyed as a teacher.

There has been throughout history, until quite recent times, a conflict between agriculturists and those who went in for pastoral land. This goes a very long way back: one of the most interesting texts in the Bible occurs in Exodus, where it remarks that every shepherd was an abomination unto Egypt. In Egypt they went in for cultivated land and not for pasture, but the Hebrews went in for pasture, and on this ground they had great difficulty in getting themselves admitted into Egypt. This enmity between shepherds and grain growers persisted through the ages, and I found it still in full force when I was in China in 1920. There were no shepherds in China, as in ancient Egypt, but there were shepherds in Mongolia, as in ancient Judaea, and so the Mongolian shepherds became Marxists, since Marx, as every one knows, had lived a pastoral life.

I have sometimes thought, when considering past epochs in history, that I should like to have been a French liberal aristocrat who died in 1788. Some liberal aristocrats of that period, even though they escaped the guillotine, were less fortunate. There was one who went to the theatre in 1788, and when Marie Antoinette came into the Royal Box, he hissed her, because at that time there was the scandal of the diamond necklace. As he was an aristocrat, he was not treated with the severity which anybody else would have been, but he was put into a lunatic asylum on the grounds that only a lunatic would hiss Marie Antoinette. He thought, 'Well, since I'm here for life I may as well settle down.' So he sent for the manager of the lunatic asylum, and he said, 'Look, I'm going to write a history of Rome, will you kindly bring me paper, ink and pens and such books as I may need.' The manager of the asylum said that he would. And our liberal aristocrat settled down to write the history of Rome. He finished it in 1820. He sent again for the manager of the asylum, and said, 'I have finished my history and I wish to dedicate it to Louis XVI.' 'The late Louis XVI, you mean.' 'Tiens, il est mort?' said the aristocrat. 'Oh yes, yes, he's dead,' he replied. 'Well, then, Louis XVII.' 'Oh, he's dead too. A lot of things have happened since you have been here. And then there was a certain Napoleon – but it would take too long to tell you about that.' And so the aristocrat retired, bewildered.

In the interval between the Jameson Raid and the outbreak of the Boer War, Lord Loch, who had been Governor of South Africa, paid a call on my grandmother; and when he was gone she said, 'It's extraordinary how living in the Colonies makes people forget how to behave.' So we said, 'What was the matter with Lord Loch?' 'Why,' she said, 'he told me that Mrs Kruger complained that Kruger never took off his trousers till after he'd got into bed.' And that shows that life in the Colonies makes people forget how to behave.

Modern international politics begins with the Boer War, or perhaps even earlier, with the Jameson Raid. When the Jameson Raid proved a fiasco, people were impressed by the vigour with which Chamberlain disowned it. Few people knew, and nobody publicly stated, that because it was being planned, British troops returning from India were brought by way of the Cape so as to be on hand if needed. Still fewer knew that this measure had been sanctioned not only by Chamberlain, but also by the previous Liberal Government. The initial ill success of the British in the Boer War encouraged the Continent to express its hostility, and there was talk of intervention in favour of the Boers by a coalition of France and Germany and Russia. This fell through because their combined navies were not so strong as the British navy, but it frightened the British Government, and made it feel that we needed Continental allies. Joseph Chamberlain offered an alliance to the Germans, but his advances were rebuffed because the Kaiser was determined to have a big navy. Consequently the Foreign Office set to work to make friends with France and Russia. I first heard of this policy before it had been officially adopted, from Sir Edward Grey, then in Opposition.

I first met H. G. Wells in 1902, at a small discussion society created by Sidney Webb and by him christened 'The Co-efficients', in the hope that we should be jointly efficient. There were about a dozen of us. Some have escaped my memory; among those whom I remember, the most distinguished was Sir Edward Grey, then there was H. J. McKinder, afterwards Sir, who was Reader in Geography at the University of Oxford and a great authority on the then new German subject of Geo-politics. What I found most interesting about him, was that he had climbed Kilimanjaro with a native guide who walked barefoot, except in villages, where he wore dancing pumps. Then there was Amery. And there was Commander Bellairs, a breezy naval officer, who was engaged in a perpetual dingdong battle, for the parliamentary representation of King's Lynn with an opponent universally known as Tommy Bowles, a gallant champion of the army. Commander Bellairs was a Liberal, and Tommy Bowles was a Conservative, but after a while Commander Bellairs became a Conservative and Tommy Bowles became a Liberal. They were thus enabled to continue their duel at King's Lynn. In 1902 Commander Bellairs was half-way on the journey from the old party to the new one. And then there was W. A. S. Hewins, the Director of the London School of Economics. Hewins once told me that he had been brought up a Roman Catholic, but had since replaced faith in the Church by faith in the British Empire. He was passionately opposed to free trade, and was successfully engaged in converting Joseph Chamberlain to tariff reform. I know how large a part he had in this conversion, as he showed me the correspondence between himself and Chamberlain before Chamberlain had come out publicly for tariff reform. I very soon found out that I was too much out of sympathy with most of the Co-efficients to be able to profit by the discussions, or contribute usefully to them. All the members except Wells and myself were Imperialists and looked forward without too much apprehension to a war with Germany. I was drawn to Wells by our common antipathy to this point of view. He was a Socialist and at that time, though not later, considered great wars a folly. Matters came to a head when Sir Edward Grey, then in Opposition, advocated what became the policy of the Ententes with France and Russia, which was adopted by the Conservative Government some two years later, and solidified by Sir Edward Grey when he became Foreign Secretary. I spoke vehemently against this policy, which I felt led straight to world war, but no one except Wells agreed with me. At one of the meetings of the Co-efficients, Amery, then still quite young, discussed various possible wars, and his eyes beamed with joy as he said, 'If we fight America we shall have to arm the whole adult male population.' I was in those days still somewhat naïve, and when the Russian navy fired upon British fishermen at the Dogger Bank, I was pleased with Arthur Balfour, of whom in general I thought ill, because he treated the incident in a conciliatory spirit. I did not then realise that he was only preparing bigger and better wars. Still less did I realise that during the General Election of 1906, when the Liberals were supported largely because they were thought less bellicose than the Tories, Sir Edward Grey, without the knowledge of the country, or Parliament, or even the majority of the Cabinet, inaugurated the military and naval conversations with France which committed us in honour to the support of France in war, although Sir Edward Grey repeatedly affirmed in Parliament that we were not committed. Our agreement with France committed us to support the French conquest of Morocco, which was a wholly unjustified imperialist venture and led to violent quarrels with Germany. Our support of Russia had even worse consequences. The Russian Government suppressed the revolt of 1905 with great barbarity, especially in Poland. The Russians also invaded Northern Persia, and induced Sir Edward

307

Grey to join them in defeating Morgan Shuster's efforts to introduce an orderly constitutional régime to that country. Every Tzarist atrocity was minimised by Sir Edward Grey, who did everything that public opinion would tolerate to discourage support for Russian and Polish rebels. I became so interested in Persian affairs that I wrote about them with indignation against the British Government. In consequence, a young man at the Persian Legation came to see me to express gratitude, and when he had finished with politics he sang Persian poems to me and explained his theological opinions. I said, 'You do not seem very orthodox.' But he replied, 'Oh, yes I am. My views are those of one of the recognised orthodox sects, namely the Sufis.' He was young, beautiful, idealistic and poetic. Thirty years later in a hotel in Cambridge, I met a fat middle-aged Persian bureaucrat who informed me that he was the Minister of Education. It was the same man.

In the days when the outbreak of war was visibly approaching, I hoped against hope that England might remain neutral. I knew the Kaiser's Germany, though it had many faults, was more liberal than any Continental régime of the present day, except those of Holland and Scandinavia. Tzarist Russia had filled all liberal-minded people with horror for a long time and I found the thought of going to war in support of it intolerable. I induced a large number of Cambridge Dons to sign a letter to the Press urging neutrality. The day after the war began nine-tenths of them expressed regret at having signed it. *The Nation,* the liberal weekly edited by Massingham, had an editorial lunch every Tuesday; I went to this lunch on 4 August and found Massingham and his assistant editors all passionately in favour of neutrality. Then hours later England entered the war, and Massingham wrote to me next morning beginning, 'Today is not yesterday . . .' and retracting everything that he had said before. Almost all those who throughout the previous years had opposed Sir Edward Grey, became overnight his passionate supporters. Their excuse was the German invasion of Belgium. I had known for years from friends in the Staff college that it was quite certain that the Germans would invade Belgium in the event of a war. I was amazed to find that leading politicians and journalists had been ignorant of this easily ascertainable fact, and that all their public utterances had been due to this ignorance.

There were various facts about the origins of the war which were kept dark. Long after it was over, I learnt that before the assassination of Sarajevo, its imminence was announced by the Serbian Prime Minister to his Cabinet. One of the crucial facts precipitating general war was the mobilisation of the Russian army which was ordered by the War Minister, Sokolnikov, without the knowledge of the Tzar. It was this that led the Germans to break off negotiations with Russia and declare war. But Sokolnikov's patriotism was of a peculiar sort. When the French and English sent supplies to Russia, Sokolnikov sold them to the Germans. Unfortunately for him, the Russian Revolution cut short his enjoyment of the proceeds.

It was my first experience of mass hysteria on a large scale and I had considerable inward difficulty in withstanding it. I used to think in buses or trains, 'if these people knew what I think, they would tear me to pieces.'

The Press was filled with untrue atrocity stories. But anyone who questioned them was regarded as a traitor. I was told later on good authority that moving pictures of atrocities were manufactured by a cinema company in the Bois de Boulogne, and sold to belligerents on both sides impartially, with only a change of captions. The story that the Germans used human corpses to make gelatine was quite deliberately invented by a young man in a Government office in London, but nevertheless it proved very effective and was one of the main causes of the Chinese entry into the war on our side. The supposed idealistic aims of the war gave people an excuse for letting loose a great deal of ferocity, which the decencies of civilised life had until then compelled them to conceal. I remember at a time when the war was going badly and there was some talk of peace, Sidney Webb remarked: 'We must keep the soldiers' noses to the grindstone.' This was a not uncommon attitude among those not liable to military service on account of age or sex or holy orders. Patriotism of course had its limits. When at the outbreak of the war a coalition Government was established, it contained Sir Edward Carson, who had recently bought arms from the Kaiser for use against the British Government, and Bonar Law, whose brother sold arms to the Germans after the outbreak of war. I wrote to a friend in America pointing out how much these men strengthened the war effort, but I think the censorship prevented my letter from arriving. I learnt many years later that in the middle of the war, the Directors of the Nobel Company, of whom some were German, some English, some French, had met in Holland and discussed the affairs of the company which was, naturally, flourishing. In 1917 peace negotiations were well advanced and would probably have been successfully concluded but for the fact that America's entry into the war was obviously imminent. If these negotiations had been allowed to proceed to a successful termination, Kerensky's Government might have survived and Russia would almost certainly have had something better than the Communist régime. Germany would not have been ruined, and there would have been no chance of a Nazi régime. It may therefore be said that we owe both the Nazis and the Communists to Wilson's determination to make the world safe for democracy. The Hang-the-Kaiser election immediately after the armistice was disgraceful both to the country and to the Government. The Government agreed, in reply to popular clamour, that an indemnity of 26 billions should be asked of the Germans. When, after the election, somebody suggested to Lloyd George that this sum was impossibly high, he replied : 'My dear fellow, if the election had lasted three weeks longer, the Germans would have had to pay 50 billions.' Lloyd George then and throughout the negotiations in Versailles was perfectly aware that a vindictive public opinion was demanding impossibilities, but he nevertheless proclaimed this awareness and was cynically willing to ruin the world for the sake of his majority.

PART FIVE

MEDLEY

'Dreams', 'Parables', 'Cranks' and 'Newly Discovered Maxims of La Roche-foucauld' were collected together and published in *Fact and Fiction* in 1961. 'Cranks' had first been published in *Saturday Review* on 11 August 1956; one of the 'Parables', entitled 'Planetary Effulgence', appeared in the *New Statesman* on 5 September 1959. Another 'Parable' entitled 'The Misfortune of Being Out-of-Date' was reprinted in *Harper's Bazaar* in January 1962.

The Good Citizen's Alphabet* and *History of the World: In Epitome*, both with drawings by Franciszka Themerson, were first published by the Gaberbocchus Press in 1953 and 1962 respectively; the latter to commemorate Russell's ninetieth birthday. In 1971 the Gaberbocchus Press re-issued both items under one cover.

' "G" is for Gobbledegook' was published by the *New York Herald Tribune* on 12 April 1953; the original title was 'The Alphabetical Atomiser, or Making Baby's Lispings Lucrative'.

'A Liberal Decalogue' was first published in the *New York Times* in 1951 as part of Russell's 'The Best Answer to Fanaticism – Liberalism', and reprinted in 1969 in Volume III of his *Autobiography*.

'Auto-Obituary – The last Survivor of a Dead Epoch' was first published in the *Listener* on 12 August 1936 and, in 1950, collected into *Unpopular Essays*.

'The Boston Lady' and 'Children's Stories' have not previously been published.

Dreams

The following dreams are exactly as I dreamt them. I offer them to the psychoanalysts in the hope that they will make the worst of them.

Jowett

I sometimes had dreams which had, perhaps, rather more of literary quality than one expects of dreams. I can remember several of these: one, when I was just at the end of adolescence. I had suffered, as many adolescents do, from melancholy, and I thought that I was on the verge of suicide. I don't think I really was, but that was what I thought. And, just as I was beginning to feel rather less of this sort of melancholy, I dreamt that I was dying and that Benjamin Jowett was watching by my death-bed. In my dream, I said to him in a die-away voice: 'Well, at any rate, there is one comfort. I shall soon be done with all this.' To which Jowett, in his squeaky voice, replied, 'You mean life?' And I said, 'Yes, I mean life.' Jowett said, 'When you are a little older, you won't talk that sort of nonsense.' I woke up; and I never talked that sort of nonsense again.

God

Another time, when I lived in a cottage where there were no servants at night time, I dreamt that I heard a knock on the front door in the very early morning. I went down to the front door in my night-shirt – this was before the days of pyjamas – and, when I opened the door, I found God on the doorstep. I recognised Him at once from His portraits. Now, a little before this, my brother-in-law, Logan Pearsall Smith, had said that he thought of God as rather like the Duke of Cambridge – that is to say, still august, but conscious of being out of date. And, remembering this, I thought, well, I must be kind to Him and show that, although of course He is perhaps a little out of date, still I quite know how one should behave to a guest. So I hit Him on the back and said, 'Come in, old fellow.' He was very much pleased at being treated so kindly by one whom He realised to be not quite of His congregation. After we had talked for some time, He said, 'Now, is there anything I could do for you?' And I thought, 'Well, He is omnipotent. I suppose there are things He could do for me.' I said, 'I should like you to give me Noah's Ark,' and I thought I should put it somewhere in the suburbs and charge sixpence admission, and I should make a huge fortune. But His face fell, and He said: 'I am very sorry, I can't do

that for you because I have already given it to an American friend of mine.'
And that was the end of my conversation with Him.

Henry the Navigator

On another occasion, I dreamt that I was a friend of Henry the Navigator,
and that I went to see him one day and said, 'Can you give me lunch?' And
he said, 'Well, I'm sorry, I can't give you lunch here because I have to go
to a diplomatic Congress, but I can take you to the Congress if you like.'
So I said that I should be delighted, and he took me to the Congress. When
we got there we found all the other delegates already assembled under a
Chairman. When Henry the Navigator came into the hall, they all stood
up as he was the only royal personage at the meeting, and the Chairman,
in a kind of ecclesiastical, intoning voice, said, 'What is the price of
Royalty?' And the congregation replied, 'Royalty has no price.' To which
the Chairman rejoined, 'But it has inestimable value.' Whereupon, they
sat down, and the proceedings continued.

P.S. Now, on reflection, I realise that this dream had two sources. On
the one hand, I had gone on a certain occasion to Desmond MacCarthy
and asked him if he could give me lunch, and he said, 'Well I cannot, but
you can come with me to a lunch at the Erewhon Society', which existed
to pay honour to Samuel Butler, whom Desmond MacCarthy had known
when he was a boy. And so I went with him, and there I found Festing
Jones and Bernard Shaw in their glory setting forth the extreme merits of
Samuel Butler. It was a rather curious occasion. That was one of the
sources. The other source was that I had been, not long before my dream,
to a meeting of the assembly of the League of Nations, and there I had
observed proceedings of various kinds which suggested to me the Assembly
at which Henry the Navigator was treated with such reverence.

Prince Napoleon Louis

I dreamt that I was travelling (as observer from the House of Lords) in a
train containing the whole House of Commons, and that I was sitting next
to the Speaker. The time was 1879. The train broke down on the borders
of Zulu-land. The Speaker informed me that he would there and then call
a meeting of the House of Commons. I inquired, sceptically, whether he
possessed the right to do so. Somewhat indignantly, he informed me that
he could call a meeting of the House anywhere, at any time. He then
began a speech to the assembled Members, but had not got beyond the
introductory platitudes when we all observed a man running at great speed
from our ranks towards those of the Zulus. A moment's observation showed
that he was Prince Napoleon Louis, the son of Napoleon III. The assembled
House of Commons concluded that he intended to promise the protection
of France against British arms and therefore, as one man, we all pursued
him.

I woke up before the issue was decided.

(Major Chard (?) hero of the Zulu War came to Pembroke Lodge and told of his campaign, much to the joy and excitement of the young Bertie.)

The Catalogue

I dreamt that I was staying in a hotel which was at the top of a three-thousand-foot precipice. It had a balustrade from which the descent was sheer. I heard a man call out in a piercing voice, 'Death to John Elmwood, Communist and Atheist!' A confused noise of fierce assent came from people whom at first I did not notice. On looking round, I observed a man tied by a rope to the balustrade, and I realised that he was John Elmwood. Again and again, I heard the same fierce denunciation, and, each time, the crowd, which I could now see, advanced a little further towards the bound man. At last, with a savage cry, they all rushed towards him. He struggled, and broke the rope that bound him. As it broke, he fell over the precipice. I watched his fall, which seemed to continue endlessly and to be slow, like the fall of a feather. At last, he fell upon tree-tops, and broke. Everybody seemed happy except a little girl some ten years old, who was crying bitterly. One of the lynchers spoke to her, and she answered. I could not hear what was said. But he announced to the assembled crowd: 'She is crying because she has not got a catalogue.' I realised that the death which I had seen was only one of many that had been arranged as a public spectacle.

P.S. This dream was occasioned by my having to listen to a panegyric on free speech in Western countries by the Father of the H-bomb.

Parables

Planetary Effulgence

Science in Mars had been making extraordinarily rapid progress. The territory of Mars was divided between two great Empires, the Alphas and the Betas, and it was their competition, more than any other one cause, which had led to the immense development of technique. In this competition neither side secured any advantage over the other. This fact caused universal disquiet, since each side felt that only its own supremacy could secure the future of life. Among the more thoughtful Martians, a feeling developed that security required the conquest of other planets. At last there came a day when the Alphas and the Betas, alike, found themselves able to despatch projectiles to Earth containing Martian scientists provided with means of survival in a strange environment. Each side simultaneously despatched projectiles, which duly reached their terrestrial target. One of them fell in what the inhabitants of Earth called 'The United States', and the other in what they called 'Russia'. To the great disappointment of the scientists, they were a little too late for many of the investigations which they had hoped to make. They found large cities, partially destroyed; vast machines, some of them still in operation; store-houses of food; and large ships tossing aimlessly on stormy seas. Wherever they found such things, they also found human bodies, but all the bodies were lifeless. The Martian scientists, by means of their super-radar, had discovered that on Earth, as in Mars, power was divided between two factions which, on Earth, were called the A's and B's. It had been hoped that intercourse with the curious beings inhabiting Earth might add to Martian wisdom. But, unfortunately, life on Earth had become extinct a few months before the arrival of the projectiles.

At first the scientific disappointment was keen; but before very long cryptologists, linguists and historians succeeded in deciphering the immense mass of record accumulated by these odd beings while they still lived. The Alphas and the Betas from Mars each drew up very full reports on what they had discovered about Tellurian thought and history. There was very little difference between the two reports. So long as each of the two factions remained unidentified, what A said about itself and about B was indistinguishable from what B said about itself and about A. It appeared that, according to each side, the other side wanted world dominion and wished all power to be in the hands of heartless officials whom the one side designated as bureaucrats and the other as capitalists. Each side held that the other

316

advocated a soulless mechanism which should grind out engines of war without any regard to human happiness. Each side believed that the other, by unscrupulous machinations, was endeavouring to promote world war in spite of the obvious danger to all. Each side declared loudly: 'We, who stand for peace and justice and truth, dare not relax our vigilance or cease to increase our armaments, because the other side is so wicked.' The two Martian reports, drawn up by the Alphas and the Betas respectively, had similarities exactly like those of the A's and B's whom they were describing. Each ended up with a moral to its Government. The moral was this: 'These foolish inhabitants of Earth forgot the obvious lesson that their situation should have taught them, namely, that it is necessary to be stronger than the other side. We hope that the Government to which we are reporting will learn this salutary lesson from the awful warning of the catastrophe on our sister planet.'

The Governments of the Alphas and the Betas, alike, listened to the reports of their Tellurian experts and, alike, determined that their faction should be the stronger.

A few years after this policy had been adopted by both the Alphas and the Betas, two projectiles reached Mars from Jupiter. Jupiter was divided between the Alephs and the Beths, and each had sent its own projectile. Like the Martian travellers to Earth, the Jovian travellers found life in Mars extinct, but they soon discovered the two reports which had been brought from Earth. They presented them to their respective Governments, both of which accepted the Martian moral with which the two Martian reports had ended. But as the Rulers of the two rival States of Alephs and Beths were finishing the drawing up of their comments, each had a strange, disquieting experience. A moving finger appeared, seized the pen from their astonished hands, and, without their co-operation, wrote these words: 'I am sorry I was so half-hearted at the time of Noah. (Signed) Cosmic President.' These words were deleted by the censor on each side and their strange occurrence was kept a profound secret.

The Misfortune of Being Out of Date

The last years of the second millennium, like the last years of the first, were filled with prophecies of the end of the world, but with somewhat more reason than at the earlier date. The cold war had been steadily getting hotter, and was felt to be rapidly approaching explosion point. Attempts had been made by both sides to make use of various heavenly bodies as bomb-sites. Astronomy, both in the East and in the West, had been made a department of the Air Ministries, and all recent astronomical knowledge was 'classified'. Each side continued to hope that the other knew less than it did, but so far this hope had proved vain. Each side had hopefully sent an expedition to the Moon and, after a few days of jubilation, had discovered that the other side had also landed there in full force. The two parties had instantly engaged in nuclear warfare and had wiped each other out. But what they had not foreseen was that the Moon was made of more explosive materials than the Earth. The brief H-bomb war started a chain reaction on the Moon. The Moon began to crumble and, within a month, was reduced to a cloud of tiny particles. A few poets regretted the loss, but they were considered subversive. The British Poet Laureate wrote a verse obituary of the Moon, pointing out that she had been the source of lunacy, and we were well rid of her. An eminent Soviet scientist published a very learned memoir pointing out the advantages of having done with tides.

Since the Moon had proved unsatisfactory, the next war effort on both sides was directed to reaching Mars and Venus. Both were reached simultaneously by both sides; but, again, the space-travellers considered it their duty to ideology to exterminate each other. But, alas, Mars and Venus, like the Moon, disintegrated under the influence of the powerful nuclear solvents that the voyagers from Earth had brought with them. Nothing daunted, the apostles of the rival faiths proceeded to Jupiter and Saturn. But even these enormous planets disappeared as the Moon and Venus and Mars had done.

The Solar System, so the zealous Governments on either side decided, is too small for our cosmic warfare. We cannot hope to win a decisive superiority over our dastardly foes, unless we can find a means of enlisting the stars.

Meanwhile, astronomy pursued researches which, both in the East and in the West, were shrouded in the utmost secrecy. Radar had proved that the distances of the nearer stars had been quite wrongly estimated, and this wrong estimate was explained as due to the bending of light-rays by the gravitational effect of dark matter in the interstellar spaces. Each side decided that the nearest habitable spot, outside the Solar System, was the Dark Companion of Sirius, which, in view of the new data, was estimated to be at a distance of fifty light-years from the Sun. Each side hoped that it alone possessed this knowledge. True, there was one astronomer in the West, and one in East, who was suspected of treacherously revealing secret information, but it was hoped that the leak had been stopped in time. Both in the West and in the East, it was found possible to launch a projectile with a velocity not far short of that of light, and it was calculated that this projectile should reach the Dark Companion of Sirius eighty years after its launching. The expense was so great that food in both East and West had to be rationed to the bare minimum demanded by health, and all new capital investment had to be forbidden unless it contributed to the Grand Design. Since it could not be expected that the passengers originally embarked in the projectile would survive their eighty years' journey, it was necessary to make provision for new passengers to be born *en route*, although this entailed a much larger projectile than would otherwise have been necessary. All this was successfully accomplished, and, with a cargo of adequately indoctrinated boys and girls, each projectile was sent on its journey on the last day of the second millennium. On Earth each side came to know that the other side also had launched a projectile towards Sirius, but, as this was only discovered after the launching, the passengers did not know it and believed that they had stolen a march on their enemies.

Year after year each projectile sailed on its way through the darkness of interminable night. The boys and girls, instructed by wise elders and removed from all subversive influences, were cheered throughout the dreary years of their imprisonment by the hope of the ideological benefit which would ultimately accrue to those whom they had left behind on Earth. The boys and girls grew to manhood and womanhood, and children were born to them. Indoctrinated by their parents, the children equally felt themselves dedicated to the sacred task. They, in turn, had children and it was this second generation, now in the prime of life, which found itself at last on the firm ground of the Dark Companion. They proceeded at once to set up radar and send triumphant messages to Earth – triumphant, because neither knew that the other party also had landed. 'Communism vanquished,' said one message: 'Wall Street overwhelmed,' said the other. Fifty years after these messages were despatched, they duly reached the Earth.

But during the hundred and thirty years that had elapsed since the projectiles had been despatched, affairs on Earth had taken a new turn. Capitalism and Communism had, alike, disappeared into the archives of history. The division of mankind into separate nations had ceased. In an uncommitted nation a great Prophet had arisen who had taught that enough to eat could bring even more pleasure than simultaneous death to our enemies and ourselves. But he had not confined himself to this hedonistic argument. He had revived an older and almost forgotten ideology which taught that people should love one another, and even that they should love their enemies. Oddly enough, this idealistic doctrine did as much to convert public opinion as did the appeal to self-interest. In Eastern and Western lands alike, mobs assembled, shouting: 'Let us all live in peace. We will not hate. We will not believe that we are hated.' At first the mobs were small and were easily dispersed by the police, but gradually the words of the Prophet found more and more of an echo, until only Governments were left preaching the old doctrines. At last even they surrendered to the immense wave of liberation and goodwill that swept over the world. Mankind had established a single Government, and had forgotten the old divisions that had kept the human race in bondage to strife. The new generations knew little of the cold war period, since all knowledge of it had been kept secret while the danger of war remained, and very few in the new world of joy cared to plunge back into the gloomy

319

abyss in which their grandparents had thought themselves compelled to live.

The messages from the Dark Companion were almost unintelligible except to historical students. They had the same musty, old-world flavour as we should feel if we got messages from Wessex and Mercia denouncing each other's abominable wickedness. When the messages from the Dark Companion reached the Earth, the World Government considered them and at last sent a brief reply. The reply said : 'Come home together and forget all this nonsense.' The reply reached the Dark Companion a hundred years after the immigrants sent their triumphant messages. Warned by the fate of the Moon and the Planets, the two parties on the Dark Companion had established an uneasy truce which was kept in being by the Great Deterrent. But neither side had abandoned hope of ultimate triumph, or had ceased to regard the other as the progeny of Satan. Each side, throughout the century since their landing, had been inspired by a great faith, the faith that they themselves were good and the others were bad. The dreadful message from Earth showed that the ideologies in which they had lived were outmoded. When it appeared that the Government not specially representing either East or West had sent identical messages to both groups, the faith of each side collapsed, and each side felt that it had nothing left to live for. In sorrow, both groups met in no man's land, and both decided that life had nothing more to offer to either. In a joint harangue, the leaders of the two sides proclaimed their common loss of faith. Sadly and solemnly, in the sight of the two assembled groups of immigrants, they set a light to two very small nuclear weapons, and after a solemn moment of waiting all were reduced to dust.

Murderers' Fatherland: A Fable

There was once, a very long time ago, a country where the murderers banded together for mutual protection. Their first step was to murder anybody who testified against a murderer. They then founded a murderers' club, open only to those who had committed a murder without being condemned. Members were expected to marry rich widows and murder them after they had made wills in favour of their beloved husbands. The club committee kept all files and by blackmail acquired half of every murderer's gains. The President of the club was the member who had the greatest number of unpunished murders to his credit. In the end, the club became so rich that it was able to decide elections and control the Government. It made a law that murder should not be illegal, but it should be illegal to call anybody a murderer, however good the evidence might be, which enabled the members of the club to proclaim loudly their detestation of murder. All went well until the President and Vice-President of the club had a quarrel. They murdered each other, and the club committee, which was evenly divided, was wiped out in the resulting quarrel.

I cannot think where this country was. My historical friend, who gave me the information, omitted to tell me the date. Some malicious and ill-disposed person rashly asserted that it was the twentieth century, but, I am happy to say, he was clapped into gaol where he remains.

Cranks

I have long been accustomed to being regarded as a crank, and I do not much mind this except when those who so regard me are also cranks, for then they are apt to assume that I must of course agree with their particular nostrum. There are those who think that one should only eat nuts. There are those who think that all wisdom is revealed by the Great Pyramid, and among these there are not a few who think that priests carried its wisdom to Mexico and thus gave rise to the Mayan civilisation. I have come across men who think that all matter is composed of atoms which are regular solids having twenty faces. Once, when I was about to begin a lecture-tour in America, a man came to me and very earnestly besought me to mention in each lecture that the end of the world would occur before my tour was ended. Then there was the old farmer who thought that all government, both national and local, ought to be abolished because Public Bodies waste so much water. And there was the amiable gentleman who told me that, although he could not alter the past, he could by faith make it always have been different from what it otherwise would have been. He, I regret to say, was sent to prison for a fraudulent balance-sheet and he found, to his surprise, that the law courts did not take kindly to his application of faith to arithmetic. Then there was the letter sent from a suburb of Boston, which informed me that it came from the God Osiris, and gave me His telephone number. It advised me to ring up quickly since He was about to re-establish His reign on earth when the Brotherhood of the True Believers would live with Him in bliss, but the rest of mankind would be withered by the fire of His eyes. I must confess that I never answered this letter, but I am still awaiting the dread moment.

There was an incident which illustrates the perils of country life : on a very hot day, in a very remote place, I had plunged into a river in the hopes of getting cool. When I emerged, I found a grave and reverend old man standing beside my clothes. While I was getting dry, he revealed the purpose of his presence. 'You,' he said, 'in common with the rest of our nation, probably entertain the vulgar error that the English are the lost Ten Tribes. This is not the case. We are only the Tribes of Ephraim and Manasseh.' His arguments were overwhelming, and I could not escape them as I had to put on my clothes.

Experience has gradually taught me a technique for dealing with such people. Nowadays when I meet the Ephraim and Manasseh devotees, I say, 'I don't think you've got it quite right. I think the English are Ephraim and the Scotch are Manasseh.' On this basis, a pleasant and inconclusive argument becomes possible. In like manner, I counter the devotees of the Great Pyramid by adoration of the Sphinx; and the devotees of nuts, by pointing out that hazel nuts and walnuts are just as deleterious as other foods and only Brazil nuts should be tolerated by the faithful. But when I was younger I had not yet acquired this technique, with the result that my contacts with cranks were sometimes alarming.

Rather more than thirty years ago, at a time when I shared a flat in London with a friend, I heard a ring at the bell. My friend happened to be out and I opened the door. I found on the doorstep a man whom I had never seen before, short and bearded, with very mild blue eyes and an air of constant indecision. He was a stranger to me, and the English in which he explained his purpose was very halting. 'I have come,' he said, 'to consult you on a philosophical question of great importance to me.' 'Well,' I replied, 'come in and let us sit down.' I offered him a cigarette, which was refused. He sat for a time in silence. I tried various topics, but at first extracted only very brief replies. I made out at last, though with considerable difficulty, what he wanted of me. He informed me that he was a Russian, but not a supporter of the then recent Communist Government. He had, so he told me, frequent mystic visions in which voices urged him to do this or that. He did not know whether such voices deserved respect or were to be regarded as delusions. It had occurred to him that he might obtain guidance from eminent philosophers throughout the world. At the moment, it was British philosophers whose advice he was seeking. When he had had such guidance as he could obtain from me, he proposed next to consult Arthur Balfour, at that time Foreign Secretary. I listened with such respect as I could command to his revelations from the spirit world, but in my replies to him I remained, for the time being, non-committal. At last he said that he would wish to read some of my books (an extreme step which he had not previously taken) to see whether they contained anything that would be a help to him. For a moment I thought of lending him some book of my own, but I was doubtful whether I should ever see it again and, also, whether he would really take the trouble to read it. I therefore advised him to go to the British Museum and read such of my books as seemed likely to be helpful. He said he would do so and would return to resume the discussion after he had got a grip on my general outlook.

Sure enough, he came back a few days later. Again I invited him into my study, and again I tried to set him at his ease. But he looked more dejected and defeated than ever, shabby and hopeless, a drifting waif, who seemed almost insubstantial. 'Well,' I said, 'have you been reading my books?' 'Only one of them,' he replied. I asked which, and found, after some trouble, that it was not a book by me, but a skit on my philosophy written to make fun of it. By this time, I had begun to think that it did not much matter what he read, so I did not trouble to explain the mistake.

323

I asked, instead, what he thought of the book. 'Well,' he replied, 'there was only one statement in the book that I could understand, and that I did not agree with.' 'What statement was that?' I asked, expecting that it would have to do with some deep philosophical doctrine. 'It was,' he replied, 'the statement that Julius Caesar is dead.' I am accustomed to having my remarks disputed, but this particular remark seemed to me innocuous. 'Why did you disagree with that?' I asked in surprise. At this point he underwent a sudden transformation. He had been sitting in an armchair in a melancholy attitude and as though the weight of the world oppressed him, but at this point he leapt up. He drew himself up to his full height, which was five foot two. His eyes suddenly ceased to be mild, and flashed fire. In a voice of thunder, he replied: 'BECAUSE I AM JULIUS CAESAR!' It dawned upon me suddenly that this had been the purport of the mystic voices and that he was hoping to re-establish the Empire which had temporarily toppled on the Ides of March. Being alone with him, I thought that argument might be dangerous. 'That is very remarkable,' I said, 'and I am sure that Arthur Balfour will be much interested.' I coaxed him to the door and, pointing along the street, said, 'that is the way to the Foreign Office.'

What Mr Balfour thought of him when he got to the Foreign Office I never learnt, but an obscure footnote to a subsequent new edition of that eminent thinker's *Foundations of Belief* led me to wonder.

The Boston Lady

Mrs Deborah Assgard was on a trip to the Antarctic with her husband
and while after a bathe she was exploring in a cave an appalling explosion
took place. The ship disappeared. On exploring the land she found the
inhabitants all dead. She realised that she had survived only because the
walls of the cave were made of lead. Day after day she sought for signs of
human life but in vain. Mankind it seemed, had ceased to exist except for
her. She, a pious young woman of twenty, educated in the strictest circles
of Boston Protestant piety, found herself in a situation to which the old
morality seemed inapplicable. She was pregnant and must do what she
could to see that the child was born alive. But what then? During the
lonely months of pregnancy she realised that if the child were female the
human race would die out, but if it were male. . . . At this point Bostonian
imagination boggled and she shelved the problem until after the birth. The
child proved to be male. She reflected on what must have been the conduct
of Adam's sons and daughters. She decided that she must prolong the
human race at all costs. Through the long years of childhood and
adolescence she brought up the boy with as stern a sense of duty as ever
actuated the Pilgrim Fathers. But it was a duty of a new sort. It was the
duty to raise up seed by her before she grew too old. The son accepted his
mother's ethic and felt himself dedicated to a great, though painful, task.
He felt at home with the animals but not with his mother whom he almost
hated. Nevertheless, when he reached maturity he did his duty. Once more
she was pregnant, once more she was filled with agonising uncertainty. She
had reached an age when she could never hope to have another child after
the one she was expecting. If this one proved male all her sacrifice would
have been in vain. But the issue was happier than she could possibly have
expected: twins, male and female. To them, she thought, I can leave the
perpetuation of my race. Her son, who only stern duty had held to his
task, fled into the woods and consorted with the beasts whom he could
love without constraint. But at her earnest entreaty he came back once a
year to make sure that all was well. For if the male twin should die, the
onerous duty would again devolve on him.

Just as the twins were reaching maturity, Deborah, by this time an old
woman, saw to her amazement a human being approaching along the
sands. He stared and she stared. 'Good God, who are you?' they exclaimed
simultaneously. She told him her name and he told her his. His Christian

name was Ulysses and his surname, to the amazement of both, was the same as hers. He discovered that she was his great-aunt who had disappeared in the Antarctic expedition of fifty years ago. A vast radio-active explosion had rendered a wide belt between North and South America uninhabitable, and he was the first human being who had been enabled by the gradual decay of radio-activity to cross the zone of danger. He found his great-aunt somewhat disconcerting; through the long years of solitude she had forgotten that privacy is expected in the indulgence of certain natural functions. When he saw the twins, he naturally inquired as to their origin and could not conceal an instinctive motion of horrified revulsion when she told him the truth. He felt, however, that family duty required him to suggest that she should come back to Boston with him. She hesitated but refused. However, when he returned to Boston and reported what he had found, the Return to Nature Women's Club, whose committee consisted of the richest and most sophisticated matrons of that cultured city, decided that an effort must be made to procure an address from her as the most authentic example known to history of a return from Boston to nature. Her great-nephew who had seen her, explained that great tact would be needed to induce her to come. At last, the eminent anthropologist, Miss Peggy Field, was induced to take an interest in the case. It was felt that she, having dealt with savages of all descriptions, might be able to tame the old lady. She made the journey. Gradually and insinuatingly, she aroused in the old woman a nostalgia for the scenes of her youth. She painted in glowing colours the eagerness with which the pampered products of plutocracy awaited her simple unvarnished truth. She had taken pains to procure, before starting on her journey, such clothes as old women had worn fifty years ago. As Deborah put on these clothes, she began to remember her great-aunts, who had been in their day great ladies lording it over distinguished social gatherings. Under the influence of the mood induced by the clothes, she yielded to the pleadings of Peggy Field. Her coming was loudly trumpeted in Boston as the most remarkable social event ever organised by the Return to Nature Women's Club. She was led onto the platform, but before she began to speak nervousness produced a return to nature which the Club had not expected. In horror the Chairwoman led her away, and the occasion collapsed. Nor was private life any better. Her few remaining relations tried to befriend her, but her uncouth ways and her frank avowal of incest were too much for them. In despair they appealed to Miss Peggy Field, who felt that here was an opportunity for anthropological study such as might never again present itself. It was agreed that Deborah should be kept a prisoner in Peggy Field's house, treated kindly, encouraged to talk, but no longer allowed to scandalise the élite of Boston by indecent behaviour. Fifty years' habit of the forests could not be overcome. She wasted away and died of unendurable misery. Her older son vanished in the forests. The twins who were determined to populate South America with a new race devoted to the cult of incest were exterminated together with their infant progeny for addiction to un-American activities.

Children's Stories

When my children were very young, we spent the summers a mile from the sea up a steep hill. At the end of a day on the beach, they would find the hill tiring and I tried to take their minds off fatigue by inventing stories. Here are three of them.

The Post Office of Pinkie Ponk Town

The Post Office of Pinkie Ponk Town had grown very tired of the small village to which it belonged, and of the very restricted outlook from its windows. It learnt from the advertisements which passed through it, that nowadays it is possible to fly, and it thought, 'If only I could fly, what journeys I could make.' It discovered that on the top of a steep and lonely cliff there lived a very, very old woman who had inherited magic powers from a long line of ancestral witches. When it asked her whether she could enable it to fly, she replied, 'Nothing easier, you must get the Post Master to stand on a hilltop at midnight when there is a full moon and to say in a loud voice "Inkie pinkie fly pie, chinkie chonkie rattle pie, up, up to the sky, one, two, three, *go*". If,' she continued, 'he can get this exactly right, you will fly and quickly be out of sight.' The Post Master, who also was tired of Pinkie Ponk Town, tried it on at the next full moon, but unfortunately instead of 'fly pie', he said 'fly tart' and so nothing happened. It was clear that nothing could be done until the next full moon, but during the intervening month he made many visits to the old sorceress, and at last became word perfect. When the inhabitants of Pinkie Ponk Town woke up in the morning after the next full moon they were astonished to find an empty gap where the Post Office had stood. The passengers on a cross-Channel steamer averred that they had seen it flying through the air towards Dieppe. They would have been regarded as lunatics, but for the fact that one of them was the Archbishop of Canterbury and another was President of the Royal Society.

Next day the newspapers reported that a building clearly labelled 'Pinkie Ponk Town Post Office' had descended upon a small village in the South of France, complete with Post Master. But, alas, the Post Master and the Post Office found their new habitat just as dull as Pinkie Ponk Town and at the next full moon they flew home again, and thence forth travelled no more.

The Great God Zoomp

Close to where we lived, there was a very large area of marsh filled with the sort of vegetation appropriate to such a place. My children explored the edges of this region, and were interested by the strange sucking noise that their shoes made as they pulled them out of the mire. In the very centre of the slough, so I assured my children, lived the Great God Zoomp, the tutelary deity of all swamps and quagmires. Once upon a time an eminent zoologist in pursuit of rare ferns had come upon the God and pulled him out with extraordinary labour. The zoologist dried him out, and put him in a glass case in the Natural History Museum, but the night watchman complained that throughout the hours of darkness he heard a melancholy voice wailing 'Zoomp, Zoomp, Zoomp'. The zoologist investigated and found that the poor God was suffering unbearable desiccation. The zoologist took pity upon him, and transported him in the dead of night to the wettest part of the swamp. After this, though the God's words were unchanged, the emotion that they stressed was entirely different, and all who heard him rejoiced in the cheerfulness of his 'Zoomp, Zoomp, Zoomp'.

Sir Theophilus Thwackum and Captain Nimminy Pimminy

My children at one time became interested in tales of the fierce beasts of the jungle, and the strange luminous fishes that live in the deeper parts of the ocean. This led me to tell them about the very remarkable zoo near Southampton which was the private property of that eminent wealthy naturalist, Sir Theophilus Thwackum. The most remarkable items in his zoo were collected for him by that adventurous explorer Captain Nimminy Pimminy, whose skill in catching animals alive surpassed all previous records. For a month or so I supplied a new animal every day to illustrate his prowess. Most of these stories I have forgotten, but I remember a white elephant which Captain Nimminy Pimminy enticed into captivity in the upper reaches of the Congo. Tales of this elephant – which was unique both for size and fierceness – had spread through native sources until at last they reached the ears of the White authorities. When the zoologist's agent in that region heard the rumours, he communicated with his employer, who at once sent Captain Nimminy Pimminy to that difficult region. At first the Captain was uncertain as to how he should proceed, but he discovered that when elephants break loose from captivity at Crystal Palace they always proceed at once to the refreshment room and eat all the buns which have been there since 1853. This gave him an idea. In the darkest part of the jungle on the banks of the river, he constructed an enormous cage on wheels which looked exactly as if it were a natural part of the forest. He constructed a trail a mile long entirely strewn with buns and leading to the concealed entrance to the cage. Sure enough the white elephant came upon the trail at the furthest end from the cage. The huge beast returned every day, and every day ate a hundred yards of buns. At last he came to the very end of the buns. Feeling secure from past experience he marched in. Captain Nimminy Pimminy closed the clanging gates. The elephant roared but found escape impossible. With the help of a hundred natives who had feared the beast, he pushed the cage on to the deck of his ship. He had laid in so large a store of buns that by the time they reached Southampton the elephant loved him, and contentedly became one of the chief ornaments of Sir Theophilus Thwackum's zoo.

On another occasion Sir Theophilus decided that his collection of animals would be incomplete until it included a whale. There were, however, certain difficulties. Sir Theophilus had, it is true, a large lake on his property, but it was connected with the sea only by a narrow, shallow rivulet. The first step, therefore, was to make a canal that could take large ships into his lake. When this was done, he sent for the gallant Captain and said, 'Can you think of any way of getting a whale into my lake?' 'Oh yes,' said the Captain, 'Nothing easier, but I shall of course need a specially constructed ship.' Sir Theophilus had a ship built with an enormous door in the stern, opening into a vast watertight tank. The Captain sailed the ship into Antarctic waters and filled the tank with plankton of a variety which whales considered a special delicacy. Sure enough, the next whale that they met swam boldly into the tank, enjoying the huge gulps of plankton. When its whole length was within the tank, the Captain shut the door in the stern, and though the whale lashed its tail in savage fury, the walls of the tank successfully withstood its utmost rage. News of the capture was published, and all the inhabitants of Southampton lined the banks of the canal as the ship sailed towards the lake. But the huge beast remained invisible until the last lock was passed, and escape from the lake had become impossible. Then, at last, the whale was allowed to escape. At first its fury was such that several houses were washed away by the waves that it created, but after a time the soothing influence of plankton calmed its passions, and it consented to rejoice the children of the neighbourhood.

Newly Discovered Maxims of La Rochefoucauld

The following, hitherto unknown, maxims of La Rouchefoucauld were lately discovered at the bottom of a well in the garden of a chateau in France that had, at one time, been inhabited by Lord Bolingbroke. It seems probable that the manuscript was given by La Rochefoucauld's descendants to this English philosopher whom they regarded as their ancestor's spiritual descendant.

I cannot pretend that, at all points, I am in agreement with the epigrammatic Duke. Indeed, there is only one of the ensuing maxims in which I wholeheartedly and unreservedly believe. This one is the nineteenth. Some readers may feel that to accept it completely is to incur a logical paradox. To them, I can only say: remember that life is greater than logic.

1. Men do as much harm as they dare, and as much good as they must.
2. The purpose of morals is to enable people to inflict suffering without compunction.
3. The advantage of duty is that it can always be neglected.
4. People never forgive the injuries they inflict nor the benefits they endure.
5. Since the effects of all actions are incalculable, actions intended to do harm, do good, and actions intended to do good, do harm. It follows that evil intentions should be encouraged.
6. Manners is the pretence that you think your interlocutor is as important as yourself.
7. Liberty is the right to do what *I* like; licence, the right to do what *you* like.
8. A pacifist is one who is always determined to annoy everyone.
9. Discipline and indiscipline are the twin children of Authority.
10. Pythagoras and Plato thought to get the better of Zeus: but they forgot that Aphrodite as well as Pallas Athene is his daughter.
11. 'Truth' is a governmental concept.
12. Religion is a department of politics.
13. Friendship may be defined as a common enmity.
14. Arithmetic is a dastardly attempt of the Administrator to impose His authority upon the flux.

15. Vagueness is the rebellion of truth against intellect.
16. We must let our opponents think – if they can.
17. Philosophy is the art of using in an impressive manner words of which you do not know the meaning.
18. An eminent philosopher has stated: 'That all knowledge begins with experience is not open to doubt.' But he would have been hard put to it to say what he meant by 'knowledge' and what by 'experience'. Familiarity with the words made him mistakenly suppose that he knew what they stood for.
19. It matters little what you believe, so long as you don't altogether believe it.
20. A Realist is a man who confirms the prejudices of the man who is speaking.

A Liberal Decalogue

Perhaps the essence of the Liberal outlook could be summed up in a new decalogue, not intended to replace the old one but only to supplement it. The Ten Commandments that, as a teacher, I should wish to promulgate, might be set forth as follows:

1. Do not feel absolutely certain of anything.
2. Do not think it worth-while to proceed by concealing evidence, for the evidence is sure to come to light.
3. Never try to discourage thinking, for you are sure to succeed.
4. When you meet with opposition, even if it should be from your husband or your children, endeavour to overcome it by argument and not by authority, for a victory dependent upon authority is unreal and illusory.
5. Have no respect for the authority of others, for there are always contrary authorities to be found.
6. Do not use power to suppress opinions you think pernicious, for if you do the opinions will suppress you.
7. Do not fear to be eccentric in opinion, for every opinion now accepted was once eccentric.
8. Find more pleasure in intelligent dissent than in passive agreement, for, if you value intelligence as you should, the former implies a deeper agreement than the latter.
9. Be scrupulously truthful, even if the truth is inconvenient, for it is more inconvenient when you try to conceal it.
10. Do not feel envious of the happiness of those who live in a fool's paradise, for only a fool will think that it is happiness.

'G' is for Gobbledegook

In these days of world organisations, of European and transatlantic unions, of dollar aid and convertibility, it is becoming necessary to modify literary style. I, in my humble efforts at English style, have in the past aimed at simplicity and lucidity. But I have now discovered that this is a mistake.

Our world-flung bureaucracies have, I find, a passion for long words. If you use short ones they think it is because you do not know any longer ones.

In a recent issue, *The Times* took note of what it called 'Giant Gobbledegook', and reported hopefully that the Mutual Security Administration was making an effort to eliminate 'such words – or "near-words" – as "built-in inflation", "disincentive", "conceptual", and "ratiocination".'

But *The Times* could not imagine a private secretary so bold as to tell a 'built-in' superior – 'We can't 'ave that there 'ere.' So probably nothing will come of it all, and Western officials will continue to exchange cables, 'which,' said the London paper, 'if they fell into the hands of a Soviet agent and were correctly decoded, would be so difficult to understand that the decoding clerk might well have the misfortune to be shot for suspected sabotage.'

I am reminded that I once gave a course of lectures in the University of Oxford which I called 'Words and Facts'. I was asked to repeat this course of lectures in America, but I was given to understand that so simple a title would not be acceptable.

I therefore altered the title (if memory does not deceive me, which perhaps it does) to 'The Correlation Between Somatic and Laryngeal Factors in the Behaviour Patterns of Homo Sapiens'. This title appeared to be completely satisfactory.

It is still, however, unnatural for me to use the kind of vocabulary that is required by present-day international affairs, and I suggest that education from earliest infancy should be revised and adapted to the modern world.

When I was taught the alphabet, I learned that A was for Archer who shot at a Frog. It would be a pity to mislead the recently-minted infant-mind with this sort of thing. The words are short, and both archers and frogs are rare in the high and far-reaching places of Government today.

I have therefore composed a new children's alphabet, which I hope will be adopted universally. In my new alphabet all the words are long, and all stand for things with which any truly modern child should be familiar.

Here it is:

Anatomically asymmetrical axolotls arrogantly affront Amerindian agronomists.

Benevolent Baluchistanis beautifully belaud Belisarius.

Crapulous Corinthians convincingly confute congressional cryptocommunists.

Deliquescent Doukobors deliriously denounce deificatory dumbcrambo.

Eleemosynary eleutheromaniacs eccentrically exterminate ectoplasmic elephants.

Fantastically fanatical Filipinos furiously fraternise.

Ghoulish Godolphin gloriously gormandises.

Horrescently hirsute Hyrcanians hilariously harass hippopotamuses.

Iridescent Iguanodons irritably infuriate ichneumons.

Jagged juggernauts juxtapose Javanese jamborees.

Kangaroos knowledgeably knock Kamchatkans.

Lilliputians languorously liquidate libidinous Liberians.

Monotonously monophysite Mongolians mercilessly mutilate Montenegrins.

Numismatically notable Nijninovgorod nostalgically notifies neolithic Novarians.

Oleaginous octopods osmotically occlude oysters.

Potentially platythliptic Patagonians ponderously proliferate.

Querulously quaternion quaggas questioningly quantify quartz.

Rarefication rapidly reduplicates Rutilian radio-activity.

Sardanapalus sardonically segregates seceding Semipalatinsk.

Tumultuously tintinnabulating Titanium titillates Timbuktu.

Ubiquitously unimaginative Uruguayans unhesitatingly understand ubiety.

Venomously voracious Voltigern vehemently vomits volcanoes.

Wearisomely Worplesdon winsomely witnesses witenagemots.

Xanadu xenophobically X-rays xenophytic xylanthrax xylopyrographically.

Yodelling Yugoslavs yearningly yowl ytterbically.

Zincographers zealously zootomise zygodactyls.

THE GOOD CITIZEN'S ALPHABET
&
HISTORY OF THE WORLD IN EPITOME

Illustrations by Franciszka Themerson

P

**is for
Pedant
who wrote
this book**

THE GOOD CITIZEN'S ALPHABET

This book, it is felt, will supply a lacuna which has long disgraced our educational system. Those who have had the largest amount of experience in the earlier stages of the pedagogical process have in a very large number of cases been compelled to conclude that much unnecessary difficulty and much avoidable expenditure of school hours is due to the fact that the ABC, that gateway to all wisdom, is not made sufficiently attractive to the immature minds whom it is our misfortune to have to address. This book, small as is its compass, and humble as are its aims, is, we believe and hope, precisely such as in the present perilous conjuncture is needed for the guidance of the first steps of the infant mind. We say this not without the support of empirical evidence. We have tried our alphabet upon many subjects: Some have thought it wise; some, foolish. Some have thought it right-minded; others may have been inclined to think it subversive. But all — and we say this with the most complete and absolute confidence — all to whom we have shown this book have ever after had an impeccable knowledge of the alphabet. On this ground we feel convinced that our education authorities, from the very first moment that this work is brought to their attention, will order it instantly to be adopted in all those scholastic institutions in which the first elements of literacy are inculcated.

17th January 1953   **B.R.**

A

Asinine

—What *you* think.

B

Bolshevik

—Anyone whose opinions I disagree with.

C

Christian

—Contrary to the Gospels.

D

Diabolic

—Liable to diminish the income of the rich.

E

Erroneous

—Capable of being proved true.

F

Foolish

—Disliked by the police.

G

Greedy

—Wanting something I have
and you haven't.

H

Holy

—Maintained by fools for centuries.

see:

IGNORANT

I

Ignorant

—Not holy.

J

Jolly

—The downfall of our enemies.

K

Knowledge

—What Archbishops do not doubt.

L

Liberty

—The right to obey the police.

M

Mystery

—What I understand and you don't.

N

Nincompoop

—A person who serves mankind
in ways

for which they are not grateful.

O

Objective

—A delusion which other lunatics share.

P

Pedant

—A man who likes his statements to be true.

QR

Queer

—Basing opinions on evidence.

Rational

—Not basing opinions on evidence.

S

Sacrifice

—Accepting the burdens of a great position.

T

True

—What passes the examiners.

U

Unfair

—Advantageous to the other party.

V

Virtue

—Submission to the government.

W

Wisdom

—The opinions of our ancestors.

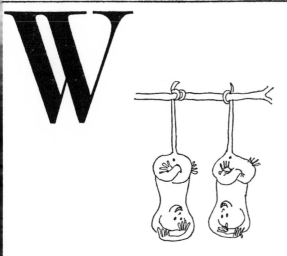

X

Xenophobia

—The Andorran opinion that the inhabitants of Andorra are the best.

Y

Youth

—What happens to the old when in a movement.

Z

Zeal

—See stool pigeon.

HISTORY OF THE WORLD

✳✳ in epitome ✳✳

{ For use in Martian infant schools }

𝕾ince 𝕬dam

and 𝕰ve ate

the apple,

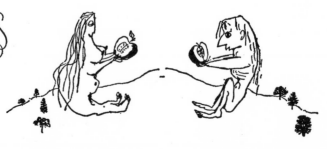

man has

from

never

any

refrained

folly

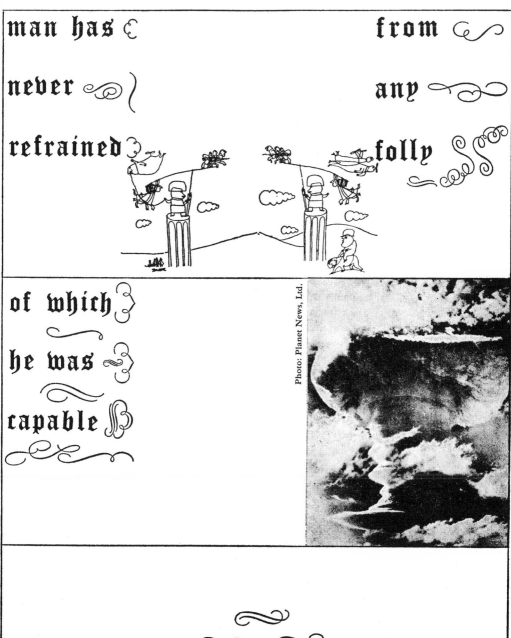

of which

he was

capable

The End

Auto-Obituary*
(1936)

By the death of the Third Earl Russell (or Bertrand Russell, as he preferred to call himself) at the age of ninety, a link with a very distant past is severed. His grandfather, Lord John Russell, the Victorian Prime Minister, visited Napoleon in Elba; his maternal grandmother was a friend of the Young Pretender's widow. In his youth he did work of importance in mathematical logic, but his eccentric attitude during the First World War revealed a lack of balanced judgement which increasingly infected his later writings. Perhaps this is attributable, at least in part, to the fact that he did not enjoy the advantages of a public-school education, but was taught at home by tutors until the age of eighteen, when he entered Trinity College, Cambridge, becoming 7th Wrangler in 1893 and a Fellow in 1895. During the fifteen years that followed, he produced the books upon which his reputation in the learned world was based: *The Foundations of Geometry, The Philosophy of Leibniz, The Principles of Mathematics,* and (in collaboration with Dr A. N. Whitehead) *Principia Mathematica.* This last work, which was of great importance in its day, doubtless owed much of its superiority to Dr (afterwards Professor) Whitehead, a man who, as his subsequent writings showed, was possessed of that insight and spiritual depth so notably absent in Russell; for Russell's argumentation, ingenious and clever as it is, ignores those higher considerations that transcend mere logic.

This lack of spiritual depth became painfully evident during the First World War, when Russell, although (to do him justice) he never minimised the wrong done to Belgium, perversely maintained that, war being an evil, the aim of statesmanship should have been to bring the war to an end as soon as possible, which would have been achieved by British neutrality and a German victory. It must be supposed that mathematical studies had caused him to take a wrongly quantitative view which ignored the question of principle involved. Throughout the war, he continued to urge that it should be ended, on no matter what terms. Trinity College, very properly, deprived him of his lectureship, and for some months of 1918 he was in prison.

In 1920 he paid a brief visit to Russia, whose Government did not impress him favourably, and a longer visit to China, where he enjoyed

* This obituary will (or will not) be published in *The Times* for 1 June 1962, on the occasion of my lamented but belated death. It was printed prophetically in the *Listener* in 1936.

the rationalism of the traditional civilisation, with its still surviving flavour of the eighteenth century. In subsequent years, his energies were dissipated in writings advocating Socialism, educational reform, and a less rigid code of morals as regards marriage. At times, however, he returned to less topical subjects. His historical writings, by their style and their wit, conceal from careless readers the superficiality of the antiquated rationalism which he professed to the end.

In the Second World War, he took no public part, having escaped to a neutral country just before its outbreak. In private conversation he was wont to say that homicidal lunatics were well employed in killing each other, but that sensible men would keep out of their way while they were doing it. Fortunately, this outlook, which is reminiscent of Bentham, has become rare in this age, which recognises that heroism has a value independent of its utility. True, much of what was once the civilised world lies in ruins; but no right-thinking person can admit that those who died for the right in the great struggle have died in vain.

His life, for all its waywardness, had a certain anachronistic consistency, reminiscent of that of the aristocratic rebels of the early nineteenth century. His principles were curious, but, such as they were, they governed his actions. In private life he showed none of the acerbity which marred his writings, but was a genial conversationalist and not devoid of human sympathy. He had many friends, but had survived almost all of them. Nevertheless, to those who remained, he appeared, in extreme old age, full of enjoyment, no doubt owing, in large measure, to his invariable health, for politically, during his last years, he was as isolated as Milton after the Restoration. He was the last survivor of a dead epoch.